W9-BMO-451

Radiant Daughter

Radiant Daughter

a novel

Patricia Grossman

TriQuarterly Books
Northwestern University Press
Evanston, Illinois

TriQuarterly Books
Northwestern University Press
www.nupress.northwestern.edu

Printed in the United States of America

10   9   8   7   6   5   4   3   2   1

The author is grateful for permission to use the following English translations of poems or excerpts from poems:

"In Memory of M. B." from *Poems of Akhmatova,* selected, translated, and introduced by Stanley Kunitz with Max Hayward, © 1967, 1968, 1972, 1973 by Stanley Kunitz and Max Hayward, originally published by Little, Brown and currently available from Mariner Books.

"But I am warning you . . ." by Anna Akhmatova, translated by Tanya Tulchinsky, Andrew Wachtel, and Gwenan Wilbur, published on the website "From the Ends to the Beginnings: A Bilingual Anthology of Russian Verse," www.russianpoetry.net.

Anna Akhmatova, excerpts from "Additions" and "The Sentence" from "Requiem" from *The Complete Poems of Anna Akhmatova,* translated by Judith Hemschemeyer, edited and introduced by Roberta Reeder. Copyright © 1989, 1992, 1997 by Judith Hemschemeyer. Reprinted with permission of Zephyr Press, www.zephrypress.org. First published by Canongate Books Ltd., 14 High Street, Edinburgh, EH1 1TE.

This is a work of fiction. Characters, places, and events are the product of the author's imagination or are used fictitiously and do not represent actual people, places, or events.

Library of Congress Cataloging-in-Publication Data
Grossman, Patricia.
    Radiant daughter : a novel / Patricia Grossman.
       p. cm.
    ISBN 978-0-8101-5199-4 (trade cloth : alk. paper)
    1. Mothers and daughters—Fiction. 2. Czechs—Illinois—Fiction. 3. Mentally ill—New York (State)—New York—Fiction. I. Title.
PS3557.R6726R33 2010
813'.54—dc22

2010008848

Radiant Daughter

Chapter One

No one in Irena Blazek's family wanted to hear about 1938.
She knew this but occasionally indulged herself anyway. "Right before
we came over in 1938, just as we were locking up the house for the last
time—"

"The minute you say the date, don't you think I know what's coming?" her daughter Elise interrupted. She was sitting at the kitchen table,
examining her skin in a hand mirror while across from her Irena peeled
and sliced potatoes.

All Irena knew was that after so many years, naming the date was
the only way she had to recognize her passage from an inevitably harsh
fate—her joints would have ached before their time, she'd been told—to
a promising future in the United States.

Elise put down the mirror. "You sound like a broken record, Irena,"
she complained. "And it's such a cliché—'only the clothes on our
backs.'"

Irena ignored this. "Your grandfather Václav—he might have been a
laborer, but he was a smart man, a forward-thinking man. If you got your
brains from anyone, it was from him. He didn't believe a word of the
Munich Agreement. The Munich Betrayal, he called it. 'You think they
care about promises?' he said. 'You think it makes a difference that we're

Catholic? In the end Hitler will conquer everyone not born Christian in the Fatherland.'"

"So you've said," Elise remarked, now dabbing her chin with makeup from a little plastic disc Irena had never seen.

"My problem is I don't remember *enough*," Irena continued. "I had already turned fourteen by 1938. You'd think I'd remember everything. Can you imagine barely remembering your first fourteen years?"

Irena was sure she saw a smile flicker across her daughter's face. "Don't be fresh," she said. "And don't call your mother 'Irena.' It's not respectful. I called my mother maminka till the day she died."

"It's not disrespectful," claimed Elise. "It just means I've reached a particular age."

"What age? Eighteen is not so much of an age anymore. I've noticed this. Every year you teenagers get younger. When my father was eighteen in Plzen, he was already married and working at Pilsner Urquell. He already had a sore back from moving barrels through the tunnels of the lagering cellar. You may know a lot up here," Irena said, tapping her right temple, "but believe me, you are *not* 'a particular age.'"

Elise lit a cigarette, then exhaled a tapered stream of smoke in that gallingly "cool" way she had. Her little cousin Miloslav entered the room, but Elise didn't bother turning his way. He pulled back an empty chair and straddled it. He was sweating and grimy from exhausting himself with the boys in the street, the rough ones who carried their hockey sticks as if they were rifles.

Irena gave her nephew a sidewise look, then laid down her peeler. "Come here, Miloslav, come to Aunt Irena."

When he came over, she pulled him closer, locked him between her knees, and wiped his broad and sweaty face with the handkerchief she generally kept in the pocket of her roomy cardigans. "Go wash. Get ready for dinner."

Glad to wriggle free, Miloslav ran to the bathroom.

"Poor boy," said Irena.

"He'd be better off if you didn't keep saying that," Elise said. "You and Daddy are taking good care of him."

Irena refrained from asking why she was "Irena" and Stepan was "Daddy." "It'll never be the way it should, though," she answered. Her eyes began to well up.

"You and Daddy are doing everything you can," she repeated.

"The water's boiling," Irena said. "Can you put these in while I finish the rest?" She pointed to the pile of sliced potatoes.

Elise took her time getting up. Back to looking in the mirror, she was doing something with her eyelashes, using her fingertips to separate them. Ordinarily she was not a vain girl. She always kept herself up but did not fuss endlessly like many Laflin girls, the ones with teased hair and so much eyeliner they looked like ladies of the night. Elise was natural looking. She had beautiful, shiny hair, a light chestnut color, that she set every night and brushed into a becoming flip every morning. Her skin had broken out a few times last year, but it was clear now, as Irena had promised her it would be.

Once Elise had dropped the potatoes into the boiling water, Irena asked her to set the table while she herself fried the blood sausage.

Miloslav reappeared. He went over to see what Irena was putting in the big frying pan. "Puke, barf, not again!"

"Stop it, Miloslav! You know it's Friday, and it's one of your uncle's favorites. And don't use the disgusting words you get from those boys."

"How can Uncle Stepan stand it?" Miloslav asked. "There's real pig's blood in there! Look, I see it!"

Miloslav couldn't see any blood. Hanus Sedlak, Laflin's butcher, made his own blood sausages and sold them already cooked.

"They're getting darker now," she told Miloslav. "See? The color of chocolate. Now move." She nudged him away from her stove.

After a few minutes, Irena drained the potatoes, then fried them up in the sausage drippings. She glanced over to the table. "Don't forget the water glasses, zlatíčko," she reminded Elise.

For her own account, Irena was happy it was Friday. She couldn't help thinking in terms of her and Stepan's nights versus Elisa and Miloslav's—Czech versus American. The four of them had worked out a deal: she would cook American every day but Tuesdays and Fridays. On those days she was free to cook anything she liked: garlic soup; sauerbraten; roasted pork, dumplings and cabbage; steak with sour cream gravy. In Quincy, Illinois, where Irena's family had settled and where her father had been a cellar manager at the Ruff Brewing Company, there'd never been any question; they had eaten Czech every night, and so had most of Irena's friends, all from Czech families. Stepan had not grown up in Quincy, but he said it had been the same in Downers Grove.

Stepan got in at 6:45, the usual time, and soon they were all seated at the oilcloth-covered table. All day Irena saved her questions and observations about the family's activities so that she might air them during dinner. As the one who prepared the meals, she felt entitled to guide the conversation when everyone sat down at the table. It was necessary that she do so; she had a silent husband, a moody daughter, and a nephew who understood nothing of civility.

"Stepan, Elise is spending the weekend in Chicago," she announced.

Stepan gave his daughter a benign smile. He looked tired, Irena thought. For twenty-one years he'd been a draftsman at Casner & Fitzbaum LLP in Chicago. He had done the renderings for countless low-income apartment complexes, strip malls, storage facilities, and medical plazas. He did not have a degree in architecture and had never mustered the ambition to go after one. Sitting behind his slanted, laminated desk all these years, Stepan had acquired a soft belly and rounded shoulders. Throughout the day he listened to lite FM, and when he came home he appeared to be listening still.

"Elise, tell Táta what you'll be doing in Chicago."

"I'm seeing a couple of performances," said Elise.

Stepan was concentrating on his sauerkraut. Irena had served it cold, in oil with onions and dill. It gave off a briny smell.

"She's going to two dance recitals and one performance at the Goodman Theatre," declared Irena proudly.

All those excursions to the Art Institute, Orchestra Hall, and the Civic Opera House had fulfilled their objective. The local dance lessons, the experimental Dalcroze method before Elise was ten, the ceramics, the music theory, children's theater, and drawing classes—these hard-won efforts of Irena's had cultivated Elise to the point where she now sought out enriching experiences on her own. Elise had been accepted by every college she'd applied to, and although Irena duly credited her daughter for being a curious and receptive scholar, her deepest pleasure came from knowing that she herself had done in motherhood what her own mother had never managed to do for her: she had fashioned a young woman with a cultured mind, a person who in a few short years would be able to fit in anywhere she chose to go.

"She's staying with Mindy," continued Irena. "You remember Mindy Wesson, don't you, Stepan? The one who moved back to Chicago when Elise was in the ninth grade?"

"Very nice. I approve," Stepan said. His smile was ironic. Everyone knew his approval was irrelevant.

Friday evening or not, Irena noticed that her nephew enjoyed a hearty appetite. "Good?" she asked him.

"Can I have more potatoes?" Miloslav asked, answering his own question by getting up to take seconds directly from the pan on the stove. Little did he know that in Kutná Hora, where his mother now lived, it would not be so easy to lay meals like this one on the table. What did he understand of communist rule, rations, the black market, deprivation?

"Of course, Mindy was not so lucky with college, isn't that right, Elise?" asked Irena. "She only got into Urbana-Champaign."

"So?" asked Elise in that tone—what was it? Yes, that *pugnacious* tone. Irena was pleased she remembered the word. She had spoken English to one degree of proficiency or another for thirty years, but she still kept a weekly log of new words. If it sounded ridiculous to smuggle these words into daily conversation, she could at least remind herself of them during opportune moments. Pugnacious. Eager to fight. In Elise's case, pugnacious for no reason.

"So, nothing. I'm just making an observation." She refused to dignify Elise's disrespect by altering her tone. "Tell Táta what you'll be seeing at the Goodman Theatre."

"*Endgame.*"

"A Samuel *Beckett* play, Stepan," Irena said, a touch of reverence in her tone. Mr. Beckett had won the Nobel Prize. He was spoken of as a genius. "A postmodern genius" was the phrase she had heard.

"Very good," Stepan said.

His weary tone made Irena sad. She knew he still felt ashamed that he couldn't pay the greater share of Elise's tuition. But to Irena, the scholarship was another feather in her daughter's cap; she was one of 148 women who would make up Princeton's first coed class. And Princeton had even given her money for the privilege!

"Who's that?" asked Miloslav, turning to Elise. "Who's Samuel Beckett?"

"A man who writes plays."

"I figured *that* out. God."

"Really? What impressive powers of deduction," said Elise.

"For heaven's sake, Elise, don't talk to him like that. He's your cousin. He was asking a legitimate question."

"I gave him a legitimate answer."

"You gave him a *rude* answer. And one that does not become a young lady on her way to Princeton."

"May I be excused?"

"You're not finished," said Irena. "Stepan, do you want the rest of Elise's supper?"

Stepan held his plate out to Elise, and she transferred the remains of her blood sausage and potatoes.

"Now can I go?" Elise asked.

"I suppose. Stepan, may Elise be excused?"

"Would *I* stop her?" he asked.

After Elise and then Miloslav left the table, Irena busied herself finishing her supper. Stepan sighed. He pushed aside his plate and discreetly opened his belt buckle. Irena knew it would be only a matter of seconds before he too excused himself and went down to his workshop in the basement. He would stay there all evening, working on his model of Karlstein Castle, the famous castle between Praha and Plzen. He had been working on it for seven years. Just as in the office, Stepan listened to lite FM as he worked. Irena did not know how he sustained this silence within himself. When she'd married him, he had been as rowdy as the other boys at the lumberyard where he had worked. She'd had no way of knowing that his sociability had been designed for the purpose of finding himself a wife.

After she had dried and put away the pots and pans, Irena went into the living room to fetch her paperback copy of *Madame Bovary*. She had just vacuumed and dusted in there, and couldn't bring herself to take up her usual place on the La-Z-Boy recliner. Instead, she brought the book back to the kitchen, her favorite room. Even though the oak cabinets and woodwork were old, their golden honey color and high varnish made her feel cozy. The bright yellow wallpaper, which she had chosen when they'd first moved in, was starting to separate at the seams in two places, but she still loved its pattern of floating red roosters.

Settling down at the table, Irena removed the bookmark from *Madame Bovary*. She was up to the overnight ball, where Emma refuses to dance with her husband but then dances with the Viscount. Irena felt sorry for Emma's husband, Charles, and wanted to find out how he'd react. But then Elise appeared with her duffel bag slung over her shoulder, ready to be driven to the train station. She stood there waiting for Irena to interrupt her reading and get her car keys.

In America, it was all about the children. Irena had been living in this country far longer than she'd lived in Bohemia, and if she didn't understand this by now, she figured, she never would. In Bohemia it had been the opposite: parents' needs were the ones that had determined their children's fate. No child could hope to surpass his parents' fortune. But here in the United States, in the state of Illinois, every child was worth priming for a magnificent future. So, tired as Irena was, she put down *Madame Bovary* and followed Elise out to the Blazeks' old green Valiant.

✦

Sunday was laundry day, and that afternoon Irena was busy with the ironing from two loads of wash. Miloslav had gone to watch a Cubs' game at a friend's house, and Stepan was taking a nap in their room. When the phone rang, Irena glanced at her watch, wondering if it could already be time to get Elise at the train station. She left her ironing to go pick up the extension in the hall.

"Is this the Blaznik residence?"

"Blazek."

"Sorry. The Blazeks in Laflin?"

"Who is this?"

"This is Officer Grogan of the Chicago Police Department. Is this Mrs. Blazek?"

"What's happened?!"

"We have your daughter Elise here, Mrs. Blazek. She's perfectly fine, but we've had to apprehend her."

"Apprehend?"

"Arrest."

"Arrest!"

"We found her vandalizing private property. She's very upset, but she's not in possession of illegal drugs. Whether she's on them is another question."

"Oh no, this is a mistake."

"Elise Katrinka Blazek? Born April 12, 1951?"

"Wait, I have to get my husband." Irena ran to the threshold of their bedroom. "Stepan! Wake up! Pick up the phone! It's the Chicago police."

In a moment, she was back on the line. "He's coming. What do you mean destroying private property? Elise would never do such a thing."

"Legally speaking, your daughter's not a minor anymore," said Officer Grogan. "But she gave us your number, and as a courtesy—"

There was a click on the line. "Hello?" said Stepan, sounding surprised to hear his own voice.

"Mr. Blazek, your daughter Elise is here at District One. She's lucky no one pressed charges. Even though she's of age, we'd prefer to release her to the custody of her parents."

"We'll take her," said Stepan, as if Officer Grogan had just offered Elise up for sale.

First they picked up Miloslav at his friend's house. Sitting in the back of the Valiant, he could not be stopped from reviewing the injustice of being carted away at the top of the seventh inning when the Cubs were ahead. It made no difference that Irena told him it was necessary, that his cousin was in some sort of trouble. Miloslav's whining didn't seem to bother Stepan, but to Irena it could have been coming full blast through a set of hi-fi speakers. After ten minutes of his complaining, she finally turned around and slapped him, not hard, but liberally, her palm striking his thigh and his upper arm before she missed twice. "Stop it! Behave or we'll leave you at the police precinct!"

"For pity's sake, Irena," said Stepan, switching lanes on I-294.

"I didn't *do* anything," insisted Miloslav, his voice threatening tears.

"It doesn't matter. Show some decency. Can't you see we're upset?"

"What'd she do, anyway?"

"We don't know yet." Then Irena turned to Stepan. "Maybe the pressure was too much. The interviews, the SAT tests, all those extracurriculars."

"I didn't pressure her," Stepan said, his tone mildly insinuating.

"They're not going to call Princeton, are they?" Irena's breathing quickened; her gaze darted about the worn interior of the Valiant.

Stepan dismissed the notion with a snort.

"Stepan, you don't know!"

"We'll wait. We'll see what's what. Nobody is going to take away her college."

It annoyed Irena the way Stepan always avoided saying *Princeton*. His modesty was a direct assault on her pride.

When they arrived at the police station fifty minutes after Officer Grogan's call, Irena ran in while Stepan and Miloslav parked the car.

"I'm Elise Blazek's mother," she told the first uniformed man she saw—just a boy, really, a bored-looking boy in a uniform. "Officer Grogan called me."

The boy gestured farther inside, where Irena approached the only man in the room—the one who had mistaken her daughter for a criminal. He looked up from the Selectric typewriter he'd been tinkering with and offered Irena a seat.

"I'll stand. Please, just tell me what happened."

"We found her in the lobby of an apartment building on the Gold Coast. The doorman called us, and so did the people, the family of the boy she'd been harassing."

"*Harassing?*"

"The doorman had been in the basement for a minute. When he came up, your daughter was scratching up people's mailboxes with a knife. We confiscated the knife. Eight ninety-two is a luxury building, Mrs. Blazek. The lobby's got gold-plated everything. The doorman dresses like he's guarding Buckingham Palace. You're lucky no one's pressing charges." At this, Officer Grogan settled his gaze on Irena, and she could see he was considering her with compassion. Compassion!

"My daughter is going to Princeton in September," Irena informed the officer.

"Irena," said Stepan, entering the room with Miloslav. "This is not relevant."

"Of course it's relevant." Irena looked at her husband—the cracked leather of his belt, the stooped posture, the small ink stain on his breast pocket. She looked at Miloslav, one shirttail hanging out of his pants, his unwashed neck, the Cubs baseball cap with the frayed bill. "It's relevant," she repeated.

"I'll get her," said Officer Grogan.

Irena stood apart from her husband and nephew. She had never expected to confront Elise in such circumstances, and she had no idea what to say. She was a strict believer in "innocent until proven guilty," and it had never occurred to her not to trust her daughter. Yet when Elise emerged from a room in the back—it could have been a jail cell, for all Irena knew—it was clear that she'd done what Officer Grogan had charged. She was looking at the floor. She seemed to be muttering to herself.

Irena, Stepan, and Miloslav simply stared. This was not the young woman who had left the house on Friday evening, her hair freshly shampooed, her flowered duffel bag slung over her shoulder. And where was the duffel bag? Elise had nothing with her.

Officer Grogan appeared, holding a Swiss Army knife with a numbered tag dangling from its stainless steel ring. "I wouldn't let her carry this for a while," he advised Irena.

"I'm hungry," said Stepan, as he started up the car. "There's a Howard Johnson's near here."

"Stepan, you're talking about Howard Johnson's *now*?"

"Me too, Aunt Irena. I'm starving. It'll be forever before we're home."

Elise said nothing, and Irena could not bring herself to turn around from the front passenger seat to look at her.

Okay, thought Irena, maybe Howard Johnson's wasn't such a terrible idea. Each of them, in his own way, was reeling. Elise was the most exemplary member of their family. She was the achiever who had never let them down. Irena saw how sitting in a booth at Howard Johnson's might gird them to deal with this dreadful thing Elise had done.

"All right," she said. "But before we go in, tuck in your shirt, Miloslav."

In a few minutes they were seated. Their booth overlooked the parking lot, their old Valiant among the cars in their view. Right away, they hid their faces behind the plastic-coated menus. It was some time before anyone made a sound, but finally Irena sighed and laid down her menu with a small slap.

"What're you having?" asked Stepan.

"The chicken-salad plate," Irena told him, and she endured listening to everyone else recite their choices, including Elise, whose hunger outraged her. After the waitress took their order, Irena clasped her hands together and leaned toward her daughter. She was helpless to stop her fidgeting thumbs.

"We're waiting, Elise."

Elise shrugged, but Irena sensed a torrent of emotion behind this gesture. There came to her a painful impulse to take her daughter into her arms. She paused to unfold her napkin on her lap and to will the urge away.

"Not here, Irena," Stepan said. "Wait till we get home."

"Here is as good a place as any. I'm sure we can control ourselves like civilized adults. Elise, I'm waiting."

Elise abruptly turned her head away.

"The policeman called it harassment. Is that true?"

"That's their opinion."

"What would you call it?"

"Aunt Irena, can I change my order? I want a milkshake instead of a coke."

"No. And sit up straight."

Miloslav squirmed but did not adjust his posture.

"Was it some boy? And what happened to Mindy?"

Elise shrugged again.

Stepan examined his spoon, then put it down. Clearly forcing himself to look Elise in the eye, he asked, "Why would you go so far as to destroy property?"

"It doesn't matter. I wish I'd done worse." Elise looked left, then right, scanning the room.

Irena's heartbeat quickened, but she pressed on. "This was a boy who . . . didn't return your affections?"

At this, Miloslav snickered.

"Where did you meet such a boy, a boy not from Laflin? Couldn't you—"

Before Irena finished her question, Elise grabbed a handful of sugar packets from the dispenser next to her place. Struggling at first, she tore through the centers of several at once. Cascades of sugar spilled onto the table. Irena grabbed Elise's wrist, but she yanked it away, jumped up, and ran out of the restaurant. Stepan went after her. Petrified, Irena watched from the window as he opened the car door, made way for Elise to get in, then leaned inside to tell her something.

Irena busied herself cleaning off their table. She picked up the empty sugar packets and jammed them into her pockets. With her forearm, she swept the granules off the table, then got up to brush them off her skirt and the seat. Miloslav just watched, his very presence making Irena feel exposed. Glancing up, Irena saw that Stepan was still talking to Elise. What should she do now? She couldn't just sit calmly across from her nephew, who was barely containing his satisfaction at the whole turn of events. She swore she could feel her blood racing, threatening to split open the fragile walls of her veins.

Irena told Miloslav to stay put and wait for his uncle. Then she rushed off to the ladies' room. Inside, she looked at the mirror but didn't quite register the face reflected back at her. How could her daughter leave the house as one person and return as another? Irena realized she was trembling. Stepan and Miloslav must not see her like this. Closing her eyes, she deliberately recalled what she had been doing before Officer Grogan's call. She had been ironing one of Stepan's oxford cloth shirts. Inside the wicker basket beside the ironing board were three more, two powder blue and one white, awaiting her return.

Back in the dining area, Irena concentrated on the soft popping noise her crepe-soled shoes made as she crossed the tile floor. Their food had arrived, and Stepan and Miloslav had begun eating it, beans and franks for both of them. Irena slipped back into the booth. When she looked out at the car, she saw her daughter's head propped against the left rear window. She appeared to be asleep.

The following Saturday, Irena went over to the house of her friends Berta and Magda Kriz for a few rounds of three-player Mariáš. They'd had a standing date at two o'clock every Saturday for almost a decade—ever since she had met the Kriz sisters at Kopecky's, the fabric shop where Irena worked as a salesclerk three days a week. That afternoon they had discovered they'd all grown up watching their parents play the Bohemian card game and had made a date for the following Saturday.

Over the years, they had probably all won equally, although Irena preferred to be paired with one of the Kriz sisters than to play against them. She experienced no pleasure in taking the highest contract and then beating them both. Together and separately the sisters had a good life, but Irena could not help feeling that as spinsters they were starting out with a losing hand.

The card games always took place at the Krizes' semidetached house, two blocks from the Blazeks' bungalow-style on Kozna Street. The sisters preferred to stay at home on weekends, while Irena liked to get out of the house. All three women treated the card game as an occasion, setting their hair and choosing their clothes carefully. Sometimes Irena made pound cake or a strudel. When it was their week, the sisters served French pastries or—Irena's favorite—homemade kolaces with poppy-seed filling.

"What's doing with Elise?" Berta asked between games. Every Saturday the sisters asked about Elise, kindly indulging Irena's pride in her daughter.

Feeling a flash of panic, Irena heard the question as if it were spoken through a megaphone; the sound waves reverberated in her chest. Since last Sunday, she had thought of little else but the scene in Chicago, had made herself ill trying to puzzle out what could have been going on in her daughter's mind. Yet as close as she felt to the Kriz sisters, this brief and nightmarish episode was a private matter.

"She had a busy time in Chicago last weekend. Two piano recitals and a play by Samuel Beckett." The moment this was out of her mouth, Irena heated up with shame.

"Wonderful," said Magda, the younger of the sisters. "I saw Beckett once, you know—when we lived in Paris. Just on the street, but I recognized him at once. Those cheekbones."

"You must have been thrilled!" exclaimed Irena, grateful to divert the conversation toward the Kriz sisters' days in Paris.

"And that hair," chimed in Berta, although apparently she hadn't been accompanying Magda.

"I wouldn't have known Beckett from a bottle of beer," Irena admitted.

The sisters said nothing. They had left Praha with their parents and lived in Paris for five years before coming to the United States. Their father had taught Eastern European literature at the Sorbonne, and Irena considered the Kriz sisters something of intellectuals, too. Berta was a reporter for the *Czechoslovak Daily Herald* in Cicero, Illinois, and Magda taught honors English and French language at a private high school for girls in Chicago. Magda's English was formally perfect, and Irena often wanted to ask her to explain certain passages of the novels she was reading in English—there were some tricky ones in *Madame Bovary,* for instance—but in the end pride prevented her.

"Has Elise heard from the Princeton housing office yet?" Berta asked, politely returning to the subject of her original inquiry.

"Yes, they assigned her a roommate, and the girl has already written," said Irena. "She's from Minneapolis, but she went to a boarding school in Switzerland. Her father's high up at Pillsbury."

"That will be so interesting for Elise," said Berta. "A whole new perspective."

"Yes," agreed Magda. "Has she written back?"

"She's been busy," said Irena, "but she plans to."

In point of fact, Elise had made a sarcastic remark about the new roommate: "Oh, great, the Pillsbury Doughboy's heiress." Irena worried that Elise had developed a chip on her shoulder, that she would judge the wealthy students at Princeton with unwarranted harshness. Such bitterness would not be good for her future, Irena fretted.

"I envy her," remarked Berta. "I'd give anything to have those days back."

Berta had gotten a B.A. from the University of Chicago, and Irena knew this to be no small feat. Magda had attended the University of Wisconsin, where she had picked up her socialist ideals—ideals she brought up less frequently with each year she stayed teaching at the Easton School for Girls.

Neither sister knew the exact truth about Irena—that she had married Stepan and worked to support him while he was in trade school. They thought she'd gone to the University of Michigan and dropped out at the end of her sophomore year to marry Stepan. A fib that hurt no one, Irena had decided, and anyway, she had married Stepan when she was nineteen, she *could* have been a sophomore.

"Those were such heady years," said Magda. "As if not a soul had ever discovered the same 'new' ideas as you." Magda drew quote marks in the air over the word *new*.

Berta laughed. Irena had never asked about their social lives in college. Not only did she fear the returned question, but she did not know what she would say if she ended up unearthing the tragic romance of one or both of their lives.

"And Miloslav?" asked Magda, flipping idly through the deck of cards. "How's he?"

Irena didn't know if Magda was just being polite, if she wanted the short or the long answer. She sighed. "Full of back talk, hard to control. I don't know if it's just that he's a boy, or everything else."

The sisters observed a respectful silence. They knew that "everything else" meant the tragedy.

A little over two years ago, Miloslav's father, Josef—Stepan's younger brother—had been killed by a gang of hoodlums in Chicago, a wretched pack of roving criminals who thought nothing of knifing a man for carrying less than twenty dollars in cash. Animals. They had left Josef bleeding on a dark side street around the corner from the tobacco shop where he'd been headed. People in their apartments had heard the animals spit out "bohunk," but no one had seen more than the sole of a sneaker fly past.

"What about Katrina?" Berta asked. "Is there anything new there?"

"No," Irena said. "I don't expect anything to change."

Miloslav's mother Katrina was perhaps the worst part of the tragedy. Only two weeks after the murder of her husband, she had gone out of her wits, beyond the state where even the most gut-wrenching grief might take a widow of sound mind. Day and night she had heard the voices of the thugs who had killed her husband—and third cousin—Josef. Katrina had always been strange, at times imagining bugs crawling over her, but such bouts had been temporary. After Josef was murdered, though, she kept hearing the voices of his killers, voices that threatened her with violence. Soon enough Stepan had to arrange for her admittance to St. Anthony's Hospital in Chicago. When Katrina's condition only worsened, he took precious vacation days from work to travel with her all the way to Vienna, where two of his cousins by marriage lived. He stayed with her there until one of the cousins delivered her to her mother, Vlasta Cizek, in Kutná Hora. When Stepan arrived home, he learned that Katrina had attacked Vlasta, confusing her for her husband's assailant, and now she was in a state-run psychiatric hospital.

In the nights after this episode, Irena and Stepan had whispered about the fate of their sister-in-law in a mental hospital under communist rule. But they had committed themselves to raising Miloslav with hardly a word about it. He had been eight. Now he was ten and lived only in the moment.

"As long as Katrina is in that horrible place," Irena continued, "she won't get better. And even if she does, they would never let her out of the country."

There was nothing left to say on the subject. They finished their coffee and went back to Mariáš. The last game ended when Irena found herself with both the king and over-knave of hearts, a *hláska*. As usual, the Kriz sisters were gracious, appearing to enjoy Irena's luck more than she did.

Irena didn't linger after their game as she usually did. Her conscience was bothering her because of the lie she had told the Kriz sisters; she didn't trust herself not to try to soothe it by telling them the real story— that Elise had betrayed her and Stepan's trust, that she had done something that would shock them, something not only shameful, but illegal.

Chapter Two

So what if the back of Milos's neck was dirty? No one but his aunt Irena had ever, *would* ever, look at it. It was supposed to be dirty—he had just slid into third base, driving a runner home, winning the game for the pickup team. It was a pickup team now, but it could become a real team with a real sponsor. Milos and his friends might not be in Little League, but they were better than half the Laflin boys who were—the ones with the uniforms that spelled MIKE'S AUTO PARTS in raised letters across the backs. Maybe they didn't have some rich sponsor taking them to Wrigley Field to see Fergie Jenkins pitch for the Cubs, but they had three players, including Milos, who could catch pop-up flies practically in their sleep. A good half of the times they got up enough guys for a game, Milos was the pitcher. His fastball was withering. Uncle Stepan had seen it once, and that's what he'd called it: "withering." On the scale of what was important and what was not, Milos put a couple of dirt creases on the back of his neck at zero.

Yet here he was, confined to his room because when Aunt Irena had told him to go wash his neck before dinner he'd said, "Why? I don't eat with my neck." A perfectly logical question which she had called "sass." Milos didn't care. In fact, he was happy; this was the best thing that could have happened. It was a Friday night, which probably meant blood sausage or deviled toasts or those dumplings like miniature bowling balls. If Aunt Irena made him miss dinner, he knew he'd be released from his room in a couple of hours, and then he could go into the kitchen and make himself a peanut-butter-and-marshmallow sandwich. Couldn't she tell she had done him a favor? Probably not. All she thought about was Elise leaving for that college, Princeton. He'd seen pictures. Dark, scary buildings, plants crawling all over them. Who would want to live in such a creepy place? What was the big deal about Princeton, anyway?

Still revved up from his game-saving slide into third, Milos picked up his bat, the one his uncle Stepan had bought him at the beginning of the season. Micky Mantle's signature was carved into the wood. Mantle had been great, but now Milos wanted to hit like Willie McCovey. The season wasn't over, but so far McCovey had the most homers and RBIs.

Milos dragged his bed out to the middle of the room and stood on it. That way he had clearance on all sides. He squinted ahead at his black-and-white poster of Jenkins winding up, then he imagined the ball coming at him at ninety miles per hour. Bam! Out of the park. He was positioning himself for another swing when someone knocked. "What?"

"Let me in."

"I'm busy."

"Right. Busy being punished. I'm coming in."

The door opened, and Elise stepped inside. "You'd better not let Irena catch you at that. Move your bed back."

"You're not my boss."

"This is true. Boss implies I employ you, when in fact you are a mere serf on my vast estate. Your use to me is only as good as the hand that scatters the fertilizer."

"Shut up."

"Mmm, didn't think of that. Astute rejoinder."

Milos felt his cheeks burn. He was never one hundred percent sure how he felt about his cousin. He knew how he felt about most people, at least basically. Aunt Irena was okay when she wasn't getting mad at him for no reason or wiping something off his cheek with that snotty handkerchief she always kept in her pocket. Uncle Stepan didn't laugh like Milos's father had, but, like him, he always kept his word. Milos could trust his uncle not to try and worm his way into Milos's thoughts the way his aunt sometimes did. But Elise he couldn't figure out. He didn't get why Aunt Irena thought Elise was superior to other people. As far as Milos was concerned, she used words like *astute* and *rejoinder* just to show off.

When Milos had first come to live in Laflin, Elise hadn't used so many fancy words, and she had been okay to him, buying him candy and helping him raise his math grade. But then something happened and she started shutting herself in her room and not paying attention to Aunt Irena and Uncle Stepan. What really threw Milos off, though— what made him have to watch her extra close—was what happened at the beginning of the summer. He was in awe that she had committed an actual crime and had practically ended up in jail, but when Milos thought about what she'd done—wrecking a whole set of mailboxes with a Swiss Army knife—he was lost. As crimes went, it seemed pointless. Still, one good thing had come out of it—he had ended up getting her Swiss Army knife. He used it to whittle branches into spears and open bottles of orange pop.

"What're you doing in here, anyway?" Milos asked Elise.

"I can't visit my delightful little cousin?"

Milos chewed his thumbnail.

"Get off of there," Elise ordered, poking the end of his bed with the toe of her sandal.

Milos figured he'd better do it. Sometimes she told on him, other times she didn't, but he could never tell in advance which it would be. He jumped down, then gave the bat a couple of half swings, just to check his grip.

Once Milos was down, Elise pushed the bed back against the wall. She sat on it, patted the place beside her for him to sit down too. Forget it. This was his room; he didn't have to sit next to her just because she wanted him to.

"What are you doing in here?" he repeated. "I'm not giving you back your Swiss Army knife. Aunt Irena said I could have it. So did Uncle Stepan."

"I'm not asking for it back."

Milos put down the bat and went over to his desk to remove his hardball from its plastic stand. He loved this ball; it had the signatures of three of the best hitters for the Cubs from last year—fake signatures, but reproduced from real ones. Then he got his new pitcher's mitt from the top of a pile of T-shirts in the corner, straddled his desk chair, and started slamming his fist into the pocket of the mitt, breaking it in. "Where'd you get that knife, anyway?" he asked Elise.

"I bought it," was all she said.

"Why'd you go to that apartment building in the first place? Why'd you wreck those mailboxes?"

"Forget about it, you don't need to know."

"Did you think you wouldn't get caught? I heard Aunt Irena say she'd have to call Princeton, and they'd tell her you couldn't come there after all."

"Oh right, I'm sure. As if she has no investment in my going to Princeton."

Milos was silent for a moment. *Investment* had something to do with money, but he didn't think Elise was talking about money. Suddenly he got it. "Why's she care so much?" he wanted to know. Aunt Irena had never said anything about *him* going to college. His father had, though. He had always said that he was going to make sure Milos went to college. As far as Milos was concerned, college was just more school, but when he remembered the pride on his father's face as he had made his promise, Milos felt a stirring deep in his gut. He tossed up his baseball. It hit the ceiling, leaving a mark, one of several up there.

"Nice play, Shakespeare."

"I'm not going to college. It's a waste of time. I'm going to be drafted for the Cubs right out of high school. If the Cubs are stupid enough not to want me, the Yankees will."

"No doubt."

"You don't believe me?"

"I believe you. The big deal for Aunt Irena, if you really want to know, is that she never went to college."

"Why not?"

"Multiple reasons. Money. Her status as an immigrant. Also, the expectations for women back then."

"Then what about Magda and Berta? They're women, and they're immigrants, and they went to college."

Elise shrugged.

Hah! thought Milos. Got you! He started to say so, then thought better of it and threw the ball up again.

Elise held her hands cupped together in front of her, signaling Milos to toss the ball to her. This made him nervous. He eyed her. After what had happened in Chicago, he thought Elise might be a little mental. He didn't know if he wanted her touching his baseball. She had never so much as glanced at it before. Besides, Milos didn't play catch with just anyone; playing catch had to do with other boys who put baseball ahead of everything else, boys who like him adored the back-and-forth of the ball—first propelling it into the air, then a moment later feeling it smack into the soft pocket of their well-oiled gloves. But this was Elise. He couldn't trust her in a game of catch. Nothing was simple with her.

Elise clapped her hands, then cupped them together again.

He'd better throw her the ball. Who knew what she would say or do if he didn't? He tossed it to her, keeping his attention on her face.

Elise held the baseball up to examine. Milos felt itchy. He socked the palm of his mitt again, this time a sign for her to toss the ball back.

"Listen, I need to tell you something," she said.

Milos knew it. She had to *tell* him something. He just wanted his ball back. Then he wanted her out of his room. He had been enjoying his punishment before she came in and ruined it. "Gimme my ball."

Elise held on to it. "You know how Aunt Irena was going to go with me to Princeton?"

"Yeah . . ."

"Well, yesterday when she was at Reyna's, UPS came and picked up all my stuff. I'm leaving tomorrow. I'm taking a bus."

"Why?"

"I have to get out of here now."

"The Princeton people aren't gonna let you in. It's not time for school to start yet."

"They'll let me in."

Elise must have told Princeton a lie. That was another thing about her. She lied. He'd caught her in a few. She was good at it, just like she was good at everything. She didn't blink. Her voice sounded normal.

"You're going to get in big trouble," Milos said, jerking his head in the direction of the living room, two rooms from his. He could hear his aunt's and uncle's voices in there, but not what they were saying. "*Big* trouble."

"I won't be here to get in trouble. So I wanted to say good-bye. I'm not sure when I'll be home again." Elise rose. She still had his baseball in her hand.

Milos glared at it. "Gimme."

She walked over to him. "Here," she said, handing him the ball. For a second it looked like she might hug him.

"So good-bye," he said as quickly as he could.

Elise went to the door. "And listen," she added, "wash your neck. A clean neck will get you farther than you think."

The next morning when Milos came into the kitchen, Aunt Irena was crying. Uncle Stepan was holding a sheet of notebook paper. The paper was thin, and Elise's handwriting showed through the back. Milos could see she hadn't written much. Before his aunt could notice, he went to the cupboard, took as many Oreos as would fit into his jacket pocket, opened the screen door, and left. He had his bat and his mitt and ball with him. He'd find somebody to play something.

Chapter Three

If they had come on Family Weekend, as planned, Elise could have dealt with it. That weekend would've been ready-made, with parent-pleasing activities arranged by the college and lots of other families around, including those of other scholarship kids—Matt Henry's father, who was a foreman at Chrysler, and Sadia Rahim's mother, who sorted mail for the post office. As it turned out, though, Elise's father had broken his ankle the Thursday before Family Weekend. Now his ankle was healed, and they were all coming, including Milos. Elise had to be at Newark Airport to pick them up in an hour.

She kept moving things around her side of the room, making sure nothing was out that she didn't want out. The black-and-white photo of Mick Jagger backstage at Madison Square Garden was the first to go; he was wearing makeup, and Elise knew Irena would make a crack. Her hash pipe she rolled up in a pair of leg warmers and stuck in the cardboard sweater box under her bed. Given how infrequently she smoked hash, it would be ridiculous for her parents to come upon the pipe. Everything else, she gauged, was okay: the Gustav Klimt poster of *Kiss,* the rattan footstool another freshman had been about to throw out, certainly the piles of books and tacked-up memos from the English department. At any rate, she planned that they would spend as little time in this room as possible.

Yet Elise didn't look forward to roaming around the campus with them either. With no other parents around, they would all be in a fishbowl. Elise dreaded running into one of her friends, who'd figure out from a mile away that her father felt uncomfortable and out of place. That startled look would come over his face, as it always did when he was off his turf. She wanted to protect him, but also to save herself from everyone's "insights." Most of her liberal arts friends were big into insights, into psyching people out on the basis of a single encounter.

The real fear was what her friends would think of Irena. Or maybe that wasn't the real fear; after all, Irena knew how to present herself. In point of fact, Elise didn't know what *she'd* make of her mother, suddenly transported to the Princeton campus. Lately, no matter how brief their telephone conversations, it took hours before Elise could shake off the specter of Irena's stiff, withholding tone. Irena still hadn't forgiven Elise for last summer, for leaving Laflin without her. For her part, Elise continued to hold to the instinct that she must keep her contact with her mother to the necessary minimum. She couldn't explain why, knew only that she detested being the object of her mother's acute attention, as if Elise were a seed and Irena some fanatical botanist, watching under the grow light for the exact moment Elise broke open and sent out her first shoot.

Standing on one leg to pull on her desert boot, Elise wobbled and then dropped the shoe. Her roommate, Debbie, turned over in bed and opened her eyes.

"Sorry," said Elise.

"It's okay, I have to get up anyway. You remember where I told you I'm parked, right?"

"Yeah, thanks again." Elise had to be nice; she was borrowing Debbie's car to pick up her parents and Milos at the airport. "I'll bring it back as soon as we drop off their stuff at the hotel."

"As long as you're back by eleven," said Debbie. She was sitting up and feeling with her feet for the plush slippers she had put in place the night before.

Privately, Elise and her small group of friends called Debbie "Nouveau-Riche Heidi"—or "Nouveau" for short. Now and then Elise felt shabby about it and told herself she must stop, but then she remembered her first two months at Pyne Hall. Every day, Elise had heard mind-numbing tales of Nouveau-Riche Heidi's tame adventures at Institut Le Rosey, her boarding school at the foothills of the Swiss Alps. And every time Elise entered or left their room, she had to pass by the full-color aerial photograph of the Institute. During the month of January, Nouveau had played The Chambers Brothers' "Love, Peace, and Happiness" so many times that Elise had been forced to sleep in the lounge. And when Elise was in her room, she had to be civil to the ROTC types who came to take Nouveau-Riche Heidi to Firestone Library. So far this semester, Nouveau—who planned to be a civil engineer—had kept up a running commentary on her course in multivariable calculus, a subject that bored and (to be fair) scared the shit out of Elise.

Next year Elise would room with Wiley Mills, a premed freshman from Tennessee who had become her best friend. Unlike most of the other female students Elise had met, Wiley was indifferent to her status as a member of the first coed class at Princeton. She ignored the fraternity men who heckled the women, and she didn't read *The Daily Princetonian* editorials that defended their place on campus. Wiley had come to Princeton under pressure from her father, an alum who'd championed Princeton's admission of women. "The female mind is as nimble as a gazelle," Wiley had quoted, exaggerating her drawl to imitate that of her father. Life at Princeton would make more sense, thought Elise, once she was rooming with Wiley.

Meanwhile, she would just have to tolerate Nouveau-Riche Heidi. And she came in handy at times like this. She was just her mother's type. Irena would take comfort in Nouveau's Villager sweaters and penny loafers, her grandmother's afghan folded at the foot of her bed, and the neat arrangement of color-coded folders on her desk. Irena would nod approvingly at the ROTC types and give Elise a smug look that said, "See, not every girl thinks she has to hide her boyfriends under a rock."

It was true that all through high school Elise had never brought boys home. Why would she? Stepan hated long hair on boys, and Irena was apprehensive about any young man who didn't have a career path in mind. So for her junior and senior years, Elise had used her female friendships to circumvigate her parents' questions about where she went on weekend nights. She had felt no guilt. The lowest her grade-point average had ever fallen was 3.9, and she'd kept up all her extracurriculars. Her parents had never doubted her—until that one weekend.

A surge of panic engulfed Elise when she recalled that weekend in Chicago. Some kind of horrible tunnel vision had overtaken her. She might as well have been in a coal mine, wearing one of those helmets with the lamps attached. As it turned out, the beam guided her nowhere but to unremitting humiliation in the days and weeks that followed. Doing little but hanging around Laflin, spending a lot of time in her room, she felt her shame inflating until it consumed the very oxygen around her. Finally, she had to get out of the house, out of Laflin altogether.

These days Elise was too busy to think much about that weekend. When she did, though—when its details came to her unbidden—she longed to escape Princeton as well.

She had gone to Chicago to see Rupert Dwyer. That he had not invited her was immaterial. She had been certain that once she showed up, Rupert would glimpse their lustrous possibilities and be overjoyed that she'd come.

The two of them had met at a statewide event for officers of the National Honor Society. They were among the few who weren't pasty-faced and asexual-looking. Rupert had had some mescaline-spiked pot with him. Their night together had been unlike any Elise had known. Every time she'd opened her mouth, a dazzling new insight had emerged. She had amazed herself. And Rupert had mesmerized her with his ability to express himself; he had applied metaphor and allusion with dead-on accuracy. His delivery had been melodic. He drew out of her revelations that had apparently lingered beyond her reach. By the time the weekend was over, Elise wanted nothing more than to see Rupert Dwyer again.

Back at home, she spoke to him on the phone twice. Each time had been a disappointment. During the second conversation, he had referred twice—both times in an irritatingly proprietary tone—to someone named Rebecca.

When Elise had arrived that Friday night at the Dwyers' apartment building on Lake Shore Drive, the doorman told her the family had just gone out for the evening. Later she had called from a phone booth at the diner where she'd gone for coffee, but no one answered. By eleven, she had panicked. Where would she sleep? She took a bus, weeping when unable to stop herself, to the neighborhood where Uncle Josef and Aunt Katrina had once lived. There she walked, terrified, hyperaware of her body, bothered by an odd metallic taste in her mouth. She remembered being bombarded by contradictory revelations and by smells and odd tastes of no apparent origin. She had entered a sphere of unfamiliar sensations. Hugging her duffel bag to her chest, she'd eventually come to a small brick building with a sign that said ROOMS. No elaboration. Elise thought the place would turn her away, but the old man behind the front desk had taken her money and shown her to a room with a grimy window shade, fluorescent lighting, and a bed whose mattress dipped in the center. Elise had slept in her clothes, not wanting to be naked in that room for a single second. The clothes she wore were all that reminded her of herself.

At noon on Saturday, Elise had finally reached Rupert. She had asked him to meet her at Grant Park, countering his reluctance with promises of "party favors," code for drugs. She had no drugs. By the time she spotted him walking toward her, a slim boy with wire-rimmed sunglasses and straight, shoulder-length hair, her body was no more than a vessel for her dread. A quiver stole into her voice and wobbled pitifully over the syllables of his name. Rupert was more beautiful than any boy Elise had known; there was a luminosity about him that Elise believed came from all he knew, all he was able to put into words.

When Rupert asked why she was in Chicago, Elise had used the same story she'd told Irena—Beckett. He had nodded indifferently. Elise asked him to sit down on the grass with her. No time, he said, he was going to meet Rebecca. Elise took hold of his shirtsleeve and clung to it. Rupert looked down at her clutching fingers. She sucked in her breath. He had to go, he repeated. He didn't ask about drugs. Merely a "see you," and he was gone. Standing in the lonely breeze of his absence, Elise had felt clammy all over. She couldn't bear to be in her body. She cringed to think what he had seen in her expression, and she wanted to slaughter herself. *Slaughter* was the only word. A brutal act, although hers need not be swift. She had walked until she was exhausted, all the way back to the room of the night before, where she slept in her clothes once again.

When she woke up that Sunday morning, her humiliation had vanished. All that was required to win Rupert over, she had thought, was to make herself unambiguously heard. He had no idea how aloof she had kept herself throughout high school, even while carrying on with this boy or that one. Rupert's attention that night had inspired her to confide in him, to describe the strange, loping energies that took hold of her thoughts, scaring her. She knew that once she reminded Rupert of their intimacy that night, the blooming of their rare affinity, he would be open to her again. Clinging to this certainty, she returned to the Dwyers' apartment building. When the doorman rang 15G, Elise could hear a woman's voice on the other end and then a rustling before the doorman clamped the phone tighter to his ear. In a moment, the doorman hung up. "Mrs. Dwyer says they're not expecting anyone."

Elise asked him to call again, to see if Rupert could come down to the lobby. She thought she saw him smirk, but he did as she had asked. This time he kept his back to her. Then, "Rupert's not at home."

"I'll wait," Elise had said, eyeing a velvet settee in the lobby.

"That's for invited guests only," the doorman admonished.

Elise had felt a stab of indignation at the doorman's slight. Before she could stop herself, she'd given him the finger. *Not becoming of a young lady on her way to Princeton,* Irena would have said. Elise had stalked off, walked around the block. She wanted a cigarette, but she was out of them. The doorman would never let her back in the lobby. She walked around some more, until she saw he wasn't at his post. When a resident left the building, Elise smiled at her and walked through the open door into the lobby, where she rang the Dwyers' intercom bell. When a woman answered, Elise hung up. A rage took hold; it started in her abdomen, and in the next moment she had her Swiss Army knife out and was dragging the tip across the bay of gold-plated mailboxes.

Elise couldn't quite cast off the image of herself in Chicago that weekend, roaming unfamiliar streets like an animal that had lost its pack. When Nouveau left to go to the bathroom down the hall, Elise lay face down on her bed, closed her eyes, and tried to breathe away her panic. At home in the weeks that had followed that Sunday, Elise had done her best to forget the whole business—her brazenness, the funny taste in her mouth, her resounding footfall on the rooming house's linoleum steps— but it was impossible. And her parents hadn't made it any easier. Irena had probed. "What was building up inside of you? . . . Please explain it to me, what would drive a girl of your promise to threaten her future . . . Who *is* this boy? I'm your mother, I have a right to know . . . Táta may not show it, but he's out of his mind with worry. It's the destruction; he just can't understand . . . Did you think or did you just act? . . . I will never comprehend it—I swear I asked myself, 'Is she a changeling?'"

Elise's father had taken to sneaking her sidewise glances. He had said little, but he developed a habit of clearing his throat before speaking to her. The day before she left early for Princeton, he had told her that that Sunday in Chicago had broken his heart.

Irena was the first to emerge off the Jetway, greeting Elise with a strained smile. Fuck her, thought Elise, what did she have to be so pissy about? Elise had done just fine her first semester at Princeton, more than fine— she had maintained a 3.5 GPA, joined two clubs, made new friends.

"We're going to the hotel first?" Irena asked on the way to Nouveau-Riche Heidi's Ford Maverick.

"Yeah, we'll check you in. Then after I return this car, I'll take you around. We can go to the Wilson College dining room for lunch."

Again Elise tensed up at the thought of showing them around. Practically everyone they might run into would have something over Elise, something they might slip and reveal to her parents. She had little to hide—her occasional hash smoking, two antiwar demonstrations in New York that had turned ugly, the time she was almost raped by a pizza delivery man with whom she'd drunkenly flirted. But how little she had to hide was beside the point. Even after all these months, she could not rid herself of the sense that Irena was always ready to take something from her, something Elise did not yet possess.

The reason Elise had to return the car by eleven was that Nouveau was driving into Trenton. There she had an appointment to be fitted for a diaphragm. Until last weekend, Nouveau-Riche Heidi had been a virgin. But Jim Goodwin, one of the ROTC types, had toppled her resistance with some line of logic Nouveau said she hadn't fully understood. Elise imagined Jim had proven himself smarter than she was. Nouveau required this of a potential boyfriend. Elise had pointed out that since she was a member of the first coed class at Princeton, her preconditions in this regard were quite interesting. Improbably, Nouveau had taken this as a compliment. If a dig was too subtle, there was always the chance Nouveau-Riche Heidi wouldn't get it.

After Elise's family dropped their bags off at the Howard Johnson's Motor Lodge on 101, they all got back into the Maverick. Sooner or later Elise would have to take them to Pyne Hall; she preferred to get it over with. She parked Nouveau's car and, after a short walk, led her parents around the outside of the U-shaped Pyne. The tour was mostly for her father's benefit. Elise explained that the building had opened in 1922 and that it was the first of a string of Princeton dorms designed in the Collegiate Gothic style. She told them that the dorm had just been renovated for the arrival of the female students. Elise wondered how the sight of so many impressive buildings affected her father, if he ever had any regrets about not becoming an architect. Nothing in his expression gave her a clue.

"Some people call it Pink Hall," she offered. "As if that were witty."

On the top floor of Pyne, Elise knocked on her door, just in case Jim Goodwin was there. Nouveau came to greet them immediately. "Welcome!" she sang out.

"Debbie, this is my mother, Irena, my father, Stepan, and my little cousin, Milos."

Nouveau swayed forward. Elise was afraid she might kiss them. Instead, she was going for her mini refrigerator to the right of the door. "What can I get for you? Juice? Soda?"

Milos was interested but looked blankly at Elise.

"Pop," Elise clarified.

Once they were all holding Dr. Peppers, they sat down on the two twin beds.

"Your daughter is quite a character," Nouveau told Irena. To prove her point, she told the Blazeks about Elise's habit of eating spaghetti with chopsticks and about the time she had spent three days sewing a really impressive dummy of Henry Kissinger, only to burn it to ash on the lawn in front of Cuyler Hall.

"Thanks so much for lending me the car," Elise interrupted, handing over the keys. "We'd better go. I want to show them around some before Wilson closes for lunch."

"But I haven't heard a thing about Debbie," objected Irena. "What are you studying, dear?"

Elise went down the hall to the bathroom. When she returned, Nouveau was still explaining to her parents why multivariable calculus was the hardest course she had ever taken. She was comparing it to honors calculus, which she'd taken at Institut Le Rosey, when Elise reminded her of her doctor's appointment, giving her a significant look.

Nouveau-Riche Heidi sprang up. Stepan stood politely. "It's been a real treat to meet you," he said.

"Thanks for the pop," said Milos.

"I hope we'll be seeing more of you this weekend," Irena added. "We'd love to get to know Elise's roommate."

Now Nouveau *did* kiss Elise's mother—more warmly than Elise herself had at Newark Airport.

"And I'd like to hear about what your father does at Pillsbury," added Irena. "I can tell you, we're sold at our house."

Nouveau went over to her desk and came back with several doughboy key chains.

"Well, *thank* you, Debbie. What a thoughtful gesture," said Irena. Her accent was thicker than usual, as if the sight of the Pillsbury doughboy had reminded her she was an immigrant.

As promised, Elise took her family around the campus. They went to the FitzRandolph Observatory and to the art museum. They toured Firestone Library. They had lunch at Wilson College, and then Elise took them to see Taplin Auditorium in the new Fine Hall and to Mercer Street to walk past Einstein's house.

By mid-afternoon, Milos began asking if he could go back to Elise's dorm to watch football. Irena forbade it. He didn't let up and began to groan every time they came to a building that Irena wanted to see on the inside. Finally Irena grabbed Milos by the arm, stopping him in mid-step, and told him that he wasn't the center of the universe, and he should try to expand his mind. Elise cringed. As they resumed their tour of the stately campus, Milos conducted a series of wordless rebellions: dragging a branch behind him on the walkway, rolling his eyes when Irena asked Elise a question that involved a long answer, gawking at a student with a big Afro, and—once—breaking out in a boxing match with an imaginary opponent. When he did this, Stepan put a hand on his shoulder to restrain him, and Irena announced that as far as she was concerned Miloslav was not a member of their family this afternoon.

Throughout the tour, Stepan was attentive, and Irena continued to be hugely impressed by all she saw. Her cheeks glowed.

In the evening they went to see a student production of *Waiting for Godot* at Hamilton Murray Theater. (Elise had thought twice about this, not eager for anyone to make the *Endgame* association, but it was the only performance on campus that weekend.) Milos, who could not be trusted to stay alone at Howard Johnson's, squirmed in his seat, waiting for Godot for his own reasons. Stepan fell asleep during the last third of the play, his chin hitting his top button before he roused himself again.

While they sat waiting for a cab to take the Blazeks back to their motel, Irena wanted to analyze the play with Elise. "Its interpretations are endless," she said. "Who is Godot? Or maybe it's *what* is Godot? I have some theories, but I need to mull them over."

Elise found herself completely dry inside, so unyielding that she could not (or would not) offer her mother a single idea with which to engage. Waiting for the cab, she and Milos—never friends before—became silent partners, and her mother eventually stopped talking and closed her eyes to reflect. Right as the cab pulled up, Irena burst out, "God! Godot is God. Didi and Gogo were waiting for God the Savior! Sleep tight, zlatíčko."

Thankfully, Elise's room in Pyne Hall was empty. With any luck, Nouveau was initiating her new diaphragm and wouldn't be home till tomorrow. Elise wasn't in the least sleepy. She had a lot of work due next week, most of it in English and Humanities: a preceptorial on Milton that she hadn't prepared for, an interpretive paper on Yeats's poem "A Man Young and Old," and she needed to work on grammar and on her pronunciation for Beginning Russian. She'd always had good study habits, but tonight she lit on one text after another, not considering the course to which each was attached. Just as a central idea for her paper on "A Man Young and Old" struck her, she felt compelled to move on to conjugating Russian verbs. Then she read some stanzas of *Paradise Lost*. Next to these, in green ink, she jotted bits of her own analysis, points she wanted to remember for the preceptorial on Thursday. From there, she thumbed through an anthology of Russian poets in translation, a book she had borrowed on her own from Firestone. A few poems she copied into her orange notebook—not so much a journal as a repository of small gems. Two poems by Osip Mandelstam. Several times over, she copied "The Sentence" by Anna Akhmatova, slowing down particularly over the lines "Today I have so much to do: / I must kill memory once and for all, / I must turn my soul to stone, / I must learn to live again— / Unless . . . Summer's ardent rustling / Is like a festival outside my window."

Elise marveled that someone could translate into English the nuance and meter of a poem. She had looked at Princeton's courses in Slavic languages and literature and knew there was a survey of nineteenth-century Russian poetry, to be read in the original. She couldn't take the course unless she moved on to Intermediate and then Advanced Russian. All at once, she was determined to do this. What would it be like to first transliterate Russian poems into English, then decipher a poet's meaning? Elise knew it usually took two kinds of mind reader to accomplish this task—a precisionist and a prophet. It came to her tonight that she could be both such people: the one who rendered the intricacies of poetic diction across languages and the one capable of looping back to the original song in the poet's mind. She was only now becoming familiar with the basic conventions of the Russian language, yet tonight Elise knew that she would conduct extended debates with dead Russian poets until she reached an agreement with them, an echoing of their first fevered awakening.

Closing her orange notebook, she saw it was after four A.M. She was too excited to be tired, but she lay on her twin bed—still made with the Indian print bedspread from her old room in Laflin—and tried to slow her thoughts.

A few hours later, Elise was awakened by a knock on the door. She reached for the bedside clock. "Shit! I'm coming!"

Irena, Stepan, and Milos stood in the hall outside her room. They had their luggage with them.

Elise was in last night's clothes. Her hair was in tangles. She glanced in the mirror by the door and saw a sleep crease on her left cheek, a smudge of green ink on the right. She had missed their date to meet at Wilson College, to have breakfast at the dining hall there.

Irena's hair was perfect. She had on a light blue sweater set, her usual pale rose lipstick.

"Shit," said Elise again.

"We waited, but Milos was hungry. Here, we brought you some coffee cake." Irena held out the piece of cake, wrapped in a napkin. "Is Debbie out already?"

The three of them walked in, tentatively at first, Irena looking around the corner for Nouveau-Riche Heidi. "What happened to you?" she asked.

"I overslept."

"You should set your alarm when you know—"

"I slept past it."

"You must have been tired."

There was that tone again. Elise told them to sit down. Preparing for the bathroom down the hall, she gathered her toothbrush and towel. She didn't want them in her room alone, but she couldn't very well make them wait outside. What would they do until six, when her parents would call a cab to the airport? Elise felt stranded. She had failed to plan for this second day. They were her responsibility. She felt an overwhelming need to flee, but then—worse—a shock of regret for last night, for not having given Irena so much as a confirming nod when she went on so eagerly about *Waiting for Godot*. Irena was drawn to almost anything she deemed cultural and had simply wanted some companionship in her quest to get at the meaning of Beckett's play. Was that so criminal? Her mother certainly could not get that kind of companionship from her father.

Towel over her shoulder and toothbrush in hand, she swooped down on Irena and enclosed her in a tight embrace. Startled, Irena patted Elise's shoulder brusquely. When Elise backed away and straightened up, she saw that Irena was struggling to hold back tears.

Milos switched on Nouveau's portable television, no doubt looking for a game. Suddenly Elise remembered that Perry Fraser, her friend from Beginning Russian, had given her the name of someone to call if she wanted last-minute tickets to see the Princeton Tigers play.

"Milos!" Irena declared. "You think you're just entitled to amuse yourself with someone else's possessions? That TV belongs to Elise's roommate."

Milos turned off the television.

"Let's not—" began Stepan.

"Milos, do you want to see the Tigers play today? I can get us tickets."

Elise waited for Milos to take this in. In a moment his eyes widened. "Seriously?"

"No. I'm making it up."

The Tigers lost to Dartmouth's Big Green. Milos had been on the edge of his seat in Palmer Stadium. Stepan seemed to enjoy himself, Irena toughed it out, and Elise had kept her eyes on the game while her thoughts raced elsewhere—to her reading last night of the Russian poets, to how she might finagle a way to live in Manhattan this summer, to Nouveau's diaphragm fitting, to her own desperate fear of turning out to be just another trapped soul waiting for Godot.

It was almost four o'clock when the game ended. They walked off campus to get a milkshake for Milos. At the coffee shop, he went on about the Tigers' loss, something about a running back fumbling at a crucial moment, an error he seemed to take very personally. Stepan engaged him briefly, then no one listened.

"I'm taking Intermediate Russian next year," announced Elise. "I might major in Russian Lit."

Irena blew on her tea. Then she turned her head almost imperceptibly to the left and faced Elise again. "And when did you come to this decision?"

"Last night. But it's been brewing."

"Why?"

"What do you mean, why? It's a fascinating culture. There's such passion there."

"'Passion' she calls it, Stepan."

"Things are changing, Irena."

"What's changing? Ever since Dubček left two years ago, all the protests have been squelched. The pansies in our window box lasted longer than the Prague Spring."

"Your family left Czechoslovakia because of the Germans, not the Soviets," Stepan reminded her.

"It doesn't matter. They both speak from the inside of tanks," said Irena. "Bullies of the world."

As if Elise weren't present, Stepan said, "We can't tell her what to study."

"Zlatíčko, why would you want to study the people who brought tanks to your homeland?" Now Irena's tone was wounded.

"It's your homeland, not mine," responded Elise, ashamed even as she said it.

"You have no idea," said Irena. "You and Miloslav have no idea what you have here in America. And what do you do with your advantages? You study the language of Bohemia's occupier, and you burn a dummy of Mr. Kissinger on the lawn. In my view it's a sacrilege to use the freedom this country gives you to mock its leaders."

Elise did not want to debate the people's right of dissent with Irena. She tapped her fingers on the table and looked around. Her fellow students all looked alike. Scruffy in a nonthreatening way. Elise decided that when her parents left later, she would avoid everyone. She would go back to copying poems into her orange notebook. Committing pen to paper, even to reproduce someone else's words, had a way of blanketing her mind.

✦

Elise and Wiley had heard that if they took a course at NYU during the summer, they might be able to stay in university housing there. The second weekend in April, they took the train to Manhattan to find out more. They stayed on Bedford Street, house-sitting for a friend of Wiley's cousin, a teacher who was on spring break in the Bahamas. As soon as they had dropped their bags by the door, Elise wanted to go out again. She didn't particularly care if they made it over to NYU. She wanted only to immerse herself in the gorgeous chaos of Greenwich Village. What could be farther from the staid and imposing environs of Princeton than the bedlam of the Village on a Saturday afternoon?

Back out on the street, the spring breeze carried myriad odors: souvlaki meat turning on a rotisserie, rotten fruit pitched into a corner trash barrel, bread baking inside Zito's Bakery, anise from somewhere, marijuana smoke. Throngs of people crowded the sidewalks, some window shopping, others weaving through the mob. Most of the people were young. They wore jeans, tie-dyed T-shirts, madras skirts, clogs, fringed vests, and—like Wiley today—flowing black caftans and lots of bangle bracelets. One man had Tinker Bell wings attached to his arms. The chaos reminded Elise of pictures she'd seen of medieval marketplaces, the Bruegels she had studied in last semester's art history course. There were rabbits, still unskinned, hanging by their feet in the butcher's window. Plucked ducks. Cheese wheels the size of tires on display in Murray's Cheese Shop. A display of trout on a layer of crushed ice, their iridescent skins flashing in the sunlight and their damp black eyeballs fixed on the sky.

Elise kept tugging at Wiley's arm. "Man, this makes downtown Chicago look like a backwater. Where do you want to go tonight?"

"I don't know," said Wiley, "but we better get over to NYU now."

"Later," said Elise, spotting a secondhand clothes store called Mamie Eisenhower on the corner. "Let's go in here."

"Ugh, it's crowded."

"So what? Come on. You might find some cool Bakelite stuff."

Once Elise was inside, she was seized by a previously undetected need to adorn herself. The place was a gold mine. Some styles Elise recognized from the early sixties, but others went back decades earlier. Yards of chiffon scarves in geometric patterns, late forties suits with cinched waists and padded shoulders, hats with netted veils, raw silk pedal pushers, and—best of all—lace-up, ankle-high shoes, the kind that Irena said Elise's grandmother Kraus had always worn, with hooks and eyes and thin cord laces. Elise made Wiley come to the open dressing room in the back as she tried on armfuls of clothes. She could have been a mannequin, that's how perfectly everything fit. She took out the credit card her father had given her for emergencies and brought everything up to the register.

"Are you crazy?" Wiley asked. "You don't need all this stuff. Where are you going to wear it, anyway?"

Elise didn't pay attention. She had spotted two more pairs of the same twenties high-top shoes she was buying—one brown, the other cordovan. Her size—she wouldn't even have to try them on. She plopped them down on the counter, along with the original pair.

"What's wrong with you?" repeated Wiley. "Your parents are going to kill you." Then she lowered her voice to a whisper. "The prices are outrageous, Elise. That suit has a cigarette burn. Look how worn the leather is in these shoes. This place is a rip-off."

Elise waved away Wiley's concerns. In less than an hour she had discovered her style, and she planned for it to last a lifetime, for at least as long as her dazzling career in Russian language and literature.

"Five hundred and fifteen all together," said the ponytailed clerk at the register. His voice was disaffected. Stoned, no doubt.

"Elise, you have to take back some of this stuff. *Most* of it."

The clerk was putting through Stepan's Master Charge.

"Why? Don't you want anything, Wiley? Look at this." Elise took a blue-and-black cloisonné broach from a basket on the counter and held it up to Wiley's chest. "This is perfect for you," she said. "I'll take this, too."

"No you won't," Wiley said. "Here, take this stuff back." Wiley gathered together all but one pair of shoes. "I'm sorry," she told the stoned clerk. "She's a little weirded out today."

"Fuck you, Wiley," said Elise, signing the charge slip. "Just give me a couple of bags," she demanded of the clerk.

He handed her two outsized paper shopping bags with MAMIE EISENHOWER scrawled in what must have been a match of the former first lady's handwriting. Elise stuffed everything into the bags and rushed out of the shop.

"God, what is *wrong* with you?" demanded Wiley outside. "I'm going over to NYU. You can do whatever you want."

Elise didn't care. She stalked off, bags in hand. She looked in some more windows, bought a box of a dozen cannoli, walked some more, then entered a bar with a sign shaped like a shamrock. In the ladies room, she changed into the pedal pushers. She stayed in the bar for about an hour, drinking with a man who called himself Dunbar. While the sun was still high in the sky, she took him back to the cousin's friend's apartment. He was a burly guy, with a scar on his upper lip. Indisputably sexy. A cabinetmaker, he had said. Probably in his late twenties, Elise thought. She told him about the model of Karlstein Castle in Bohemia that her father had been working on for many years. Dunbar was impressed.

When they reached the apartment, he coaxed her easily onto the bed, kissed her hurriedly, pulled off her pedal pushers, then picked her up and pinned her against the wall, hoisting her legs up and around his waist. His strength was a revelation. Elise adored it at first, moaned loudly, but Dunbar soon overrode her, and then she couldn't block out the rhythmic slapping of her ass against the plaster. When it was over, Dunbar asked if she had any beer. Elise went to the refrigerator. Inside was nothing but yogurt and a jar of wheat germ. She offered him a cannolo. "A what?" he asked. "Singular of cannoli," she said, laughing. "Not this time, sweetheart," he answered, then kissed her forehead and walked out of the apartment.

Wiley returned just after sundown and walked right past Elise, who sat on the teacher's corduroy couch, going through her new purchases.

"I'm taking a bath," was all she said. She stayed in the bathroom for a long time.

After a while, Elise knocked.

"I'm reading."

Elise went in anyway and sat on the toilet. "Please talk to me," she begged the shadow behind the drawn shower curtain. Although she hadn't felt herself start to cry, a tear plopped onto the back of her hand.

"I don't know what there is to say," answered Wiley. The water made a swishing sound when she placed her book, open facedown, on the floor beside the tub.

"I brought some guy here," confessed Elise.

"Great. I really needed to hear that."

"I know, but I had to tell you. You're my best friend. I have to tell you things."

"No you don't. There are things I don't tell you."

"Like what?"

"*Elise.*"

Elise heard Wiley stand up and take a towel off the rack.

"Please don't be mad at me," Elise said. She heard her beseeching tone, so unlike herself, but couldn't control it. "Please. I don't know what I'd do without you. You're my rock. Shit, you're going to be a *doctor.*"

"That's the plan, anyway," mused Wiley, pulling aside the shower curtain and stepping out of the tub to dry her feet. When she looked up, she said, "God, Elise, what are you wearing?"

Elise lowered her head to confirm. She had on the chintz shirtwaist dress, the cordovan high-top shoes (only one laced), and a chiffon scarf printed with octagons.

"It's the new me," she answered.

Wiley broke out laughing. Once they had started, it went on for a while, Wiley stopping for several seconds, then chuckling again. Despite the pains that shot up her side, Elise was helpless to stop her laughter until ten minutes after Wiley made her take a Valium.

It was still early evening, and they sat down together to watch whatever was on TV. Elise could not focus. Though feeling wobbly from the effects of the drug, she was nonetheless shot through with an aimless sense of dread, with a metallic taste at the back of her tongue, and with the sudden conviction that she could just as easily be any of the passersby on Bedford Street or one of their dogs or a trout laid out on ice. Her body was all but borderless. That weekend in Chicago she had felt the same. She wanted to tell Wiley about that time, and she wanted to ask her if she knew the borders of *her* body, but it all became too intricate and too burdensome to phrase. Instead, she gathered the teacher's afghan around her, reached out to rest her hand on Wiley's knee, and submitted to the Valium—to the seduction of sleep.

Chapter Four

"This just came in," Irena told Sylvie Vanek. "We've been order-ing from a new supplier. They have everything teenage girls like. They make it their business to keep up to date."

The fabric was a mustard-colored paisley. Ugly, even atrocious in Irena's view, but the girls in Laflin were wearing a lot of paisley these days. Sylvie sewed for all three of her girls, two in high school and one still in elementary.

"Michelle might like it, but I don't know. What else do you have?"

From the shelf Reyna Kopecky had set aside for the new wholesaler's goods, Irena pulled out five fabrics suitable for dressmaking. The bolts had just arrived; all had their full yardage. Pulling them down set off Irena's bursitis pain, but what could she do? Furthermore, she didn't enjoy having to make a fuss over fabrics she would never let touch her own body. The 1970s were turning out to be a terrible fabric decade. If Irena took a match to three-quarters of the bolts in the store, they would melt into a sticky puddle. Polyester, acrylic, acetate, rayon blends—why was everyone so crazy about parading around in plastic?

Reyna Kopecky had spoken to Irena about dressing in fabrics more like the ones the shop sold, but Irena thought there were limits to how much she would do for the sake of the shop. Weren't American women supposed to have freedom of choice when it came to their bodies? Wasn't that what *Roe v. Wade* two years ago had been all about?

Irena still sewed most of her clothes, but only from the bolts of pure cotton or loose-weave linen that she periodically dusted off at the back of the store. In the summer, she preferred her clothes to breathe. The new fabrics had no pores. In winter she chose wool gabardine. What was so complicated? She had learned a lot about people from working at Reyna Kopecky's. As soon as a new customer walked in the door, Irena could easily tell if she would jump on the latest bandwagon or hold fast to her own taste.

Whether Irena liked it or not, there was no doubt that her daughter, Elise, had her own style, one she had discovered while still a freshman at Princeton. Although Irena approved of the fabrics Elise selected (most patterns from the forties and early fifties were woven through, not surface printed), she would never get used to her daughter's style. Half the time she looked simply outlandish. Why did she have to draw such attention to herself? It had all started during that weekend in Greenwich Village when Elise had abused her credit card privileges. She and Stepan had been shocked when they'd received their Master Charge bill. They had phoned the company to report a theft, but finally had to call Elise. She had never been so extravagant before; they couldn't understand it. They had called the shop, Mamie Eisenhower, to confirm Elise's claim that the clothes could not be returned. Stepan and Irena had agreed the best thing to do was make Elise pay back all the money. Elise had wanted to live in Manhattan that summer, but they'd made her return home. She had worked at Reyna Kopecky's and at Dairy Queen. If a Princeton coed was humiliated working at a Dairy Queen, Irena was sorry, but she and Stepan had both taken the shopping spree as a sign that the values reflected at Princeton did not live up to their academics. Ivy League or not, they couldn't let a college with too many children of the rich undo the effects of their careful and principled child rearing. Stepan had even spoken of not sending Elise back, but in the end Irena persuaded him they would be depriving their daughter of a precious advantage—that Elise simply had to learn how to resist temptation, that doing so was part of growing up in a materialistic country.

Thankfully, by the time September came, Elise appeared to have regained her ground, and Irena sent her daughter off to her sophomore year with her own hope restored.

Sylvie Vanek pointed to the bolt of jade-green Dacron. "That would look good on Jana, but she doesn't really need any new clothes. I came in here for Michelle. You'd better put a leash on me, Irena," she said, winking.

"Oh, *pish*," said Reyna, appearing from nowhere. "You aren't going to find a fabric that will better bring out the color of Jana's eyes. And she's so slim you could probably get away with less than a yard."

Sylvie Vanek looked from Reyna to Irena. "Dano wouldn't like it. He said 'Michelle only.'"

Dano Vanek had been out of work for six months. He was one of the proudest men in Laflin, a shoemaker whose store had not been able to sustain itself. People said he had started drinking.

Irena rolled out the beige rayon blend with the pattern of the see-hear-and-speak-no-evil monkeys. Michelle was still young enough to wear it. "What about this?" she asked. "Michelle would look adorable in this."

Reyna walked off, clearly irritated that Irena had steered Sylvie back to her original intention.

"Maybe just a *little* less busy," Sylvie said. In the end, she chose a bright madras and a zipper and buttons to go with it.

Irena started to measure and cut.

"How're Elise and Miloslav?" Sylvie asked.

"Just fine. Elise is in graduate school at Northwestern now, completely taken up with her studies. She plans to get her Ph.D., then apply for a tenure-track position."

"Really? Well, I can't say I'm surprised. She was always so advanced. What's her field?"

"Literature."

"Oh, I'm so glad she didn't pick one of those silly fields that are coming up these days. Communications. What's that? Isn't that what they teach in kindergarten? Or, what's that other one? Industrial psychology. My nephew in Bloomington is studying that. He explained it to me once, but it sounded like something right of out of the Office of Propaganda. I didn't tell him that, of course. What kind of literature is Elise specializing in?"

"American," lied Irena, plucking some loose threads from the madras.

"The Jazz Era. You know, F. Scott Fitzgerald and Hemingway and those writers."

Now that Magda Kriz had helped her so much with novel reading, Irena had joined the sisters' book group, five women and two men. This month they were reading *The Great Gatsby*. Irena loved it. Not that she didn't know that Jay Gatsby would turn out to be someone else by the end of the book, but if Nick Carraway and the others could be captivated by him, so could she.

"It must be wonderful to have her so close by," said Sylvie. "Tell her I wish her the best of luck."

Irena folded the madras and wrapped it in a sheet of white tissue. She smiled but didn't answer Sylvie. Let her think that she and Stepan saw Elise regularly. Let her think the four of them, Miloslav included, had Sunday dinners and that Elise was really studying American literature.

"Is there someone special?" Sylvie added tentatively.

"You mean Elise? Not that we know of. Stepan and I have decided that one day she'll just walk in the door with a ring on her finger, a good-looking man by the hand, and that will be that."

"America," concluded Sylvie and waved good-bye.

When the store was empty, Reyna came up front again. "Irena, would you please try to team up with me a little more? You should see the books this month. Do you want us to go the way of Dano Vanek?"

Only recently had Reyna Kopecky started to talk this way. For years she had said she thought of Irena as a partner, not an employee. But things between them were changing. It wasn't Irena's fault that people weren't sewing as much these days. It was the inexpensive ready-mades, the wash-and-wears, the American need for ease. The shop wasn't doing as well as it had, but Irena couldn't change her sales approach now. And she knew her customers. Despite years of hard work to reach the middle class, most of them were barely hanging on to its bottom rung.

Irena didn't know what to say to Reyna. She busied herself replacing the bolts she had pulled down earlier.

In bed that night, rubbing Bengay onto her bad shoulder, Irena said to Stepan, "I don't know if Reyna has changed or I have. After seventeen years, I'm not sure I like her anymore."

"Quit, then," said Stepan, bending over on his side of the bed to untie his shoes.

It was eleven o'clock on a Karlstein Castle night. Irena had come to see that it was unlikely Stepan would finish Karlstein Castle within the next five years, and she had imposed a rule that three nights a week he stay upstairs with her. Occasionally she wished that she had never raised the issue, since they usually ended up watching situation comedies that were beneath them—or any full-grown adult.

"You know I can't quit."

"Yes, you can, Irena. We'll be fine."

"We won't be so fine, Stepan. We're not so fine even now. And we have Miloslav's education to think about."

"He'll get a baseball scholarship, you watch."

"Maybe and maybe not. But even so, who knows what'll come up with Elise?"

This was what really worried Irena. Northwestern had given Elise only a quarter of her first year's tuition. The remainder came from student loans that Elise would have to start paying back out of her first-year teaching salary. Irena sighed. Certain things had gone wrong, and contemplating the reasons exhausted Irena. Throughout Elise's years at Princeton, Irena had continued to fade from the center of her daughter's life. She could have been one of the complicated cartoon figures the eight-year-old Elise had drawn with the knobs on her Etch A Sketch set, then unceremoniously shaken away. One shake faded; two shakes dimmer still; three shakes gone. Irena was not yet gone, but she frequently experienced a dread that she might be soon. Never mind how close Northwestern was to Laflin; that had turned out not to matter.

Over the years, Irena had grown to expect a secondhand education simply from being in Elise's company. That was how it had been when Elise was a little girl. By scrupulously seeking out a cultural education for her daughter, Irena had improved her own tastes, brought into the house new ideas to filter out the stale ones that came of being uneducated. If not for Elise, how would Irena have happened upon Dalcroze's Eurhythmics, the harmonious movements and improvisation that delivered to Irena a wondrous sense of permission every time she watched it in action? How would she have discovered the magical floating figures of Chagall if not through her daughter's eyes? Or found out about the sonata form, if they hadn't brought home those instructive LPs from the Young People's Concerts Elise had attended at Orchestra Hall? Stepan would never have accompanied Irena to Chicago to seek out such experiences, and he preferred that Irena did not take public transportation alone. But he hadn't seemed to mind Irena taking Elise. She had convinced him that exposing Elise to the cultural life of Chicago was part of her obligation as a good mother.

"Everything's fine," Stepan assured her again, yawning.

When he got under the covers, Irena wanted to sidle up to him, but he had been too tired to take a shower, and he smelled of the contact cement he used for his model making. Of course, she smelled of the Bengay she'd rubbed on her bursitis shoulder. Irena smiled to herself. Would Daisy Buchanan have entered the marital bed smelling of Bengay?

Unable to fall sleep after an hour, Irena got out of bed and headed for the living room. First she checked on Miloslav in his small bedroom off the kitchen. He had kicked off the covers. He was growing so fast it was as if his bones lengthened as he slept. She pulled up the zipped-open sleeping bag he liked to use as a blanket. Only a few months ago his cheeks had been smooth. Now he was shaving once a week. Miloslav was turning out to be a good-looking boy, and not a bad one compared to some his age. She and Stepan were doing right by him. Josef, thought Irena, would have been satisfied. Katrina, God knew. Miloslav had stopped asking about his mother a few years after she'd left. In any case, Irena and Stepan knew nothing. For years their letters had gone unanswered. The KSC, no doubt.

Irena turned on the bronze floor lamp in the living room and picked up *The Great Gatsby*. She sat down in her La-Z-Boy recliner and flipped the book over. "F. Scott Fitzgerald was born in St. Paul, Minnesota, in 1896, and attended Princeton University." There was a time when that sentence would have given Irena a proprietary thrill. "Just like my Elise," she would have thought, but the luster had been taken off her hopes for her daughter. Elise had been rejected by Princeton's Ph.D. program in Slavic Literature. Northwestern had accepted her, but Irena never found out the reason for Princeton's rejection. Turning down one of their own? There must have been grounds of some kind. After all, Elise had done respectably as an undergraduate. Yes, there were the unaccounted-for times after she and Elise had argued that Irena hadn't heard from her daughter, once for four weeks, another time for six. Irena could only suppose there were things she did not know, but she was quite sure that Elise's grade-point average had never fallen below a 3.2. Probably, Irena had to concede, that wasn't good enough for Princeton's program. If Elise *had* gone into American literature, as Irena had told Sylvie, perhaps she would have had a better chance of staying at the very apex of her field. (*Apex*—the uppermost point—a word from last week's log.)

Irena tried to concentrate on *The Great Gatsby,* but now she had an uneasy feeling in the pit of her stomach from lying to Sylvie Vanek. But how could she tell her and Stepan's friends, all Czech, that Elise was studying Russian? What would she say to the few relatives Irena and Stepan both had in Plzen? What the KSC was doing there and throughout Czechoslovakia was unspeakable. "Normalization," they called it. Normal according to whom? Normalization meant no newspapers or radio stations that weren't controlled by the party, no art they didn't approve of. It meant all kinds of persecution, more than Irena and Stepan probably knew. Every single citizen, even Irena's fifteen-year-old nephew Martin, had to carry a red book with all sorts of information in it. And the ŠtB, the KSC's national security police, had a file on every adult in Czechoslovakia. That terrible Gustáv Husák had gone from being Dubček's deputy to a patsy of the Central Committee. He was a typical politician, Irena thought, grabbing power from whoever dangled it in front of him.

Irena simply could not tell her friends that Elise was in love with Russia and its literature. The Kriz sisters, for example. Their younger brother Petr, still in Bohemia, was a famous violinist who had been arrested by the ŠtB for performing in an unsanctioned concert. Almost everyone Irena knew had some version of this story. Did the Russians write beautiful and heartrending poetry? Yes, but the Germans during Hitler's rise had also excelled in the arts, a cruel contradiction that Irena had no interest in pondering.

But lying to her friends? She had done it once or twice before, but never easily. How many times had she used that quote, the one Elise had told her was actually *not* from Shakespeare but from another English writer, Sir Walter Scott: "Oh what a tangled web we weave / when first we practice to deceive"?

"What are you doing out here?" Stepan interrupted.

Irena shuddered. He'd crept up on her. "You scared me."

"I'm sorry. It's past one."

"I couldn't sleep."

Stepan groaned, expressing his own weariness, his own dread of facing tomorrow with not enough sleep. He looked defenseless in his buttoned-up pajamas and bare feet.

"You can let me worry about the money," he said. "Haven't I always?"

"It's not the money."

"Come to bed."

Stepan held out a hand, and Irena took it. Back in bed, she moved close to him. "I lied to Sylvie Vanek. I told her Elise was studying American literature."

"So? Tell her you were mistaken."

"Stepan, how could I be mistaken!" Irena started to move away. "What mother wouldn't know a thing like that?"

Stepan tightened his grip. "Russian is an academic subject, like math or science. It's nothing personal against us."

"You're wrong, Stepan. I think it *is* something against us. But anyway, it's too late. You and Miloslav have to lie also. If anyone asks, you have to say Elise is studying American literature."

"You're going to drag Milos and me into this, too?"

"What choice do I have now?"

Stepan loosened his grip, and Irena took her place on the other side of the bed.

On her way to the Kriz sisters' house, Irena glanced down at the saran-wrapped pan of Pillsbury brownies she carried. What a depressing sight. Maybe it was her just due for having once told Elise's freshman roommate that Pillsbury was a hit at their house. True enough—Miloslav had been crazy about the refrigerator biscuits Irena popped in the oven when she didn't have time to bake real ones. But now she couldn't get away from Pillsbury. The Kriz sisters served it at every Saturday Mariáš game. Their first had been a marble cake with chocolate frosting from a can. As time went on, the sisters made fewer kolaces with poppy-seed filling. Then they made none. As a consequence, Irena worried they would think her homemade strudel was a reproach, so for the sake of the friendship she had stopped making it. Now at the Saturday games they ate nothing but cakes from a mix and cookies from refrigerator dough. Appallingly good at first bite, but then a chemical aftertaste.

Just after Irena let herself in and laid the pan of brownies on the kitchen counter, she heard a raised voice and the slamming of a door. When Magda and Berta approached, their steps were heavy.

The sisters hugged Irena as usual. Berta announced that today they would dispense with selecting the contract—Magda wanted to take Open Durch. Magda looked tired, Irena thought. She doubted Magda really wanted to play Open Durch, the highest possible contract and the most difficult to win.

As they began to play, Irena and Berta against Magda, Irena tried to distract the sisters from whatever was bothering them. She raised her voice over the sound of cards slapped too vigorously onto the dining room table. "How can anyone be expected to put a child through college?" she complained. "We helped Elise as much as we could with Princeton. To do it all over again with Miloslav, I just don't see how we can."

"You need to invest your money," said Berta, not for the first time.

Both sisters had told Irena this before. But the savings interest rates were good, and Stepan believed in putting aside money they could always count on. Moreover, Irena was just plain scared of the stock market. No one in Bohemia would have thought up such a thing, a legitimate game for people to gamble their paltry earnings.

"I wouldn't know where to start," answered Irena, trying to dismiss the topic with a tone of finality.

"I'll sit down with you," offered Berta.

Irena took note of the *I'll*. What had happened to the usual *we'll*?

"I'd never be able to take it all in," she claimed.

Berta glanced up from her cards. "I'd be embarrassed to tell you how much we've made since we started in the early sixties." A trace of a smile appeared.

At least the *we* was back. Still, Irena thought boasting about money was vulgar.

"The best choice we made," continued Berta, "was McDonald's. Personally I would never eat at one, but did you know its founder is from Plzen?"

This *was* surprising. Irena looked up from her hand. "Is that so?"

"Ray Kroc. He was born here in Oak Park—he's another Chicago Czech—but his family emigrated from Plzen."

"I never knew that."

"Concentrate," directed Magda. "Are we playing or not?"

Berta ignored her. "We invested out of a sense of Bohemian pride," she said, "but you would not believe how well the stock has done. And we got in late—I can just imagine the people before us. You really should think about buying it, Irena. By the time Miloslav is ready for college, you'll be able to help him."

Even Irena knew that it wasn't wise for people to invest in stocks when the price was high, as McDonald's must be. Rather than be negative, she joked, "I'd prefer to bet my money on Pillsbury. We've raised their stock all by ourselves."

"The kind of success Ray Kroc has had could only happen in this country," Berta went on. "He never finished high school. He had a few failures, but they didn't doom him. He was already in his fifties when he founded McDonald's. It gives us all hope. A captain of industry with a grade-school education."

"I didn't know captains of industry impressed you so much," said Magda without looking up at Berta.

Again Berta ignored her. "Just last year Ray Kroc bought the San Diego Padres. You know, the baseball team. Tell that to Miloslav. He'll be so impressed, he'll beg you to buy McDonald's stock."

"It is impressive," conceded Irena. But it was easy to be impressed, she thought. She was impressed multiple times a day by the accomplishments of strangers. Being impressed, though, was not the same as being inspired; it was not what mattered.

"Stay afterwards," said Berta. "I'll show you how to get started."

Before Irena could politely decline this offer, Magda placed her cards on the table, faceup. Astonishingly, she had the highest outstanding cards in all four suits: Hearts, Bells, Leaves, and Acorns.

Berta stared at her sister's hands. "For Christ's *sake*!" Her tone brimmed with accusation.

"You two were talking," defended Magda.

"As if that mattered. It's your luck. Your despicable luck."

"Berta, please." Magda was embarrassed. "Irena does not have to hear..."

Berta turned to Irena. "It turns out she's a mistress, the lover of a married man. What do you think of *that*?"

Was Irena expected to answer?

"And she says he's going to leave his wife for her."

Irena looked at Magda, her winning hand still spread before her.

"I'm sorry," Magda said, her tone measured. "This was going to be a conversation for another time."

Berta was crying. She turned her back on Magda to talk to Irena. "I'm trying to see it from her perspective, I really am. I know how ungenerous I must sound."

"I'm not judging you," said Irena. "Please. It's not for me to judge either of you."

"You should have heard how she sprung it on me," Berta continued.

"There's no easy time," interrupted Magda. "Let's not get Irena involved. She's our steadfast friend."

"Forty-nine years old," said Berta, tilting her head to acknowledge Magda behind her, "and behaving like a teenager ready to elope."

Irena was grateful for this information, never having known the ages of the Kriz sisters—only that Berta was the older by three years. It was a comfort to confirm they were all so close in age. For years she had thought of her herself as something of a third Kriz sister.

Irena rose from her seat. "What should I use to serve the brownies?"

"The china plate with the grape bunches," Magda answered eagerly. "You know where it is. And we moved the cake knife to the top side drawer."

When Irena came back to the dining room with a pyramid of brownies and three dessert plates, Berta stopped whispering and went back to the kitchen to percolate the coffee. She did not look at Irena as she passed.

"I *am* sorry," Magda said after Irena sat down. "I'd planned to talk to you alone."

Irena shrugged.

"He's another teacher at my school. The biology teacher. He's Czech."

Irena nodded, then held herself still.

"Half Czech, actually, since his mother was Hungarian. His marriage has been bad for some time. He has no children."

Irena was relieved that at least the man had no children, but surprised by Magda's naïveté about his marriage. She sounded like any self-deluding mistress on one of those lunchtime soap operas.

"Are you really moving out?"

Magda smoothed the front of her blouse. Maybe she wore old bras on weekends, but it looked to Irena like Magda's breasts were sagging. She wondered if the biology teacher minded.

"It seems to be headed in that direction." Magda sounded contrite yet smiled in spite of herself.

As far as Irena knew, Magda and Berta had lived together ever since their separation during college. "This is a milestone, then," said Irena, choosing the neutral term carefully.

"Yes, and like all milestones, it carries its freight," said Magda.

Berta walked in with three coffee cups on a tray. She looked older than fifty-two, Irena thought, and so sad that Irena had to hold back her own tears. Drinking their coffee together, they avoided the topic of Magda's news. Berta told a brief story about one of her colleagues at the *Czechoslovak Daily Herald,* a man they were accustomed to making fun of, but her mournful tone blurred the point of the story. Then Magda announced she had a pile of papers to grade. She'd had her fourth-year honors students translate a passage from *Swann's Way,* and she had to be alert, she said. She hugged Irena and left.

Still tense, Irena and Berta helped themselves to second brownies.

"When I was nineteen," Irena started, "my mother found out that my father—my own otec I loved so much—had a girlfriend, a bookkeeper at the Ruff Brewing Company. When Maminka figured it out, she yelled so loud that all of Quincy got their gossip for the month. She made my father break it off. They don't want to leave their wives, Berta. If they go to Mass or not, most of them remember they're Catholic when it comes time to actually leave their wives. And most men, if you want my opinion, are too lazy to go. Stepan I don't believe cheats on me. He has his model making, a lover who doesn't talk back. But if he ever did start up with another woman, I know that in the end he'd be too scared to leave. It will probably blow over with the biology teacher."

"It's not for me to say," answered Berta, identifying the very truth from which Irena wanted to protect her—that Berta's opinions would have little influence over Magda from here on in.

Irena put her hand on Berta's. "Listen to me," she said. "I have some money Stepan never asks about, from the dressmaking I do at home. It's more than Stepan thinks. Do you really think McDonald's is going to keep going up?"

"I do!" said Berta, rousing the part of herself she apparently trusted most. "It would be a smart thing to do, Irena. Here." She pulled a pen from her pocket and wrote on her paper napkin. "I'm giving you the number of my broker."

Irena tucked the napkin into the zipper compartment inside her purse. Never on her own would she invest in a stock. But who knew? In America, great profits could come from anywhere, from ugly fabrics that made you perspire in winter or from skimpy hamburgers with too much gristle.

Chapter Five

December 1976

Elise forgot to check the time. She simply picked up the phone and dialed. She had been outside, moving about so she could think more clearly. She had circled Norris, the student center, in the moonlight. Afterward she'd returned to Engelhart Hall, the dorm for graduate students where she lived, and paced around the parking lot, wondering—not for the first time—how she had ended up in such a nothing building, a brick mid-rise with ugly juniper shrubs out front. Now she was back in her room. Carla, the moron who lived below her, had banged on the ceiling twice. Tomorrow morning she would leave a nasty note about the sound of Elise's heels. It was too much trouble for Elise to unlace her shoes—all those eyelets. Besides, she needed to be ready to go out again; she never felt quite right unless she was ready to go out again.

"This is the last time I'm answering," said Wiley Mills. "*The* last. I mean it. Maybe you don't need sleep, but other people do."

"Are you in bed?"

"No, I'm having afternoon tea. At three in the morning."

"Sorry. Don't be mad. It's really important this time. I'm getting married."

Wiley sighed. Elise hated that Wiley acted so blasé about vitally important changes in her life, as though she were just being melodramatic. "Did you hear me?"

"Yes. Elise, did you talk to Dr. Brinner about giving you something to sleep?"

"I don't remember. Who cares? I like not sleeping. So Viktor wants to marry me. It'll be so much easier to go to Leningrad if I just marry him. And he's not so bad, right? You said so, when we came to New York. You said you were expecting worse, remember? And older looking."

"Don't marry him," said Wiley.

"That's easy for you to say!" Elise accused, her tone mounting in that way that Wiley had told her she had to control. "Everything's going like clockwork for you. Two more years at Columbia and you'll have your pick of neonatal residencies. You'll go on record as saving the youngest preemie ever. Then marriage, affluence, kids. Tick, tock, tick, tock."

Elise flashed on tomorrow morning, when she knew she would wake up to regret the very tone she was using now, the one Wiley had told her would alienate everyone, including Wiley herself, if Elise couldn't get a grip on it.

"You're flying, Elise. You need a medication adjustment. Call Dr. Brinner. Don't marry Viktor."

"He loves me."

"You don't love him. Anyway, you have to be stabilized before you can make such a big decision."

"Lithium makes me fat."

"No it doesn't. And even if it did a little, the rewards outweigh the drawbacks. Excuse the pun."

"Viktor is good for me. *He* stabilizes me."

"Men are not medicines," said Wiley. "*Medicines* are medicines. Go get your blood levels checked."

"He thought my Princeton thesis on the Acmeism movement was brilliant. Which is more than *Princeton* thought."

"Get over that already. Northwestern has a highly respected program."

"He loves Akhmatova as much as I do," continued Elise. "In his seminar on Russian poetry last year, he devoted more time to her than to any other poet. His analysis was prosaic, but still."

From the heap of books on her desk, Elise pulled out a volume with a torn dust jacket. "Listen to this. It's from the Stanley Kunitz, Max

Hayward translation: 'Here is my gift, not roses on your grave, / not sticks of burning incense. / You lived aloof, maintaining to the end / your magnificent disdain.' That's the first stanza of 'In Memory of M. B.' Don't you love that—*magnificent disdain*? I told you, the best translations are collaborations."

Elise went on to recite the rest of the poem, interrupting herself twice to comment on words she could tell were Kunitz's. Then she delivered the poem in Russian, hardly faltering, although there was no text in front of her.

"I'm hanging up now, Elise."

"No! Please. I'm scared. I don't want to marry Viktor. He's boring," Elise complained. "And he has a small dick. Boring with a small dick—what less could one ask for?" She began to laugh hysterically.

"Elise, you know I hate to just hang up on you, but I'm going to."

"Wait! Wiley, I'm sorry . . ."

Too late. Wiley had cut her off. Elise put down the receiver, looked around her cluttered room, then once more dialed Wiley's number on West 110th Street, where she lived with her boyfriend, Michael, a hematology resident at Columbia-Presbyterian Hospital.

Wiley picked up before the first ring had ended. "I will not speak to you again until you see Dr. Brinner," she said, and hung up again.

"*Fuck* her!" shouted Elise to the empty room. Furiously, she began untying one of her high-top shoes. After she worked it off, she flung it against the opposite wall, feeling supremely enriched by the smacking sound when it made contact, then again when it fell to the floor.

In a moment came Carla's broom handle banging on her ceiling. Elise crossed the room, picked up the shoe, and pounded its heel on the floor as hard as she could. Let Carla call campus police, as she had done twice before. Who cared? Who could stand the peppiness of the early childhood ed students anyway? Elise would marry Viktor Frolov. He had tenure. He had published a textbook on Russian syntax and style as well as translated two obscure nineteenth-century Lithuanian poets. He understood Elise and wasn't threatened by the mood disorder that Dr. Brinner called manic-depressive illness but that Elise called "It." Viktor was the only person besides Wiley who knew about It, and he didn't take certain of her behaviors personally. Viktor would never hang up on Elise.

Fuck Wiley. Nothing was hard for her. She swam downstream. Elise was going to marry Viktor and live in Leningrad with him next semester, while he was on sabbatical. She would travel to nearby Tsarskoye Selo, where Anna Akhmatova had grown up. She would go to the Russian Museum to examine the portraits of her there and visit her grave at Komarova back in Leningrad. She still could not believe that Akhmatova, among the greatest Russian poets, had died as recently as Elise's sophomore year at Laflin High. Yet Elise had not heard of her until she'd come across an anthology in the poetry stacks at Firestone Library. After reading the anthology, Elise had borrowed books by others of the Acmeism movement. She remembered the first Osip Mandelstam poem she had ever read, "Sisters." "Sisters—Heaviness and Tenderness—you look the same." It had made her think of her mother's friends, the Kriz sisters. Berta was Heaviness. Now the sounds in the first line attracted Elise, beckoned her, even. The emphasis could go in any number of places, she thought, and still convey power. She began to recite the line over and over, stressing first one syllable, then another. She sang it, finally making it absurd, turning Heaviness and Tenderness into two of the Seven Dwarfs. She did this until she was exhausted. By the time she stripped off her clothes and got into bed, a tint of morning light had exposed the shape of the single window in her tiny bedroom.

Viktor Frolov, Elise knew, was not the most beloved of the professors in the Slavic languages and literature Ph.D. program. Competent but uninspired, people agreed. By reputation, he was a more interesting teacher of language studies than of literature. Attendance at his Applied Linguistics class was better than at his seminar in Russian poetry. A couple of students had imitated his tone-deaf reading of lyric poems. One or two others had pointed to Viktor Frolov as an example of what was wrong with tenure.

Viktor and Elise's relationship had started the day after she had overslept and missed his course "Development of Russian Phonology, Morphology, and Syntax." She had been up most of the night studying the grammatical structure of Serbo-Croatian.

The doctoral program required that its students be competent in a second Slavic language. Elise's mother had lobbied for Czech. "Think how much easier it will be for you," Irena had pointed out. "You already know the basics." And besides, Irena had added, the two of them could converse in Czech, something Miloslav couldn't do and Stepan had no interest in doing. But Elise had wanted the challenge of Serbo-Croatian, which had some different declensions than Russian and a total of seven verb tenses. She had stayed up that night trying to recognize these tenses, but on her way to lunch the following day, Professor Frolov had stopped her.

"We missed you in class this morning, Ms. Blazek," he had said in his heavily accented English.

"Professor, I'm sorry. I had a personal thing."

"Those are always useful. It is not considered appropriate for us to inquire about those."

"You can inquire." Elise felt her guard slipping. Without warning, her guard did this from time to time. One blink, and gone was the bulwark against all who would invade her. "I get these horrible period cramps, at least the first day. I promise I'll be there next week."

Viktor had reared back just perceptibly, enough to signal the usual mix of embarrassment and disapproval that men try to conceal when women they don't know very well forget themselves and mention menstruation. He had looked down at his open and overflowing briefcase, then back up at her, his eyebrows raised. It wasn't hard to guess his chain of thought: "period, body, sex, me." Elise had smiled back, run her hand through her newly dyed red hair. Clearing his throat, Viktor had maintained his wide-eyed expression. His eyebrows were thick and his chin stubbly, even by noon. He was shorter than Elise, not a handsome man, but the years hadn't touched the clarity of his pale blue eyes. Elise could sleep with those blue eyes, she had decided, focus on them to the exclusion of all else. She had cocked her head and asked Viktor if there was any chance they could meet at the Golden Coach that night to go over what she had missed.

Viktor had agreed instantly. In the early evening, they'd met at the bar, a block off campus. An hour later they were in Viktor's apartment, an unremarkable one-bedroom in faculty housing. They drank vodka on the rocks. Keeping the striking blue of his eyes in mind, Elise gave Viktor a blow job he deemed among the top ten of his life. Then she had stood up, curtsied, and asked him for another vodka. After he poured one for each of them, she began to question him about his childhood in Leningrad.

Two weeks later, Viktor was still talking, and Elise was no longer distracted by his shaggy eyebrows or the hair peeping out of his ears. The deprivations he had suffered forgave his less elegant features.

Elise wanted to go with Viktor to Leningrad. He was signed up to teach at an exchange program there next semester, the CIEE Russian Language Study Program. It would be his first return to the Soviet Union since his emigration in 1963, and Viktor said it had been next to impossible to arrange. When she asked how he'd done it, he had given her an enigmatic smile. Now that he was in, he said, he could probably get her in too. She could be his TA, teaching intermediate Russian to American students.

By the third week of their relationship, Viktor knew everything. He knew about Rupert Dwyer and how Elise had been arrested for vandalizing his parents' apartment building on Lake Shore Drive. He knew about Elise's first shopping binge, at Mamie Eisenhower in the West Village, when she was a freshman at Princeton. He knew that Elise's best friend, Wiley Mills, had tried to get her to go to the counseling center but that Elise had opted instead to break off the friendship. Elise had told Viktor how finally her roommate—whom she had privately called Nouveau-Riche Heidi—had called the counseling center after Elise had stayed in bed sleeping or eating peanut-butter crackers and watching *The Phil Donahue Show* for two straight weeks, speaking only to ask her visitors what they thought made their lives worth living. In front of Elise, Debbie had asked about the legality of committing someone against her will. Embarrassed for Nouveau, Elise had grabbed the receiver and set up her own appointment at the center. There she had seen a Dr. Shelley Weiss for three sessions, the last coinciding with Elise's complete and inexplicable recovery, her enthusiastic reentry into Princeton's academic and social life.

Viktor knew also that Elise's sophomore year had had its trials but that it wasn't until Elise was a junior and rooming with Wiley, once again her best friend, that she was forced to consult a psychiatrist in Manhattan. A bribe, essentially. Wiley had confronted Elise with the draft of a suicide note she had run across among the papers on Elise's desk. "It's just a draft," Elise had claimed. "You know what a slow writer I am, how much I revise. I probably won't finish it for years." Wiley had not been amused.

She had called her father, the Nashville neurologist who thought the female mind was as nimble as a gazelle, and he'd given her the number of his med school friend, now a psychiatrist with a Park Avenue practice. "Call him now," Wiley had threatened, waving the suicide note in the air, "or I go to the counseling center *and* to the dean of students. Who will in turn go straight to your parents."

And Viktor knew all the rest—that the Manhattan psychiatrist had diagnosed manic-depressive illness and started Elise on lithium. Elise had seen him only a handful of times after that, but in the late spring of her senior year, he had referred her to Dr. Jonathan Brinner, the Chicago psychiatrist who was treating her now.

Listening to this tale, this case history, Viktor had stroked Elise's hair. "The Eastern European temperament is in your veins," he had told her.

With Viktor, Elise's condition—"It"—was a mere footnote to her personality. She wondered if half the Russian population wasn't manic-depressive. In their first few weeks together, Viktor had seen behavior from Elise that only Wiley had seen. Nothing seemed to faze him, not her excesses or her self-recriminations. Elise began to think it was no wonder she was attracted to Russia—the national psyche seemed to mirror her own.

Still, Wiley was right that Elise was not in love with Viktor Frolov. In truth, her mind often wandered as he spoke. But who else would walk open-eyed with Elise into her future, and who else could get her to Leningrad?

✦

Fifteen minutes before Patten Gym opened on the second Saturday in March, Elise was already standing outside with her nylon mesh bag. Inside the bag were her Jensen racing suit, two latex bathing caps, swim goggles, a bottle of aloe vera and one of vitamin E, a pair of rubber thongs, and a Northwestern towel. In her view, the Patten pool—not lithium—was her true mood stabilizer. Every day of the week Elise showed up at Patten. Plenty of days she showed up twice. One day last month, when her careening thoughts threatened to permanently separate her from her body, Elise had gone to the pool three times. The entire day had been taken up with undressing, covering her hair in a protective coat of aloe vera gel, doggedly swimming her twenty-five laps, showering, drying her hair, lacing up her high-top shoes, then doing it all over again two hours later. Pursued by ineffable terrors, Elise had distrusted the earth's gravity that day. In the water, she had been able to transfer the energy from her prickly nerves to the muscles in her arms as she coursed evenly up and down her lane. Today she had to get her swim in early. It would be her one chance all day, and it had to fortify her for the long journey ahead.

By noon, Elise and Viktor were in Laflin. They had rented a car. They would eat lunch at the Blazeks', then drive to O'Hare Airport. Eighteen hours later they would land in Leningrad.

Normally on a Saturday, Stepan would be napping or in the basement working on his castle. Milos would be at baseball practice, and Irena would be cleaning. But when Irena opened the door, Elise saw that she and Stepan and Milos were dressed in their best clothes. Irena's good linen tablecloth had been spread over the dining room table. When Elise noticed that the silver goblets from Plzen had been polished till they gleamed, the sunlight showing off their resplendent surfaces, she wanted to rush into her mother's arms and apologize for the last seven years of her life. "Maminka," she would call Irena, as Irena had called her own mother, Maminka, take me back. Instead, she took Viktor's hand and declared, "This is Viktor Frolov. I'll be his teaching assistant in Leningrad." She paused to harness the calm from her early-morning swim. "Actually, he's my husband. We got married last week, but I'm keeping the name Blazek."

Milos ran his finger under his starched collar, then looked down at Viktor's canvas deck shoes.

Stepan looked off to the side.

Irena clapped a hand to her mouth before she recovered and addressed Viktor. "Elise has always been one to shock," she told him.

"We'll answer any questions you have," said Elise.

"I should think *so*," Irena snapped.

"I am delighted to meet you," Viktor tried belatedly. He held out his hand. "Elise has told me much about you. You, Milos, I hear you're a very talented pitcher."

This was good enough for Milos; he blushed with pleasure.

Stepan hung up their jackets, and Irena rushed them in to lunch. Once they were all seated, she offered every dish to Viktor first. She didn't look at him, though, and didn't bring up the subject of the marriage. She had known for some time about the trip to Leningrad but didn't ask Elise and Viktor anything about it. She ate in silence. Stepan was known to be socially disabled, but Irena never behaved this way with company. The single sound in the room, cutlery tapping china, began to resemble the rat-a-tat-tat of a machine gun.

It was Milos who broke the silence. "Can you give me a theme analysis of *Silas Marner*?" he asked Elise.

Elise laughed. "Do I look like a set of Monarch notes?"

"No, I mean it. I have a game tomorrow, and we have a paper due at ten o'clock on Monday morning."

"I haven't read that book since junior high, and I didn't want to read it then."

"Come on, Elise. You could tell me if you wanted to."

The clicking from Irena's place continued. Stepan was soaking up gravy with a wedge of brown bread.

"Elise doesn't know about American literature, Milos. My book club knows more," Irena said.

"Sure she does; she's in that program."

"No, she's not," Irena reminded him.

"Oh." Milos blushed. "Sorry, I forgot."

"Why did you think she was going to Leningrad?" Irena asked testily.

"I *said* I forgot. It's your fault anyway, for making me tell everyone she was studying American literature."

Elise bunched up her linen napkin and tossed it onto her plate.

Irena stared stone-faced at the napkin, shaking her head.

Elise turned to her mother. "There's barely a writer I study who was not a dissident at one time or another," she said. "What do you think we're all doing, deconstructing the Party's propaganda writing? Celebrating the reign of Joseph Stalin? Maybe you think we're stockpiling arms."

"I don't know what you do, but we won't discuss it at the table."

Viktor rose and asked the way to the bathroom. When he was gone, Elise said, "You're being willfully ignorant. And by the way, Viktor left

Russia because, like most émigrés, he couldn't tolerate the Party's interference in his intellectual life. It wasn't much different from you and Daddy leaving Czechoslovakia to make a better life here. Your distrust is completely unwarranted. Viktor is not the one making everyone in Plzen show their little red books, and I'm sure not."

Throughout this little speech, Elise had managed to control her tone. She really *was* in a good place, she reminded herself. Her own master. Maybe the rebalancing of her lithium played a part, but she gave most of the credit to her daily swimming regimen. She had already identified a pool near where they'd be staying in Leningrad.

"You come here a married woman," answered Irena as though she were merely continuing Elise's train of thought. "You marry a man with about as much ceremony as it takes to brush your teeth, and you expect us not to react? To just welcome you and your new husband with open arms? This little Russian man twice your age?" Finally, Irena laid down her fork and looked her daughter in the eye. "Elise, I've never felt so disrespected in my life. You may as well throw me and Táta out with the trash."

During her first visit to the Hermitage, three days after their arrival in Leningrad, Elise went to see the drawings done during the siege of Leningrad. She had learned about these drawings as an undergraduate, but seeing them was another thing. As the Germans had encircled Leningrad in 1941, the curators of the Hermitage—along with ordinary citizens—began to strip the walls of masterworks. They had packed as many as they could into crates for shipment to Siberia. When Elise had first learned this, it had struck her as the noblest expression of cultural pride. When she had then learned about the five artists who had committed themselves to recording the destruction of the Hermitage, carefully drawing the damaged galleries even as shells exploded in other parts of the Winter Palace, she could not imagine such depth of loyalty to one's heritage.

Whether rendered in color or black and white, all of the drawings were beautifully executed by artists clearly trained in rendering perspective. Some showed empty galleries, their walls and marble floors and gilded molding covered in frost. A grand staircase was littered with pieces of fallen ceiling. Others showed Hermitage staff members clearing up the exhibition halls. In one of these, empty frames lined the wall—their pictures perhaps already in Siberia.

Returning to their tiny apartment, Elise told Viktor what she had seen. He nodded sadly. His uncle, he told her, had been among those who had prepared paintings to be shipped north. No rest, no food, Viktor said, not for any of them. He himself had regularly taken refuge in the bomb shelter at the Hermitage. Then he had quit his classes at the University of Leningrad and fled with his family to relatives living outside the city. Leaving Leningrad, they had stepped over dead bodies.

Elise was in awe of Viktor, enthralled with his strife-ridden history. When he pulled her toward him at night, she felt the cold burden of the years he had lived before her—few of them happy, he had claimed. She was often unsure what she felt for this man who had become her husband, but she knew that for him she was innocence itself, the embodiment of America.

A few days later, Elise returned to the Hermitage. She was edgy and didn't feel well. Also, certain things had begun to irritate her. The students she helped Viktor teach at CIEE were not serious; the majesty and pathos of Leningrad did not touch them. They smoked grass in front of Savior of the Blood Cathedral, then went up to the various coats of arms and announced, nearly in unison, "far fucking out." Another problem was that Viktor expected Elise to cook for him and do his laundry. She felt tired all the time, and often her head ached. She couldn't get used to the cold. The excessive amount of starch in the Russian diet was having its effect on her thighs. Furthermore, the pool near where they were staying had unreliable hours. And she and Viktor were constantly on top of each other in the minuscule apartment the school provided.

Elise couldn't concentrate as she had during her first visit to the Hermitage. By the time she reached the boudoir of Alexander II's wife, Empress Maria Alexandrovna, her temples buzzed with a sense of foreboding. The Baroque room could not have been more splendid or uglier. A sign said that the red brocatelle used for the curtains and walls was purchased from the Cartier Company in Paris. The gilt bronze chandelier was reflected in the many mirrors. Elise was also reflected. There she was in her black leotard, black jodhpurs, the cordovan high-topped shoes she'd had made for the trip, her wide silver belt, and several chiffon scarves, the top one lime green. She saw herself from three angles. In the background, a loose part in an unseen ventilator rattled annoyingly. Elise felt queasy and then cold in the overheated gallery.

"What are *you* doing here?" asked a woman in Russian.

Elise spun around but saw no one.

"You want to know me, but do you think yourself capable of it? A sheltered American girl who has lived through nothing? A Cold War baby. Please. One thwarted crisis in Cuba. Nothing."

Elise recognized the voice she'd heard on recordings, Anna Akhmatova's voice.

"Writing papers on what I've lived through, a girl like you. Princeton? I'm not impressed. Now a Ph.D. program in 'Slavic Studies'?" the voice mocked. "What's *that*?"

Elise kept looking around, but she was alone in the empress's boudoir.

"American female graduate students, you violate me. You do the same to Sylvia Plath and Virginia Woolf. All of you—raised in radiance, drawn to darkness."

Elise had always thought it a gift of hers—that she could relate to others, especially women, who knew deprivations she had never known. This sense of identification, she had thought, promised to lend gravity to her translations.

"You are here in my city because you could afford the plane ticket." The voice was one of loathing.

Elise closed her eyes. "I am alone in this room. No one is here, no one is speaking to me. Akhmatova is in her grave in Komarova."

"What do you imagine you have to do with *me*?" the voice continued.

Just walk away, Elise told herself. Motion clears the head. Go to another gallery. Leave the Hermitage. Walk along the River Neva. Yet as she gave herself these instructions, the weight of her terror held her in place.

Shortly Elise heard another voice, a man's, also speaking Russian. She didn't know how long the uniformed guard had stood over her, an anxious expression on his face. Elise was on the floor, though she didn't remember falling. He helped her to her feet, his touch unexpectedly tender.

Elise had only a spotty memory of what happened after that. The return of the voice, the guard's panic. Someone's car. An iron bedpost. An injection—or was that an image from some forgotten film noir? When Viktor arrived, his face loomed over hers, his blue eyes cloudy, his expression gentle but insipid.

✦

What had they put her on? Elise knew it was something. Why else would she be stuck to this chair? She was back in Chicago, at Northwestern Memorial Hospital, where Dr. Brinner had admitted her. She knew she should be grateful for Viktor's insurance. But she couldn't get off the chair. Too much strain, and anyway, where would she go? She had already seen the Ping-Pong table, both in and out of use. She'd seen the library with its donated westerns and soft-boiled mysteries. In occupational therapy she had seen the plain copper octagon that she was expected to hand glaze and turn into a ceramic trivet. To whom did Elise owe the perfect gift of a ceramic trivet? Maybe Professor Gunther, she reflected, the Tolstoy authority who had won a Guggenheim last year? Or maybe the only other Slavic studies grad student living in Engelhart Hall, Benjamin Sharpe, whose dissertation on the Soviet political economy was already promised to Yale University Press? She could send the glazed trivets, personalized by her individual design, as gifts of congratulation for their accomplishments.

She let her eyelids drop. She would make no trivets. Rather, she would just sleep here in this chair until Dr. Brinner assured her the voice would not return, told her it was safe to go out again.

Chapter Six

They had been together for four years, so after the divorce came through, their marriage was inevitable. Still, it marked the beginning of the end of the Mariáš games with the sisters, and Irena had to hide her disappointment when Magda and the biology teacher, Frank Masik, announced they'd had a private ceremony at city hall. The two of them set up housekeeping in an apartment two blocks from the Easton School for Girls in Chicago.

At first, Irena and Berta kept up the Saturday games without Magda. Eventually, though, they admitted to each other that two-handed Mariáš did nothing for them. Yet without the excuse of Mariáš, Irena wasn't sure she would see Berta every Saturday. Too many empty weekends, Irena worried, and Berta would simply languish. So as they were drinking coffee after their last game, Irena said, "I'm thinking of taking Miloslav to Vienna, if I can get us there. Would you come?"

"Vienna!"

"Yes," said Irena, who had only gotten the idea for the trip the day before. "We can't go home, but at least we could go to Vienna, which isn't all that far. Miloslav has been asking about Kutná Hora lately. I wish I could take him there."

"For heaven's sake, Irena, Vienna is nothing like Kutná Hora."

"I know, but two brothers of Stepan's cousin's wife live in Vienna," Irena claimed feebly. "And it's the closest we can get."

"Has Miloslav been asking about his mother?" Berta inquired.

"He's just started to ask again. I couldn't tell him much."

"Do you know where she is?"

"Since Vlasta Cizek died we haven't heard a word. What was that, three years ago? We think she either had to move back to that hospital or in with one of Stepan's distant cousins."

Berta nodded. "Imagine her life."

"I can't."

"When would you go?"

"This summer, when Miloslav is out of school."

"How's his team doing?" Berta wanted to know.

"I don't keep up," Irena admitted. "I think fine. Stepan says that the coach starts Miloslav more than the other pitchers."

To Irena's surprise, Miloslav's pitching arm *had* gotten him a baseball scholarship. The Blazeks were paying less than half of his tuition to Michigan State, not such a burden now that their house was paid off. Irena was still getting used to the idea that being good at a game could get one's tuition paid. Elise had gotten a scholarship to Princeton on the weight of her scholastic achievement. *This* made sense to Irena. The rest was nonsense.

"It's more his grades I care about. He has to maintain a high B average to even have a hope of going to law school."

"A lawyer? This is news. How exciting, Irena."

Irena shrugged. "I don't know if he'll get in." The idea had been Stepan's, not hers. Miloslav seemed to go along with it. "So what do you think?" she went on. "Would you consider going to Vienna with us? An adventure for the three of us?"

Berta would know better than to ask Irena if Stepan was going. He hated to travel, even short distances. He didn't even show an interest in going to Alaster College in western Massachusetts, where Elise had been teaching. Not that she had invited them.

"Just think about it," Irena said before Berta could answer. "It would do you good."

Berta finished her coffee.

"Don't you wish we could go back home?" Irena mused, looking away from Berta.

"I never think about it. Since Petr finally got out, there's no one left. They're either dead or here."

Her brother Petr had waited years to get out. Like many defectors, he had come through Yugoslavia, paying off petty officials as he went. Now he lived in Chicago but was mostly on the road, performing as a guest soloist for various orchestras.

"Some people say Vienna is the most beautiful city in Europe."

"It wouldn't be for me. Now, if you wanted to go to *Paris* . . ."

But Irena didn't want to go to Paris. The very idea of Paris intimidated her. If she went to Paris, Berta would speak French. She spoke as well as Magda, who had been teaching it for twenty years. Speaking French regularly was one of the things Irena imagined Berta missed most about Magda's absence. She had little doubt that if she went to France with Berta, Berta would spend much time pointing out all the places that had meant something to Magda and her during the five years they had lived there. Irena didn't want to be led through Paris by a ring in her nose, even if allowing it would call Berta back to the carefree spirit of her youth.

"Maybe going to Vienna is a little ridiculous," Irena admitted, "but I'm just afraid I'll never be able to see Plzen again. Sometimes I swear I smell the yeast coming from Pilsner Urquell. And I can remember my mother there better than I remember her here. She never really adjusted to America. She missed her sisters and her cousins. Most of them are gone now."

"I can't remember the yeast smell," said Berta. "I remember only that for all my father's academic training, there was no opportunity for him. The one smell I *can* remember is cabbage and boiled potatoes. The smell of steam, really—practically no smell at all."

What could Irena say to this? She tried to think of an argument to convince Berta the trip would be good for her.

"*You* should go, Irena. You and Miloslav should go to Vienna on your own if you have people there."

"Maybe," Irena said, losing heart, "but I don't actually know the two brothers there. And now that I think of it, Stepan wouldn't like it. Who would take care of him?"

"For two weeks? Three at the most? I'm sure he could manage. I'll have him over for dinner once or twice. Probably Sylvie Vanek would too. In no time, you'll be back."

Despite herself, Irena felt a prick of doubt. Stepan's defenselessness might embarrass her, but he was hers to protect. "I suppose if I cooked and froze all his meals, he might be all right. And he would have more time to put the finishing touches on Karlstein Castle. Did I tell you the historical society wants it by Labor Day?"

"That's wonderful!" said Berta. "After all these years."

Irena wished she could be as enthusiastic as Berta. She *was* impressed. Anyone would be. The replica of the castle was perfect. Part of it was a cut-away, revealing scale model rooms and their furniture, fashioned out of balsa wood stained to approximate various rich surfaces. The wall coverings and upholstery were made from scraps from Kopecky's Fabric Shop, and were the closest approximation of the materials used in Karlstein Castle that Irena could find. Wearing his headband magnifier, Stepan had mounted them with impeccable care; there wasn't a ripple or bubble on a single wall or chair. The board of the Laflin Historical Society had been thrilled to accept the model castle on extended loan. They planned a big reception for Stepan. Irena longed to be swept up in the excitement, the sense of fulfillment her husband clearly felt. But as much as she admired the completed castle, it left her cold as a stone at dawn. And what, she worried, would replace Karlstein Castle for Stepan? Irena had been married to a man married to a castle. She could hardly remember when he had been hers alone.

✦

When Miloslav returned from Michigan State in early June, Irena found herself looking upon a full-fledged grown-up. It was possible, she thought, that her strictness in the early years had paid off. She had not been averse, as so many parents were, to the occasional slap. And she had put herself out to repeat to Miloslav, until she could barely stand it anymore, that he was not the center of the universe, that others breathed the same air he did. He had been an exasperating child, always wheedling for his way. His persistence had exhausted her, and it was all aimed at such insignificant ends—a pair of shin guards, an aluminum bat, a special wax for polishing his baseball glove. Miloslav had wanted only to be outdoors, participating in one team sport or another, and he had behaved with civility only when he was looking for permission to join some neighborhood pickup game.

In the early years, Stepan had told Irena she needed to be easier on Miloslav. But she knew that if one of them didn't exert some discipline, Miloslav would think that the tragedy with his parents entitled him to a lifetime of indulgence. Stepan insisted they should never forget their nephew's misfortune, they must never make him feel unloved. So even though she had been the disciplinarian, Irena had also made a point of showing her affection. Deep down, she knew Miloslav could not be fooled; he knew her kisses and hugs had been drawn from a surplus, that she was merely being charitable. By contrast, Stepan's manly hugs were never effusive, yet Irena could see that hugging Miloslav, his brother's boy, meant everything to him.

Since Irena had last seen him, Miloslav had acquired a new attentiveness to those around him. Now he asked about Irena's attacks of bursitis, and he no longer rolled his eyes when Stepan talked about the completion of Karlstein Castle. Most encouraging, he seemed to realize that his talent for baseball would do nothing to carry him beyond his college years. No doubt the pleasing changes were due to the influence of Dawn Layton, his girlfriend of the past year. Irena and Stepan thought Dawn was a sensible, sweet young woman, and they were grateful to her for pushing Miloslav outside his narrow, childish ambitions.

Two days after Miloslav's arrival home, Irena booked their tickets to Vienna. A letter had come through from Pavel Blazek, Stepan's cousin who lived in Kutná Hora. Yes, he had confirmed, Katrina had returned to the institution after Vlasta Cizek's death; no other relative had the means to take her in. In Pavel's view, her condition had never been properly treated, and she sometimes had violent or self-destructive episodes. Pavel and his wife visited her regularly, though, and during good periods Katrina occasionally stayed with them for the weekend. He had closed his letter by telling her that his friend in Chicago, Josef Hanek, had known Katrina as a girl.

Irena had thought this last remark strange. She'd shown the letter to Stepan. When he got to the part about Josef Hanek, he had tapped two fingers on it. "This man has something to tell you. Look him up."

Irena knew that scheming and conspiring was the way of life for many decent Czech citizens. She called Mr. Hanek. She assumed he was the man who answered the phone. "I'm Irena Blazek," she said. "My husband's cousin is Pavel Blazek."

"I understand. Give me a minute."

He sounded very old. Was he getting a piece of paper? Or perhaps he just needed to collect his thoughts.

In a moment he was back. "Yes, thank you. Pavel says he will meet you in Austria. He will bring the boy's mother with him."

Irena gasped. It was just the sort of message she should have expected, yet she hadn't. This poor man, she thought, this Josef Hanek, who was he? A lonely old man delivering messages to strangers. And if it was not safe for Pavel to give Irena this news, then why had it been all right to give it to Josef Hanek? Had they established some kind of code over the years? To whom else did Josef Hanek deliver messages? Was it like a hobby of his, delivering dramatic news to strangers?

"Excuse me? You are still there?" asked Josef.

"Yes. I'm sorry."

"I'll mail you the details. I have your address."

"Thank you very much." Tough as it was, Irena refrained from asking questions. She hung up.

Stepan walked into the room and looked at her. She told him what Mr. Hanek had said. Again he nodded. "There are ways to get through."

The next afternoon Miloslav agreed to the plan of meeting his mother in Vienna. The Saturday before their departure date, he asked Irena some basic questions he had long avoided. "What's wrong with her?" "Did she love my father?" "Did she ever write asking about me?" "Did she want to come back to Chicago?"

Irena told Miloslav she wasn't sure exactly what was wrong with Katrina, it had not been spoken about frankly in the family. She reminded Miloslav that his parents were third cousins, as well as husband and wife, that their marriage might have been as much about practicality as romance. As far as Katrina writing to ask about him, she told Miloslav there were many places in Czechoslovakia where one couldn't be sure that the KSC wasn't interfering with the mail.

"Once we meet her," she told Miloslav, "I'm sure you will find out more. It won't be easy, but in the end I think it will make you a more complete man."

Over the next few days, Miloslav put himself to work around the house. He fixed Irena's toaster oven and took down the storm windows. He tore out the kitchen linoleum and helped Irena lay down adhesive-backed tile squares. He replaced a corroded drain pipe under the bathroom sink. Irena admired his strength and his dexterity. Had she failed to observe him all these years? In the evenings, Irena and Miloslav made plans for their trip.

Two days before they were to depart for Vienna, Irena got a call from Josef Hanek. She and Stepan and Miloslav were playing three-handed Mariáš in the dining room. When Irena answered, he got right to the point. His voice was more animated than during their last conversation. "The mother Katrina is in a terrible state. Pavel cannot bring her to Vienna."

Irena's heart raced. "She should pull herself together!" she told the stranger, Josef. Stepan and Miloslav turned to look at her. She pivoted around so that her back was to them.

"The hospital won't let her out. Pavel and his wife are not permitted to visit. Pavel says this has happened before, that she'll be better, but it's hard to know when."

There was nothing Irena could say; she was left to keep her reactions to herself. Once again she thanked Josef Hanek and hung up.

At the dining table, Miloslav shuffled his cards, made them ripple in a pretty arch. Finally he said, "So?"

Irena explained. She saw red inflame the tips of Miloslav's ears, and, for an instant, his lower lip quivered. She had never seen an outward display of emotion from her nephew about anything that mattered. She reached for his hand, but he pulled it away.

"Milos," said Stepan, "let's go for a walk. Let's go get some ice cream."

Miloslav refused and left the house on his own. The next morning he told them that he was going to visit Dawn at her parents' house in Dearborn.

"But the trip," Irena had said. "You shouldn't let this stop you from seeing Vienna."

"I can't help it," Miloslav said. "I know it's unfair to you, and I'd probably be mad if someone did it to me, but I just can't help it."

"You do what's best for you," said Irena, and she rushed off to the kitchen before she had the opportunity to add another word.

That week at Reyna Kopecky's, Irena shorted a customer by over a foot of polished cotton, snagged a piece of expensive raw silk, miscounted the weekly deposit money, and stabbed herself with a seam ripper. Such mistakes were unlike her. Since she had cancelled the trip, she had been edgy and unable to concentrate. She had roused herself for a great adventure, one that might give birth to a relationship with Miloslav after all these years, and now there was only her life at Reyna's, Stepan finishing his castle in the basement, and her routine visits to Berta Kriz. Rather than give in to the full sway of her disappointment, Irena sped up. She spoke faster, moved faster, thought faster. At home she told Stepan, "I'mgoingtogovisitElise."

"What? Speak slower, I can't understand."

"I think I'll go visit Elise."

"Did she invite you?"

"Grown children don't invite their parents. If you want to see them, you take the bull by the horns."

"I don't know about that. I'd wait."

"Till when? Stepan, her accomplishments didn't spring from nowhere. We provided the foundation."

"And? To what does that entitle us?"

"To a little sense of satisfaction, if nothing else!"

"You can be satisfied from here. What difference does it make if you're here or there? The accomplishments do not exist in space. They exist in time."

"Don't get philosophical."

"What do you want? To see her teach a class? She'd never let you."

"No, maybe not actually teach, but . . ."

"Let her adjust. She hasn't even been there a year."

"She's probably lonely," Irena speculated.

"I doubt it. She's never been lonely before."

"How do *we* know? She's been alone for almost two years."

Stepan said nothing.

Irena seized upon his silence. "You're still brooding about the divorce, aren't you? As if she should have stayed married to a man twice her age. You don't remember he'd been married two times before Elise? I always found him entirely unpleasant. Thank God he's gone."

"I have no opinion," said Stepan. "As long as she's happy."

Irena sighed. It was impossible to argue with Stepan. These things he said—these bromides. Irena didn't keep her word list anymore, but she had recently circled *bromide* in a magazine article. "An unoriginal or trite statement." Irena hated her husband's bromides. To her, they were small iron curtains blocking off the possibility of a true exchange. Who could penetrate such commonplace remarks? People didn't so much *say* bromides as erect them.

"Well, it was fine by me," Irena said. "Good riddance to him."

Irena didn't normally approve of divorce, but this little man with too much body hair was dragging her brilliant daughter down. He had wanted her to stay in Evanston, to be his teaching assistant even after she had gotten her Ph.D. From what Irena had read in newspapers over the past few years, she would never call herself a feminist, but this man had been self-centered enough to expect Elise to hold back her intellect and her career for the sake of his. Even Irena, who had not gone beyond high school, could see that Viktor Frolov's intellect was nothing compared to Elise's.

Irena moved away from the sink, where she had been stacking dishes in the countertop drying rack. "I'm going to call her. Do you want to come? The flight's not long."

"Not before the historical society reception," said Stepan.

"I'll be back in plenty of time," Irena assured him, getting herself to smile. "It will be a wonderful occasion."

"Zlatíčko, I'm so glad I reached you. No classes?"

Elise was teaching a month of summer-school classes. One was for matriculating students; another was an evening class in Alaster College's extension program.

"Oh, hi. No."

Not a very welcome tone, but if Irena wasn't used to Elise's moods by now, she never would be. "Our trip to Vienna has been cancelled."

"What happened?"

"Poor Miloslav. Katrina went into some kind of tizzy. I think the idea of seeing Miloslav must have touched off her mental illness. Now the hospital won't allow her out."

Elise made some kind of noise. Irena thought for a second she might be humming. Her attention seemed elsewhere.

"Miloslav was very upset. He's visiting Dawn now. I feel so sorry for him, don't you?"

"Sure," Elise said flatly.

"Just as he was beginning to show some real maturity, too. I hope this doesn't—what's the term—arrest his development?"

"He'll be fine. You said that Dawn's been good for him."

"I had to cancel Vienna, but I kept my two-week vacation. It's the first time in years I'll have two weeks together like that."

"That's good."

Elise had turned on some music in the background. She had a wide-ranging taste in music. Irena recognized a composition by Erik Satie. Some years back, she had picked up one of his albums in Elise's dorm room at Princeton. One of the pieces was called "Three Dried Up Embryos."

"So I thought maybe—"

"Why can't you go yourself?"

"I'm going to wait. Czechoslovakia can't stay under communist rule forever. One day it will open up, and I'll be able to go back to Plzen. It's just as well. You know, zlatíčko, I still haven't seen where you live."

"I know, but this isn't such a good time. My Russian Language One is not a problem, but I can barely keep up with the syllabus for Pushkin and His Time. And I'm working on a paper to submit to one of the Slavic literary reviews. I wouldn't be able to show you around."

"I don't care about that, Elise."

Irena didn't believe that Elise was having trouble keeping up with her syllabus. It was true the Pushkin course had been thrust upon her— Irena knew Elise didn't much care for Pushkin—but she would wager her daughter had a thorough knowledge of her material.

"Well, I care. You wouldn't have a good time. And I'm going to see you in just a few weeks anyway, at the reception for Daddy."

"I know, zlatíčko, but that's a quick trip, and I thought we could have some alone time." With this last remark, Irena's heart raced. The adrenaline release caught her by surprise, and she put a hand to her chest.

"Why don't you come in the fall? I'll be more set up then."

Of course Elise wasn't set up. She had rented a ballroom on the second floor of a former dance studio in town. How does a person go about making a home out of a ballroom?

"What would you like to do when you come here?" Irena asked. It was time for her to stop talking about the visit to Alaster College. The visit was not going to happen.

"There's a new restaurant, just two stores from Reyna's. Thai food. Laflin is getting very sophisticated." Irena snorted. Elise needed to be reminded that her mother was capable of irony. "We could eat there and maybe go to a concert at Orchestra Hall. Should I see what the program will be?"

"Sure," Elise said.

Irena would have to keep her daughter busy that weekend, she thought. It wouldn't be good if she slipped down to Evanston to see Viktor.

✦

At first it didn't register with Irena that the man in the center of the room was her husband. She recognized the new beige linen suit, as Stepan had left the house in it an hour earlier, but she had to stare to confirm the man wearing it was Stepan. Holding a glass of champagne, he stood to the right of Karlstein Castle, talking to a small group of people Irena didn't recognize. And what she truly didn't recognize was Stepan's animation.

The Laflin Historical Society's main gallery was crowded with people. Irena estimated maybe fifty or sixty, and more were coming in the door. Berta's nice feature in the *Czechoslovak Daily Herald* must have drawn this crowd.

Stepan had gone early to make sure that the castle had been set up to best advantage. Now he bent over its roof to look at what a guest was pointing out. He nodded vigorously. From twelve yards away, Irena still had to tell herself it was him. His belly was concealed beneath the flattering lines of the tailored jacket. Perhaps it was the distance, but Irena couldn't detect the crease at the bridge of Stepan's nose. Gone was the usual pallor that she put down to the endless hours he spent in the basement. She had not seriously appraised her husband's appearance in a long while. Half the time she saw him, there was a red stripe across his forehead, branded there by the headband magnifier he wore to work on the castle. She had grown used to his threadbare black sweatshirt and the ever-present smell of contact cement. The sight of this man with the healthy complexion and the respectable linen suit startled her so completely that she had to pause in her progress toward him. She held onto Miloslav's arm.

Standing to the left of Karlstein Castle, Elise waved to Irena and Miloslav, beckoning them over. Irena wanted to smile, she told herself to smile, and when she saw her daughter's sweet, lit-up expression, her heart lurched. Yet she could not overcome her reaction to Elise's costume. She had wanted to ask her to change before she left the house with Stepan. But Elise was twenty-eight years old. If she thought it acceptable to show up in public with those ridiculous grandmother shoes and all the rest— the green toreador pants and black satin vest and the purple and violet chiffon scarves wrapped about her neck, what could Irena do about it? If she insisted on leaving the house in that ruby-red lipstick, so startling against her pale complexion, she was of age, and it really was her own business. At the moment, Elise's costume seemed designed to point out the blandness of Irena's navy suit and single strand of Majorca pearls.

"Let's go say hello to Magda," Irena told Miloslav. She pointed in the opposite direction, toward Frank and Magda Masik, who were accepting canapés from a waiter.

"But we haven't said hello to Uncle Stepan yet."

"He's busy now. We'll go over in a minute."

Dawn was on Miloslav's other side. Irena saw her give him a look.

"I don't know, I think he saw us come in."

"You two go, then," said Irena. "I'll be right over." She let go of Miloslav's arm and approached Magda and Frank. Magda was wearing a rose-colored silk suit; she was more dressed up than Irena.

"Isn't this wonderful!" Magda exclaimed. "This is just splendid, Irena. Did you ever think you'd have such a famous husband?"

Frank smiled. "We came early," he said. "He's a very talented man, your husband. His precision is remarkable. Does the Czech government know?"

"The KSC? I certainly hope not."

"Actually, they'd be proud," said Frank. "This is just the sort of thing they champion. Historical preservation."

Irena didn't know what to say. Was Magda's new husband a communist?

"You must be proud," Magda put in. "And really, you deserve credit, too. You've been so patient all these years."

Tears sprung to Irena's eyes. She wiped them away. Magda would think they were tears of pride.

"Who's he talking to?" asked Irena.

"I don't know," Magda answered.

"He introduced me to them," Frank said. "They're his colleagues."

Colleagues? The architects at Casner & Fitzbaum had traveled out to Laflin on a Sunday evening? Irena was surprised they even knew about Karlstein Castle. Her impression was that Stepan, the only draftsman in the office, was not held in esteem by the licensed architects. Stepan had left her with that impression, but when she glanced over now, she saw one of them heartily shaking Stepan's hand and another slapping him on the back. They were big men. Next to them, her husband looked small and eager, at age fifty-five the agreeable little brother being chucked under the chin.

"You've never met them?" Magda asked, clearly surprised.

"Oh, a couple times at the office," she said. "You know how different people look outside their usual places."

Berta came over. She was holding a sausage canapé on a cocktail napkin. "You must be so happy to have both the children home at the same time," she told Irena. "How long has it been?"

Irena again forced herself to smile. "I can't think," she said.

Magda and Berta's silence on the subject of Elise's outfit roared in Irena's ears. She felt herself condemned, but how could she answer a silent charge?

"Did Berta tell you her news?" asked Magda.

Irena looked at Berta. She had seen her just two days ago. Berta blushed.

"No, what news?"

Before Berta could answer, they heard the amplified sound of someone tapping the microphone up front. "Everyone! Everyone, may I have your attention now?" called a beautiful baritone voice.

Presently the room quieted down.

"That's right, thank you," said the nice-looking bald man standing at the podium. "For those of you who don't know, I'm Jiri Mueller, president of the board of the Czech Historical Society. Thank you all so much for coming." Mr. Mueller paused. "Tonight is a very special occasion for us. Our longtime member Stepan Blazek has made us a loan of his remarkable replica of Karlštejn Castle."

There was some applause from the front of the room.

Mr. Mueller went on to remind the crowd about the history of Karlstein Castle. *Remind* was the word he used, although Irena could not believe everyone in attendance was familiar with the castle. Over half the people in the room were clearly second or third generation. Mr. Mueller talked about Charles IV, whom he called a mystical thinker. He told the gathering that King Charles had not lived in Karlstein Castle, that—hard as it was for us to imagine today—the castle was used largely as a secure storehouse for the crown jewels. As he spoke, his gaze landed repeatedly on Stepan's model. Then he introduced Stepan, to much earnest applause.

Stepan added to Mr. Mueller's historical introduction by talking about Karlstein Castle during the two world wars. Then he discussed the building of the actual castle and of his own scale model. Irena had told him repeatedly that he would need to project, but from where she stood she could barely hear him. His sentences began fine, then trailed off. "The structure of the Well Tower . . . Even though the drop to the water was two hundred fifty feet . . . For the well crank, I . . . The biggest challenge about trying to replicate the Hall of Knights was . . ." His monotone stood in contrast to his alert expression. After twelve minutes, he didn't seem ready to wrap up. Irena tried to signal him that people's attention was wandering, as they had planned, but he didn't look toward her.

Finally, as Stepan paused in his explanation of how he had simulated the leaded windows, Elise raised her glass to toast him. In contrast to her father, her voice was commanding. Of course, Irena thought, she had to be heard in the back of lecture halls. She toasted him with evident affection, joked about Stepan escaping his family to go work on a castle that no one lived in. The applause that followed Elise's toast clearly signaled the end of the audience's attention. Stepan looked a little baffled, but he put his arm around Elise's shoulders, raised the glass someone had put in his hand, and thanked everyone for coming.

The Kriz sisters beamed. If Irena could only conjure such pride herself. She found medieval castles intimidating, and the knowledge that soldiers threw their enemies from the turrets did little to soften her attitude. The very last word she had entered on her final word list had been *soporific,* the perfect adjective, she had confessed to herself, for the subject of Karlstein Castle.

"So Berta, what is your news?" Irena asked now. "Why don't I already know it?"

"I was going to tell you tonight," said Berta. "The paper is sending me to Paris next week."

Irena immediately felt sorry for herself. Shameful, she knew, but self-pity never waited for an invitation.

"How wonderful," Irena managed, thinking she had wasted her time worrying over the uncertainty of Berta's future.

"I'm going to write a series of stories on the Czech community there."

"You're going alone?"

"Yes. Although, since Vienna fell through, maybe you'd like to join me."

Irena saw that Berta was bracing herself; she didn't really want Irena along.

A six-piece brass band had materialized and started to play the Dukovanska Polka. Irena turned away from the Kriz sisters and watched Elise trying to pull her father out to dance. A ceiling fan whirled overhead, rippling Elise's scarves: one purple, one violet, and underneath a third one, flaming orange with gold stars.

✦

In the middle of the night, the last of Elise's brief stay, Irena thought she heard the distant notes of her daughter's weeping. She got out of bed, crept to the door of Elise's room—slightly ajar—and stood there.

Elise's old nightlight was turned on in the corner of her room, and Irena could see she was lying facedown, her head bobbing. She was pitching her sobs into the center of the pillow she had pressed to her ears. The sound snaked through Irena, taking with it every last fragment of what she thought of as her maternal energy, a special energy that allowed her to identify a need and fill it with precisely the type of attention required. But Elise was not wailing for food as when she had been a baby, nor—a few years later—for comfort when she had fallen and hurt herself. The sounds that came from her grown daughter were terrifying. They angered Irena. Couldn't we all give in to this kind of hysteria, if we permitted ourselves? She turned and felt her way down the dark hall and back to her bedroom.

In bed, Irena worked her arm around Stepan's waist and pulled herself as close as she could get, burying her head in his neck, just as Elise's head was concealed within the hollow of her childhood pillow.

Chapter Seven

November 1980

The moment she entered consciousness, Elise knew she was too low to the ground to be in her bed in the ballroom. Her own mattress was mounted on a high iron bed frame and a box spring. There was no daylight in this room, not yet. She must have thrust her arm out in her sleep; her rings had clinked against a linoleum floor, waking her. It didn't take long to figure out that, career-wise, she was in the worst place possible, on a futon in an Alaster undergraduate dorm. A dull pain pulsed over her eyes. When she sat up, nausea rose. The sight of two empty wine bottles told the story. Visual representation, an underrated learning modality according to Darryl Perleman, a critical studies instructor out of the English department. Maybe he was right. The sight of the two empty bottles on the floor allowed Elise to acknowledge her recent past and to forecast her future.

No one was beside her. Sasha might be off waking up everyone to tell them Professor Blazek was in his bed. At least Elise *thought* Sasha was his name. It could be Pasha. She remembered he was Russian, recently come from Belarus, and that last year he had audited a session of her class on nineteenth-century Russian prose. Elise got up, looked for the bathroom, and saw that it was behind her. Thankfully there was only this one bed in the room; the boy was a junior, and the room was a single with a bathroom.

Where was this boy, Sasha/Pasha? Did he have the nerve to sleep with a tenure-track associate professor and then abandon her in his boxy dorm room? Had he made good on an undergraduate bet? As Elise sat on his toilet, wearing only an Alaster T-shirt that was not in her wardrobe, was he rounding up a campus full of witnesses to entrap her? Would they bring their Instamatics and Sony tape recorders? Elise got up, grabbed the sequined cashmere cardigan she had bought at a DAR thrift store the day before, put on her pants, jammed on her shoes without lacing them, and ran into the cold predawn air.

During the next week, Elise braced herself to hear from her department chair—a tap on the shoulder, a call on her home phone, a message in her faculty box.

To contend with her mounting anxiety, she picked up her swimming schedule. On her way to the Alaster Sports Complex for her second swim that Friday, she passed him, Sasha or Pasha, exiting with a squash racket in his hand. He gave her a bemused look, neither triumphant nor curious. She saw what she should have known in the first place—that he had the insouciance and furtive manner necessary to survive in the black market. He was virtually programmed not to betray himself or his consorts. To him, Elise was just another item of contraband; he had already erased his path to her.

Elise's sense of relief that Friday evening lasted until she returned to her ballroom and saw her three sets of living room furniture. She had bought them at a flea market outside Springfield. Two were blond wood and one teak. All faintly Danish Modern. There were three upholstery colors: olive, mustard, and burnt orange. Of these, one was a tapestry fabric and the others tweedy. Over the last five days, Elise had arranged and rearranged the sets around her two-thousand-square-foot ballroom. She liked the way the furniture looked under the two glass chandeliers, a satisfying juxtaposition of ornate and sleek, but she couldn't get their arrangement right. After many failed attempts, she began to plot on graph paper each pattern she tried. Maybe Bella Howard in mathematics could tell her how finite the possibilities were and how much time it would take to exhaust them. This was the kind of challenge Bella enjoyed. But

Elise wanted only to draw and arrange, draw and arrange. To broaden the possibilities, she mingled the three sets, combining their colors.

Was it so much to ask, she thought, to come in from a class and be purely satisfied by what she saw before her? She was a grown-up, a professor, an accomplished woman; shouldn't she have command over her environment? Yet every time she stepped inside her ballroom, some aspect of her furniture arrangement mocked her with its conspicuously poor placement. As soon as she walked in the door, she had to get right to work. In fixing the problem, she invariably caused another. After a while, she would try to go back to her desk, where she was translating the work of the late Yugoslav poet Sanja Kenovic. It was a coup for Elise that Kenovic's U.S. publisher had given her this book. But she was behind on her deadline, and she could never work for long. Soon she would be lured back to move an orange chair to the left or the mustard couch eight inches forward. Elise knew she should call Dr. Orell, her new psychopharmacologist in nearby Northampton, but she always seemed to remember at two A.M.

After the first week of moving around couches and chairs, Elise found it too anxiety-provoking to leave her ballroom in its imperfect state. Twice, she had missed a class. The department chair had called to ask why she hadn't given him advance notice. Salmonella, she had said. A death in the family.

Sometime later one of her favorite students called, wondering why Elise had missed three classes. Three? Elise had told him something, she didn't remember what, then stopped answering the phone. During the day, numerous calls came in. Alaster didn't like students having professors' numbers, but Elise had given out hers, and now more students called, needing clarification of an assignment or requesting extensions on their papers. Faculty members called to remind her of committee dates, her mother called with some detail about Milos's wedding, and Wiley called from New York.

When the ballroom was finished, thought Elise, she would call these people back. When she walked in her door and was truly welcomed by the sight of her furniture, she would go back to her translation, show up to teach all her classes brilliantly, and call everyone back.

More time passed; she wasn't sure how much. Then came Wiley's voice again on the answering machine. "Enough already, Elise. You know damn well I'm worried. If you don't call me back within twenty-four hours, I'm calling the Alaster police to go in and see what's wrong."

Elise picked up. "*All right.* Jesus."

"I've been calling you for days."

"Really?"

"As if you didn't know. What's going on, Elise?"

"Nothing."

"I doubt that."

"So? No one asks you to keep tabs on me."

"Not entirely true. There have been times you've asked me to do exactly that."

"Well this isn't one of them."

"How have you been sleeping?" Wiley asked.

Elise noticed that the orange chair with the arms was too close to the olive one without arms. She tried to stretch the phone cord close enough to move the orange one out a bit.

"What's that noise?" asked Wiley.

"Me moving something out of the way."

"In a *ballroom*?"

"So tell me what's new with you," said Elise. "Save any five-ounce preemies lately?"

"Do you really want to know why I called? Or would you rather go into your preemie spiel?"

"You know I love what you do," Elise apologized. She settled into the orange armchair. "You're not mad, are you?"

"Just indulge me and answer your phone, okay?"

It was almost insulting that no matter how obnoxiously Elise behaved, Wiley never got offended.

"I was calling to tell you that Michael and I are going to have a baby at the end of February."

Elise sprang up. From where she sat, she could see that if the mustard chair was positioned closer to the couch diagonally across from it, the chair would bring out the gold in the couch's tapestry upholstery. "Hold on a minute!" she said. She walked to the other side of the ballroom to make the adjustment, then saw that in fact the two colors clashed. For a moment she felt paralyzed. With great effort, she forced herself back across the room.

"Sorry." She kept her eye on the chair and couch.

"Elise, did you hear what I said?"

"Sorry. Repeat it."

"I'm pregnant. We're having a baby at the end of February."

"Oh, my God, Wiley! Do you mean it? A miniature Wiley or Michael? What does Michael say? How long were you trying? This is so great! And *so-o-o-o* legitimate!"

Wiley laughed. They had both recently heard news of Nouveau-Riche Heidi. She had used the oldest trick in the book to get her latest boyfriend, a first lieutenant in the Navy, to marry her. But the lieutenant was stationed in Hawaii, and by the time Nouveau had gathered the courage to give him the news, she was at the end of her second trimester, and he was engaged to a Filipino girl. Nouveau had slipped off somewhere to have the baby. "The Princeton-educated daughter of a leading executive at the Pillsbury company has disappeared," Elise had announced at the time, imitating the rich timbre in a male anchor's voice. For Wiley's benefit, she had added in her own tone, "How *Howard's End.*" Even as she'd said it, though, she had felt a pang of conscience. Debbie Curtis had been kind to her. For someone as deeply conventional as Debbie, the latest event in her life was nothing short of tragic.

"When's it due?" asked Elise.

"I just said. The end of February."

"I'm coming!" Elise declared. "Can I come? It'll be right during my semester break. I'll be your nanny! I'm so excited, Wiley."

"We'll be inundated at first," Wiley said, ignoring the nanny offer, "but then you can come. When the baby's doing more than sleeping eighty percent of the time."

A sob rose from Elise's throat; she had no idea where it had come from. "I didn't mean that about the five-ounce preemies. It's not funny," she said. "I'm such an asshole."

"Elise, *I* don't care, for heaven's sake."

But Elise couldn't get control of herself. The crying escalated until she was lost within it, frightening herself with sharp intakes of breath that emitted no sound.

"Do you want me to come up for the weekend?" Wiley asked finally.

"No," Elise managed. "It's a mess here."

"So I'll stay at the Marriott. Who's been prescribing for you?"

Elise still sobbed. Wiley had to wait.

Finally: "The same guy. Orell."

"When did you last see him?"

Elise closed her eyes. Little constellations of olive and mustard and burnt orange pulsated behind her lids. She didn't want to talk about Dr. Orell. *Wiley* didn't have to see a Dr. Orell or a Dr. Brinner or a Dr. Weiss. Wiley prescribed for herself: successful medical practice, good-looking, equally successful husband, pregnant with her first child at age twenty-nine.

"I don't need to see Orell! I'm fine. Look, why don't you worry about your *baby,* not me? If I have a problem, I'll let you know."

"Elise, I'm on your side here."

"Don't patronize me. You sound like you're talking me down from a fucking bridge."

"I know you're not on a bridge, but something is clearly not right. And you're leaving me in a difficult position. Will you give me permission to talk to Dr. Orell?"

"Oh, I'm leaving you in a difficult position? Poor you. Poor one of New York's top ten neonatologists, financially secure, physically and mentally healthy, married, expectant mother you."

Silence on the other end. Elise didn't care. She was sick of being Wiley's charity case. Wiley hadn't prevented her from marrying the only Russian who, to quote Dorothy Parker, ran the emotional gamut from A to B. She hadn't prevented Anna Akhmatova from talking to Elise in the Hermitage, hadn't prevented Elise from being admitted to Northwestern Memorial Hospital, from which she'd been discharged with conflicting diagnoses, hadn't prevented her from sleeping with undergraduates or from trapping herself in a ballroom full of mismatched furniture.

"I can't stay on if the abusive thing starts," said Wiley.

"Don't stay on, then," Elise answered, but crossed her legs and lit a cigarette. "I've started smoking," she confessed. "I haven't smoked since high school."

"I'm not surprised. You're trying to calm yourself. Please, Elise, just set up an appointment with Dr. Orell. If you really feel better when the time comes, you won't have lost anything."

"What's he going to do, up the lithium? My students stare at my tremor as it is. Or maybe he'll give me one of those antipsychotics

Dr. Brinner tried. My favorite was the one that had me frothing at the mouth when I was defending my dissertation. The committee only passed me so I wouldn't give them rabies."

"What exactly *are* you feeling?" Wiley tried.

Elise ignored the question. "I slept with an undergrad. Fortunately he's a recent Soviet immigrant and rats on no one."

"Don't change the subject."

"Okay, let's trade feelings. You're feeling thrilled that you're going to be a mother. We both know I should never be a mother. I'm only relieved I'll save a child by not having it. You're feeling secure in your husband's love. My ex-husband once made me feel secure for forty-five seconds. You're looking forward to an open future. My future is open, too; maybe I'll hear a voice telling me to shoot my parents, or maybe thinking about the furniture in my ballroom will reduce me to catatonia. Or I could fuck my way through Sig Delta Phi and get blacklisted by the MLA."

"What I've absolutely never understood is how you can be so objective about it all. Like you're narrating it."

"Maybe I'm faking it," said Elise.

"I didn't say that."

"Right. You're on my side."

"Elise, I have to get off. This is one of our famous going-nowheres. Call me tomorrow if you want."

✦

In the end, discipline prevailed, as it had so many times. Wiley was right. Where her illness was concerned, Elise had a penchant for objectifying. If she pushed herself to the furthest degree, like an athlete straining beyond preset limits of endurance, Elise could read and interpret her symptoms as she read and analyzed Akhmatova's poems. She could sort her symptoms into categories as she once had the verb tenses of Serbo-Croatian, deciding which she had to master first. This time it was the business with the living room furniture. The day after she talked to Wiley, she carried all three sets out to the sidewalk. When she went out later that evening, only the burnt-orange ottoman was left, a string of its shredded fabric dangling like a visceral appendage onto the sidewalk.

The ballroom was bare again, save for the bed, the chandeliers, stacks of books, and Elise's writing desk. She could breathe. She could resume her classes and speed up her work on Sanja Kenovic's poems, even turn in her translation just two weeks past its original deadline.

Back on track, Elise returned her mother's call.

"Zlatíčko! Where have you been?"

"You only called once, didn't you?"

"How many times should I try before you return my call?"

"I was busy. I got your message about Milos and Dawn's wedding, though. I'm glad it's all set up."

"It's set up, yes, but a Buddhist temple? Did you ever hear of anything so ridiculous? The Laytons call themselves Buddhists. Miloslav said that last year they were Unitarians. What if they become something else before the wedding date?"

"Don't worry. It'll be fine."

Elise didn't take anyone's wedding seriously. Pomp and ceremony, signifying nothing. The best thing about her marriage to Viktor was that it hadn't been launched by a wedding.

"Elise, a Catholic Czech marrying in a Buddhist temple? Instead of saying, 'I do,' they're going to bow to each other. Then they're going to offer flowers to Buddha. How can I take this seriously?"

"What does Daddy say?"

"What does Táta ever say? Like you, he says 'Don't worry, it'll be fine.'"

"Weddings are secular in Buddhist countries. The big difference will be the bowing. And there's nothing wrong with that. We should all bow to one another more often."

"How do you know these things?"

"What?"

"About Buddhism."

"That's all I know." Elise felt guilty when her mother made these oblique references to her own lack of education.

"Well, at least everyone will wear normal wedding clothes. None of those saris or anything."

"That's India," said Elise before she could catch herself. She knew what was coming: the "what are you wearing?" question.

"So now we have to talk about the wedding party," Irena announced.

Shit, thought Elise. She hadn't dared to allow herself to think about the wedding party. The wedding itself was in June, almost eight months away. Elise didn't know where she would be in eight months, what shape she'd be in. Her heartbeat quickened. She lit a cigarette.

"Of course Miloslav wants you to be a bridesmaid. There'll be you and two of Dawn's college girlfriends and her sister Suzanna. Then her married sister Laurie will be the matron of honor."

"I don't need to be in the wedding party. I'll call Milos and tell him."

"You can't do that. You'll hurt his feelings."

Elise exhaled noisily. "He didn't even ask me to be a bridesmaid. I'm sure he doesn't care."

"Elise, are you smoking a *cigarette*? After all these years?"

"What makes you say that? Listen, Milos won't care, take my word for it."

"He's *changed,* zlatíčko. He's become very family oriented. I won't let you hurt his feelings."

"What, suddenly you're his protector?" said Elise. She shouldn't have said it, but if it ever came up, Irena wouldn't be able to deny that she had been too severe with Milos when he most needed protection, when his father had been killed and his insane mother had moved back to Czechoslovakia. Stepan had been the one to take in Milos with no reservations, to treat him like a son.

"Just please do me this favor. Is it so much to ask? People will wonder if you're not in the wedding party."

Elise had never given much thought to what people did or did not wonder. Still, she was feeling fine, there was no reason to think she wouldn't be feeling fine in eight months, and how would it harm her to stand at a Buddhist altar for ten minutes? "Have Milos call me," she told her mother.

"*Dawn* will call you," Irena said, virtually singing. "I'll have Dawn call you as soon as we hang up. She'll give you the address of where to order the bridesmaid's gown."

Elise had managed to forget about the bridesmaid's gown. Of course, she remembered, identically dressed maids in waiting; that was the whole point.

"Oh, forget it, I can't do this. I'll call Milos. He'll appreciate me spending money on his wedding present instead of a gown. Believe me, he won't care."

"Elise, you just agreed to do it! The gowns are already picked out. Turquoise chiffon with matching bonnets. Reyna will do all the fittings, including Dawn's. It's her wedding present to Miloslav."

"Bonnets at a Buddhist wedding? *That's* embarrassing."

"This is why I reserved the church on Malvek Avenue," said Irena conspiratorially. "I bet in the next few weeks they'll drop this whole crazy Buddhist idea."

"Mother, I'll be there, I'll be full of good cheer, I'll buy them the most expensive present on their registry, but I'm not standing up there in a bonnet. Didn't you raise me to abide by the limits of my integrity?"

"What *are* you going to wear, then? Those hideous grandmother booty things? One of those outlandish outfits of yours?"

Elise snuffed out her cigarette. Temper, she told herself. Beware. The only way to get across to Irena now was to address her strictly on her home territory. "Mother," she said, "doctorates in Slavic studies don't wear bonnets."

Elise waited for her department head, the septuagenarian Adrian Levitsky, to speak. It was ten minutes after three on the third Tuesday in November, just before Thanksgiving. She had just finished teaching her class in nineteenth-century Russian prose and had gone on to Levitsky's office, as Rita, the department secretary, had earlier asked her to do.

"Dr. Blazek, thank you for coming in," Levitsky said. He had a habit of attaching *Doctor* or *Professor* to faculty members' names, implying he expected the return courtesy. Now he continued to look down at her file, open before him. "You've been with us a year and almost three months now," he finally said, leafing through some papers. He withdrew one with the letterhead of Sonja Kenovic's U.S. publisher, the Fogel Press, and held it up for a second.

"This is impressive," Levitsky said. "I won't deny it, this counts for a great deal. But I must tell you that if it *weren't* for this, we'd be having a serious conversation right now. Alaster puts great stock in faculty publication, you know that. We had confidence you would gain some significant publications, that's a large part of why we hired you. But were it not for the Kenovic translation and the more visible of your articles, I'd be in a position of telling you that you weren't on track for tenure."

Too bad you can't tell me that, thought Elise. You'd be in your glory.

"Would you like to know why?"

"I'm sure I know why."

"Why, then? I'm interested in your perspective."

"My attendance could be better," said Elise quickly. "But I've had some extenuating circumstances."

"How many times have we all heard that from our students? I'd think you could do better than that."

"The Fogel Press is going to publish a new translation of selected Mandelstam poems," Elise said. "They've asked me if I'm interested."

Adrian Levitsky reddened. "Attendance is a problem particularly when you don't call. We've had to cancel two of your classes, and that is completely unacceptable. Alaster parents are paying money to the college, Dr. Blazek. They are getting nothing for their money on the days you don't show up."

Elise wasn't sure what was expected of her now. The dressing-down was all the more humiliating for being called "doctor." "Maybe the best thing would be if next semester you gave me one less class," she said at last. "I'll need time for Mandelstam—more time than Kenovic required. There are twice as many poems."

"This is not about granting you privileges!" Levitsky sputtered. "And I should let you know there's been talk about liaisons with students. We can't prove this point, but be aware that disciplinary action for that particular infraction is severe. You would be subject to immediate discharge."

Elise tried to remember what Levitsky had published in the last ten years. From her hiring interview she recalled something about a chapter in a level one Russian grammar book and a translation of a Polish folktale for children.

"Making accusations without any evidence amounts to slander, Dr. Levitsky," said Elise.

Again Levitsky reddened. "Kindly keep your absences to a minimum," he said, "and be professional enough to give us ample notice when you absolutely must be absent."

"Understood," answered Elise and got up to leave.

"Good to see you, Dr. Blazek," said Levitsky, apparently unable to suppress the small formality.

Elise had the Kenovic; in all probability she'd get the Mandelstam. The high road stretched before her. She extended her hand. "Thank you, Dr. Levitsky."

Chapter Eight

"Jesus, what time is it?" Milos had kept his cousin waiting while he transferred to the phone in the kitchen. Still, his tone rose barely above a whisper. "You probably woke everyone."

"I'm sorry. Sorry, sorry, sorry. Listen, I need to borrow some money. Not a lot."

From the other end, Milos heard the sound of a bus or a truck accelerating.

"Where are you?"

"At a pay phone. I'm running out of change, I can't stay on."

"You know my situation."

This was the third time since she'd left Alaster College that Elise had asked Milos for money. As if he had any. The other two times he'd given her a little because Dawn had convinced him that something was wrong. She'd said she didn't know what the real story was, but obviously what Elise had told the family—that she was on sabbatical—was pure fabrication; she had been away from her college for far too long. The other two times Milos had wired a few hundred to Elise's account. But that was before they'd had Kristy.

"What's going on?" Milos asked now.

"I might need to move out of my apartment."

"Why?" Milos knew only that Elise was living in a studio apartment on Avenue C in New York's East Village. Once he had gotten her to tell him the unlisted number there, but when he'd tried to call her a month later, the number had been disconnected.

"It's a long story."

"Why can't you borrow from that friend of yours, Wiley? Or break down and call your *parents,* Elise."

A recorded voice interrupted, telling Elise to deposit more quarters.

"Milos? Milos?!"

"I'm here."

"You can do a wire transfer. It's not like I don't have an account. Let me give you the number."

"Elise, you can't call here at three in the morning just because—"

Click. Milos wasn't sure if they had been cut off or if Elise had hung up on her own. He turned the ringer off, then went to the bedroom and unplugged that extension, his fingers tracing the cord in the dark.

"Elise?" Dawn asked.

"Oh, shit, I thought you were asleep. I told her she can't call here at three in the morning."

"What did she want?"

"Money."

"Oh."

"She should get a job."

"I doubt she can," said Dawn groggily.

"If I fail my Construction Law test, I'm sending her a bill. Elise Katrinka Blazek, care of No Man's Land."

Dawn didn't answer. She had the enviable capacity to weave in and out of sleep without ever getting stuck at the margins. Maybe she had acquired it from that first year of getting up to nurse Kristy. For his part, Milos was probably awake for good. He had to admit he couldn't imagine what kind of job Elise could get. Her field, if it could be called one, was not exactly a gold mine of opportunities, and Milos couldn't picture his cousin behaving in a normal enough way to hold a real person's job.

Contemplating Elise's fate was terrifying. But wasn't her predicament her own fault? Dawn said no, that Elise had complicated problems. In Milos's view, Elise's chief problem was that she turned everything into a major production. Everything had equal weight on the importance scale.

If this was the result of her reputed brilliance, Milos was just as happy to have a lesser intelligence that he knew how and when to apply. He knew which events in his life should be taken seriously and which must simply be endured. He knew, for instance, that his course in Construction Law was important because he could well end up representing real estate developers. On the other hand, his part-time job as a telemarketer for an outfit selling condo timeshares was merely to be withstood. He had learned that right off the bat, the first time he was handed the script, which began, "How would you like to open your curtains right now and look onto miles of white sandy beach?" Instead of commenting on the ridiculous "sandy beach," Milos had decided on the spot to become an automaton for however long he needed to sit in cubicle number thirty-eight. Knowing where to assign different experiences on the importance scale was vital to success. That's where Elise went wrong. For her, bagging up recyclables was as big a deal as getting married. Buying shampoo was right up there with securing a teaching job. Every goddamned little thing sent her into a tailspin.

"Stop it," Milos told himself. "Sleep. You have a test tomorrow." He had barely managed a seventy-five on his last quiz in Construction Law. This was his final semester at John Marshall Law School, and he couldn't afford any slips. He had to be out by the spring and well placed by early summer. Maybe he had been too ambitious, enrolling in John Marshall's joint JD-master's program. He had thought the specialty master's would cinch him an associate spot in the real estate department of one of Chicago's top firms. Now he wasn't so sure. He didn't feel like the eager and exploitable young attorney he knew he would have to offer up on interviews. He didn't believe the senior partners would look into his eyes and assure themselves they had a live one who would ace the seventy-hour week required of a first-year associate. Most of his fellow law students weren't yet married, let alone parents. Their faces didn't show the strain of dividing their energies among doing coursework, bringing in income, and soothing the regular tantrums of a three-year-old.

Milos turned onto his side and pressed his face into Dawn's hair. The scent of her new conditioner was cloying; he flipped onto his back again. Since Elise's call, he knew he wouldn't be able to still his thoughts. What was he supposed to do about her? He realized Dawn was right, that something was truly going wrong, had been to one degree or another since that time they'd had to pick her up at District One police headquarters in Chicago.

Even in her absence, for the seven years Milos grew up in the house without Elise, she still managed to suck up half the air in the household. There were times she went AWOL, not calling and not answering messages. A few times she had done crazy things. It was hard to forget the day his uncle received his Master Charge statement with an outstanding balance for a fortune's worth of secondhand clothes. Aunt Irena had stayed up all night pestering Uncle Stepan with the same questions about Elise's motivation—questions his poor uncle had no way of answering.

Early on, Milos had decided he wouldn't be drawn into any turmoil centering on Elise. This hadn't proved difficult because when Aunt Irena was most distracted over her, the Laflin High baseball team was on the rise, and Milos was its biggest star. He knew that the team counted on his pitching arm to take them to the state championships. In reality, he didn't much care what Elise did. If he resented her during the years she was in college, it was only for turning his aunt into a broken record about Elise and her goddamned future.

Four fifty A.M. by the bedside digital clock. Milos got out of bed and went into Kristy's room, a converted pantry off the kitchen. He hated to see his daughter sleeping in this makeshift bedroom. It had no window and only a scatter rug that kept bunching up over the linoleum floor. He lifted her out of her narrow bed. She stirred on his shoulder but did not wake. Milos took her into his bed and placed her between Dawn and himself. Tucking her close against his side, he timed his breaths to coincide with her deep and steady ones. He couldn't quite manage her rhythm, and his thoughts continued to shift between the details of construction liabilities and what could happen to Elise, roaming around by herself in who-knew-what kind of neighborhood in the middle of the night.

Chapter Nine

December 1985

Irena was not surprised. Really, how could she be? It was her sixtieth birthday and Stepan had asked her to the movies, a rare enough event, without mentioning dinner afterward. Before they had left, she'd opened the freezer and taken out two pork chops to thaw. Stepan had frowned slightly. Too bad, thought Irena, wasted pork chops was the price he would have to pay for surprising her when he knew she was a woman who didn't like surprises.

Still, when Stepan opened the front door to their house at ten minutes after seven and a chorus of "Surprise!" rang out and camera flashes went off, Irena wasn't altogether unhappy. She'd had the presence of mind to apply a fresh coat of lipstick in the car—Stepan of course hadn't noticed—and she looked presentable enough in a merino wool skirt and her English mohair cardigan.

And how could Irena fail to be charmed when Kristy, her four-year-old granddaughter, gingerly approached with a small tray bearing two pigs-in-the-blanket on a Happy Birthday napkin and a tumbler half filled with wine? When the handover was completed with no spills, everyone applauded. Irena bent down and asked, her eyes wide, "for *me*?!"

"Happy birthday, Babička," Kristy managed. Miloslav and Dawn emerged from the crowd to praise Kristy for her pronunciation of the Czech *grandma,* and the party began.

Although Miloslav had never quite settled on what to call Irena, she was *babička* to his daughter, and Stepan was *dědeček,* grandfather. Irena knew Miloslav could have instead had his daughter call her grandaunt, *prateta,* and she was grateful that he hadn't.

Irena looked back at Stepan, who was arranging coats in the closet, making more room. Even from behind, he looked tired. Since the pace-maker had been implanted last year, it seemed to Irena that Stepan's movements had become more guarded, as if he were afraid to jostle the mechanism. She went over to embrace him. He turned around and smiled.

"Were you surprised?"

"Of course. Have you ever thrown me a surprise party before?"

Stepan appeared pleased with himself. "Milos and Dawn had a hard time convincing Kristy the party wasn't for her."

"Poor baby," said Irena. Then she called, "Where's my zlatíčko, my koťátko?"

Kristy left Dawn, who was wiping something off her face, to join Irena. She went over readily, yet if any guests had looked closely, they would have seen that Kristy felt the burden of Irena's love, that she was in fact a little afraid of it.

"Can you say *koťátko* for Babička? It means 'kitten' in Czech."

"Koťátko," whispered Kristy.

"That's right, my little koťátko. Now come show Babička around. Take her to all her wonderful guests." Irena held out her hand.

Kristy latched on but looked up at Irena, puzzled.

"There! Take me to Berta Kriz, right over there." Irena pointed to Berta, who was over by the dining table, laying out silverware that had been rolled into the Kriz sisters' Madeira linen napkins.

Obediently, Kristy led the way. She was a small-boned brunette child, darker than Elise had been, both her hair and skin tone. She had the green eyes that usually went with lighter hair, and long lashes that accentuated her femininity. She insisted on wearing only skirts and dresses, no matter how impractical. Dawn worried she was too vain, but Miloslav got a kick out of seeing his daughter so dolled up.

"Kristy!" exclaimed Berta. "Thank you for bringing over our guest of honor."

"Babička," corrected Kristy.

"That's right, Babička." Berta looked at Irena. "She's so adorable. So tell me, were you surprised?"

Irena turned around to see if Stepan was nearby. "Big surprise," she said. Then, taken aback at her own acid tone, she quickly added, "But it's such a pleasure to have all of you here together."

"It's a big accomplishment, turning sixty," said Berta.

Where, thought Irena, was the accomplishment? Murderers turned sixty. Vegetables in the hospital turned sixty. "What are you doing?" she asked. "Can I help?"

"No, no, we brought everything, you don't need to lift a finger."

Irena looked around to see who Berta meant by *we*. There were Magda and Reyna, of course, and Dawn. The guests included a few of the women from the old book club, with their husbands. There were Jiri and Ana Mueller from the Laflin Historical Society; since the reception for Karlstein Castle, they had become steady friends of Stepan and Irena's. There were a good five sets of neighbors. Petr Kriz was in town, and he had come with his latest young blond girlfriend. Kristy was the only child there.

"Now let's go say hello to Petr, koťátko. He's over there, in the blue shirt." Again Kristy led Irena by the hand.

"You're in town, Petr! I thought you were in Argentina."

Petr kissed Irena's cheek. "Such a beautiful little girl," he told her, looking at Kristy, who beamed. It didn't matter how old the woman, Petr would have her in his thrall within thirty seconds, even if she knew nothing of his great musical talent. The Kriz sisters' little brother, now in his forties, was a real charmer and an adventurer besides. As a violinist, he traveled all over the world, but while he was away he also climbed mountains and struck out on his own for long distances on small sailboats—skiffs, Stepan had called them. He had friends everywhere, on coffee plantations in Brazil and in the diamond industry in South Africa. Ever since he had defected, nothing daunted him, and Irena had never seen him anything but cheerful and in love with his life. There had been a time she'd thought of Petr Kriz for Elise.

"This is Heather Rose," said Petr. "She's just moved to Chicago from Miami."

"Oh, the weather must be a terrible shock for you. It's nice to meet you, dear. Thank you so much for coming."

Heather Rose wished Irena a happy birthday but did not manage to fully conceal her wish to be elsewhere with Petr. Heather Rose didn't sound like a real name, Irena reflected. It was probably a modeling or a musical-stage name. Or a stripper's.

"Babička, can I open your presents?"

Irena laughed. "Soon, koťátko. First take me to some more of my friends."

Kristy sighed dramatically. Irena didn't like to see such affectation in children, but Miloslav encouraged his daughter's theatrical streak. Irena hoped dearly that he wouldn't turn her into just another spoiled American child. He'd had her so young, Irena didn't think he knew enough about child rearing. Still, she had to admit that both Miloslav and Dawn seemed awfully grown-up for their ages.

"Don't forget it's *Babička's* party. Don't you want her to have a good time?"

Kristy nodded. Tears were gathering.

"You have a very important job to do, koťátko. You're coming with Babička to meet all her friends." Irena looked about the room. She wanted to talk to Magda, who was here alone. Frank's ileitis must be acting up again. Yet Magda was talking animatedly—flirtatiously, Irena thought—to Sam Karr, the Blazeks' neighbor on the west side of the block. So Irena pointed toward Sally Fitzhugh, her friend from the old book club, and Kristy took her over.

Sally hugged Irena. "Many happy returns," she exclaimed. Then, almost whispering, "Will Elise be here?"

The question, timed and asked in an ordinary way, sounded to Irena calamitously sudden. "She's in Belgrade," she answered.

"You don't say? I knew it had to be something very important to keep her away."

"She felt terrible," muttered Irena. "But—"

"Babička?" Kristy interrupted meekly.

"What, koťátko?"

"I'm hungry. I want pigs in sleeping bags."

Irena smiled. "That sounds like one of her daddy's jokes. Okay, you've been very patient. Let's go get you some pigs in sleeping bags. Come, Sally?"

"I've had plenty," said Sally, patting her stomach.

Irena left to get food for Kristy, but her mind was not on the task. That would be the first question of a long evening, she told herself. Another reason she was uncomfortable about this surprise party; how could she and Stepan reach an agreement beforehand on how to handle questions about Elise? Irena had used the Belgrade answer in front of Stepan before, but he hadn't liked it, and who knew what he was telling people tonight? She needed to corner him. It was her birthday; she would insist he go with Belgrade.

As Irena put pigs-in-the-blanket and pasta salad on Kristy's plate, her chest felt leaden. She still couldn't believe that so much time had passed since she had last spoken to her daughter. Not a day went by that she didn't reflect on the sheer unnaturalness of it. Irena didn't know how she could get through the rest of her party, much less the rest of her life. This surprise party had undermined her attempt to downplay her sixtieth birthday. The more her birthday was on display, the less she felt able to forgive Elise for ignoring it.

Miloslav appeared beside Irena at the buffet. "So were you surprised?"

"Are you kidding? Do you know this is the first surprise party of my life?"

Miloslav smiled. "We all planned it," he said.

"Daddy! Look at my pigs in sleeping bags!"

Miloslav glanced at his daughter's plate. "Very nice. If you eat some pasta salad and a little piece of chicken, you can have birthday cake."

"Shh-h-h-h!" Kristy's chin trembled. Her eyes filled with tears, and she stomped her foot.

"It's okay, Kristy. Grandma knows about the birthday cake."

Kristy looked at Irena, who said, "It's okay, koťátko, Babička knows. You'll get a big piece."

"But you don't know the *flavor*," claimed Kristy, holding fast to her shred of power.

"She went with Esmeralda to pick out the cake," Miloslav explained.

Irena nodded. Esmeralda was Kristy's part-time nanny. Miloslav was a first-year associate in a big Chicago firm, and Dawn had just been promoted at her public relations company. They both left the apartment early, and Dawn dropped Kristy off at the Rogers Park Montessori School on Thorndale Avenue. Esmeralda picked her up there at one P.M. In the evenings Kristy watched videos of animated movies, and on the weekends she went to what Miloslav called play dates. As far as Irena was concerned, something was missing. As much exposure as she had given Elise to the city and its culture, she had also given her time to herself. "Go gather wool," she would say to Elise when they got home from Eurhythmics class or from one of the Young People's Concerts in Chicago. When Elise was small, she would run off and come back minutes later to drop a heap of sweaters at Irena's feet, laughing hysterically. By the time she was seven or eight, though, she would go off to her small room to read or draw pictures or daydream. Yet maybe the woolgathering had been the start, had marked the beginning of whatever it was that had caused Elise's problems.

"Elise is in Belgrade, that's why," Irena overheard Sally Fitzhugh tell Rhonda Carroll, another member of Irena's old book club. Then the two of them approached her.

"Tell us, birthday girl," declared Rhonda. "What is your daughter doing in Belgrade? She's really something, isn't she?"

"Teaching," said Irena. "She's there as a visiting scholar at the university, teaching nineteenth-century American literature." Irena felt her cheeks blaze. She had no idea if the University of Belgrade even offered such a course. Though who among the people in her living room would check?

"What about Alaster College?" Rhonda asked. "Does she have tenure yet?"

"These academic institutions," said Irena. "She's practically guaranteed, she just has to pass her fifth year there." Irena tried to catch Stepan's eye. He was standing with Harv, Rhonda's husband, showing off one of his books on medieval European castles. He might as well be in Siberia, for all Irena's chances of making contact with him. The room suddenly seemed stifling. "Excuse me, please," she said to Sally and Rhonda, then fled to the bedroom.

Behind her locked door, Irena was seized with a nervous, prickly energy. She rifled through the nightstand for the last number she'd had for Elise. No matter how slim her chances of making contact, she had to try. After

she dialed, a recording advised her that the number had been disconnected or was not in service. Then, before she could talk herself out of
it, she called Wiley Mills. So what if Irena put her on the spot? It was
her birthday, and calling Wiley was her present to herself. After three
rings, though, she heard another recording: "You have reached the home
of Wiley Mills, Michael Stefano, and Travis and Sabrina Mills-Stefano.
We're sorry we missed your call. Please leave a message." Irena hung up.
She would be damned if she'd leave a message for Wiley, her husband,
son, and a baby Irena hadn't even known existed.

A wave of dizziness passed over her, a lightheadedness she associated
with being at high altitudes. Until recently, she hadn't gotten dizzy since
childhood, since that time before they came to America when her father
had taken her to the Krkonoše Mountains in northern Bohemia. She'd
passed out, and Václav had had to revive her with a bitter-smelling flower
and a slap on the cheek. Now, fifty years later, Irena was in her bedroom
in Laflin, Illinois, feeling as robbed of oxygen as she had that day in the
mountains. She sat down on the bed to recover herself. For the thou-
sandth time, she recalled the conversation she'd had with Wiley Mills
three months ago. Three months, yes, but it still seemed to Irena to have
taken place outside of time, as if on one of the space stations in Miloslav's
old science-fiction comic books.

"Mrs. Blazek? Irena? This is Wiley Mills, do you remember me?"

"Of course I remember you. My God, just tell me she's all right."

"She's safe, yes."

"She's back at Alaster? She's finally back? I know nothing about
anything. I can't tell you—"

"I know. I've put myself in your position; it's absolutely awful. I've
tried to get her to call you. She just—"

"What? She just *what*? My husband says we should hire a private
eye. How ridiculous, I thought at first, but then—what am I doing? Tell
me everything you know."

"There have been many times I've wanted to call you myself, but
Elise always managed to talk me out of it. Then things got better. This
time is different."

"*Tell . . . me.*" Irena's throat might have been coated with mortar for
all the difficulty of repeating these two syllables.

"I'm sure you've long since stopped believing the sabbatical story. The fact is, Elise was fired from Alaster."

Irena had clutched her left breast. "No! When?"

"At the beginning of 1982. The campus police caught her in her department chair's office in the middle of the night."

"She'd probably forgotten something in there."

"That wasn't it."

"Are you saying my Elise is a burglar? You're supposed to be her friend."

Why was Wiley telling her this? What had happened to *her*? She was still young, but maybe trying to save so many premature babies had toughened her, had turned her into a cold fish. "I'm sure she had a good reason to be there," Irena defended.

"Once she was inside," Wiley had continued, "she broke into a locked file cabinet to find her records. She'd gotten it into her head that everyone in the department was trying to sabotage her, that there was some big plan afoot to keep her from getting tenure."

"But that's ridiculous! She had the Sanja Kenovic translation that won that big prize. And wasn't she working on a bigger book? Yes, Mandelstam, she told me about the Mandelstam poems. That's why Alaster gave her the sabbatical."

Wiley had already said there was no sabbatical, but Irena hadn't believed her.

"She never finished that project."

"But no one in that department has published more than Elise, she told me, and she was the youngest by far! They would never have fired her."

Irena had heard a shuddering breath from Wiley. When she began to speak, though, her tone was clinical, a doctor's tone. "The truth is, Elise hasn't been right for many years. I've known her now for sixteen years. She's so wonderful in so many ways, Mrs. Blazek, but I saw trouble from the very beginning."

How dare Wiley say this? Was she saying she knew Elise better than her own mother did? The beginning? Wiley *had not been there* in the beginning; she hadn't come into Elise's life until Elise was in college. Yet as soon as Irena had thought this, a memory had arisen—the scratched mailboxes, the bizarre act of vandalism that came out of the blue the summer Elise was eighteen.

"At the end of grad school," Wiley had continued, "she was finally diagnosed as Bipolar I. Actually, with psychotic features. She was put on lithium, which helped some. But over the last couple of years, she's been fully functional for shorter periods."

"I don't believe you. Elise functions better than most people do. Look at that Kenovic translation. Did you read what the *Los Angeles Times* said? They said Elise may as well have lived in Sanja Kenovic's brain, that it was a brilliant translation."

"She finished it when she was manic," Wiley had explained. "But when her mania spins out of control, that's when the trouble starts. Paranoia, sensory delusions. She was in very bad shape when Alaster fired her."

Irena still had not believed Wiley, but she needed more information from her. "Why didn't Elise tell me all this? She would have told me this. I'm her mother."

"She wanted to protect you and your husband. She still does—she doesn't know I'm calling. But lately things have gotten a good deal worse. I literally had to drag her to get her evaluated at Columbia Presbyterian last week. She was admitted for several days, but now she's back here, with us. Michael and I are trying to decide what to do next. She refuses inpatient treatment."

"Let me talk to her!"

"She's sleeping. And it wouldn't be—"

"Stepan! *Stepan!*" Irena had called, then remembered he'd gone out for his Saturday walk. "I can't understand all this. If she'd only gotten married and settled down! Not that awful Viktor Frolov, good riddance to him, but someone her own age, someone steady. What would it have taken? Very little. She's an attractive girl, a brilliant girl, Wiley, you know that. If only she dressed like a normal person . . ."

"Mrs. Blazek, Elise's clothes are not her problem. It's a great credit to her that she's held up as long as she has. But things are worse now. Last year she developed what's known as a rapid-cycling specifier. It sometimes happens in intractable cases of bipolar disorder. In essence, it means she runs through mood cycles far faster than the typical manic depressive. It happens in about ten percent of cases."

Wiley had come at her with a tidal wave of information. Rapid cycling? Irena had pictured her daughter in one of those bike races, the

Tour de France, leading the others up a hill, drops of sweat being flung into the air every time she looked back to see who was gaining on her.

"I don't know about this rapid cycling," Irena had said, her voice still half stuck in her throat.

"I have literature on it. I'm going to put it in the mail to you."

"I don't want literature! I want my daughter. I'm going to come up there, with Stepan. We're coming immediately."

"Please don't. She needs to be stabilized. I understand how you feel, I truly do, but it's a very bad idea to come right now. It would be bad for Elise."

"Bad to see her parents?"

"I know how painful this must be."

"No, you don't. I'm sorry to say it, but you just don't," said Irena.

"Michael and I decided that at this point we were being irresponsible in not trying to contact you. First off, we wanted you to know that Elise is safe with us. But at the same time we thought you needed to know what it's like for her, that Elise's life is sometimes a nightmare to her."

"You say that to her mother, who raised her? That her life is a nightmare?"

"I'm sorry, I shouldn't have put it that way. But another thing is that if you come now, Elise will know I was the one who called you. Because of everything that's happened, she's lost many friends, most of them, in fact. If she finds out that I went behind her back while she's in this state of psychosis, it would be disastrous. So I'm asking you—please don't come. I promise you that when she's stabilized, I'll let her know that we've talked, that you know what's happened to her."

Psychosis? A minute ago Wiley had said bipolar disorder. Then that cycling thing. Or maybe she had said something else; Irena couldn't remember. "What do you mean, psychosis? Now you're saying—"

"It's temporary. It can happen when bipolar patients are off their meds."

The most profound exhaustion had taken hold of Irena. She had thought she might fold in on herself. Still, she had understood that Wiley was *it* for her and Stepan, their sole connection to Elise, and that she had no choice but to do as she asked.

In the three months since that call, Irena had only once summoned up the strength to phone Wiley Mills. She'd found out that Elise had finally agreed to be hospitalized, that now they were saying something about a kind of epilepsy Irena had never heard of, temporal lobe epilepsy. The word *lobe* had leapt out at her. She knew that word; she'd heard about the prefrontal lobotomies performed on political prisoners in Russia. Surely this operation was outlawed in America. Still, the very mention of the word *lobe* had made Irena feel sick. She couldn't call the hospital and ask for Elise, and she hadn't been able to call Wiley again. Instead, every few days she had tried the Avenue C number, the last number she'd had for Elise. Each time she'd called, an old woman answered. Maybe, Irena thought, Elise had sublet her apartment; maybe she would be back in a few days, back and returned to herself.

Tonight was the first time Irena had gotten the message that the Avenue C number had been disconnected or was out of service.

While Irena was in her bedroom, someone had softened the living room lighting. A lamp had been switched off and two lavender-scented candles had been placed on the buffet. Irena looked up at the loop of stringed letters that spelled *Happy Birthday* hanging from the entryway to the kitchen.

"Babička, watch this!" shouted Kristy from the other side of the room. She had taken off her little Mary Janes and now, after a running start, skidded in her white anklets across the polished wood floors, stopping at Irena's side.

"Very good, koťátko, but be careful."

"What is 'careful' to a four-year-old?" asked Magda, laughing.

"Ach, what is it to any of us? Just a word. There's no such thing as being careful," Irena reflected.

"Then why did you say it, Babička?"

"I don't know, koťátko, maybe your babička is not so smart now that she's sixty."

"Time for presents!" trilled Berta, standing by a pile of wrapped packages on the cleared dining table. These latest preparations had also occurred while Irena was in the bedroom. All these people, she thought disbelievingly, buying and decorating and cleaning and cooking for her. She was shown to her La-Z-Boy recliner, and before long, colored tissue and ribbon gathered around her feet. Directly in front of her, Kristy sat blowing bubbles from the bottle someone had thoughtfully included among Irena's presents: two silk scarves, a silver picture frame, costume jewelry, a pair of gardening shears, a deck of cards in a leather case, a decoupage recipe box and—to Irena's complete astonishment—an indigo fox coat from Stepan.

✦

"Where *is* she?" Irena sobbed in bed that night, burying her head in Stepan's pajama shirt. It was only a few hours after he had surprised her with the luxurious calf-length coat that Reyna must have advised him on and that surely cost in the thousands, a gift such as Stepan had never made to her. Yet now she cried against his poor, sunken chest.

Stepan sighed and patted her head. "If we don't know, we'll be unhappy, and if we find out, we'll be unhappy. What can I say? Did you enjoy your party at all?"

Irena pulled her arm tight across his narrow body. He didn't feel to her as he used to. He had contracted, his shoulders hunched more toward his torso. "I did enjoy it. Don't think I'm ungrateful, Stepan. You've been wonderful to me. I just—"

"You can't dwell, Irena. You have before you perhaps another twenty or thirty years. They are yours, not hers."

Chastened, Irena fell silent, thinking of the years before her. Thankfully Stepan had not embarked on a project as ambitious as Karlstein Castle, but he still spent long hours in his workshop, building and fixing things—sometimes just fussing, it seemed to Irena. He would retire in a few short years, maybe sooner if that thing he kept talking about took over his office. CAD, he'd called it—computer-assisted drafting. But whenever he retired, Irena didn't imagine their life changing much. Stepan would not suddenly develop a taste for travel, and it was too late for Irena to better her estate in the world. Maybe she would reduce her week from three to two days at Reyna Kopecky's Fabric Shop, take a course or two. Miloslav and Dawn talked about moving to California, but they had not suggested that Irena and Stepan join them. They would probably have another child, yet how often would Irena see them?

Presently Stepan's hand grew still on Irena's head. When it fell away, she heard the wheeze that would be followed by his snoring. She'd had too much wine, and lay sinking one moment, awake the next.

Trying to get her mind off Elise, Irena shifted her thoughts to 1938, her passage to this country, her father robust with youth and a hundred determined dreams. To this day, Irena remained impressed that Václav, merely a laborer at Pilsner Urquell, had understood in 1938 what Hitler was capable of. Even as a Catholic, he had known. The Kraus family was not devout; Irena remembered worshipping only on holidays at the Church of St. Bartholomew, an imposing Gothic structure with one of the highest towers in all of Czechoslovakia. Since coming to America, Irena had wondered if her father had had some Jewish blood—if she herself might.

Václav had often been angry in those days. He was angry at whole nations—England and France and Italy for signing the Munich Agreement and bargaining away his national identity. When the Germans came to occupy Plzen, Irena remembered that Václav had scoffed at the agreement, saying Hitler would never make good on his promise not to start a war in Europe. The people of Plzen, he'd said, had been sacrificed for a principle that would not be honored. The sight of German soldiers in his city enraged him, and he began to make plans—the details of which Irena had never learned—to leave for America.

A year later, in the spring of 1939, after they were all settled in Quincy, Illinois, Václav's letters home began to come back unopened. They were marked, "Return. Connection interrupted. Territory occupied."

The Nazis destroyed thousands of houses in Plzen and killed many hundreds of its people. By then, Irena's father was a different man. He looked as if he had shed years. Like many immigrants, like Ray Kroc, the founder of McDonald's, he came to realize he could change his estate in life, become successful. He was introduced to a new feeling—ambition. Václav began to hatch business schemes that would enrich his family and give him a chance to become a respected community leader. In the end, he didn't have the discipline to turn any of his ideas into reality. But at least while he was scheming he had known enough to hold on to his job as cellar manager at Ruff Brewing. With his union wages, the Krauses lived comfortably. Václav never lost the sense that his lucky break was just around the corner, and Irena loved him for that. She believed he relished his life until the day he died, shortly after her marriage to Stepan.

But now was now, and if you worked in manufacturing, enjoying life was more complicated. Even if they had wanted to, the second-generation descendants of her parents and their friends at the brewing company would not be able to settle into a secure factory job while they nurtured their dreams—they had to take the next step. Most of them ended up taking ten. To a person, Irena's old friends in Quincy had raised successful children. Irena and Stepan had themselves raised a college professor and a lawyer.

And yet Elise. In the United States, what had become of the granddaughter of the man most responsible for ensuring her bright future, the man who'd had the foresight to escape the war in Europe? What had become of the only American-born member of his family? She had achieved a high status in the most open society in the world, then had given in to a diagnosis of "rapid cycler," a term no one in Plzen would ever have dreamed up.

Irena got out of bed and went to the living room. Magda, Berta, and Reyna had stayed late to clean, and the house was spotless. Her three good friends—they were all doing fine. Reyna's shop had known better years, but it served a loyal clientele of immigrants who believed handsewn clothes were superior. Irena had been wrong about Berta; she had really gone places since Magda's marriage. Her series on Czech life in Paris had been so widely read that the *Tribune* had offered her a job as features writer. Last year she had moved to Chicago and bought an apartment in Magda and Frank's building. And Magda, too, was happy. She was now head of the languages department at the Easton School for Girls.

Wondering how her life would have turned out if—like the Kriz sisters—she'd had no children, Irena went into the kitchen and poured herself a glass from the last bottle of birthday-party wine. Then she headed over to the hall closet to take out her indigo fox coat. It had a sharp smell, from its packing. She put it on, examining her reflection in the full-length mirror on the door. Except for the sleeves, it fit her well, and she felt a pulse of excitement that this gorgeous coat with the fashionable shawl collar was hers. She must not take for granted the fact that after all these years of marriage her husband still loved her. He had bought her a deluxe fur coat because he believed she deserved it.

Chapter Ten

April 1986

"It's actually six stories," Elise said, standing alongside Wiley.
They were in the flower district, looking at a gray brick building across the street. "You can't see the other two because they're set back from the street."

It was early spring, and they both wore leather jackets that they had opened to better appreciate the first warm breezes of the season. Wiley's was a three-quarter-length calfskin from Barney's. Elise had gotten hers, a grainy brown leather, at a flea market twelve years before. In the back, a frayed section of lining dipped below its hem.

"It's nice. I like the casement windows. But honey . . ."

Elise took hold of Wiley's shoulders and made Wiley face her. "I am not manic."

"I hope not. Except an undertaking on this scale—"

"Do I seem manic?"

"Not in the way you've been before, but that doesn't mean you aren't."

"Call Dr. Massie if you don't believe me. She'll tell you."

Wiley turned her attention back to the building. "How did you find out about this, again?"

"I told you. Tomás. He works at Milstein's." Elise pointed to the gray building's storefront. MILSTEIN'S WHOLESALE FLOWERS was stenciled across the top of the glass.

"Not a family business, I take it."

"All the workers are Puerto Rican. So what?"

"How did you meet Tomás, anyway?" asked Wiley. "Oh never mind, don't answer that."

They had crossed the street, and now Elise was looking at the building entry from up close. Then she peered inside the window of Milstein's.

"Is he in there?" asked Wiley.

"He's not working today."

"And how did Tomás find out the building's for sale?"

"He heard Ray Milstein talking about it. Tomás gave me the name of the realtor, so I called."

"If the building's such a good deal, why doesn't this man Ray Milstein buy it? Wouldn't it be in his interest?"

"Maybe he doesn't want to be a landlord, how do I know? Tomás says the store has a ten-year lease, and the rent is very low for this street. Probably Ray Milstein just doesn't want to bother. He's old, he's got plenty of money, why does he need the responsibility? Let's go in."

Elise led the way into Milstein's. The walls were lined with glass-doored refrigerators in which large vats of tulips and lilies sat on deep shelves. The floor was crowded with hyacinth in clay pots. An enormous table with a chopping block surface took up half the center floor space. There, one worker was assembling identical freesia arrangements, and another was trimming gladiola stems. Elise liked the sound of his shears snapping through the stems and the fresh smell the cuts released, a fragrance that mingled with the occasional whiff of the damp sawdust covering the floor.

The second worker held a batch of dripping gladiolas away from his body. "Elise! *Buenos días! Tomás no está aquí.*"

"*Yo sé,*" said Elise. "I'm just showing my friend around. Is that okay? Wiley, this is René. And this is Hector."

The heavy man working on the identical arrangements looked up and smiled at them. "So are you going to buy us, Elise?" He and René exchanged a look and started to laugh. Their eyes were full of fun. "*Compra, por favor. Cómprenos todos.*"

Elise let loose one of her deep-bellied laughs, so unrestrained that the two men exchanged smiles once more.

"*Lo veremos,*" she said, then turned back to Wiley. "I wish I could show you upstairs. I've only seen the spaces once myself."

"Do the tenants know the building's for sale?"

"I don't know. But any new owner would get rid of them. They pay next to nothing, and they're illegal anyway. These lofts aren't zoned for residential."

"You'd do that, Elise? You'd evict them?"

"I'd have to. I'd want only commercial tenants. I have it all figured out."

Then she began to explain to Wiley her plan, such a farsighted yet simple one that she savored its telling. She would get an advance against her inheritance from her parents, use it as down payment on the building, borrow the rest from somewhere—she was willing to go to one of those private mortgage lenders so she wouldn't have to verify income. Once she was in, she would get a home improvement credit line, pay the tenants' moving expenses, then act as her own designer and general contractor to renovate the whole building, including putting in a new lobby, intercom, and security system. As soon as possible, floor-by-floor if she had to, she would fill the building with commercial tenants. To prove their solvency, the tenants would have to show her five years of tax returns. Within two years, Elise calculated, she would be able to get the building out of its renovation debt and have enough solid income to refinance a better mortgage, this time from a bank. Thereafter, her monthly income would be huge and her overhead small.

"What experience have you had as a G.C.?" Wiley asked.

"None. But I changed around the plumbing in the ballroom and put up drywall and replaced the hot water heater myself. I can do it."

"You did all that when you were manic," Wiley reminded her. "Let's leave. There are a few minor details you haven't considered. Such as how it might be a bit touchy to approach your parents for your inheritance when you haven't had three conversations with them in four years."

Elise's expression grew resolute. "Let me worry about that."

Wiley looked at her watch. "Let's get lunch. I told Michael I'd be back at two. Sabrina can't say a word, but she's mastered all the nuances of whining. Michael and I spell each other."

*　*　*

At the diner around the corner, Elise ordered a bran muffin and a fruit salad. At one diner or another, she had eaten this same lunch ever since she'd moved to New York. "Why are you being so negative about this? I could get off disability—completely free myself."

"Elise, think about it. You can't blame me for being skeptical. I'm just worried about you. It wasn't four months ago you were so depressed you couldn't get out of bed."

"You'd be depressed, too, if you lived in a two-square-inch basement apartment with a bookie on one side and a crack dealer on the other." Elise was doing her best to control herself, but she felt her anger mount. Wiley and Michael and their children had just moved into a large three-bedroom on Central Park West, overlooking the park.

"Come on, sweetie. That apartment's horrible, and I'd love to see you out of it, but we both know it wasn't the apartment that caused the depression."

"Well, it's going to take something radical to get me out of there. This is an amazing opportunity. The owner, this guy Vizzini, lives in Florida. He's some kind of a shut-in, and he has no idea what he has in that building. He hasn't even seen it in ten years; he thinks the block is still a pit. The realtor's disgusted with him for not raising the price, but she can't force him to. If Vizzini is loony tunes, is that my problem?" Elise paused. "Maybe we're meant for each other."

They both laughed, but Wiley quickly sobered. "What if you get sick again?"

"Dr. Massie said Depakote could maintain me for years."

Elise knew Wiley was skeptical. Depakote was an antiseizure drug. By prescribing it for Elise's psychiatric condition, Wiley thought Dr. Massie was playing fast and loose. But how could she deny Elise's obvious improvement?

"Come on," Elise continued, "Anna Akhmatova hasn't said a word to me in years."

Wiley laughed. "But what about Osip Mandelstam? Before you left Alaster, you were working on the translations at twenty-four-hour stretches. You were obsessed."

"*The Science of Departure*," recalled Elise, the name she had given her translation. She had taken it from the title poem of Mandelstam's second book, *Tristia*. She had pored over previous translations of the first two lines: "I've acquired the craft of separating / in the unbraided laments of the night" from Bernard Meares; "I have taken to heart the lessons of good-byes / In bareheaded laments in the night" from James Greene. In the end, she had settled on "I have studied the science of departures" but had not been able to come up with a satisfactory interpretation of the second line, rejecting "in a woman's uncoiled hair at night," "in sleepless nights beside her wailing" and "deep at night beside her unraveled hair."

In, at, in, on, an. The choice of every article and every two-letter preposition had become a torment. Anna Akhmatova had declared that translating was like eating your brain. In the end, Elise had been overwhelmed by the project and had written to the Fogel Press, returning her advance.

"I never *literally* heard his voice, though," Elise insisted now.

"Maybe not, but you blocked out the world during that period, and you also drank too much."

"Why are you bringing all this up?!" Elise snapped. "You know I haven't looked at a poem by a Russian since the day I left Alaster. No more of those dismal existences under Stalin. Dr. Massie thinks I'm right. She said I chose to specialize in oppression because it's the idiom of my illness."

Wiley rolled her eyes. "Since when do you listen to a word your psychiatrists say?"

"She's fine with this idea," Elise continued, ignoring this last remark. "She gets it that if I can pull this off, I can free myself to do whatever I choose. I'm still young, right? Maybe I'll go to medical school, become a really *good* shrink, like Dr. Massie."

"And what if you don't pull it off? Then what?"

Fury rose so fast Elise felt it pressing against her eardrums. Was Wiley deliberately trying to banish her back to her hideous little apartment, exile her as Mandelstam had been exiled to Cherdyn? Was Wiley becoming like the others, her old psychiatrists with their low expectations? Elise no longer paid attention to those who did not take an optimistic view of her situation. The quality of Dr. Nan Massie's attention was utterly crystalline; she was about Elise's age and enthusiastic and believed that with a little help, Elise had a unique capacity to push back otherworldly mental states—ones that were native to her illness, not to her character. Dr. Massie had high hopes for Elise, and Elise knew that she herself had inspired those hopes.

"What is *with* you, anyway?" Elise threw down her fork. "My Ph.D. came to naught, my life is like a worm's. Should I just accept it? Would that make you happy?"

"That would make me very *un*happy, Elise. It's just that this is a huge venture, and I'm afraid you may be underestimating it. The whole idea frightens me for you, if you really want to know."

Elise relaxed and gave Wiley a look she had given her many times— a determinedly calm look, neither happy nor unhappy, a look that conveyed her pure appetite for survival. "Oh, fear again," she said. "That old thing."

Wiley's husband, Michael, had been the one to refer Elise to Dr. Massie. Last year, the day after Elise had gotten out of the hospital for the second time, Michael had tracked down Nan Massie, a friend from his residency days. Right before their move, Elise had been staying with them—Wiley and Michael, five-year-old Travis and the new baby—in their cramped apartment on 97th Street off Amsterdam Avenue. At Columbia Presbyterian, Elise had just gotten another feature added to her diagnosis. Not only was she Bipolar I with psychotic features and a rapid-cycling specifier, but she also had temporal lobe epilepsy. ("My high-octane upgrade," Elise had later called it.) During the afternoons Wiley and Michael were at the hospital, she had done little but sway on the rocker in their room.

On Elise's third afternoon in the apartment, while she was there with the children and their nanny, Travis had opened the door to his parents' bedroom and scrambled in on his hands and knees. Each hand bore down on a toy truck, an ambulance in his left hand and a fire engine in his right, and he'd entered screeching like a siren. Elise had stared at him.

Travis had imitated a siren wailing for a while longer, then stopped and waited for Elise to react. When she didn't, he stood up to face her. "Retard!"

Deep down, in a recess she couldn't possibly get to, Elise had wanted to tell Travis that in fact she had an undergraduate degree from Princeton, was a Ph.D. in Slavic studies, had been the youngest full professor in the history of Alaster College, and had won the coveted Kaminsky Poetry Translation Prize. She had wanted to tell this towheaded little boy, the insufferable son of her best friend, that she was *not* a retard—that she was merely undone by the smells no one else smelled, the recurrent feeling that she had stood in the precise same spot, wearing the exact same outfit, thousands of times before. She wanted to tell this five-year-old how she sometimes whirled right out of her body to become no more than an accumulation of molecules, then whirled back in, transformed into a vessel for all means of sensation: ringing in her ears, metal in her mouth, particles raining on her, voices in her head.

She'd wanted to repeat that she was not a retard, that Dostoyevsky had had the very same disease, that he'd described it in *The Idiot*. Elise couldn't find the voice to tell Travis all this. She had rocked silently instead, but she remembered how in *The Idiot*, Prince Myshkin had described something that appeared to burst open before him, an astonishing inner light that illuminated his soul. Elise knew that light, and longed for it, but rather than tell Travis about the light, she had given in to tears. That was when the nanny ran in, scolded Travis, and dragged him from the room, bawling.

Two days later, Michael had set up the appointment with Dr. Massie. Elise had shown up only for Wiley's sake. But Dr. Massie had immediately distinguished herself from the others. Her office was full of Mexican pottery and Aboriginal art. She seemed to know all about Elise—not only her immediate diagnosis from Columbia Presbyterian, but all her previous diagnoses, true and false. She looked Elise straight in the eye. She told her that this was an exciting time for intractable bipolars like herself. Elise could see how turned on Dr. Massie was by science, how she saw neurotransmitters and hormones and pharmaceuticals interacting in a dance of never-ending variation.

Dr. Massie had promised Elise they would find the variation for her, the precise synergy that would stabilize her. She had told Elise that the new diagnosis, the temporal lobe epilepsy, was heartening; it opened up a whole new avenue of treatment. Most of Elise had remained back in Wiley and Michael's bedroom, rocking to nowhere, yet she had left the office with another appointment and an uncertain ripple of hope.

✦

Elise's mother had cried when Elise announced she was coming to visit. Her father had been formal. "We'd be glad to have you," he had said.

Elise arrived late Friday afternoon, three days after she had shown Wiley the building. At six o'clock, Milos and Dawn walked in with their little girl. Kristy had looked at the carpet when she was introduced to Elise. She had turned her attention to Irena and Stepan, eager to tell them a joke about an alien in underpants. Stepan chuckled. Irena's smile was halfhearted and a touch censorious. Elise, though, had exploded in laughter. That was all Kristy had needed. She settled nearby and began to ply Elise with questions: Why was her hair the orange-red of the crayon in a Crayola box, why did she wear those lace-up shoes with all the little hooks? And why did her hands shake like that?

Elise had answered all of Kristy's questions: her hair was orange-red so she could pull a chunk out whenever she wanted to color; her shoes had all those hooks to keep her feet from wandering away; and her hands shook because before she arrived, she had outrun an alien in underpants. Kristy had giggled but stared all the same at Elise's tremor—a side effect of the 1,500 milligrams of Depakote a day.

By seven o'clock, everyone was seated, plates of Irena's roast pork with dumplings and cabbage before them. Not a word was said about the length of time that had passed—nine years—since Elise had sat at this table.

"I don't like this, Babička," said Kristy, holding up a dumpling she had speared with her fork. "It tastes like an old sock."

"Honey, you like dumplings," said Dawn. "You had them just two weeks ago, and you liked them."

"Pee-u," said Kristy. "I did not." She put her thumb in her mouth. Dawn didn't tell her to take it out.

Elise liked Dawn. It was evident she was that rare creature, a truly nonjudgmental person, and although she knew the truth of Elise's situation, or something close to it, she was treating her with a casualness reserved for family. By contrast, Milos would not—or could not—look at Elise. Whenever he spoke to her, his gaze fell somewhere between her and his wife.

"Could you pass the butter?" Stepan asked Elise. At least *he* looked at her.

"Stepan, there's margarine here for you," said Irena, a warning in her tone.

"I'm celebrating Elise's arrival."

"I shouldn't keep it in the house," Irena explained to the others. "I got it for all of you. Besides the pacemaker, the doctor says his cholesterol is too high."

Kristy had dropped her head on her arm beside her plate. She was playing with her dumpling. "I wish this was a pig in a sleeping bag," she mused.

Everyone laughed.

"A pig in a sleeping bag?" Elise asked.

"From Babička's sixtieth birthday party!" declared Kristy, clearly irritated that Elise didn't know.

The rest of them continued eating.

In a moment, Irena said, "Of course, to be fair, this is not exactly a cholesterol-free dinner. Don't get used to it, Stepan. Tomorrow we're back to skim everything."

"You are a heartless woman, Irena Blazek."

"And you're a stubborn man, Stepan Blazek."

"Mommy, are Babička and Děda calling each other bad names?"

"No, sweetie, they're just teasing."

Irena picked up the platter of pork and offered it to Milos. Elise noticed the tight set of her mother's jaw, a tension in her face she had never seen. But neither had she seen Irena in bifocals nor her father with a bald pate. Irena's neck was thicker, and she had lost height; her father's face was more gaunt, and it seemed to Elise that one of his hips was lower than the other. Every time one of her parents turned away, she stared, but for all the basic familiarity of their appearance, there was nothing about their identities that resonated inside her. The illness, Dr. Massie would have said. The illness makes the familiar foreign.

✦

Elise had planned to bring up the topic of the building during breakfast on Saturday, but when she woke the next morning, her parents had eaten breakfast and were dressed to go out. Irena got up from the table, offered Elise oatmeal and coffee, and without taking a breath, told her the agenda for the day. They were to go to the Art Institute to see the László Moholy-Nagy show, have lunch at the museum, then on the way home go to the Laflin Historical Society so Elise could see the society's placement of Karlstein Castle. Stepan said nothing. Irena might not care greatly about the Moholy-Nagy show or Karlstein Castle, but it was clear that she was in charge, that she had carefully paced the events of the day and intended no deviations. And Stepan would go with them, even though he never went into Chicago on weekends. Plainly, he had been ordered. We will do this, and then we will do that. Irena sounded like a drill sergeant. Elise could virtually see her drawing this unfamiliar bossiness out of herself, a thing of weight, a burden that needed to be carried.

Fifteen minutes later, when Elise emerged from her old room wearing her brown leather jacket, Stepan was helping Irena into a calf-length fox coat that looked real. Elise took a step back.

"A gift from Táta for my sixtieth birthday," said Irena, her voice rich with sorrow.

Elise closed her eyes and rubbed her temples. Cold as it might be for early April, Irena was clearly wearing this coat as a rebuke to her daughter. An endless stream of the most sincere apologies would never suffice, so she merely acknowledged the coat with a nod.

During lunch at the museum, Elise again looked for an opportunity to bring up the building. Her parents had started right in talking about what was going on in Czechoslovakia. It was clear that Irena had orchestrated even the topic of their lunch conversation. Elise was only half listening. Her status as a Czech-American was so remote from her consciousness that she barely recalled it. Another label was the last thing she needed. Her parents were discussing Václav Havel. The Blazeks belonged to a discussion group, and they were all reading Havel's essay "The Power of the Powerless."

Elise had noticed from an early age that the greatest share of her parents' intellectual curiosity was reserved for the politics of their homeland. On this subject, they always kept current. Now Irena said she was sympathetic to Václav Havel's viewpoint, that maybe a revolution, terrible as it would be, was the only hope. Stepan, as usual, was waiting until he learned more, a moment in time that Elise knew would remain elusive.

When they finished lunch, Irena stood up and gathered her coat and bag. "Let's get going. We still have a lot to do."

"Wait," said Elise. "I have something to talk to you about."

"Not here," said Irena.

"Yes, here," Elise said.

"Sit down, Irena. Let her talk," said Stepan. He took another sip of his coffee. "I want to hear what she has to say after all this time."

"Thank you, Daddy. Let me start by saying there's a lot I don't want to get into."

"Good," said Irena.

"I know that Wiley spoke to you last year. When I was sick. So I know you know that I haven't taught at Alaster for four years now."

Irena's eyes began to well up. "What you do is your business now. You've made that perfectly clear."

"Not out of anything negative toward you, Irena," Elise replied. "What did you think, I plotted this separation?"

"You are torturing me with this talk, Elise. I will not listen."

"Irena, if she has something to say after all this time, don't you think we should hear her out?"

"No. I've adjusted my life."

"I'm still your daughter," said Elise. "Believe me, you wouldn't have wanted to know me over the last ten years."

Irena's face was flushed. Elise saw she was struggling to regain her sense of authority, the one she had manufactured to get her through this visit.

"I don't believe in this rapid cycling," Irena got out.

"You don't get to choose whether to believe in it. It's not God, it's science."

"And this other thing. This temporal lobe epilepsy. It's ridiculous."

Elise put her head in her hands. Don't fail me now, she implored the Depakote in her bloodstream. "I can't make you accept it. But it's physiological."

"You were fine as a girl."

"That's not unusual," said Elise.

Dr. Massie had helped prepare Elise for this conversation. She had told her over and again not to make excuses for herself. If anything, she should point out all she had accomplished while battling her illness.

"Elise," said her father. "We're your parents."

Elise didn't know what he meant by this, but it seemed as good a segue as any.

"I know, Daddy. And that's why I'm coming to you. At first, you'll think it's extreme. But I'm not manic, you can talk to my doctor. So here goes: I want to borrow my inheritance money to buy a building in Manhattan. I would never ask if I didn't know your house was paid off. It would be a good investment for both of you." Now Elise looked only at Stepan.

"A building?" he asked, "What for? A building in Manhattan costs a fortune."

"Not this one. You'd be surprised. I found an amazing deal. A twenty percent down payment of forty thousand dollars would do it. There are six units. I'd live in the smallest one and rent the others out to businesses. Once the spaces are renovated, the mortgage payments will be nothing next to the income."

"Where will you get the renovation money?" asked Stepan. "This is not sound thinking, Elise."

"Stepan, put on your muffler, it's cold outside. If we don't get going, the historical society will close."

"Shh-h-h, Irena."

"Once I have the building, I can borrow against it. I've already investigated. If I work fast, I can have one of the units ready to go within the first three months."

"And what will you live on in the meantime?"

"What I have been living on. Disability."

"Oh my God," said Irena.

"Ask Milos about this plan," Elise said. "He'll see it's tenable."

"Don't involve Miloslav in this. He's just starting out."

Elise looked steadily at her mother. How far they had come since it was Milos who was to steer clear of Elise and her sterling future.

"Forty thousand dollars is a lot of money," said Stepan. "It's not that we absolutely don't have it. It's that I may be forced into early retirement, and we need to make our money last."

Whatever Elise thought about her father's limitations, she had always trusted him, but she wasn't sure about this argument. What about the fox coat he had just bought her mother?

"You've been at Casner & Fitzbaum for what, forty years?"

"It doesn't matter. Companies are doing it all the time now—forcing out their older employees with reduced pensions. And they'll have a good reason I won't be able to fight. Computer drafting is going to take over."

So? Elise wanted to say. Learn it. Here she was, about to completely change her life, embark on a complicated new venture. How hard could it be to learn a software program?

Elise sighed. "I'm doing this for a reason," she said. "This is not for adventure's sake. And keep in mind the benefit to you. This building could set you up for a very comfortable retirement. Just give me a couple of years."

"Didn't you hear your father, Elise?"

Elise shifted in her seat. She was thirty-five years old and being asked, "Didn't you hear your father?"

"Daddy, I could hire you. You could draft all the renovation plans. It would be great. We'd be partners." This seemed to Elise a real brainstorm. She smiled at Stepan, reached over and squeezed his forearm.

Stepan frowned.

"And what about your Ph.D.?" asked Irena. Preparing to leave, she had put her fox coat around her shoulders. "What about your teaching and all your translation work?"

Finally, Elise shifted her attention to her mother. "This is the best I've been in years," she said, speaking slowly. "You may not believe in my diagnosis, you may reject it as some other country's fanatical religion, but you're only right on one count. It is another country. One that thankfully some people understand, even though they don't live there. Dr. Massie for one. Wiley for another. Teaching became unendurable and unrealistic for me. Maybe it'll change, if I keep doing well on this drug. But right now I have the most reliable perspective I'm going to get, and I know that this building can set me up for life. No more disability, no more hell-hole apartment. I'll spare you the details."

Irena was crying, but Elise wasn't finished. She hadn't felt quite so clearheaded in a long time, and she couldn't let the moment slide by. "And if I let this opportunity go, it could very well be that you'll have to take care of me in your old age, ultimately a much bigger investment than forty thousand dollars and a much bigger burden. With the building, the worst-case scenario is that you'll sell it and put the money in a trust for me. And I'm very optimistic that's not going to happen. These new drugs are my saving grace."

"I can't take another second of this," said Irena, her voice barely audible. She rose and reached to put her arm in the right sleeve of her fur coat. Before she got her left arm in the other sleeve, she was out of the museum café.

The Depakote did not do its usual job of helping Elise to fall asleep. It was no match for the memory of the afternoon's events, the memory that crashed right through the border where the drug usually took hold.

Irena had taken the train back to Laflin on her own. Following on the next train, Elise had prevailed on her father to get Irena to take the building plan seriously. She had been able to convince him that her plan had some merit, but he refused to get between Elise and her mother. He had said that no amount of intervention from him would make a difference. Elise knew he was right. For the rest of the trip her father seemed lost in sadness. Two stops before Laflin he had put Elise's hand in his and held it there.

Elise's flight home was at 4:45 the next afternoon. Her mother, recovering slightly after dinner, had laid out the plans for the next day. Kristy had a round of birthday parties coming up, and she needed a new dress. Irena and Elise would join Dawn and Kristy at Marshall Fields. After the shopping trip, they would take Kristy for hot chocolate. Fine, Elise had thought. Fucking fine. I'll go back to my wretched piece of shit apartment next to the armed heroin dealer because instead of giving me the support I need, you were drinking hot chocolate with a five-year-old.

Now at two A.M., she knew she must find the time to give her plan another try. She would exchange her ticket for a later flight, revise and present her argument once more. Shortly after she had resolved to argue her case one final time, Elise passed over her nervous exhaustion and fell asleep.

A voice was coming from very nearby. Elise's eyelids fluttered. Wafting toward consciousness, she flipped around to face the wall. No voices. Voices were not part of her present-day life.

"Turn around and wake up for a minute, zlatíčko," she heard now. She opened her eyes to complete darkness. "I need to talk to you."

Elise turned to lie on her back. Her mother, it seemed, was sitting on the edge of her bed. Now she was switching on the bedside lamp. Elise saw she wore a cotton nightgown and the same kind of hairnet she had always worn to sleep, blue mesh with a white starburst at the crown. Just to satisfy herself, Elise reached out to touch her mother's arm. After all, she had been just as convinced that time she'd heard Anna Akhmatova's voice, just as certain the real was upon her when the voices of strangers had accosted her on streets of the Lower East Side.

Then Irena used that old name again. "Zlatíčko, listen."

Elise blinked against the light.

"I can't stand it, any of it, but you are my daughter, the one who danced Dalcroze for me and the one who was smarter than anyone in her class. You're still that daughter, aren't you?"

How could Elise answer this? No, she was not that daughter and never would be again. How much she might like to be was beside the point. Since leaving home, Elise had too often inhabited a cold terror her mother could not begin to imagine. She had been invaded by sensations that she shuddered to recall—a sudden panic that the street was rising up to swallow her, an energy so overwhelming she could not move fast enough to contain it. Once she had been the person who had experienced this, there was no part of Elise that could be anything so straightforward as Irena Blazek's daughter. Yet she took a breath and answered, "Yes, of course I'm still your daughter."

"I have the money."

Elise sat up. A slick layer of overnight cream coated her mother's face. When Irena brought her face closer, Elise smelled eucalyptus.

"What do you mean?"

"I've had McDonald's stock since 1975."

"McDonald's! You hate McDonald's."

"Their food, yes, but did you know the founder comes from Plzen?"

"No," said Elise. "I haven't been keeping up."

"Shhh! Don't wake Táta. He doesn't know about the money. Most of what you ask for is there. I'll tell him when it's necessary to tell him."

Elise didn't know what to say. How could this be the same woman of the day's long afternoon?

"But you must promise me never to float away again, zlatíčko. To where Táta and I can't reach you."

"I promise," Elise said. She knew she could betray this promise, no matter how determined she was to keep it. She looked at Irena's face, the wrinkles and creases obscured by her face cream, and for the first time that weekend truly recognized her, the old her, a vestige of the eager young woman whose singular mission was to expose her small daughter to every shred of potentiality she dreamed was on offer beyond the front door of her plain bungalow-style house.

"I won't float away," she assured Irena. "I'll call you and Daddy every week and give you a progress report. I'm going to pay you back, too, at twenty percent interest. And that's just for starters." Then she sank down and lay her head on her mother's lap, closed her eyes as Irena laid her hand, for only a moment, on Elise's forehead.

Chapter Eleven

Unfastening her pants, Irena settled down for a nap on the made-up bed in the guest room of Berta's apartment. It was the middle of the afternoon. Berta was at the *Tribune.* So what? Irena told herself. She was entitled to lie down. She was a sixty-four-year-old widow who had recently lost her job. So what if Berta Kriz had just renewed herself with a weekend stay at a beauty spa, wore expensive suits, had thrown out all her old housedresses, never napped, declined to play Mariáš, and went to Scandinavia and China with groups of University of Chicago alumni? So what if Magda and Frank spent every Saturday night playing bridge with a couple they had met on their honeymoon ten years before? Maybe Berta and Magda didn't have the time for Irena they'd once had, but they were still her friends. Berta had been quick to offer Irena the guest room for as long as she needed it. Neither sister had forgotten about her, and when Stepan had died last month, they'd both been kind—baking a poppy-seed kolache like in the old days and helping Irena with the funeral arrangements.

Miloslav, too, had been attentive, returning from San Francisco with his family: Dawn, Kristy, and two-year-old Samantha, who looked so much like her father. Kristy no longer called Irena "Babička," claiming that at eight years old she was not a baby, but she had let Irena teach her two-handed Mariáš. And Miloslav had stayed after the others returned, helping Irena to clear out Stepan's workshop and file the necessary papers for Irena to claim the life insurance money.

Elise had come for the funeral also, but had left the next morning. She had cried throughout the funeral and at the graveside service, twice letting her nose run unchecked, and she had keened in a way Irena hadn't heard since her own childhood in Plzen. Yet after the funeral she had seemed distracted, eager to return to her building, which she now called "the business."

For the most part, Irena had gotten the attention due her, and she didn't know quite why she was still in Berta's apartment. This morning, rushing around looking for her keys, Berta had been brusque with her. Irena would soon return to Laflin, whether she liked it or not. She closed her eyes. Through Berta's double-pane windows Irena didn't hear a thing, though she knew that outside gearshifts grinded, horns blared, and sirens sounded all day long. Stepan, thought Irena, would have commented on the windows. He would have told Irena what kind they were and explained the design that allowed them to completely block out noise.

Irena turned her head to the side so quickly her cheek bounced on the pillow. The truth was she would barely have listened to Stepan's explanation, and this knowledge was more than she could bear. Where was he now? Irena attended church for all the holidays but was not convinced there was an afterlife. When she had told Berta this following the funeral, Berta had looked at her sympathetically, as if wondering how she had ever entertained such an idea in the first place.

It was the thought of Stepan's utter aloneness that tortured Irena. He had died at the Laflin train station, waiting on the platform for the commuter train, as he had for forty years. ("They haven't sacked me yet," he would tell Irena just about every week, the tough talk of a weary man.) Irena imagined he knew the other commuters by sight, had registered their faces hovering above his own as he lay on the cement in the moments before he was gone. He might have recognized even the hands that yanked loose his tie and tore his shirt open, but Irena knew he wouldn't have admitted them into his reality. In his panic, struggling to grasp the probability of his death, he would only have wondered why his wife had not materialized. Irena had no doubt that Stepan had died confounded by this—that in his moment of terror he might have hated her for shirking her duty, for not arriving as if by magic to cradle his head, to whisper in his ear.

Irena removed the folded *Czechoslovak Daily Herald* obituary from her sweater pocket and sat up to reread it.

Laflin Model Maker Dies

Stepan Blazek, 64 years old, immigrated from Plzen with his parents in 1927. Raised in Downers Grove, Illinois, Mr. Blazek married Irena Kraus, also originally from Plzen, at the age of 19. He worked as an architectural draftsman in Chicago for many years but was known locally for his model-making skills, which had their greatest expression in the elaborate scale replica of the 14th-century Karlstein Castle, 17 miles northeast of Prague. The model has been on display at the Laflin Historical Society since 1980 and will become part of its permanent collection. Mr. Blazek is survived by his wife, Irena, and two children, Miloslav of San Francisco and Elise of New York, as well as two granddaughters, Kristen and Samantha. In lieu of flowers, please send donations in Mr. Blazek's name to the Laflin Historical Society at 193 Dubcek Avenue. A funeral will be held at St. Josef Cross Church in Laflin on Saturday, October 7 at 10:00 A.M.

There it was, her husband in 159 words, if she counted the numbers. At least Irena had made sure that Miloslav appeared in the obituary as Stepan's son—a small but critical alteration of fact. Irena got up, splashed water on her face, and went into the living room. Since Reyna Kopecky had closed her shop, time had never hung heavier. Along with Sylvie Vanek and a small group of other loyal customers, Reyna and Irena had gone out to dinner and ordered expensive wine. They had toasted their years at the shop and berated the cheap clothing offered at Kmart, which had finally driven Reyna out of business.

Irena turned on the TV. When one soap went to a commercial, she switched to another. Black, white, or Spanish, everyone was good-looking and comfortably off. Everyone put on a show of resisting temptation, then yielded to it. Irena knew that even the admirable spinsters would soon be distracted by romantic possibility, just as Magda had been distracted by Frank Masik.

Irena had Stepan's small monthly pension benefit, and she had a CD she could cash. She was trying to hold out for a few years so that she could get her widow's social security at its full rate. However modest her income might be, though, her time was hers. If she let it, her greatest challenge could be deciding which of these three daytime soaps to devote herself to. But no, she had worked her whole life—she could not, would not, stoop to being seduced by these ridiculous people who idled away their lives. To Irena, watching soaps amounted to drinking on the sly. She put the television on mute and looked at her watch. It was late morning in California. Miloslav had said it was fine to call him at Wessel & Doyle, his law firm in San Francisco. She would do it now, before she lost her nerve. After two rings, he answered.

"Miloslav?"

"Hi! How are you?" After all these years, he still avoided calling Irena anything.

"Oh, you know, I've been doing all right. I'm planning to go back to Laflin in a day or two. But I've been thinking about what you said, before you left."

"Hold on," said Miloslav.

Irena heard nothing. Then, "Yes, sorry, I'm back."

"I've decided there's no harm in trying it out."

"That's wonderful. Dawn will be so excited."

"I don't have the energy I once did," Irena warned.

"That's fine. It's not as if we're in bad straits. We'll hire a part-time nanny to relieve you. Just having you around will be so good for the kids. They need family."

"The three of us will have fun," said Irena, barely able to force out the words.

"Samantha is going through a stage right now. Maybe you can help her."

"What kind of a stage?"

"A little tantrum prone. It'll pass. When are you coming?"

"When do you want me?"

"As soon as you can make it. I'm going to call Dawn now."

"Miloslav, how did you grow up to be such a good boy?"

Miloslav laughed. "Hold again," he said. This time he was off the line for a while. Irena stared at the mute television. Two women, dressed and made up to the nines on a weekday morning, were yelling at each other in a designer kitchen.

Back on the line, Miloslav said, "I have to go. Call as soon as you have your reservation."

Even as her plane landed in San Francisco, Irena couldn't shake the memory of her last glimpse of her house in Laflin. Fully paid off, it was there to serve her, yet she had turned down the heat, covered all the furniture in muslin, canceled her phone service, and arranged to have the *Czechoslovak Daily Herald* forwarded. Leaving for the airport, she had sensed her house reproaching her. Confronted with her own disloyalty, Irena had felt her heartbeat quicken, and she'd fled down the short front walk to the waiting cab. But now she was moving along with the rest of the passengers through the Jetway, and she had to transfer her allegiance to another home, one she had never seen.

"There she is!" Dawn pointed out, nudging Kristy in front of her.

From a distance, Irena noticed that Dawn was poking out a little in her middle. She couldn't tell if she had gained weight or was pregnant again.

Kristy approached Irena cautiously. Irena knew that their relationship was about to change. Irena would no longer be a treat for Kristy but a daily presence, someone her family would "have around." This was how it was in America. Live-in grandparents were regarded either with suspicion or not at all. When Irena's grandfather in Plzen had moved in with the Krauses, it had been different. Irena and her parents had catered to him.

"Hello," said Kristy softly. "Welcome to San Francisco." She withdrew from behind her back a red rose encased in a stiff, clear plastic cone, doubtlessly purchased from an airport stall. Her smile was nervous.

"Thank you, Koťátko! How thoughtful." Irena took the flower.

Miloslav and Dawn approached with Samantha. They leaned over the stroller to kiss Irena's cheek. Samantha had been crying and was straining to escape her seat belt. When Irena bent down to greet her, she started to scream.

*   *   *

The apartment, thought Irena, belonged to the children. It was a sprawling floor-through in a neighborhood called Noë Valley. All the rooms reflected the children's imprint. With its two marble fireplaces and ornate woodwork, the apartment itself was stately, but everywhere Irena looked she was distracted by brightly colored plastic: small vehicles, a high chair, a beach ball, a pink radio (a boom box, Irena had heard it called), a child's stove set in the kitchen, and puzzles, beads, and board books in Miloslav and Dawn's bedroom. Irena knew Miloslav had hopes of buying the whole house. Was the goal to have more children and fill more rooms with their things?

At least the small room that was deemed Irena's, a freshly painted one off Samantha's bedroom, was fit for an adult. It had a bed with a down quilt, an old-fashioned porcelain washbasin and pitcher set, a desk, and a tufted easy chair that appeared to be new. But the room overlooked a driveway, and Irena suspected it had originally been a maid's room.

Miloslav put Irena's luggage down. "Do you like it?"

"It's very nice," answered Irena. Her throat swelled, and her voice wobbled. Tears moistened her eyes. Dawn stepped forward to hug her.

Free of her stroller, Samantha was circling the apartment, pulling her earlobe and dragging a big naked doll by her hair. She circled and circled. Irena watched.

"She does that with her ear," Dawn apologized. "At first we thought it was an earache, but the doctor says no."

"It's because she's a mental case," added Kristy.

Miloslav gave Kristy a warning look, which she returned with an exaggerated pout.

The next day, Irena stayed alone with Samantha while Kristy was at school. Miloslav had three back-to-back closings, and Dawn, despite being pregnant (almost seventeen weeks, she'd confided to Irena the night before), had started a new job. As much as Irena explained to Samantha that she was her grandmother, her very own babička who loved her, the child did not warm up. She screamed for Dawn, ran around in frenetic circles tugging her ear, refused to eat what Irena put before her, and shrieked in her room when she should have been napping. Finally at two thirty, Irena put her in her stroller and went out to explore Miloslav's neighborhood. Exhausted and lulled by the motion, Samantha fell asleep.

Irena wasn't used to this kind of neighborhood. To her, it didn't seem like a real neighborhood at all. It was part city, part town. On some streets there were several Victorian houses in a row, but then there would be a vacant lot or a house of an entirely different style. There was a run-down shoe repair shop and an old Laundromat, but there was also a brand-new café filled with standing plants and a modern coffeehouse where young people sat around looking uninterested in life. A good number of the neighborhood residents were some kind of Oriental, and others were Spanish. Asians and Latinos, Miloslav had said to call them. As she walked along pushing Samantha's stroller, Irena became aware of several young men who were obviously homosexual. Gay, Irena knew she was meant to say. They made no bones about it, either, wearing tight T-shirts that made immature references to what they did with their bodies and talking in loud, attention-getting voices. One was even dressed as a woman, a glamour-puss type. Irena supposed they came from the neighboring Castro, a section that Miloslav had told her about, his tone deliberately neutral. Irena tried not to stare—partly out of politeness but also because she didn't want to give them the satisfaction.

What would Stepan have thought of this place Miloslav had moved to? He would not have offered an opinion to Dawn and Miloslav—he wasn't a critical person—but with his exacting need for order and visual harmony, Irena thought he would have felt particularly lost in this changing area of the city. He would have clung to her.

After Irena had covered eight or ten blocks, she hurried back to wait on Miloslav's corner for Kristy's school bus. When it came, Kristy emerged holding the hand of a schoolmate, a little girl whose race Irena couldn't quite identify.

"This is my grandmother, sort of," Kristy said by way of introduction.

Irena was taken aback. Who had explained to Kristy the real situation and, more importantly, why?

"And this is the famous brat, Samantha Ellen Blazek," Kristy continued.

Irena couldn't see Samantha's face but knew she was awake because she was kicking the stroller's footrest.

"Wanda's coming over to our house," Kristy told Irena.

"This is something you ask, Kristy. You do not command Babička."

"Well . . . so okay. Can Wanda come over?"

"I suppose. For a little while."

Once home, Irena let the two girls go to Kristy's room, where in a moment she heard rock music blaring from the pink radio, the boom box. Should she be telling Kristy to do her schoolwork? In another half hour, should she go in and courteously tell Wanda it was time for her to go home? Irena did not know the range of her authority.

For two weeks, every day was much the same. Besides caring for the children, Irena cooked the family dinner. Miloslav and Dawn told her not to, but if she hadn't, they would have brought in takeout or ordered a pizza, as they had apparently done ever since they'd moved to San Francisco. Whenever Miloslav or Dawn asked how she was getting along, she told them fine. They did not bring up hiring a part-time nanny, not even for after the baby was born, and Irena wouldn't dream of raising the subject. They were grateful and affectionate, and Irena supposed they thought they had found a perfect solution all around, what Miloslav might call "a win-win."

Samantha continued to be whiny and impossible to please, consumed with wanting to leave wherever she was—the bathtub, her stroller, the apartment, her car seat, the store, even the playground. It wasn't that she had a desired destination; she simply longed to be elsewhere.

Although Irena and Kristy fared a little better, Irena had once overheard Kristy imitating her accent in the school playground. She had kept her hurt feelings to herself, but she acquired a new self-consciousness around Kristy.

If the letters that Irena and the Kriz sisters exchanged every week were not filled with all that was happening back in Czechoslovakia, she would have written them the truth, that she was not adjusting well to her new life, that she was thinking about returning to Laflin. She knew they would understand her detour in California, the depth of her reluctance to face her loss. In the early days, she had confided to them about Stepan's limitations—how unadventurous he had turned out to be, how few subjects truly interested him. But after the children left home, after all that had happened with Elise, Stepan's mildness had become a comfort to Irena, and she knew the Kriz sisters recognized this. They knew that although Stepan never took the slightest risk, he respected those who did.

Irena had told Magda that when she had finally confessed to Stepan that she had made thirty-nine thousand dollars on the McDonald's stock she'd had for almost twelve years, almost all of Elise's down payment, he had surprised her by patting her behind and calling her the brains of their operation. The Kriz sisters had always liked Stepan, and they would understand how impossible Irena found it to be alone since his death. If she had written to them pouring her heart out, they would have responded with tender words.

But those were not the letters Irena wrote. The letters that flew back and forth between Chicago and San Francisco were all about what was going on in Czechoslovakia. Students had started it with their demonstration in Wenceslas Square. Riot police had charged at them, but the students held their ground. Some of them passed flowers to the police. There were pictures of this in the newspaper. Soon Irena and the Kriz sisters were reading about the playwright Václav Havel, who wanted to bring down the KSC. They all did. There were strikes, big ones, general strikes that grew by the day. When Irena and the Kriz sisters could not keep up with events through letters, they began to call one another every two or three days.

Last year, when Irena was still in Laflin, Gorbachev and his ministers had come up with a policy that allowed the Eastern Bloc nations to control their own futures. They named the policy the "Sinatra Doctrine," after Frank Sinatra's song "My Way." Irena remembered reading about it in the *Czechoslovak Daily Herald*. It was a joke, and when was the last time there had been a joke about what was going on in Eastern Europe? Hundreds of Czech Americans, the article said, were buying Frank Sinatra's album from 1969.

Visiting her from California, even Miloslav—who did not make a point of keeping up with news about Czechoslovakia—had bought the album. Irena remembered Kristy giggling as her father sang and acted out the lyrics of the title song, alternately clutching his heart and gesturing to the heavens until he finished up with a drawn-out and histrionic "... *my* way!"

As much as everyone made fun of the name, the Sinatra Doctrine ended up weakening the KSC. How else could this revolution now happening in Prague succeed? So little blood was shed that it became known as the Velvet Revolution. Irena thought it a splendid name. She had always had a weakness for velvet. For the sheer pleasure of it, she would sometimes pass her fingers over the bolts of plush velvet that were set upright near Reyna Kopecky's cash register.

The only time remotely like these last couple of months in Czechoslovakia had been Prague Spring in 1968, but then before the celebrations could begin, the Soviet Union and its allies had invaded. The reformers hadn't had a chance. This time everything was different. Irena and the Kriz sisters were overjoyed when President Husák resigned. Everyone said Václav Havel would be the next president.

At breakfast on the third Sunday in December, Irena interrupted Miloslav and Dawn's conversation about last year's Christmas tree stand. "You know," she said, "I could go back now. They're starting to let people in. I mean people from the West."

Miloslav turned to her. "Why would you want to?"

"Why? Because! To see."

"You don't know anyone there."

"Yes, I do. There's my cousin Martin, the carpenter. Remember I used to tell you he couldn't go anywhere without that ID book they all had to carry? And there are some grade school friends I still know of."

Irena did not mention Stepan's cousin Pavel, in Kutná Hora, who had years ago tried to arrange the meeting in Vienna between Miloslav and his mother.

"Know *of*?" he asked.

"And there are *places* that meant something to me, Miloslav."

"You're talking about a visit?"

"A visit, a stay, whatever it turns out to be."

Miloslav glared at her. Kristy shifted her attention from her plate; she had just poured two syrup circles onto her pancakes and set a blueberry at the center of each. Nipples.

"A visit," Irena corrected. "Just a visit, of course."

"She's curious, Milos," said Dawn. "Wouldn't you be?"

Miloslav didn't answer.

"I'm going to the hardware store for a new stand," Dawn finally said. "I don't trust that flimsy one. Who's coming with me?"

* * *

That night in her room, Irena reread the *Daily Herald*'s piece on travel visas. If she understood it correctly, she was free to visit Plzen. She would have to go as a U.S. citizen whose Czech naturalization had been revoked, but she could get in on a travel visa, like anyone else. If only Stepan were alive. He had been a baby when he'd come to this country, but prodded by her, he had never forgotten his roots. Irena imagined he would have overcome his distaste for travel to accompany her back to Plzen. He had those cousins in Kutná Hora and a distant relative in Plzen. When Stepan had died, Irena had written to them all. She would look them up when she visited. Family was honored in Czechoslovakia. People were eager to meet any relative, no matter how distant.

Irena stayed up imagining herself back in Bohemia. She would visit the Krkonoše Mountains, where she had gone with her father. Back in Plzen, she would knock on the door of the small house, the converted stable where she had lived as a child. The owners would let her right in, delighted to welcome home a national at last entitled to return.

Elise must come, too. She would want to. As a young child, how many times had she asked Irena about the tunnels in Plzen, the multi-storied underground where during the Middle Ages water had been pumped up to the city, where during both world wars scores of people had gone for protection? Elise had never tired of hearing about the tunnels. Irena had hated telling her seven-year-old daughter that it was impossible for them to visit the tunnels in Plzen, that Elise was too young to understand why. She still remembered the look on Elise's face, her bafflement at being introduced to the notion of impossibility. Surprised, she had studied Irena's face, waiting for her *no* to turn to *maybe*.

Irena left her room and went into the entry hall to use the phone there. She dialed her daughter's number. It was late. Miloslav's household was asleep, but Irena guessed Elise would be up. When she answered, Irena said, "Zlatíčko, I'm glad you're awake. I just had a wonderful idea. Would you like to go to Plzen together?"

"What?"

"The travel ban has been lifted! I can go back. I want you to join me. Now that you've been doing so well, you can travel like you used to."

"Irena, what're you talking about?"

"What do you mean? Haven't you been reading the news? You know what's going on over there, all the great things that have been happening."

"Yes, but that doesn't mean I can just pick up and go."

"It won't be right away. Everyone wants to go now. We'd have to wait for visas."

"Jesus! Do you know what's going on here?!" Elise demanded. It was a dare. Her voice was climbing to that level of belligerence that made Irena's heart sink.

"Whatever it is," she said, "I'm sure you can handle it."

Irena meant this. Three years ago, with Irena's help from the McDonald's money, Elise had bought the building in the flower district. Things had worked out much as she had promised. She had gotten a line of credit and paid the building's tenants to move before their leases expired. Irena had visited earlier in the year, had managed to talk Stepan into coming, too. He and Elise spent most of their time poring over blueprints and discussing solutions for the spaces under renovation. During the day, there was the constant noise of buzz saws and hammering. Plaster dust was everywhere. Elise had stomped around in those outfits of hers, her mouth and nose covered by a paper mask. In the galley kitchen of Elise's small apartment on the sixth floor, Irena had done her best to cook their meals. At night Elise had gone over the building's expenses. Irena had tried not to think about her daughter's education and her academic gifts. Stepan thought that any kind of job well done was a meaningful one—an unsurprising position coming from the maker of the miniature Karlstein Castle. He had been honestly proud of Elise. Try as Irena had, though, she could not think of Elise's building as a worthwhile contribution to society. Twice during that trip they'd had dinner with Wiley Mills and her husband, and twice Irena had looked at the two doctors and been consumed with thoughts of what Elise could have been.

"You think that, don't you?" Elise continued. "You think that whatever it is, I can handle it. My plasterer is suing me because he *ignored* my huge sign and walked right into the empty elevator shaft on floor one and fell into the basement. I was only three weeks late on renewing the building's liability insurance. The guy broke his pelvis. You know how much my lawyer charges an hour? And the PR tenant on three hasn't paid her rent in two-and-a-half months. Like I can afford to carry her.

Do you have any idea how long it takes to evict tenants for nonpayment of rent? And what else can I handle, Irena? Oh yes, the under-the-table payments to city inspectors and the private garbage collection company. And having to spend thirty thousand dollars on new window gates for all the units because cheapskate Vizinni put in illegal ones. And all the red spider mites flying around the halls from the orchids Milstein brings in from Arizona. Milstein with his goddamned ten-year lease and his pittance rent. I can handle all of it."

It was cold in the entry hall, and Irena was wearing only her cotton nightgown. With her free arm, she hugged herself. "I'm sorry you're having trouble, Elise. But I'm sure that you *can* work out these setbacks. You're very resourceful."

"Right," said Elise. "That's me."

Irena could hear her daughter exhaling cigarette smoke. Whenever things weren't going right, she took up smoking again.

"It's fine if you can't go to Plzen now. I'll go by myself, and next year, when the building's more settled, maybe I'll go again, and you'll come with me."

"Have a good time," snapped Elise.

"Elise, what do you want me to do? I just lost your father."

"Uh-huh."

Wiley had once told Irena that a sign of Elise slipping into dangerous territory was that she became altogether self-absorbed, incapable of even a moment of empathy. Everyone else's troubles paled next to her own.

Out of the blue, Elise began to sob. Long, wrenching sobs with silent holes at their centers—the alarming pause that occurs when too much air has entered the lungs too quickly. She kept it up for a long time, losing and regaining her breath, and Irena stayed on the line, trying to comfort her. After a while Elise's wailing diminished to soft whimpers. "You have no idea," she interrupted herself to tell Irena.

"Do you want me to come there?" asked Irena.

"No, no, I'll be all right. I just need something to go right. Just one single fucking thing."

"Something will go right, zlatíčko." Irena's tone was forceful in a way she rarely managed, as though she had the power to make her prophecy come true. "It's not necessary to use that language—something will go right very, very soon."

Chapter Twelve

Milos and Dawn had let the girls stay up to watch the ball drop in Times Square and to toast in the New Year with grape juice—Kristy's in a fluted champagne glass, Sam's in a Cabbage Patch Kids sippy cup. The girls had blown noisemakers and run around kissing their parents and each other repeatedly. They had each kissed Dawn's belly and wished their future baby brother or sister a happy New Year. Yet the evening hadn't felt particularly festive. For one thing, Irena had gone to bed before eleven, claiming she didn't feel well.

"I think she's miserable here," Milos later confided to Dawn. It was after one A.M., and they were in bed.

"She's still in mourning, sweetie. This was her first New Year's without him."

"I don't think that's it. She never cries, and she hardly mentions him."

"Oh, come on. If something happened to you, perish the thought, do you think I'd go around blubbering all the time?"

"Of course. Without a break, and for years." Milos smiled and lopped his ankle over Dawn's.

"As if that's how everyone expresses their grief. I haven't seen you crying lately. For instance."

"That's different." As soon as Milos said this, tears from nowhere filled his eyes. Uncle Stepan had died alone on a train platform.

Dawn took Milos's hand. He had held back the tears, but she'd probably sensed them hovering. There was little about his emotions she missed. "They were married for how many years? Forty-five?" she asked.

"Something like that."

"Can you imagine?" Dawn asked.

"They weren't always the closest, as you know."

"That can make the grief worse."

"Maybe. But I still think something else is going on."

"Such as?"

"Or it's more like what *isn't* going on."

"I hate it when you make me pull things out of you," Dawn said.

"If you really want to know, I think she's dropping Kristy like a hot potato because she's not precocious like Elise was. And as far as Sammy goes, I think they have a pact of mutual indifference."

"A sixty-four-year-old and a two-year-old?"

"Yes."

Milos and Dawn had thought the move to San Francisco would be good for Irena. She would have two little girls to look after, and Milos had every reason to believe that his aunt preferred female children. When Kristy had been born, he'd thought, "Good, Aunt Irena will be thrilled." And she had been, for a good long while. But now Kristy was almost nine, and his aunt seemed barely fond of her.

"You're just comparing how she was with Elise to how she is with Kristy and Samantha. You should be glad she's not that intensely devoted. A little distance might not be such a bad thing."

"Okay, so maybe I'm misjudging. But I still think something besides grieving is going on with her."

"She's still finding her way, sweetie. The problem is *you* want to drive her there."

Milos didn't want to consider this unflattering perspective. "If I'm driving, it's because she's lying down in the backseat," he countered.

Dawn suppressed a yawn. She turned on her side. "We should all take a three-day weekend, maybe drive up to Napa." With that, she drew up the quilt as far as it would go.

Rain. Not what they had bargained for, of course. And Milos had business on his mind. He couldn't believe he was going to court with the Remnick case on Monday. Charlie Remnick had given him hell yesterday. He had expected an eleventh-hour settlement. So had Milos. Yesterday he had told Charlie they'd probably settle the first day of hearings, maybe even before the thing got going, but now he wasn't all that sure.

Tom Wessel gave Milos all of Charlie's cases having to do with his tenant disputes, and they were all variations on a theme. This time the plumbing subcontractor on his latest condo development had used second-rate materials, and two months after the owners had moved in, they'd had to move out. Milos had always been successful with Charlie's cases, but this one he just couldn't get a handle on.

"Daddy, I *said* stop."

"Sorry, sweetie, I didn't hear. I'm concentrating. See how slow everyone's driving in the rain?"

"I have to pee."

"I can't pull off right now."

"Yes, you *can*."

Strapped in her car seat between Kristy and Irena, Samantha woke up from her nap and started crying. The sound built to a shriek that was uniquely Samantha's.

They were on their way to Calistoga. The plan was to go to the Petrified Forest.

"You better get out at the next exit," Dawn said.

Milos didn't answer but drove onto the closest exit ramp. In the backseat, Irena was having no luck trying to soothe Samantha.

Figuring they might as well have an early lunch, Milos pulled the car into a Denny's parking lot. "Now you can use the bathroom," he told Kristy. She opened the door and bolted out.

They got a booth facing the parking lot. Samantha had calmed down some and was merely sniveling. Milos got her settled next to him. He was seated across the table from his aunt. She had aged, he thought, in the expected ways: Her face and neck had thickened some, the skin becoming loose and ruddy. There was a tiny web of broken blood vessels beneath her right eye. She had been dyeing her hair for some time, and it had acquired a dry, frizzled look. Right now she seemed faraway in her thoughts.

During lunch, Dawn tried to tell Kristy about what they would see in the Petrified Forest, but Kristy was more interested in blowing her crumpled straw wrapper at Samantha. The third time she tried to do this, Dawn took hold of her wrist to stop her.

Milos sighed. He had not settled on a strategy for defending Charlie Remnick because he never banked on it getting this far. His cases never went to court. He had not been in court for almost two years.

"What's the matter, honey?" asked Dawn.

"Nothing. Just Charlie's case on Monday. And I wish this rain would stop."

"It's supposed to."

"Aunt Irena, don't you like that?" Milos gestured to the taco salad on his aunt's plate. She had barely touched it.

"Did I tell you Elise might have to go to court, too?" Irena asked. "Someone's suing her."

"Really? Why didn't you say anything? What's going on?"

"One of her construction workers fell down the building's elevator shaft. Only one floor, and it wasn't Elise's fault. She had a great big sign on the wall next to the elevator, saying it was out of order. She says nobody could've missed it. How do you prove that, Milos?"

"Why isn't her insurance company settling?"

His aunt shrugged. Samantha was climbing out of her booster seat. Milos got her reseated.

"I think the policy might have lapsed," said Irena.

"You have to be joking."

Milos knew his cousin was doing well on a new combination of drugs, but surely they had to question her stability now. Who in their right mind would let their liability insurance lapse in the middle of a construction project? Milos would have paid her premium. That building was worth a fortune. "Why didn't she come to me for the money?"

"Don't ask me anything. I only know what I'm told."

"And why didn't she call me about the lawsuit?"

"She got someone in New York. And you represent the construction companies."

Milos didn't buy this argument. Elise hadn't called him because she never would have admitted needing his help. Now that she had this building, she was back to being Girl Wonder.

"Which is exactly why she should've called me. I know all the counterarguments. What happened to the guy? How much is he suing for?"

"He broke his pelvis. I don't know the amount."

Samantha whined and punched Milos's shoulder. She started climbing out of the seat again. Milos reached to put her back in.

"Let her go," said Dawn. "They need to be separated."

Milos helped Samantha get down, and he watched her toddle away. "Go keep an eye on her," he told Kristy. Then, to his aunt, "This is serious stuff. She could lose everything."

"She'll be fine," said Irena. "I think she has some sort of scheme."

"A *scheme*? Now she's an attorney, too? In addition to being a professor and a real estate whiz, now she's an attorney?"

"Milos . . ." Dawn warned.

From the other side of the restaurant came the sound of glass shattering and a scream. They all turned to look. Samantha had knocked a glass off someone's table. She was running back to the booth.

Milos took his two-year-old in his arms. She shrieked into his ear, her cheek wet with hot tears. He stroked her hair.

The people whose table it had been were leaving. A couple in their fifties. The woman glanced down at Dawn's pregnant belly. "That's what happens," she said, "when parents let their children run wild."

Milos didn't look at the woman. He kept his gaze on his aunt. There was an earnestness about her expression, an exaggerated innocence that telegraphed her solidarity with these two departing strangers.

The trails were fine for walking but not for wheeling a stroller, especially after the rain. Milos had to carry Sam. When Kristy saw that the ground was muddy, she refused to step on it, claiming she would ruin her new sneakers.

"We didn't come all this way for you to sit in the car," Dawn said.

"Why didn't anybody ask if *I* wanted to see these dumb trees?"

"Poor, put-upon Kristy," Dawn commiserated.

The rest of the group was assembling: a couple with binoculars, three teenage boys wearing Sierra Club T-shirts, several retirees, and a young couple who kept kissing. The tour guide was beckoning everyone to come closer.

The guide introduced himself as Ranger Matt. He told the group they would see trees eight feet in diameter that had been knocked over like toothpicks in a great volcanic eruption millions of years ago. Motioning everyone to follow, he set out on the trail, then turned to tell them about Petrified Forest Charlie who had single-handedly unearthed the first petrified tree and started charging admission for people to come see it.

The group progressed along the trail, stopping now and then to listen to Ranger Matt. Kristy plodded along behind them, her head bowed, stripping twigs of their young leaves. Samantha slept on Milos's shoulder, growing heavier by the minute. Ranger Matt stopped again to explain the molecular process that turned wood to stone. Milos noticed that although Irena was looking at the stone tree, her eyes were glazed over. She was probably still focused on Elise's troubles, Milos thought.

After another two hundred or so yards, Ranger Matt stopped the group in front of a fallen trunk he called the Queen. He told them the Queen had been two thousand years old when it died. The three teenage boys crouched down to examine the quartz formations on the surface of the Queen's trunk. Ranger Matt began to explain how the quartz came to be there.

"Daddy!" yelled Kristy from behind.

Milos spun around and saw that his aunt was on the ground. He gave Samantha to Dawn and ran over. Kristy had backed up and was staring at Irena. "Babička," he heard her say.

"It's okay," Milos told her, an automatic response. He hated this place, this primeval forest. Its air was close and ancient and could turn sap-filled bodies to stone.

Milos slapped Irena's cheeks. "Aunt Irena! Wake up!" He had never seen anyone unconscious.

Ranger Matt knelt on Irena's other side and quickly removed a walkie-talkie from his backpack. "One of my women has passed out," he said into the speaker.

Milos loosened his aunt's collar. Her shuddering breaths frightened him.

"Daddy, is Babička dead?" Kristy asked.

"Don't move her," cautioned Dawn.

In less than two minutes the medics were there. They had a stretcher. As the rest of the group looked on, one of the medics leaned over his aunt and passed a small vial beneath her nose.

Milos saw Irena's lids part, revealing the whites of her eyes. Then she blinked and opened her eyes. When she realized where she was, her cheeks went from livid to deep pink. She started to rise.

"No, no, Aunt Irena, stay there, don't move. What happened? How do you feel?"

Irena sat up anyway. "Nature makes me faint," she said. "Just like in the Krkonoše Mountains with my father, my táta. I can't take too much Mother Nature."

Milos took Route 29 back in the direction of San Francisco. He and Dawn wanted Irena to be checked over at Queen of the Valley Hospital, twenty miles south of Calistoga. "You don't just faint for no reason," they said.

"I told you, it's the woods," answered Irena, now in the passenger's seat. "It's the smell of all that nature."

"That's ridiculous," Milos said, losing patience.

In the hospital ER, Milos sat with his aunt while a young doctor checked her over, ignoring Irena's protestations that it wasn't an emergency. He quickly determined she was dehydrated and gave her a quart-sized bottle of lemon-lime Gatorade, which he told her to drink slowly while they waited for the urinalysis to come back from the lab. When it did, the doctor told them that Irena's glucose was at the high end of mildly elevated and that she should have her doctor at home give her a glucose tolerance test. He said she had two options—he could hook her up to an IV for rehydration, or her family could make sure she finished the Gatorade in the car and then saw her doctor in the coming week.

✦

At home that evening, Milos listened to the messages on the answering machine. The last was from Tom Wessel. He had settled the Remnick case. Milos was relieved, until it struck him that his boss had taken over his case on a Saturday. He hoped that Tom would not remember this incident when it came time to review Milos's prospects for becoming a partner.

It was still early evening, and Milos was at loose ends. Remembering there was a lamb chop in the refrigerator, he went into the kitchen, where his aunt was eating cereal and doing one of Kristy's word-search puzzles.

"How are you feeling? Are you okay?"

"Yes, Miloslav, I told you I'm fine now. I'm sorry I ruined everyone's weekend."

Milos removed the lid on the Tupperware container; the sight of the plump lamb chop glazed by a thin layer of chilled grease cheered him beyond measure. "You didn't ruin our weekend. I was glad to get out of that place. It gave me the creeps."

Irena kept working on her puzzle. Milos noticed that her hand was trembling.

"Are you sure you're okay? I was . . . I wasn't sure what had happened." He wanted to say more, but couldn't. His aunt must have an idea what he was trying to express; here she was living in his home—didn't that say all that had to be said?

Irena put down her pencil. She clasped her hands together, apparently to still them. "Miloslav, you and Dawn have been so good to me. You turned into such a decent man behind my back. It didn't take much with you, did it?"

Milos was embarrassed. "This is even better cold," he said, holding up the lamb chop. "Here, have a bite."

Irena shook her head. "I think it's time for me to go home."

"What do you mean?" Milos had planned to talk to her this coming week about selling the house in Laflin.

"I needed some time, and I've had it, thanks to you and Dawn. But now I'm ready to go home. I have a flight on Tuesday."

"What's wrong? Is it too much? We can get you help. We can—"

"Nothing's wrong, this has nothing to do with any of you."

What did she mean? She had moved into his house, and now she was moving out. How could that have nothing to do with them? He didn't know the right thing to say. Dawn was taking a bath; it was just the two of them. "But you have to follow up on today with that glucose test."

"I can do that at home. I have to go back and get to things."

"What things?"

"Don't you think I have things?"

This stopped Milos. He had never thought about it—his aunt having things to do. He wondered if she was going to see Elise. "I know you have things."

"Well don't you think it's time I got back to them? I can't take a break forever."

When Milos finished the lamb chop, he was still hungry. On the way out of the kitchen, he took a handful of Samantha's animal crackers from the plastic tub on the counter. "Okay, I guess there's not much I can do about it, then," he said. "But if you change your mind . . ."

Chapter Thirteen

February 1–March 5, 1990

"Elise, it's Dr. Massie again. Please pick up. If you don't respond, I'll be obligated to call the police. You don't want—"

Elise picked up. "I told you I was through with you, and I meant it." She slammed down the phone beside her on the bed. Fuck Dr. Massie. Elise should call the police on *her*. Did Dr. Massie think Elise didn't know that she was in on the whole scheme? Elise could have her license revoked. She picked up the pad on the other side of her and noted, "Write to APA about Dr. M." Then she added to the note, reminding herself to say that Dr. Massie only wanted to get her back on medication so she would calm down about her building. Meaning not notice that the guys at Milstein's Flowers were trying to take it over and that Dr. Massie was in on it. The idea was that with the Depakote and that other thing Massie had started her on, Elise would just go along her blissful way, thinking she was still in charge.

Tomás had definitely been the instigator. Elise was certain it had been his idea, and he'd roped in Hector and René.

After Elise had closed on the building in February 1987, she had brought them—one by one—upstairs to celebrate. Once she had brought Hector and René together. Neither of them wanted the other to see him naked, so it wasn't really a threesome. Homophobes that they were, they were probably afraid of accidentally touching, skin to skin. One watched, getting himself worked up, and then they changed roles. It was fine with Elise. She preferred Hector's cock, but René seemed to genuinely care about her pleasure. Afterward they had all gone out for a beer.

A month later, when she was deep into building business, Elise had stopped inviting the two of them upstairs. That, naturally, was when they'd started trashing her. Passing by the open door of Milstein's Flowers, Elise had heard Hector talking about her: *puta loca.*

Elise knew why Tomás had started the scheme to take the building. Had he actually thought she would marry him? What did he imagine they had in common? When all the building units were rented, Elise had plans to go on an archaeological dig in Yugoslavia or the Ukraine. In a *National Geographic,* she had read about a place that matches up volunteers with sites. Elise had remembered that when she was sixteen, archaeologists had excavated the underground tunnels in Plzen, turning up all kinds of artifacts from daily medieval life. She had longed to go. Now she could dig as a volunteer! Not only dig, but talk to the lead archaeologists and listen to them lecture. Elise thought she could leave by January, when the building would be humming. Did Tomás expect they would get married and he'd come with her? He wouldn't be able to understand a lecture even if it was delivered in English. He and Elise spoke mostly in Spanish. Had he thought he would eventually take her home to San Juan, and she'd look after his sick mother? The first few times he had brought up marriage, she had said he was sweet and laughed. He had laughed too. But he had kept at it, week after week, until she told him he was out of his mind, it would never be. From that day on, she had been strictly a landlady to them all.

The rats were the first sign. They had come because of the half-eaten Big Macs Milstein's guys kept leaving out overnight. No one but building owners knew the true extent of the rat problem in Midtown. Elise had a contract with a rodent exterminator, and she had reinforced the lids on the basement drains, but when Tomás and the others left their food out, the rats found a way. Elise had taped a tersely worded note on their door. Three nights later, when she had unlocked their door and entered with a flashlight, there was a rat, running away from an overturned carton of lo mein on the cutting table. "Fuckheads!" she'd yelled, and the next day she had called Milstein in Little Neck.

After that, the guys stopped leaving out food, but the rat problem persisted. Elise knew Tomás brought them in. One one week, two the next. To freak her out. To get her to do what, walk away from the building? Let RNJ Finance get it? Then they would sneak in and take over? No, they would still have to buy the building from the mortgage company. It was worse than that. Elise was all but certain that Dr. Massie was advising them. Her husband was a real estate developer. Big time. Elise knew he swindled people out of their buildings all the time. He had his minions scanning deeds downtown. He knew what to do and to whom. Elise had read about someone just like Norman Massie, another developer who worked with a lawyer to identify the oldest and most enfeebled real estate owners in the city, then have them declared incompetent and take control of their buildings.

Elise bought a handgun. She was a woman with a building; she needed self-protection. A worker from the sanitation company she used told her where to go. Nothing to it. For two weeks she had gone down to Milstein's space after midnight. If she saw a rat, she shot it. Over those two weeks, Tomás, Hector, or René had to dispose of a total of seven rat corpses when they opened up in the morning, tossing them into three-ply trash bags, along with the empty shells from Elise's Heritage Rough Rider.

Wiley had been shocked when Elise told her about killing the rats. She had shuddered, made a face, hidden her eyes. How could you do such a thing, she had wanted to know. Elise merely shrugged. Wiley's life was free of menace; no one was poised to dismantle the haven she and Michael had built together. The two of them had no reason to worry about New York's rat problem; they hadn't taken the subway in years. Elise decided not to confide in her about Tomás and the others' plan to take over the building. She knew Wiley wouldn't want to hear it. During the past few months, Elise had gotten the feeling Wiley was pulling away. One of her other friends, Elise thought resentfully, had probably told her to "set boundaries."

Dr. Massie had been very sympathetic about the rats. Naturally— her sympathy was all part of the plan. But last week, after Elise was sure Milstein's guys had gotten the message, and she wouldn't be seeing any more rats, she had quit therapy. She told Dr. Massie she intended to report her to the American Psychiatric Association and her husband to the city agency that granted real estate contracts. Dr. Massie had ignored her. "Why did you stop taking your medication?" she had asked, her broken-record question. "You took your medication when your mother was here last year. And then for months afterwards."

"She had to go back," Elise had said by way of an answer.

"Do you think she'd want you to stop taking it?"

"Am I five years old?" Elise had shouted. "Are we talking about my Flintstone vitamins?"

"Hardly."

"*You* know your husband's a crook," Elise had accused. She had stayed in her seat, not quite ready to walk out.

"Elise, I can't force you back on medication. I'm begging you, though, to look at what's happened. You're sabotaging yourself with imagined crises. At the time your mother left is when we should have been looking at rebalancing your meds. It was the worst possible time to stop. You have to work with me on this."

"You and your swindler husband probably live in the Dakota. You send your kids to Dalton and go to the beach for a month every summer. *You* don't have to kill rats to survive."

"This is your illness talking, Elise. Let me prescribe for you. We'll adjust the meds until we get them right. I guarantee you we'll find the right balance. We can't continue our therapy until you're stabilized."

Elise had looked around the office. "All these paintings. I know you bought them from that place on Columbus Avenue, the one that pays the Aborigines five dollars a painting so that Upper West Side shrinks like you can impress chic neurotics with their appreciation of primitive cultures. These paintings make you seem *so* cool. They lure in the patients that keep your kids in Dalton."

Dr. Massie had sighed.

"I'm sorry I'm disappointing you," Elise had declared, jumping up from her seat. "Consider yourself unburdened of my tragic case."

That was a week ago. She had not shown up for her next two appointments and would never see Dr. Nan Massie again. Now that Dr. Massie had ascertained Elise wasn't dead, and she would not have to account for her to any legal authorities or, worse, report her suicide to the American Psychiatric Association, she was free of accountability. And Elise was free of Dr. Massie.

There were no lovers in Elise's bed; there had not been for several months. Rather, building papers and neglected bills surrounded her. There were letters from both attorneys trying to settle the plasterer's case, an invitation to increase the building's liability insurance, a new inspection certificate, the design she had drawn for a banner announcing commercial space vacancies, bids she had requested from three elevator manufacturers, and two packages of magnetic letters she had bought to make a building directory for the lobby. Elise had planned to deal with the piles of paper this morning, but after slamming the phone down on Dr. Massie, she felt drained.

She swept aside her papers and got up. She was already dressed, although she didn't specifically remember putting clothes on. She smoothed out her capris, beautiful silk-lined ones, identical to the other five pairs the tailor on 27th Street had made for her. She straightened the black tights she wore under them and then worked on her shoes. Lately her feet had been hurting. When her mother had visited last year, she had been upset about Elise's hammertoes; she'd gone on and on about the kind of shoes she wore. Elise could not imagine another kind of shoe. She had tried others, but none were hospitable to her feet. A little pain was nothing next to a pair of shoes that didn't commune with Elise's feet.

It was late, but Elise made herself start the day as she always did, by sweeping the sidewalk in front of her building. Tomás was filling the store van with the enormous arrangements he delivered every few days to Milstein's corporate clients. Elise kept her head down and swept vigorously. The agent of her destruction, she reflected, handled glorious sprays of flowers all day long.

Tomás drove away, and Elise set off to do the day's building business. She had to xerox some papers for Jack Feinstein, her lawyer, take her banner design to the sign maker on Tenth Avenue, and buy a new accounting ledger. First the copy shop on 23rd Street. She started out fine, but soon grew panicked. Various influences were holding her back today. The recurrent taste of garlic was annoying. She had eaten nothing with garlic in it, had not eaten anything at all this morning, yet the unmistakable taste persisted. She knew she was going to Macky's Copy Shop where her building had an account, but every twenty-five yards or so Elise had to stop in the middle of the sidewalk to check her bearings. Something wasn't quite right. The juxtaposition of stores had changed. Or no, some stores had migrated from the previous block. Her confusion set off her adrenaline. Twenty-third Street, she reminded herself. Copy the papers in your briefcase for Feinstein.

"Elise? Elise, it's you!"

Elise looked down. She kept walking. No one was calling her; it was just the disorientation that had come from her morning nap.

"It *is* you!"

Elise heard this at the same time as she felt someone's firm touch on her arm. She looked up. At first she couldn't make the connection.

"I can't believe it! I wasn't totally sure it was you, but then I saw your shoes! How *are* you?"

Elise knew who stood before her in a pristine double-breasted rain-coat, undoubtedly a Burberry, but she needed a moment. "*Nouveau,*" she finally said.

"I beg your pardon?" said Debbie Curtis.

Elise broke into a wide smile. "Nouveau, how the hell are you? We were just talking about you the other day."

"Excuse me?" Debbie Curtis looked confused.

"Wiley and I," Elise wanted to say, but couldn't quite seize on Wiley's name. She sensed it in her immediate range, but every time she lunged, it escaped—a butterfly bent on survival. "You know, she hung out with me all the time."

Debbie Curtis removed her hand from Elise's arm. "Who?" she asked. "Those weren't my best years. I don't think about them that much anymore."

"*These* are your best years?" Elise heard herself ask. She wasn't sure about her facial expression. She wasn't sure she was actually speaking. Nouveau backed up a little. "Let me guess. The hubby, the two-point-three kids, the mind-numbing suburb."

"I'm sorry," said Debbie Curtis. "I thought you were someone else." Nervously, she added, "You have a double."

Elise laughed. Nouveau had hit it right again; Elise had a double! She reached out and hugged Nouveau-Riche Heidi. She shouldn't have said that about the two-point-three kids. Years ago, Elise remembered now, Nouveau had had an illegitimate baby. She had to remember not to say everything that crossed her mind.

Debbie Curtis managed to free herself from Elise's hold. "I'm sorry for the mistake," she said. "Have a nice day."

Elise stared, trying to make sense of this encounter, the divine purpose of which eluded her. "A nice day? You expect me to *have a nice day*? With those thieves trying to get hold of my building? You were always a Pollyanna, Nouveau."

Debbie Curtis was already at the curb. Elise saw only her profile. She was tapping one foot and staring down the DON'T WALK sign.

"That's right," yelled Elise after her. "Get away! Hurry back to your house in Complacent Compound! Stuff your kids with jelly beans. Juju beans. Everything bright and phony. It's too gray out here at the margins. Take yourself back to where candy colors reign, Nouveau!"

Before Elise reached Macky's Copy Shop, a cold drizzle began. She had no umbrella. Icy needle points struck her forehead and cheeks, the sides of her nose. The papers in her briefcase no longer seemed important. She turned back in the direction of her building. By the time she got there, the legs of her soaked capris glistened on her thighs, and water dripped into her lace-up shoes. She took herself up in the manual elevator as she did several times a day, first shutting the inner gate, then putting down her belongings in order to pull back the lever with both hands. As the elevator rose, the smell of damp sawdust from Milstein's Flowers grew fainter. Elise looked up through the open ceiling where she could see the cables moving. She didn't like the sound they made. When she got upstairs, she would call the maintenance company.

Once inside her apartment, though, she went directly into her bathroom and filled the tub with hot water, sprinkling in citrus bath oil. The bathroom was the only part of her sixth-floor unit where the renovation was complete, and Elise loved it. She'd had a skylight put in over the tub. The floor was glass mosaic: tiny deep iris blue tiles interspersed with pale green ones that glimmered white in the sunlight. Sleek Boffi sink and tub fixtures. A stainless-steel console with a built-in cassette player. On top she had set two rows of votive candles in milky glass holders and a telephone, a brushed nickel speaker model.

After removing her wet clothes and settling into her bath, Elise dialed Wiley. She knew Wiley would be at the hospital, but she had to tell her what had happened. When Wiley's answering machine signaled, Elise said, "You'll never guess who I just ran into. Nouveau-Riche Heidi! Can you fucking believe it? She looked incredibly insipid and at least fifty. But I behaved, didn't even ask which fascist ROTC guy she ended up with. All very civil. Toodles."

When she hung up, Elise soaped herself, then remembered Wiley would yell at her for leaving a swear word on the answering machine. Tough, she thought. If she had children, she would teach them to swear at an early age. Swearing was the doorway to catharsis. It was pure as an herbal remedy. It didn't cause a tremor like Depakote or leave you with hollowed-out bones like that other one, what's-its-name.

Next Elise called her mother. The phone rang eight times. Elise had bought her an answering machine, but Irena claimed something was wrong with it. Elise panicked; she needed to talk to her mother right now. She was ready to tell her the truth about the building—how Milstein's guys and Norman Massie were planning to take it over.

Finally giving up, Elise sank deeper into the bath, lying back against her inflatable headrest. She closed her eyes and tried to fall asleep, but not a single nerve ending would permit it. There came again that inexplicable sweep of adrenaline. A disaster was around the bend, and it was up to Elise to identify it, but she couldn't. She stretched out to reach the cassette player, pressed PLAY, and submerged herself again. Her heart was pounding as if she had run for blocks.

In a moment Akhmatova's voice filled the bathroom, reading on a recording she had made toward the end of her life. Her voice was husky, her tone shrewd. Elise spoke Russian along with Akhmatova. When the recording ended in the static that had accompanied it, Elise recited her favorite English translation:

> But listen, I am warning you
> I'm living for the very last time.
> Not as a swallow, nor a maple,
> Not as a reed, nor as a star,
> Not as spring water,
> Nor as the toll of bells . . .

Will I return to trouble men
Nor will I vex their dreams again
With my insatiable moans.

For the first time in a week, Elise felt calm.

✦

The next day, Elise again gravitated to water. She had not been to the Y
for weeks. In water she found herself a most amiable companion. She
admired her own form and the steadiness of her forward motion. The
longer she swam, the more her lungs expanded and the more she felt
she was truly breathing again. It wasn't merely that water buoyed her, it
was that water was her true element, her respite, the place from where
she should conduct her life. Her adrenal glands resumed their natural
function in the water. Bodily fear, those visceral blasts of doubt, did not
thwart her in the water. Daydreams were only euphoric, forecasts only
hopeful.

Each time Elise reached an end of the small pool, she did a flip
turn—accomplished it majestically. She had forgotten how fast she was
in the water. Maybe she would drop the idea of the archaeological dig, she
thought, become a swim coach instead. A trainer of future Olympians.
Right as she thought this, as she rose above water in the shallow end to
execute her turn, she felt a heavy hand on her shoulder. She went for the
turn again, but the hand pulled her back.

"Didn't you hear me? Lap swim is over," said a young woman wearing a McBurney Y T-shirt. "The kids' lessons are now."

Elise pulled up her goggles and saw she was the only one left in
the pool. Behind the swimming instructor, a group of children stood
jostling one another. They should all be watching her, Elise thought. If
they want to learn, they should start by watching her form. Why weren't
they? Obviously the instructor didn't recognize an opportunity when it
presented itself. To hell with them. She got out of the pool and stalked
off to the locker room.

Five minutes later, she was back on Eighth Avenue. Too bad she'd had
to get out of the pool before she was ready, but—once out—she remembered she had an appointment. She was due to meet a roofer at three,

and it was three already. She had dressed hastily and slicked her hair back with the restorative aloe vera gel. Now, from the corner of her block, she could see the roofer, Sam Barsotti, getting back into his truck.

"Wait!" she yelled, running to catch up with him. "I'm sorry I'm late. Building business. Let's go in."

In answer, Sam Barsotti glanced at his watch. Punitive, thought Elise. A glance as the last, indignant word. Silently, he followed her into the building, into the manual elevator. Along with Elise, Sam looked up through the opening in the ceiling to the cables and the gears. "You let your tenants use this?" he asked.

"No," she lied. She kept looking up, but could sense him appraising her—her gelled red hair, her nipples outlined beneath her leotard, her firm abdomen, the worn leather of her cordovan lace-ups. Outside, when he'd consulted his watch, Elise had noticed his wedding ring. As far as she was concerned, wedding rings were mere identifiers—symbols of social data, like Burberry coats or Boffi bathroom fixtures. They meant different things to different people.

"We'll go up through my unit," Elise told him when the elevator opened directly onto her galley kitchen. She led the roofer through her small apartment, for the most part still a construction site, and past her bed piled with building papers. She showed him the stains and moist spots on the ceiling, then climbed the ladder to unlock and open the hatch lid.

On the roof, Elise raised her head and watched the gathering clouds. Nothing made her feel as triumphant as standing on her roof in the middle of Manhattan, surrounded by other rooftops and their fixtures—water towers, plumbing vents, exhaust fans, various kinds of chimneys, antennae, and skylights. It was all a glorious tumble of energy, a meticulous chaos generated by strangers united in their love for New York. Elise still couldn't believe this roof and its sky rights were hers.

Sam Barsotti walked around, inspecting parts of the roof with the reinforced toe of his boot. He shifted his weight over certain areas. He knelt to look at the silicone caulking by the bathroom vent and the chimney. Then he approached her.

"I'd say you've got a year, two tops, before you need a whole new roof."

"What? The roof was inspected before I closed! The engineer said ten years."

"Do you want to see?"

Elise followed Sam Barsotti to see where metal work had rusted and water had pooled, to other spots where the asphalt was becoming mushy. He pointed out some peeling patches. "You could wait and risk interior damage," he said, "or you could do it now." Elise noticed his eyes were light blue.

"Shit," she said softly to herself.

Sam shrugged.

Elise climbed down the ladder and Sam followed. Once inside, he held up a vinyl-covered notebook and looked around for a free surface. Elise cleared off the bed.

"Here's what I can offer you," Sam said, sitting down and unzipping the portfolio he had brought in. He showed her pages of colored photographs in acetate sleeves. He told her the story of each roof, its location, how many of his men had laid it, the materials they had used, the term of the roof's guarantee. Elise looked and listened. Since she'd bought the building, she had cultivated an appreciation of industrial materials, had learned how to discriminate between kinds of pipes and fittings, cement sealers, wood planks, electrical wiring, window sashes, on and on. She knew the best and always chose it for her building.

Sam Barsotti turned to the last photograph. His shirtsleeve was rolled up to his elbow. A muscle in his forearm twitched. Elise wanted to touch it, to still the muscle and feel the lovely blond down that extended to his wrist.

"This is the top of our line," said Sam. "The roof itself is the best quality thermoplastic formulation, and we install it with copper flashing. The roof comes with a thirty-year warranty, the longest you're going to get, and the flashing will last you a lifetime."

As Elise was sitting next to him, he dissolved into the scent he was wearing. Old Spice, the aftershave that boy Rupert Dwyer had worn. Elise closed her eyes and breathed it in. Rupert could have been sitting right beside her, as he had been over twenty years ago at the National Honor Society meeting in Peoria, the one where she had stayed overnight and fallen in love with Old Spice, mescaline-spiked pot, the revelation of her own quick wit, and Rupert Dwyer. What had happened to him? What would he make of her path since that day in Grant Park—to Princeton, to Northwestern and Leningrad in Russia, to a campus of old elms, from there to a tenement where drug addicts urinated in the hall, and now to this property that would soon make her a multimillionaire? What had become of Rupert, the boy who'd shown her that Laflin High was not the world? She had to know. She inhaled the Old Spice again.

"This roof," Sam Barsotti was saying, "will cause you zero trouble. With the way we install it, it'll be like you're looking at a glassy pond. I'm telling you, you'll want to live up there."

It took Elise a moment to get her bearings, to realize she was not after all much attracted to this man who was describing the picture open on his lap, the thermoplastic roof and the copper flashing.

"I'll measure," he said. "I'll get you a price. It won't be cheap, but you'll have the best roof on the block."

Good, thought Elise. Let Tomás, Hector, and René see Barsotti's roofers go up with their thermoplastic and their copper flashing. Let them see she wasn't going to be intimidated by them or by Norman Massie, that she was buying a roof that would last years beyond the expiration of Milstein's lease, a roof that would not deteriorate even as they were caught out for some scam that would send them to jail or back to San Juan, even as they had heart attacks from the junk food clogging their arteries. Let them see that the future of the building was hers to plan. Let Rupert Dwyer, the boy who had failed to acknowledge her love—let him see her gorgeous new roof in the middle of Manhattan.

"That's fine," Elise said. "Send me the estimate."

"You fucking capitalist bastards!" Elise declared to her empty room. She had just received the third notice from RNJ Finance, the company that held her mortgage and her credit line. "As if you're not milking everyone out of a fortune with your insane interest rates."

She lit a cigarette, dragged her folding chair to the phone, and called Jack Feinstein. She explained that Milstein's three workers and Norman Massie were in cahoots with the mortgage company to take over her building. Jack Feinstein, who was doing a reasonable job settling the plasterer's case against the building, listened to her without interrupting. Then, very patiently, as if talking to a child, he told Elise it was not a case he could handle.

Elise snuffed out her cigarette, lit another. "Do you know how much this building is worth, the equity here? You'd be a fool not to take this case, Jack!"

Still, Jack Feinstein kept up his patronizing tone. Elise knew he was a major sexist. She told him so and slammed down the phone. Then she reached for her address book. She hadn't spoken to Milos since her father had died. The thought of calling him intensified her anxiety, but it had to be done. She reached him at his office.

"Milos? It's Elise. Are you busy?"

After a pause, Milos said, "No, I'm sitting here waiting for your call."

"Don't take it personally," Elise said. "You have no idea what I've been through. I haven't spoken to anyone but Irena. How are you? How's Dawn?"

"We had another child," he said. "A boy. We named him Stephen, after your father."

Milos, thought Elise, would know that Irena had already told her this news. "Congratulations. I'm going to send him something great. I've been meaning to."

"Why are you calling, Elise?"

"I need a favor." She might as well be direct.

"No! I don't believe it!"

Elise ignored his sarcasm. She told him what she had told Jack Feinstein, except in greater detail. She included more about the progress she had made on the building and her plans for more improvements.

Milos didn't say much, but his occasional question showed how closely he had been following. Once he asked how many units were rented. Elise told him all but one. He didn't need to know that four leases were pending, the units still empty. Finally, he said, "If those people are trying to get your building, then why are you continuing to spend money on it? Why are you getting that expensive new roof?"

Elise had the answer to this but couldn't call it up. Rather, she focused on the skepticism in Milos's tone. "You don't believe me? You think I'm making this up to entertain myself?"

"Elise—"

"Milos, this property is going to quadruple in value in the next ten years. Who do you think will inherit it? Aren't you interested in protecting your children's inheritance?"

"Aunt Irena told me that you've gone off your medications."

"You wouldn't even *be* a lawyer if my parents—"

"How can we talk rationally if you're not on your medications?"

"Rationality was always your downfall," she accused. "Your belief in the governing power of rationality and the American dream. From day one. From the baseball obsession to the early marriage to the law practice to the kids. One of the throngs."

"How can I help you, Elise? You know you have the willpower to get right again. You've done it before."

The word *right* threw her. Elise began to cry. Her nostrils clogged up, and her temples throbbed. She couldn't stop.

"There's very little I can do, Elise. I've tried to help you in the past, but—"

"That's not *true*!" she managed. "You can protect me, Milos! You can stop them from taking my building."

"Do you need a loan?" he asked. "We're a little tight with the new baby, but I could talk to Dawn, see if—"

"No," said Elise, managing with great effort to get herself under control. Several times in the past she had gone to her little cousin for money, and once or twice he had come through for her. No more. He could not be counted among those on her side. "No, I'm fine. I have to go, but I'll send the baby something. Say hi to Dawn."

✦

For three weeks that February, Elise considered her bed the only safe haven. When Irena called, Elise spoke with her, but she didn't answer anyone else's calls, not Wiley's or her former students', not prospective tenants' calls, certainly not contractors looking to be paid, or RNJ Finance threatening foreclosure. At least her mother believed her, understood the value of the building and how it made Elise quarry for the slick operators who penetrated all levels of society.

During those late winter weeks, Elise created a small fortress around herself: a portable refrigerator, cardboard boxes full of crackers, peanut butter and dried fruit, a television and radio, heaps of books. She ventured out only to replenish her food supply.

The only contact she had was with Dimitri Shiroff, the manager of Krshinev Bookstore on Brighton Beach Avenue. For months, he had been sending her the latest Russian-language essay and poetry collections. In the last three weeks she had read these over and over, sometimes translating them for her own amusement. She did this between long crying jags, spells of tears that finally served to relax her shoulders and loosen the clench of her jaw, yet tears that left her hollow as gutted prey.

One morning after she had cried so long she could virtually feel her strong swimming muscles contract and slacken, Elise rose shakily, took herself to the bathroom, then returned to bed to call the bookstore. She remembered a book she wanted to read, and she needed it right away.

After Dimitri said hello, she asked him if he had a copy of *Grey Is the Color of Hope,* a memoir by the poet Irina Ratushinskaya.

"Give me a couple of weeks, and I'll place the order," Dimitri said.

"Why? You always order my books right away."

"Let's just say gray is the color of my hope these days. But I'll be able to order it in a couple of weeks. I just need to clear up a bill that's in the way."

"Oh." Elise panicked. Getting her books on time was crucial; it was what she had right now.

"No one reads anymore," Dimitri complained. "Everyone browses, but no one reads. When émigrés first arrive, they gather here and talk to me for hours. They look at the spines and the covers of all the poets and writers they once read. Their eyes mist up. Then they leave."

For the first time, Elise could visualize Dimitri. A lover of literature, a modest and peaceable man who needed only to pay his bills to approve of himself; he would have the lean, pale face of an ascetic.

"The literate like to be near titles," Elise agreed.

Dimitri laughed. He told her that he would call her when he ordered the book and again when he shipped it. When she hung up, the clarity of their exchange hung in the air like a murmur of congratulations.

Two mornings later, shortly after waking, Elise looked at the bar of sunlight falling across the foot of her bed and was charged with an unexpected thrill, with more energy than she'd had in months. The oxygen that had abandoned her now filled her lungs, traveled where it needed to go. She looked at the sunbeam and remembered Akhmatova:

> I pray to the sunbeam from the window
> It is pale, thin, straight.
> Since morning I have been silent,
> And my heart—is split.
> The copper on my washstand
> has turned green,
> But the sunbeam plays on it
> So charmingly.

That afternoon, she called Sam Barsotti to schedule the installation of her new roof. Over the next two weeks, her energy still at its height, Elise took care of building business. Besides dealing with the mounting piles of paperwork, she showed her vacant spaces to prospective tenants. She found that all of their businesses fascinated her. Even as the owners were counting electrical outlets and inspecting her new thermostats, she felt a pressing need to learn everything about their fields. She plied them with questions: the corporate brander, the food stylist, the osteopath, and the Japan travel specialist. All their professions seemed to beckon to her. They were right for her, and in successive revelations she foresaw her great success in each of them. The owners all wanted to know when they would hear from her about the rental space, but Elise had found their inquiries irritating. She told the food stylist she could have the space rent free for the first six months in exchange for letting Elise apprentice to her. The woman, who for a stylist had no imagination, seemed taken aback and left without giving Elise a commitment.

When the roof was finished, Sam Barsotti invited her up to inspect it. He had not exaggerated; it was as taut as could be and perfectly level. With the sun shining, its polished copper flashing reflected glints of white light, distinguishing Elise's roof from the surrounding ones with their dingy aluminum flashing.

Elise was thrilled. It occurred to her she could hold a sunset party to celebrate the installation of the block's most spectacular roof. She would invite Wiley and Michael and their kids. She would invite all her favorite students from Alaster College, and she'd track down old Princeton and Northwestern friends. She could even invite her ex-husband, Viktor Frolov, whom she hadn't seen in fifteen years but knew had retired and was still living in Evanston, Illinois. His third wife was a refugee who spoke no English, but of course Elise would invite her, too. Most importantly, she would invite the other building owners on her block. She would also send invitations to her old neighbors from the East Village tenement; they would be bowled over that this building with its nearly half-million-dollar roof was hers. But the invitations she most looked forward to sending were to Tomás, Hector, René, and to Dr. Massie and her husband, Norman. Let them marvel at the copper flashing on the gorgeous roof they would never come close to owning.

Chapter Fourteen

March 6–June 6, 1990

Irena hadn't even prepared her coffee when the phone rang.

"Mrs. Blazek? This is Wiley Mills. I hate to call so early, but you've asked me to call if—"

"What's happened?"

"She had . . . an episode. Her meds needed some adjusting."

"What are you telling me?" Irena demanded.

"I went to visit her last evening. She wanted to show me her new roof, and—"

"Her roof! You went up on her roof?"

"No, no, nothing happened. It's a bit hard to explain out of context. She just had this very expensive roof laid, far more than she could afford, I'm sure, and I think it hit her what she'd done once we were up there together. She became really terrified. Whatever she was feeling up there set off a psychotic episode."

A "psychotic episode"? Wiley said this as if it were nothing. Then she began to talk too fast; it was hard to keep the details straight. Irena didn't know what to believe. Her daughter had told her in the past that when it came to Elise's problems, Wiley had her own set of peculiarities. She had used some new word—*codependent*. During her last visit to

New York, she *had* noticed that Wiley seemed strangely animated when Elise wasn't feeling herself.

"Where is she?"

"She's at a hospital downtown. St. Vincent's. I don't know how long—"

"Thank you. I'll call right now, thank you."

Without waiting to hear more, Irena hung up and got St. Vincent's number on Sixth Avenue. When she finally got through to patient information, the lady there told her Elise had just been discharged.

When Irena tried her daughter at home, she got no answer, just that awful machine that made her sound like a child or a dimwit every time she tried to leave a message. She called Wiley back, but her machine was on too. All day long she tried Elise, hanging up every time her recording came on.

Early the next morning, Elise called her.

"Where were you yesterday?" Irena asked. "I tried you all day. Your friend Wiley called me. I was crazy with worry."

"It's getting worse," Elise declared, her tone pitched to a key Irena didn't like to hear. "Hector and Tomás got up on my roof. I heard them up there."

"Elise, why would they do that?"

"*Why?*" she demanded. "Why do they do anything? Why did they get the rats? It's just another sign."

"Oh, I don't think they'd—"

"So *don't* believe me."

Irena didn't know what to say. Even over the phone, she sensed her daughter's trust slipping away, a trust as flimsy as the gossamer Irena used to unspool at Reyna Kopecky's. Maybe Hector and Tomás *were* up to no good. Married to Stepan all those years, living in quiet Laflin, Illinois, what did Irena know of the ways of hoodlums?

"Where were you yesterday?"

"Never mind. I was gone, now I'm back, here in the building. *My* building that those crooks will never get. All I need is a good lawyer. With a good lawyer, it'll all turn around. You know what this building is going to be worth? Six times what Daddy made in his entire lifetime. But I need the best real estate lawyer in New York, and right now I'm short of cash."

Irena hung on the line, listening. All of her McDonald's stock money had gone into that building. Now her only savings was the money from the CD she had sold, and she'd been using it to supplement Stepan's small pension income. Last month she had decided to start collecting his social security checks, even though it meant she would never get the full benefit. She felt powerless to help Elise.

"They're all going to move in for the kill—all of them: Milstein's guys, Norman Massie. And I'm pretty sure Milos is in on it, too. I have to get a lawyer who knows the particulars of—"

"Miloslav would never—"

"Will you come here?" Elise pleaded, her voice quivering. "Come help me fight?"

"Yes, zlatíčko, if you need me, I'll come," Irena said. Why hesitate? Clearly Elise was in trouble. The two of them would save her building. "I'll get a one-way ticket, and then we'll see."

Before she left for New York, Irena called the Kriz sisters to come meet her for lunch at Risa's Kuchyně, their favorite Czech restaurant. Berta was traveling on one of her assignments, but Magda was free. Irena had not been to Chicago for months, and it took some planning. Several times she changed her mind about what to wear. When she arrived at the restaurant and saw the other customers, she decided she had overdressed. Why didn't she know how to dress anymore—she, who had a mastery of good fabrics and which colors worked together?

While they were looking at their menus, Irena said, "I'm going to New York on Saturday. Elise needs some help."

Startled, Magda looked up from her menu, then back down again. Irena never mentioned Elise, and Magda in particular had long since stopped creating openings.

The waiter came and took their orders—roast duck and sweet pickled cabbage for both of them.

"It's complicated," Irena continued, then leaned across the table. "Terrible things can happen, Magda. You wouldn't believe how many people there are out there ready to rob a person of everything."

Magda folded her napkin on her lap, then glanced away.

"Do you think I'm imagining things?"

"No, of course not. I just . . ." It seemed as if Magda might cry.

"I know things have not been easy for you since Stepan . . . and then California . . ."

What did Magda know, Irena asked herself. And what did "not been easy" mean? Didn't she remember, as Irena well did, the real significance of "not easy"? Not easy was half a population out of work, Germans approaching, whole countries with futures too desperate to imagine. Irena would never claim things were not easy for her. It was true that since returning to Laflin she had discovered herself to be less adventurous than she had expected—inclined, in fact, to go nowhere, a little nervous about leaving the house to do her errands or attend her monthly discussion groups at the Laflin Historical Society. But she had her house, for heaven's sake, her paid-off house! And she had her occupations at home. The new correspondence with her childhood friends from Plzen, for instance, and with her third cousin Martin and his sister. The stamps on their recent letters had been specially issued by the Czech government to mark the forty-fifth anniversary of the year the United States had liberated Plzen—1945, seven years after Irena had emigrated with her mother and father.

Now the news from Plzen was of another long-awaited liberation. In their letters, Ivena and Kate, her friends from their years at Gymnázium Ludka Pika, asked many questions about life in a democracy. Irena answered them as best she could, the whole while shamefaced for not relishing her own freedom, for feeling dry as the bones she swore she could feel rub together when she rose from her La-Z-Boy.

"Things have been fine since I got back," Irena told Magda. "But you would not believe what Elise has been through. There are people trying to take her building away from her."

Magda nodded hesitantly. "A building? In New York City? She's not in New England anymore?"

Was Magda trying to get Irena to tell her everything that had happened? She and Berta might still be Irena's best friends, but Elise's story was none of their business. "It's complicated," she said. "I can't say more." She was relieved when the waiter brought their food.

"When will you be back?" Magda wanted to know.

"It's impossible to tell," Irena said. "I'll have to see."

"Well," said Magda, "of course Berta and I will miss you."

Irena did not believe this but said she would miss the Kriz sisters as well. She had never been an impolite woman.

During the plane ride, Irena couldn't help but feel sad about her coat. It would take her a while to get used to the idea, but how much had she really worn it anyway? Once a year, to the Laflin Historical Society fundraiser, where she was an honored guest. Still, she'd had the coat only five years, since her sixtieth birthday, and Stepan had intended for her to have it for the rest of her life. It was only a material thing, but it stood like nothing else as testament to Stepan's years of constancy and love. Selling the indigo fox coat had felt like a terrible betrayal, as if she were deliberately casting off her husband's memory.

The captain announced they had reached their cruising altitude of 27,000 feet. Irena tilted her seat back, closed her eyes, and reminded herself she was not a religious woman; she did not believe that any form of Stepan existed to witness what she had done. Nevertheless she addressed him in her thoughts. "For Elise," she told him. "It was the right thing to do, my manžel, my good sweet husband, because it was to help our Elise."

As Irena stood watching for the large, gray Samsonite bag with the piece of red yarn tied to its handle, she spotted Elise beyond the baggage carrousel, running toward her.

"Sorry, sorry, sorry," Elise said when, out of breath, she reached Irena's side. "The whatchamacallit bridge was backed up. A real mess. Why don't they do their work after midnight? The unions, probably. I believe in unions, but not to the extent of them fucking up my life."

"Hello, zlatíčko." said Irena. It seemed to her that even since the last time she had seen Elise, less than a year ago, her daughter had aged, that the skin on her forehead was more tightly sealed to her skull. The clothes, of course, were the same. Every outfit different, all of them the same. This one was a fuchsia leotard, a fitted pearl-gray jacket with large filigreed buttons, a long chiffon scarf the bright copper color she insisted on for her hair, those pants that made her look like a horsewoman, the shoes. Irena thought briefly about going upstairs to book a flight home, about recovering her indigo fox coat.

Elise did not embrace her. She concentrated on spotting the bag with the red yarn tied to its handle, which she did almost immediately.

"We'll take a cab. The building's a mess. You wouldn't believe what's been going on."

Elise spoke without looking at Irena. As Irena thought about it, her daughter almost never looked at her. In fact, she took only fleeting looks at everything, glimpses that darted about, and Irena thought Elise would be happy for a pair of eyes at the back of her head.

"A bus is fine. I can take the bus."

"We'll take a cab. The buses smell like vinegar."

"Vinegar? All of them? I can't believe *that*."

"Are you going to start out questioning everything I say? Because—"

"—I was only saying."

"If we see any of Milstein's guys when we get back, just act normal. This is very important. We want to keep them off guard. We want them to think we're a couple of dupes."

We, thought Irena. When was the last time someone had said *we*, meaning to include Irena? Miloslav, but he had meant it superficially and perhaps for his own ends. This was a real *we*, she thought, the kind of *we* that installed Irena at the core of another life.

The manual elevator was in no better shape than during Irena's last visit. Elise still hadn't covered the square ceiling hole through which Irena could, if she cared to, watch the mechanical operation. The lever that opened and shut the outer door was squeaky. The walls were a chipped metallic green. A single low-wattage lightbulb dangled too close to their heads. Irena knew Elise wanted to replace the elevator with an automatic one, that she'd had a couple of companies out to give her an estimate. Irena thought the elevator should be taken out of operation, but she knew better than to say so. A month ago, over the phone, she had suggested that Elise make replacing the elevator her top priority. That had been a mistake. Now she looked straight ahead as the carriage shimmied its way up the shaft, twice grazing the wall on her side.

"I've got you all set up," said Elise, pulling back the door that opened onto her kitchenette. "Come see."

Elise led her mother to the far corner of the room, by the ladder to the roof, where she had made up a cot. She had put a little blond wood end table and a lamp next to it, and sectioned off the area with a folding rice-paper screen. On the bed stand was a blue glass vase that held one of the most beautiful bouquets Irena had ever seen. She gasped when she saw it.

"Chaing Mai orchids," said Elise.

"Here? In March?"

"I took them from Milstein's early this morning. They get stuff flown in from all over."

Irena wanted to point out that this was stealing—moreover, stealing from the very people she wanted to sue. But maybe she was wrong. Maybe there was something in Elise's relationship with the people who worked in the store downstairs that she was missing. The fine points of her daughter's dealings with the building frequently eluded her.

"And I've made room in the closet," Elise added.

"Very nice, zlatíčko."

"Why don't you get yourself together, and we'll go down for lunch?"

Just as last time, Irena couldn't understand why Elise was always ready to go out. She thought of her granddaughter Samantha, forever wanting to be where she was not, and wondered if she had inherited the tendency from Elise. Yet Elise had not been that way as a child. On the contrary, her teachers were always praising her ability to sustain concentration. Hanging in Irena's bedroom to this day was a paper mosaic of an underwater scene that Elise had made when she was only six—finishing it in one four-hour sitting, amazing Irena and the Kriz sisters, who had happened to be over.

"Why can't we eat here?" Irena asked.

"Where?" asked Elise, looking around.

Irena surveyed the room. It was true that over half of it looked like a construction site, and the rest was a mess, much worse than when Irena visited last. There were papers and mail and ledgers everywhere. Books, also, were all over the room, stuck precariously on overflowing shelves and stacked in towers on the floor. The sight of all the books pricked Irena with a sorry pride. She must do whatever she could to help Elise, to release her back to the lofty world she was meant to occupy.

Riding down the elevator, Irena again resisted looking up at the cables. Silently, she followed Elise onto the street. Outside was one of Milstein's men, Irena couldn't remember which one. Balanced on his shoulder was a stack of giant-sized bags of potting soil. Like her father, her own otec, he would die early, thought Irena. Manual laborers so often did.

"You remember my mother, don't you, René?" Elise asked him.

"Yes, yes. Mrs. Blazek, Elise's mama, come back to see us." Even in the cold, sweat rolled down the side of René's face.

"I have," said Irena. What was she supposed to say? She hoped it was all right with Elise.

They stood awkwardly on the sidewalk until René shouted for Hector to bring him the hand truck.

"She's hungry," Elise told René, taking Irena's arm.

"Nice to see—" Irena started before she found herself already turned toward Sixth Avenue.

"Shhh," said Elise. "Did you notice that little smile? He thinks it's all a joke. To him, my life is a joke."

"I didn't really—"

"They're all like that. They love to run into me so they can play their little game."

When they were seated in the coffee shop around the corner, Irena took the envelope out of her purse. "This is for you to get a lawyer," she said, pushing the envelope toward Elise.

Elise opened it, removed the check, and stared at it. She began to cry.

Irena was embarrassed. "There are *people* here," she said.

Elise wept louder, waving away her mother's protest.

"Zlatíčko, this is a public place."

Elise blew her nose into the paper napkin but didn't stop. "I'll pay you back," she promised through her tears. "Every penny, with twenty percent interest."

That twenty percent interest again. An insult. "It's a gift," Irena said. "You are my daughter, and you have troubles. But I must tell you, Elise, there is no more. This is all I have." There's nothing left except my home, she thought, frightening herself.

"I know!" Elise exclaimed. "Do you think I don't *know*?"

A man in the booth behind them turned around to look. Elise didn't seem to notice. Abruptly, though, she stopped crying. "You wait," she said. "Within two years you'll be a rich woman. Once I get those guys behind bars, the building will run like clockwork. And don't forget—"

"Zlatíčko, let's order."

"Sorry," said Elise, then called the waiter over. She did not have to give him her own order.

When the waiter left, Irena nodded toward the check Elise had left out on the table. "Put that away," she whispered.

Elise looked at the check on the table beside her fork. She seemed surprised to see it. She folded it in two, stretched out the top of her leotard, and stuck it inside.

"Elise!"

"Listen," Elise said. "Here's what has to be done. I'm not so worried about Milstein's guys. They think they're going to get a fat piece of the building, but Norman Massie is just using them. He slips them a couple hundred every now and then. That's how these upper-echelon guys work. They don't get their hands dirty."

"Massie? Massie was the name of your psychiatrist," said Irena, lowering her voice to a whisper over this last word.

"Yes, but I've told you about her husband. He's a big developer. I'm sure he got a gold mine of information from her."

"No, this can't be. It's just the boys, the young men from the flower store who have nothing. Professionals would not do such a thing. It would be very unethical."

Elise burst out laughing, a laughter as raucous as the crying had been. Irena squirmed on her seat and gave Elise a pleading look.

In a moment Elise settled down. "You should know that Norman Massie has been in touch with Milos. Milos is starting to work with him."

The waiter set half a cantaloupe and a toasted bran muffin in front of Elise and a mushroom cheese omelet with french fries before Irena. Irena wanted to start right in, but eating now would be unseemly. What was that expression? Fiddling while Rome burned.

"Please don't start with that again. So maybe it's true about Mr. Massie, I have no way of knowing. But Miloslav would never, ever . . . You're his cousin he grew up with. He cares about you. He is a good man, Elise, a family man."

"You think so?" Elise asked in that tone Irena found so galling.

"Yes. Táta and I raised him right."

"I'm not accusing you. Just look at the facts. First of all, what does he do for a living?"

"Real estate law, but that doesn't—"

"—mean anything in and of *itself*," finished Elise. "We can put aside that he makes his living basically from money changing hands. There's a lot more going on, though."

Irena wanted to stop Elise, but instead she took a bite of her omelet. She found it uncommonly delicious, more than an omelet—a revelation and a relief.

"He's always hated me, and he's always been jealous. Jealousy can drive people straight to hell."

"Jealous? He has his three children. The baby is named after Táta, Elise. Here, I brought his picture for you." Irena put down her fork and opened her purse.

"I'm sure he's adorable, but so what?" said Elise. "Another baby is all the more reason for him to acquire what he can, by whatever means."

"Stop this! Real estate law is a perfectly decent profession. There's not a thing wrong with it. Berta used Miloslav when she bought her apartment."

"Think what you will," said Elise, working her spoon into the cantaloupe.

If Irena were home, she would eat every last bite, but she was in public. She left a scrap of omelet, a few fries. She drank some water and looked at her daughter, who was scanning the room, staring openly at everyone who entered the diner.

"You can afford not to believe me," Elise finally said. "You have nothing to lose. It's fine. You and Daddy raised him, I can understand."

"You're wrong about him. He would never go after your building. Why on earth would he do such a thing?"

Elise began to whistle, keeping time by rocking her head from side to side. In a moment, Irena recognized the tune from the movie *Cabaret*. Liza Minnelli and Joel Grey singing the chorus "money makes the world go round." It was one of the few movies she and Stepan had seen together, and she'd enjoyed it.

"All right, you can stop now," said Irena.

"Well?" Elise challenged.

"They have money. Both of them have good jobs. You forget."

"More money equals more power. Milos has always wanted to play in the major league. The only difference is that this isn't baseball."

"This is ridiculous. Why don't you call him? He doesn't talk to me about it, but I know how seldom you two are in touch."

"I did call him. I asked him to represent me. Why do you think he said no?"

Irena considered this. "Because he's all the way in California."

"No . . . think again."

"This is all a terrible misunderstanding. Táta would roll over in his grave."

Elise signaled the waiter for coffee. She now seemed thoroughly at ease with herself. She turned to the side and draped her arm along the back of the seat, keeping her gaze on Irena's face. "Think about it," she said, her voice lulling in its grace and authority. "Milos came into our household when he was already eight, under tragic circumstances. His father had been killed, his mother went crazy and had to be taken away. What could be worse? You and Daddy didn't bargain for him, and there he was. And he was a pretty wild boy. Now and then you had to slap him to get him to behave."

How could this be a correct assessment? It was nothing like what had happened. Yes, the depth of Miloslav's tragedy was undeniable, but under the circumstances he had adjusted well to Laflin. Irena didn't remember wildness beyond that of the usual boyhood. As for the rest, an occasional slap to correct his manners; she and Stepan cared about the kind of person he would turn out to be. And what did Elise mean to imply by mentioning Katrina's illness? Years ago, when all the terrible trouble with Elise had started, Irena had remembered that Katrina was Stepan's cousin and thought about her in relation to *Elise,* wondered about the meandering path of genes in a family's blood. And now here was Elise implying that his mother's illness had affected *Miloslav.*

"I don't think you're right about any of this."

"He grew up resenting me," she continued. "Justified or not is beside the point."

The waiter came by with Elise's coffee. Irena ordered herself tea. If this awful conversation were going to continue, she couldn't sit there with nothing to reach for.

"It's nice you're so trusting," Elise said. "But do you think all the world's evil was bundled up into 1938, that when you came to America that was the end of it? It only got worse, Irena. It never went away."

"What's the matter with you, Elise—you think I don't know my history? You are turning everything around. I taught *you* about the evil in Europe. You and Miloslav both. What did you two know, with everything Táta and I gave you—not a moment's deprivation in your lives?"

"Once Milos gets my building he can start on his real plan," Elise continued. "I bet he thinks he'll leave Helmsley and Tisch in the dust."

Irena closed her eyes and blew on the tea the waiter had set down. She had no idea who Helmsley and Tisch were and didn't care. Never had Irena been so deeply weary. Right at this moment, waiting for her tea to cool, she knew nothing but the pain in her shoulder—bursitis again, probably from lugging her suitcase to the ticket counter at O'Hare Airport, and a fatigue so deep she could not put up an argument about anything.

"Norman Massie must have made him a really tempting offer," Elise continued. "Since I stopped seeing his wife, he needed a source of information on me. And since I talk to you, and you talk to Milos . . ."

Irena squeezed a lemon wedge over her tea. She could not understand why the six-story building with that dreadful elevator was attracting all this attention. In New York, buildings were so much more valuable than they looked. "Things will get easier for you, zlatíčko. You'll see."

A terrible expression of bitterness crossed Elise's face. "So you've always said," she responded, looking quickly away. Then, as if to herself, "'I drink the turbid air as if it were dark water.'"

"What? Don't say these strange, ugly things to me. I can't take it today."

Elise looked back at Irena. "It's not me, it's Mandelstam. From a poem in *Tristia*. The James Greene translation."

Irena finished her tea. Was Elise's mind jammed with the words of all the poems she had studied, the translations she had done and the ones she'd abandoned? Those books on the floor of her apartment—Irena had not seen them during her last visit. They were all in Russian. How much poetry still hovered in her daughter's mind, and how deeply did she miss her life with it, her professor days? There were all kinds of tragedies in the world. Who was to say the tragedy of a little boy abandoned was worse than that of a scholar parted from her subject? Irena was no longer put out with Elise for taking up the Russians. Since the Soviets had released their hold over Czechoslovakia, Irena had begun to imagine the Soviet Union as a whole other nation. Gorbachev talked about universal human values. Irena's cousin Martin had heard a Gorbachev speech that had made him weep. Maybe in reading the poetry of its people, Elise had seen this other Soviet Union all along.

"Let's not talk anymore, zlatíčko. Tomorrow we can talk. Let's just please go back now."

Irena took out her pocket calendar to verify how long she had been in New York. Her flight number was marked on the space for three Tuesdays earlier. If she hadn't looked, she wouldn't have known for sure. Time had a different way of passing here in Elise's building. She couldn't describe it if she tried.

"I've been here three weeks already!" she called to Elise, who was working at a card table she had set up near her bed.

Elise didn't answer, so Irena brought over the pocket calendar. "Look, zlatíčko, this is from Sedlak's, the butcher shop on Third Street, remember? Hanus used to give them out every Christmas. Did you know he's not there anymore? He had to shut down when the new A&P moved in. Sad. He was there when Táta and I first moved to Laflin."

"Can you go xerox these?" Elise asked her mother, giving her a sweet smile.

Elise had been preparing for the lawyer, and Irena was helping her. She made frequent trips to Macky's Copy Shop, searched through disorderly piles of paper to find the ones Elise needed, and—under Elise's direction—ordered and reordered all the evidence. She had been repeatedly amazed at the sheer quantity of building-related papers. Was life in New York that much more complicated than anywhere else? In Irena's safe deposit box at the branch of her bank in Laflin was a deed to the house on Konza Street and the contract for its purchase almost twenty-five years ago. Those were all the papers she remembered.

Although March was almost over, an icy wind blew down Sixth Avenue as they tried to hail a cab. Irena wished she had left enough money out of the check she'd given Elise to pay for a decent new coat for herself. Nothing fancy, just one of those warm quilted ones that went down to the ankles. Then she scolded herself. In good time she could buy a new coat—ten new coats. Another indigo fox if she wanted. The only thing that mattered now was this afternoon's visit to Mr. Gordon Kruger, the lawyer Elise had paid a pretty penny to evaluate their case.

Once inside their cab, Irena repeated what she had told Elise earlier, that there was nothing wrong with public transportation, that Elise should be watching her money. Elise ignored her. She was looking out her window, no doubt rehearsing what she would say to Mr. Kruger. This was the one man, Elise had said, who could save them.

If only Elise weren't wearing that awful thrift-store raccoon coat with the huge shoulder pads. At least she had let Irena stick the stuffing back in and sew up its torn shoulder, but Irena could swear she smelled the blood of the raccoon, never mind for how many decades it had been dead.

The reception area of Alstead, Kruger, and Wishart had an air of male authority that frightened Irena. She didn't have to lay eyes on the partners to know they belonged to a class of man that had no time for the likes of her husband. Stepan's answer to this type of man was to retreat to a dank basement and use his hands, over which he had ultimate control. Merely by sitting in this reception room, on one of the law firm's deep leather sofas, Irena felt a twinge of disloyalty. "*Táta*—" she began.

"Shhhh!" cautioned Elise. Once again she was rummaging through a fat accordion file that contained the papers she had selected for the meeting.

The receptionist showed them into a conference room and told them Mr. Kruger would be with them in a minute. Elise got busy organizing the papers into neat stacks at the center of the table. She whispered to herself, reciting the categories of the various documents.

When Elise was finished reviewing the stacks of paper, she walked about the room, scanning the spines of law books, playing with the dimmer for the track lighting, even adjusting the vertical blinds to subdue the light in the room. Irena was about to tell her to sit down when Mr. Kruger entered, hand extended.

"Gordon Kruger," he announced in a deep baritone, almost a bass from what Irena knew about men's voices. He shook hands with both of them. "What have we got here?" he asked, regarding the piles on the highly polished conference table.

Elise began to tell the story of her building. As she did so, she walked about the room, rubbing her palms together, gesturing, and adjusting her chiffon scarf. Irena was amazed at the sheer quantity of words coming out of her daughter's mouth. Many were legal or real estate terms Irena didn't know. Whatever Elise turned her attention to, she mastered.

Gordon Kruger sat across from them, the fingertips of both hands pressed together over his lips as he listened. His gaze followed Elise wherever she moved. Irena wasn't paying strict attention to everything Elise was saying, but she became alert every time she heard Miloslav's name. Periodically Elise handed a document to Mr. Kruger, who reviewed it quickly. For all her movement and fidgeting, Elise's voice was measured, even as she spoke the names of the people who plotted against her. Irena blinked back tears.

At a certain point Mr. Kruger turned to Irena. "Do I understand, then, that this Miloslav is your nephew? That you were the one to raise him?"

"Yes, my husband and myself. But—"

"She's not part of this suit," interrupted Elise.

Mr. Kruger had the most penetrating stare—the gaze of the fully self-possessed, the ones who never fell far, whose losses could always be recouped.

Elise kept talking. Gordon Kruger broke in to ask a question Irena didn't fully understand, something about liens and debt. Elise grew agitated. She launched into a lengthy explanation, all the while riffling through her papers. Irena noticed her daughter's hands shaking, something she hadn't seen since Elise had been on those drugs she used to take. Why was Mr. Kruger trying to increase her anxiety? Couldn't he see how much she had been through?

When Gordon Kruger finally rose, he produced a false-sounding sigh of regret and told Elise he couldn't be of help to her.

In the course of handing over a notarized document, Elise stood motionless. Then she recovered, laid the paper on the table in front of her, and said, "You must not have taken in all I was saying. This is not your everyday case." An expression of pride passed over her face. "That's why I did my research and came to *you.*"

"It just isn't the type of case I handle."

"What do you mean?" The pitch of Elise's voice was rising. "Of course it is. This case is right up your alley, and it's newsworthy. This case would be good for your career."

"I'm sorry to disappoint you, Miss Blazek, but I thank you for coming in." Gordon Kruger turned politely to Irena. "And you as well."

"I can't believe this!" shouted Elise. "You charge us a huge fee and then send us on our merry way?"

"My consultation fee is the same regardless of whether I take a case. You're paying for my assessment of the value of your claim."

"Please, don't you see how my daughter is being pursued?" Irena heard herself saying. "It's a terrible thing that's happening to her."

Gordon Kruger looked at his watch. "I do see a building in trouble," he said, turning again to Elise. "You need a bankruptcy lawyer, Ms. Blazek. We deal only in corporate bankruptcy here, but I could see if one of the associates could recommend someone."

"Haven't you been listening to me for the last half hour? Fuck, is Massie behind this? Did he get to *you,* too?"

"I'll shut the door on my way out to give you and your mother a chance to gather yourselves," Mr. Kruger said.

He left immediately, simply evaporated, it seemed to Irena. She got up to help Elise with the papers. "Don't worry, zlatíčko, we'll find another lawyer," she said. "That man, he just wants the easy cases."

Elise was collecting the papers without looking at them. Her stare was inward. Her lips were moving.

"There's still money from the check," continued Irena, thinking there was actually very little. "Mr. Kruger is not the only lawyer in New York City."

Elise abandoned the papers and began to walk around again, back and forth, the length of the room. Her lips were still moving.

"Zlatíčko, let's go. We'll find another savior, a lawyer who understands. This Mr. Kruger, he just doesn't understand."

Irena said this despite the fact that *she* did not understand many aspects of her daughter's case. Her inability to take in all the fine points of a topic was nothing new, though. That was why she had always made a point of associating with educated people, people she trusted to grasp the important details of a matter, to make decisions—especially ones affecting her—based on their command of all the pertinent facts.

Elise appeared to be reading the spines of the law books again. Her head was cocked. She said something Irena could not hear.

"Tell me which compartment to put this in," Irena said, holding up one of the sheaves of paper.

"He took away my ration card," said Elise.

"What?"

Elise faced her mother but looked past her, at the closed door. "He called me 'half nun, half harlot,' and he took away my ration card. How am I to live?"

"What are you talking about? There are no ration cards. There haven't been ration cards since World War II. Stop this, now, you're frightening me."

"If my friends don't support me, I'll starve to death."

"Don't be ridiculous, Elise. You have me. We'll get another lawyer."

"After all I've been through, they're kicking me out of the Writer's Union. It was the Central Committee and that fiendish Shawano."

Elise must be talking about the Soviet Union, Irena thought. She was so upset that she was identifying with one of her poets. There was that Anna Akhmatova. Irena went over to the bookshelves and made Elise face her. "No, zlatíčko, that was the old Soviet Union. There is a brighter one today. Today things are looking up for the Russians and the Czechs both. You're just distressed from your situation. All these awful people going after your building, how could you *not* be upset? But we'll hire a good lawyer to protect you."

Someone knocked on the door. Irena and Elise ignored it.

"I have no means to support myself," Elise repeated. "They're throwing me out."

"We'll get it all fixed, Elise. They won't throw you out."

"Stalin despised me, now so does the Central Committee."

What should she do, Irena asked herself, the blood rushing to her ears. Should she slap Elise? Maybe she should call Wiley Mills. Or Miloslav. Oh, but she could no longer count on him. She had no idea what to do.

"Stop this! We have enough troubles with your building. You're not some dead poet, you're Elise Katrinka Blazek. You can overcome these visions of yours. You've done it before."

There came a louder knock and the receptionist walked in, a young woman in a tailored suit. "We're going to need this room in just five minutes," she said, her tone all business.

"Don't worry!" snapped Irena. "We'll be out of your way."

The receptionist did not leave. She stood inside the room, near the door, as Elise and Irena gathered the rest of the papers and placed them into the accordion file.

Elise was the first to stalk past. Irena followed her out the double glass doors of the firm's reception room and down the hall to the elevators—the gleaming, safe, automatic elevators.

Sitting with Elise on a bench in Madison Square Park on the second Monday in April, Irena tilted her head back and breathed in the fragrant air, savored its sweetness. As soon as she looked ahead again, though, her thoughts drifted back to Miloslav, and the mild breeze passing over her might just as well have been an arctic blast.

Over the past few weeks, Miloslav had left messages for her on Elise's answering machine. She had told Elise she needed to call him back, it was not right to ignore his calls, but Elise had flown into one of her rages. "Do you *still* not get it?! He's not concerned about you, Irena, he's only looking for what you know."

After the visit to Gordon Kruger, Elise had changed her mind about Miloslav's role in the scheme to take over her building. She now said he had been the one to engineer the entire thing. The addition of Nan and Norman Massie and the boys from Milstein's Flowers was merely what she called a gambit, Miloslav amusing himself.

Irena could not exactly say that she was close to Miloslav, not in the way she was to Elise, but he had been kind to her when Stepan died and again during her stay in San Francisco. If Irena did not appreciate all his character traits, if she sometimes thought he was a bit of a follower or didn't have the world's most exciting personality, that did not make him what Elise said he was—a con artist and a traitor to his family.

Last week when Elise had been out copying some building papers, Irena had called Milolav's house. She called when she knew he and Dawn would be at work, even though that meant leaving a message. To prevent herself from going on and on like an imbecile, she had written down what she would say and read from the paper. "Hello, Miloslav, it's Aunt Irena. I am fine. Elise is fine. You don't have to worry. I'll call you when I get home." Irena had felt herself flush when she hung up; she knew how unnatural she had sounded. But at least Miloslav would stop leaving messages and upsetting Elise.

"This is a nice park, zlatíčko. Lean back and smell the air. I smell hyacinth, don't you?"

Irena had forced this trip to the park; poor Elise had not left the building in days. Back at the apartment, one hour was the same as the next as Elise organized and reorganized her papers, as she studied the law books she'd had delivered to her. When she wasn't surrounded by papers, she was roaming the building. Except for Milstein's Flowers and Sara Mantel, the public relations tenant, the building was still empty. An osteopath had moved in, but he'd left after five months, his rent not paid up. Added to that, his careless movers had put gouges in the walls of the stairwell.

"How will you feel about visiting Milos in jail?" Elise asked now.

"Let's not think about anyone in jail," she answered. "Let's just try to enjoy the day." Irena's stomach had been queasy for days. She peeled more foil off the roll of Tums in her hand—two more left.

Elise shot up from the bench and swung around to face Irena. "You've spoken to him, haven't you?"

"Of course not. You didn't want me to, so I didn't." Irena put a Tums on her tongue.

"I *need* my building. You understand that, don't you, Irena? It's about security and freedom for the rest of my life. Not just mine, yours too."

"Zlatíčko, who would understand this better than I? You are a special girl, and you need security to thrive. I know this. When the building is all settled, you'll go back to your Russian. You'll get a job at a prestigious university. You'll get many assignments to translate books, and you will write your own. Russia is a different place now. Your field will be very popular, and people will know who you are."

Irena was not sure Elise had been listening. Her gaze was roaming, as it so often did. It came to rest on a small dog urinating against a tree trunk.

"Oh, go back to the Brodyachaya Sobaka," Elise said to the dog and then started in on her hyena laugh.

Irena waited it out. She was used to doing this. When Elise sat back down again, she complained, "You *know* I don't understand Russian."

"The Stray Dog, the café in St. Petersburg—his namesake."

"I don't know what you're talking about. Let's walk. Let's go see the hyacinth."

They started to walk inside the bounds of the park. After only a minute, Elise stopped and demanded, "What are we doing here?"

"We're walking, for heaven's sake. We came to see the hyacinth."

Elise frowned. "Everyone here *has* a place to live. They don't know. They can get out here on a sunny day and soak up all there is to soak up. I have to go back and fight for my building, get ready for the new lawyer."

"Not right now, zlatíčko. Not before we see the hyacinth and the tulip buds over there." Irena pointed to the new blooms several yards away.

"*Yes,* now. This is about survival. Do you want me back on disability? Do you want me working at McDonald's?"

"Don't be ridiculous. That won't happen."

McDonald's, reflected Irena, had paid for her daughter's building. Ray Kroc, the Bohemian who had succeeded spectacularly in America, had taken care of a fellow national without knowing it. The golden man with his golden arches would soon make them rich women. They would be able to buy whatever they wished. Irena could send money to her cousins Martin and Olina and to her old friends from the Gymnázium Ludka Pika.

There was a whimpering sound behind them. Irena turned around and saw the same dog from before. She shooed him away, but he didn't leave. Elise crouched down and scooped him up. He was dirty and didn't have enough hair. Irena was repelled.

"Elise! Put him down."

In Elise's arms, the dog was wagging his tail. Elise buried her face in his patchy coat, rubbed her nose along his side. This instant intimacy with an unfamiliar creature was repugnant to Irena. "Put him down! You don't know where he's been. He has no collar."

"Brodyachaya Sobaka," she told him. "Let's take you home. You need a home."

"This is not a good idea at all."

"It's still my building," claimed Elise. "Brodyachaya Sobaka is coming home with us."

"Who knows what diseases he has? And someone is probably looking for him."

"No one is looking for you, are they, Brodyachaya Sobaka? You're just a poor orphaned poochie."

The dog licked Elise's face. Elise had always loved dogs, but they had never gotten one. Stepan had been allergic, and so was Miloslav.

"You're going to be our good luck charm, aren't you? I'm going to save you, and you're going to save me. Quid pro quo. There is symmetry in the universe."

"Oh, my God," said Irena. "Something else to weigh us down."

"Brodyachaya Sobaka won't weigh us down. He's a sign. Don't you believe in omens?"

"He is not an omen."

"Yes, he is. He's just like the dog from the Stray Dog Café in St. Petersburg, where all the revolutionary poets read."

Irena knew the mangy animal would come home with them. She had never heard of the Stray Dog Café until this afternoon, and anyway she didn't believe in omens. "We don't need good luck charms, zlatíčko. We are right, so we will win. We just have to tell the truth."

Elise turned to Irena. She was red in the face. "The truth? These men are criminals. They *eat* people who tell the truth."

"You must not think that way. You must think only good thoughts."

"I'm finding a vet for Brodyachaya Sobaka. We'll see you later." Elise turned to go.

"No, zlatíčko, don't go without me!" Irena called after her. "The sun is hurting my eyes. Spring is making me heartsick." Once this was out, she looked around, as if to locate who had spoken such foolishness.

Elise sighed. "So come with us."

"Not to the vet. Let's go back to the building," Irena pleaded. "Put the dog down."

Elise tightened her hold on the dog. "We'll go back to the building afterwards. First we have to take care of our little good omen."

"Vets cost money," said Irena. "We have to save our money for the lawyer."

The overdue bill notices were mounting. Elise did not ignore them; she put them in categories, along with the previous notices: mortgage, taxes, utilities, garbage service, renovation. Every time Irena mentioned the bills, so many that they panicked her and muddled her thoughts, Elise had something different to say; when they won their claim against Miloslav and the others, she would pay back her creditors and give them an advance to boot; when her new tenants moved in, she would catch up. Once she had said that possession was nine-tenths of the law—her creditors couldn't do anything to her.

Irena didn't know what was right and what was wrong. Her stomach churned. She rummaged about her purse for the last of her Tums.

✦

Irena was making dinner for the two of them, and Elise had that terrible dog in the bathtub when Miloslav called again. The volume on the answering machine was turned up.

"Aunt Irena, I got your message. You don't sound like yourself. Call me back tonight."

Elise came running out of the bathroom. The soaked dog ran after her, shaking himself and getting water and suds on a pile of important papers. Elise came up next to Irena and looked into the pan of sausages she was frying. "I knew it," she said slowly, not in anger but—worse—in the tone of someone who had never in her life known a moment's love.

"Zlatíčko, I had to be polite. Only an uncivilized person would not have called back. But I purposely called when I knew no one was home. I said nothing on the machine. I only told him that we were fine."

"You have to leave," Elise said. "You have to go home tomorrow."

"For heaven's sake, Elise, you're just tired. You've been very upset today."

"In the morning. Brodyachaya Sobaka and I will solve our problems ourselves."

The dog was licking its wet haunches.

"This is ridiculous. We're talking about Milos, your cousin."

Elise was silent. She stood in the same spot, shaking her head.

Irena did her best to concentrate on the sausages. She transferred them from the pan to the waiting plates.

"If he had only wanted to know how you were, why would he call back once he found out?"

"*I* don't know, zlatíčko. Because he's a decent man." Irena spoke with little conviction. Why *had* Miloslav called back? She had made it clear she would be the one to call him.

"I don't care *what* you think anymore," Elise said. She returned to the bathroom and came back with a towel. She began to dry off the dog.

"Come eat," said Irena. "If there's sausage left over, maybe we can give a little to him."

"Brodyachaya Sobaka doesn't want any sausage," said Elise. "Neither of us is hungry."

How could Irena eat now? Every nerve was on edge. She felt nauseated. She thrust the hot sausages into the trash and walked past her daughter to her bed behind the screen. When she noticed Elise had filled the blue glass vase with white roses, she turned on her portable radio and broke into tears.

All through her sleepless night, Irena thought about Miloslav, about his remoteness as a child, about the time in college he had begun to open up but how he had closed down again when he found out his mother was too sick to meet him in Vienna. She remembered how on rainy days, when he couldn't play one of his sports, he used to sit cross-legged on his bed and sort and stack up his coins for hours. What if Elise were right, what if he cared only about getting rich? That on top of the jealousy she had talked about *could* drive him to hound Elise, to go after her building. Irena wished she had paid more attention to Miloslav when he was a child. If she now had no idea who he was, she had no one but herself to blame.

When she awoke in the morning, having slept no more than two hours, she heard Elise in those shoes of hers. She was getting ready to leave the apartment. Still in her nightgown, Irena followed her to the door.

"I was wrong, zlatíčko. I won't call him again, I promise."

Elise looked baffled. "We'll talk later," she said and left the apartment.

Irena returned to her bed. After all these hours, she was still nauseated. She no longer knew anything with certainty. Since coming to New York, she found herself unable to form hard-and-fast impressions. She tried to organize her thoughts, but more and more they went flying in different directions. It was up to Elise to educate her about the levels of complexity beneath the surface of people's affairs. Had Irena been naive for her whole life, accepting all her experiences at face value? She closed her eyes and sucked on a Tums until she felt it melt away—along with her unwanted consciousness and its endless stream of worries.

Irena and Elise finally had an appointment with a new lawyer. Adam Sawicki, an attorney in private practice in Queens, had agreed to see them for a free consultation. They would have to take the subway. It was a shame that Irena's back ached so much this morning, but nothing could be done about it. Maybe an aching back was what she got for not admitting she was too old to lug around heavy things. Yesterday she had helped Elise carry up to the apartment five stacks of design magazines that Distinctive Identity had left behind, a space heater from Two Front, and a footlocker someone had abandoned in the basement. Elise wanted the footlocker to store the pottery that had been delivered last Friday.

Nine cartons of Shawnee pottery had come from somewhere in the Ozarks. Elise was sure that many of the pieces were more valuable than the owner, a farmer's wife, had known. Her plan was to pay someone at the 26th Street flea market to sell them for her. Easy cash, Elise had assured her mother. Irena had no idea how her daughter had even found out about the pottery, but she helped her carry the cartons to the elevator at the back of the building and then drag them around the pile of glass bricks in Elise's apartment.

Once inside, Elise had removed many of the pieces, trying to match them with pictures in a collector's book. Now they were all over the floor, silly pieces that irritated Irena: an elf pushing a wheelbarrow, a horse-drawn fire truck planter, a smiling pig cookie jar. They mocked the seriousness of Irena and Elise's troubles.

Sitting up in bed, Irena massaged the small of her back. Forget the pain, she told herself, get up and face the day. For starters, the dog needed to be taken out. He was drilling his snout between her calves. Elise was up most of every night, so each morning Irena had to take this ugly creature out on his leash, stand around in whatever kind of weather until he was ready, then pick up his excrement with nothing but a little baggie. Every time she stooped to do this, she had to exert all her will not to gag. Afterward, she took the dog down to the basement where the trash cans were kept so she could dispose of his business. The routine would be an ordeal even if Irena were doing it for an animal she loved. For this dog she loathed, the routine was nothing but a punishment missing a crime.

The pottery pieces were everywhere. Irena stepped around them to go into the bathroom, the only finished part of Elise's apartment. A bathroom like out of a magazine, it must have cost thousands. The clock there said ten minutes past eight, late for Irena. She would dress quickly, take out the dog, return him, and then go out for coffee at the diner around the corner. She looked forward to this one half hour of peace.

Drying her face, Irena looked up when she heard a banging on the front door. She quickly flipped the bathroom lock closed. The pounding continued. The dog barked, there was a final bang, and then all was quiet. Irena didn't know what to do. She remained in the bathroom for five minutes; she timed it by the clock. When she emerged, she didn't dare go near the door. She crept over to her daughter's bed.

"Someone was here," she hissed, shaking Elise's shoulder.

"Uhhn, I'm sleeping."

"It's morning. Someone was at the door, banging."

Elise bolted up. "*Them*," she said, as if in triumph, and rushed to the door in her nightclothes—a tank top and thin cotton bottoms that looked like pantaloons.

"No! They might still be there," Irena warned.

Elise paused long enough to pull yesterday's pants over her pajama bottoms. She opened the door. Irena saw only the lower half of her daughter's body as she strained forward to survey the landing. In a moment she came back inside, holding an envelope that had been taped to the door. She opened it, read the first sheet contained there, and thrust it at Irena.

The letterhead read "Supreme Court, New York County." Underneath was typed "*RNJ Finance vs. Elise Blazek,*" and their respective
addresses. Once Irena saw this, she couldn't read on. The words meant
first one thing, then another. "How did they get up here? You can't just
enter a person's building."

"They can do whatever they want."

"What is it?"

"A summons."

"What are they going to do to us?"

Elise reclaimed the letter and read it aloud, so quickly her words fell
into one another:

" 'A lawsuit has been filed against you. You have twenty calendar days
after this summons is served to file a written response to the attached
complaint with the clerk of this court. A phone call will not protect you;
your written response, including the case number given above and the
names of the parties, must be filed if you want the court to hear your
side of the case. If you do not file your response on time, you may lose
the case, and your wages, money, and property may thereafter be taken
without further warning from the court. You may want to call an attorney right away. If you do not know an attorney, you may call an attorney
referral service or legal aid office.' "

When she was finished, Elise balled up first the letter and then the
remaining contents of the envelope and threw them, overhand, onto the
dish drainer next to the kitchen sink.

"What are you *doing*?"

"You think this is real? It's more intimidation from your nephew
and his gang. They think I'll just pack up and move out."

"But it says it's from RNJ Finance."

"It's not. It's forged. That's why it says a phone call won't protect me.
It's a trap. They want us to think we're about to be evicted."

Having spoken these words in a reasonable tone, Elise now went
over to the Shawnee pieces on the floor and lit into them with a barrage
of kicks. Ceramic fragments and shards flew everywhere.

Eyes protruding, whipping his head back and forth, the dog looked
for a place to hide, then ran into the bathroom. With almost the same
side-to-side motion of her head, Elise scoured the apartment. Irena

closed her eyes and waited. The next sound she heard was the pile of thick glass bricks tumbling to the floor. Above even the terrible clatter came Elise's howl of pain. When Irena opened her eyes, her daughter was hopping about, holding onto her right foot.

"Zlatíčko, you cannot hurt yourself! This you cannot do!"

Elise hopped into the bathroom. Looking in behind her, Irena saw the dog in the tub.

"Brodyachaya Sobaka, I'm sorry!" sobbed Elise, trying to gather up the frightened animal. She examined his paw pads to see if they were bleeding.

Everything had moved too quickly; Irena could not make sense of it. So much was going through her mind at once. She had to make an ice pack for Elise. She needed to make her try to wiggle her toes—those poor hammertoes, one might be broken. Maybe her whole foot was broken. Another flash of thought was shameful—that she would have to skip her morning coffee and the moment's peace it provided. These terrible rages Elise had; they would not help solve their problems. Irena needed to talk to her daughter, tell her to count to ten every time she felt an impulse to destroy something. Also drifting in the fog of Irena's thoughts was that the worst was coming to pass. She wasn't clear on what was a forgery and what was not, but she knew that in twenty days' time something would happen; some men—big men with bulging muscles—would put their belongings out in the street, like the Germans had done to the Jews in Bohemia right after Irena and her family had settled in America.

✦

At the hospital, Irena found out Elise had no medical insurance. The emergency room fee had to be put on Irena's credit card. It was high; there were X-rays, the orthopedist, the cast that went up to Elise's shin. During the time they were supposed to be meeting with the new lawyer, Adam Sawicki, an intern in the ER, was making a mold of Elise's foot and lower leg.

Once home, Elise discarded her crutches. Except to go to the bathroom, she stayed in bed that day and during the ones that followed, repeating the same complaints about Miloslav, Massie, and Milstein's boys. The M&Ms, she took to calling them—laughing unduly when she first thought of this. More than once she talked as if she were one of those poets she had translated when she was still at Alaster College.

Irena knew that the fight for the building could not go on unless she summoned up her energy and took control. Adam Sawicki was going out of town and wasn't able to see them until the end of June, which would be too late. Irena began to call one attorney after another. Before each call, she took a Tums and counted backward from twenty, until she got her courage up. Most of the time she couldn't get past the receptionists. If they did put the lawyers on the line, then Irena couldn't get the story straight. She told Elise she needed her help, that Elise should write down what needed to be said. Elise had waved her away. "Let the M&Ms come and get us," she said, daring them. "When all my friends on the block see our stuff out on the street, they'll save us. They'll band together and vanquish the M&Ms. You'll see."

"What friends on the block?" Irena had asked. She knew of none. She kept trying with the lawyers. After a while, though, she came to agree with Elise; what did lawyers care about a middle-aged scholar and an old lady immigrant who were slowly being whittled into oblivion? Irena could not believe it, but as Czechoslovakia was becoming the Czech Republic, a free and open society, her adopted country was degenerating into a heartless culture ruled by greed.

Irena gave up on the lawyers. She spent her days tending to Elise and writing lists of tasks she never managed to get through. In the evenings, she tried to get Elise to reminisce with her about their many shared adventures: all the concerts and art exhibits they had attended; the spring of 1961, when they had hatched chicks in an incubator built by Stepan; the time eight-year-old Elise had tried to get a patent on an invention that would enable people in comas to communicate with one another. These memories were sharp and steeped in a sense of life being lived; Irena found herself drawn to them night after night. Elise claimed to remember nothing.

Occasionally the phone rang, but they never answered it. Wiley Mills left several messages. When Elise heard her voice, she momentarily brightened, but still she did not pick up the phone. Wiley's last message, though, was of a different sort. She said she had gotten a call from Elise's cousin Milos. He was worried about Elise's mother and wanted her to get in touch with him.

The two of them stopped going out. Getting dressed, the dangerous elevator, navigating the crowded streets—it was all too much. They ordered in their meals, then ate the food still in its cartons. Joy Luck Szechwan and Ajanta Indian were the two restaurants they ordered from. After a few days, Irena found herself looking forward to dinnertime. Hadn't she cooked enough for a lifetime?

The dog was still a problem, though. He begged tirelessly throughout the meal. And three times a day, Irena had to take him down to 2R, where he did whatever business he had to do on the newspapers she had spread on the floor. Then the dog would sniff around the empty unit while Irena went down to the trash cans in the basement.

Irena thought it imperative that they find the dog another home. He needed fresh air, she told Elise, he needed to run. Every time Irena mentioned this, though, Elise called the dog over and threw his worn tennis ball across the apartment. The dog ran around the glass bricks, navigated the empty cartons Irena had yet to throw away and the broken pottery she had swept into a pile, then landed back on Elise's bed with the ball in his mouth, his tail wagging.

✦

Three times that morning Irena looked at the appointment time written down for Wednesday, June 6, on her calendar from Hanus Sedlak. Today was the 6th, and the appointment was for one o'clock. They had been talking about it for days. One of the lawyers Irena had tried weeks before had left a message. He had been away, he apologized, and asked Irena to call for an appointment.

Under the sway of a new optimism, Elise once again took charge. She had scheduled the appointment and every day since had spent time walking on her crutches through the empty units of the building, trying to build up her muscle strength. For the last two days, she had stopped her never-ending loop of accusations against the M&Ms and had gotten interested in the new attorney, Josh Birnbeck, who was freshly out of some law school in Queens and who had told Elise that her case sounded fascinating. Elise had taken to calling him Flash Gordon. Maybe she had forgotten that Flash Gordon had been a boyhood favorite of Miloslav's, Irena reflected. He had seen the movie over and over, collected the comics, and worn a wrist compass he showed to anyone in his vicinity. Nevertheless, here was Elise talking about Josh Birnbeck as Flash Gordon and speculating about the kind of lover he would be. Irena didn't like this kind of talk. She kept reminding Elise to keep these thoughts to herself and concentrate on the building.

Twenty minutes before they were due to leave, as Irena was dressing behind her folding screen and Elise was fitting the slit leg of her pants over her cast, the downstairs buzzer sounded. They ignored it. When it came again, the harsh ring more sustained, Irena heard Elise say "shit" and then walk on her crutches over to the window.

"Who is it?" Irena called from behind her screen.

"I can't see. Probably just the sanitation guy."

After Elise left the window, there was a brief silence, and then that awful Janis Joplin came blasting through two sets of speakers. Elise had lately been listening to the same album she had played continuously through the summer before she entered Princeton. Irena had not felt bad when the woman had died of an overdose. And now here she was again, her grating voice an assault. Elise was screeching along. Irena wanted to come out and shut off the stereo, but she was wearing only her bra and panties and had never been the type to parade around half-naked in front of her children.

"*Please,* zlatíčko!" she shouted.

In the next second, Janis Joplin and Elise's singing stopped.

"Oh, my God. God, *God, GOD!*" Elise said, the words coming out mangled, as if she were suffocating.

"Zlatíčko, what's wrong?!"

"It's all right, Elise. You gave me your key, remember?"

The voice sounded familiar.

"Elise! What's happening out there?"

"It's Wiley Mills, Mrs. Blazek!" called the woman. "Everything's fine."

Irena looked around her tiny quarters for her bathrobe. It wasn't there.

"Oh, my God," Elise repeated. Then came the sound of her cast thumping on the floor.

"You didn't answer the phone or the door, so what choice did you give me?" asked the woman who claimed to be Wiley Mills.

"Elise!" called Irena. "Who is it? What's going on?" Her daughter was in danger. Wasn't that why Irena had come to New York, to get Elise out of harm's way? Behind the folding screen, though, terror immobilized her. She would be a casualty of the kind of violence her father had so shrewdly seen approaching their homeland. It didn't matter what the country or continent, the soulless ambition that brought forth violence emerged sooner or later. In the weeks or years before it came, everyone sensed it lurking, even the people of this still young country. Now here it was, just beyond the partition, directly upon her as Irena had imagined her whole life. Standing next to her bed, she began to feel the pain that was about to sear through her.

"Come . . . here," she was somehow able to instruct Elise. "Come to Maminka."

"Everything's fine, Mrs. Blazek," the woman repeated. She both did and did not sound like Wiley Mills. "Do you want a few minutes to dress?"

"Come, zlatíčko!" Irena commanded, reaching deep for the wind that conveyed her words. "*Right now.*"

When Elise did not appear, Irena, wearing only her Maidenform bra and flesh-toned nylon panties, came out from behind the folding screen.

There stood Wiley Mills. Next to Wiley, ashen but for the dark pockets under his eyes, was her nephew Miloslav. He took a single step forward. Something crunched beneath his foot. The noise it made, although it caused Irena to shudder, was really no noise at all. It was a vibration that reached her ears by way of the blood somehow still coursing through her veins.

"Aunt Irena," he said, not much above a whisper. "How could this be?"

Chapter Fifteen

June 6–8, 1990

In a matter of seconds, Milos had lost all confidence in himself as a man of action. He had flown to New York with the expectation that he would find a situation of some kind; he'd predicted that his cousin's illness had gotten out of hand and his aunt was hard-pressed to manage it. Yet he was in no way prepared for what he saw when he and Wiley Mills entered Elise's apartment on the sixth floor of her building. Immediately, he had felt his knees buckle—a phenomenon he had associated only with cartoons—and he'd had to brace himself against the nearest wall.

Now, in the drugstore an hour later, shopping for the things he needed to take him through the week, he felt no more able to cope than he had standing in that disaster of a room, with Elise limping about, a cast on her leg, and his aunt Irena standing before him in her underwear, at least ten pounds thinner, some kind of rash blooming on her forearms.

In aisle four, Milos picked up a pack of razor blades and dropped it into his basket. In another aisle, he reached for two packs of Jockey briefs, a kind he disliked, but what did it matter? He knew he would need some other things, and he moved along, dropping items into his basket without examining them. Deodorant, shaving cream, shoelaces, two bags of trail mix, a toothbrush, travel-size toothpaste and shampoo, a miniature flashlight. He had already checked into a hotel just off Ninth Avenue, turning down Wiley Mills's invitation to stay with her family.

After Milos completed his purchases, he walked to his hotel. It was impossible to banish that apartment, really just a large room, from his mind. Or forget its smell, which had caused Wiley and him to look at each other even before she'd opened the apartment door, the smell of rotting perishables and who knew what else. Inside, Milos had seen no furniture but a bed, a room divider, a metal folding chair, and a battered old footlocker. Some kind of card table piled high with newspapers. There were scattered tools and construction materials, a box heaped with empty pet food cans, broken pottery, small towers of takeout cartons nesting one in the other, many pairs of those shoes his cousin wore, and a great profusion of books and papers. The dog that was living with them looked scruffy and anxious, like the dogs in the Booth cartoons Dawn sometimes showed him in the *New Yorker*.

Most impossible to get out of his mind was the terror that had showed on his aunt's face when she caught sight of him, and then her screaming. Even as the screaming continued, he and Wiley had conferred in the tiny kitchen area. They had decided that he should leave immediately. In the briefest possible exchange, they had agreed to talk again this evening.

Milos reached the hotel and went inside. The lobby could not have been drabber. It exuded a sense of defeat, the pointlessness of trying to stand out in a city full of unique statements. It reflected Milos's sense of despair.

Inside his room, Milos put his things away and went to call Dawn in San Francisco; she would still be in her office. He did not look forward to hearing her upbeat work voice. Still, he knew she wouldn't take long to accurately assess what was needed of her, to give it without reservation. She exhibited this emotional suppleness with her friends and still—after twelve years together—with Milos.

Milos removed his shoes, sat propped up in bed, and reached to put the phone on his lap. His idleness at the very moment Wiley was undoubtedly going through hell back at Elise's building made him feel awful. He had pictured himself flying into New York, handily appraising the situation and devising its remedy. He'd had no idea.

"It's me," he said when his wife answered.

Dawn excused herself to close her door. "So?" she asked, back on the phone.

Milos found himself unable to come up with the words.

"Honey?"

"It's worse than I'd expected," he managed.

"Why? How?"

"My aunt is a whole other person."

"What do you mean?"

"She's like Elise. And Elise is worse than I've ever seen her."

"*How?*" repeated Dawn.

Milos knew his wife thought he minimized problems, that she would be alarmed at his words. He got a hold of himself. "Wiley Mills and I are due to talk later. I had to leave Elise's apartment."

"Leave? Come on, exactly what happened?"

Milos described the events of the afternoon as best he could. When he got to the part about his aunt's emergence in her bra and underwear, her weight loss and the rash, Dawn blew out her breath.

"She's terrified of me," he said, his voice breaking.

"And Elise?"

"On top of everything else, she has a broken leg. Or maybe it's her foot. She hardly has any tenants left. And there's this mangy dog."

Twice during the conversation, Dawn excused herself to go to her door, but she stayed on with Milos for a good fifteen minutes, asking questions, making suggestions for tomorrow. At the end of the conversation, she said, "I can't imagine how awful this must be for you." Milos knew she was alluding to his mother, Katrina, to behavior he had seen many years before.

"I wish I could just come home," he heard himself say, veering dangerously close to baby talk.

"I know, honey," Dawn answered, "but you can't." Then Milos heard her call, "I'll be right there, Todd."

"Go," he said. "I'm going to stay up long enough to talk to Wiley, and then I'm going to sleep."

For Wiley's convenience, Milos had agreed to meet her in a cafeteria at Mt. Sinai, the hospital where she worked, at seven A.M. He had slept poorly. Judging by her appearance, so had she. Like Dawn, Wiley Mills was in the thick of balancing motherhood and her career, and she had the look of someone with whom you dare not waste a word, someone who by natural inclination was meant to both reflect and say more, but did not have that luxury. Nonetheless, Milos needed to speak with her, needed some context in which to understand what was happening to his family.

"Did you have *any* idea?" he asked.

"Yes and no," said Wiley. "With her history, the only constant is volatility. I've certainly seen her close to this bad."

"My aunt, I meant," clarified Milos.

"Oh, of course, I'm sorry. No. Since she's been here, I haven't seen much of either of them. You need to understand that I've managed my relationship with Elise by withdrawing when I've had to. It's the only way I can do it. Our friendship has always been a delicate dance."

Milos was grateful to Wiley; he imagined she had something to do with whatever level of functionality his cousin had been able to manage all these years. But he hadn't come to New York for Elise's sake.

"You've seen my aunt before this visit, though. What about the way she looks, this new thinness and the rash?"

"Both could be related to the situation, but she should get checked out. It could be nothing; lots of rashes are stress-related, but others are a symptom of something more serious, like diabetes or a suppressed immune system."

Milos nodded, remembering his aunt's elevated glucose from six months before. That her fainting episode and their visit to Queen of the Valley Hospital had been a mere six months ago was astounding. "And what if it *is* diabetes? How long could she go untreated?"

"If it were insulin-dependent, you'd know it," Wiley assured him.

How would he know it, Milos wanted to ask. Neither of them had been aware of what was going on in that single room at the top of Elise's building. How would they know anything?

Last night when they had spoken on the phone, Wiley had told Milos what had happened after he'd left. She had been unable to get either his aunt or Elise to calm down, so she had called a friend from Mt. Sinai, a nurse named Rhonda who worked on the inpatient psychiatric unit. When Rhonda got there, she managed to inject Elise with Haldol. (Not strictly legal, Wiley had confessed, but she knew EMS was hobbled by the books in these situations, knew not to bother calling them.) As Elise was quieting down, they were able to talk Irena into taking ten milligrams of Valium. By the time they had left, Elise and Irena were both asleep.

The cafeteria's strong coffee was kicking in, stirring Milos to action, never mind that none was to be had. He looked at his watch. "They must be getting up by now."

"I need to check in upstairs, but I've cancelled the rest of my day," Wiley said. "They'll probably still be groggy when I get over there. It's a long shot, but I'm going to try to convince them to get admitted to Mt. Sinai. Let's try that first and take it from there."

"My aunt has to get out of that building, back to her normal environment."

Wiley looked at him, her expression unreadable. "She's not going to go voluntarily, and she's not going to let you near her. Apparently she thinks you've masterminded a plot against Elise."

"Oh, come on."

"The very best thing you can do in the next forty-eight hours is nothing. It won't be easy, I realize, but you have to take her delusion seriously. She certainly does."

"Nothing? I can't do nothing."

"Nothing is everything in this instance," said Wiley. "Trust me."

Milos had met Wiley a long time ago, when he had visited Princeton as a boy with Irena and Stepan. He didn't remember much about her. Now she seemed awfully sure of herself, but how could he know what she had been through with his cousin over the years?

"I have to do *something*," Milos insisted. "I didn't come all the way out here to sit on my hands."

Wiley took an address book out of her handbag, copied down a number, and handed him the paper. "This is Nan Massie, Elise's last psychiatrist. She was treating her up until last January. You might want to see if she has a free hour."

Milos looked at the name. He didn't put much faith in psychiatrists, but he couldn't think of a better way to find out how his aunt could have strayed so far from her root self—and how to bring her back.

Above Dr. Massie's head was a painting in blues, browns, and white dots. It showed two figures, drifting, their arms reaching to the sky. The figures looked to Milos like a cross between gingerbread men and some sort of tribal icon. A title, "Biric Dreaming," was mounted beneath the picture, as if it were a museum piece. The figures appeared to be carefree, even rapturous. Milos kept his attention on them as he told Dr. Massie why he was there and what had happened yesterday.

"How long has your aunt been in New York?" Dr. Massie asked.

"About two and a half months."

"And when did you start to have trouble reaching her by phone?"

"Not so far along into the visit. Since my uncle died, we'd been talking once or twice a week. My wife and I tried to have her live with us in San Francisco, but she seemed restless there."

"What was she like when you talked to her at the beginning of her visit here?"

Milos shook his head. Had he noticed a difference in his aunt? Their conversations were generally brief, of a checking-in nature. Irena didn't confide in him.

"Look," Milos said, forcing his attention off the painting, "something is horribly wrong here. You know better than I that Elise has terrible problems. Ever since college—it started the summer before, actually— she's had major problems. That she's gotten this far, in terms of functioning, is a miracle. But Elise is one thing, and my aunt is something else. My aunt is a sane woman. She doesn't have a mood disorder. If anything, she doesn't have *enough* moods." Milos regretted this immediately; he was sure it carried a meaning he didn't intend.

Dr. Massie looked so concerned that Irena and Elise might have been members of her own family. "Tell me more about your aunt," she said. "Why do you think she's stayed here for this length of time?"

Milos shrugged. "Since my uncle died, she's been floundering a little. But that can't be so uncommon."

"What was that relationship like? What kind of man was your uncle?"

Enough, thought Milos. This was what he hated about therapists. They could never reach back far enough. He had once read an article about one who treated people for the psychological trauma they had endured while squeezing through the birth canal.

"Look, I don't mean to be rude here, but Elise's place is a hellhole. My aunt looked . . . it was not to be believed. She's lost ten or fifteen pounds, she's got this rash—she came out in dirty underwear for Christ's sake! There's no time to sit here and analyze my dead uncle."

"Fair enough," said Dr. Massie.

"What is this? What do you call this, that's happened to my aunt? What's the treatment for it?"

"Apparently your aunt has adopted some of Elise's constructed realities. It doesn't occur often, but I did see one case, during my residency."

This told Milos nothing. "What is it?"

"It's called induced delusion disorder. You understand this is a provisional judgment only; I don't have all the facts. But there are ways in which the profile fits substantially. Your aunt is particularly vulnerable, probably lonely, living at loose ends, and we know that Elise has a special talent for vivifying her imaginings. It would not be hard for her to take over a person who might already be in thrall to her."

"But my aunt is essentially a sound person."

"I don't doubt that."

"There's nothing *to* doubt." Probably Dr. Massie was making a mental note of how hostile Milos was, but he didn't care. He hadn't flown across the country to impress her. Yet right now she was his only resource. "What if she comes in to talk to you? I couldn't bring her—she may not be ready for that—but she seems to have at least some degree of trust in Elise's friend Wiley Mills. *She* could bring her in."

This was a spontaneous idea, but it seemed to Milos like a tenable plan B if his aunt and Elise did not agree to admit themselves to Mt. Sinai, which he doubted they would.

Dr. Massie edged up in her seat again. "I don't know if you're aware that Elise has implicated me in her paranoid delusion. It's not at all unusual for paranoid patients to put complete and exclusive trust in someone and then suddenly turn on that person. But because that's what has happened here, and for other reasons, I obviously can't play a role in treating your aunt."

Milos experienced a moment of breathlessness, as he tended to on the rare occasions he felt himself running out of options.

"So then what *do* you suggest?"

"At a certain point, you'll be able to take your aunt to someone. I can give you several referrals, all practitioners with extensive experience working with people with delusional disorders, if not this particular one. But patience is critical. If you force the issue, she'll use it as evidence that the perceived plot against her and Elise is advancing. Do you understand?"

Milos resented being spoken to as if he might not grasp such a plain point. And Dr. Massie's manner, the way she kept switching the side on which she crossed her long legs, her obvious infatuation with her appearance, was beginning to irritate him.

"That may be true, but I can't just put my life on hold. If she's not ready for treatment, then what will *cause* her to be ready? I can't just sit around and wait for the ideal conditions to line up."

"My suggestion in the short term would be that you use your only asset to the greatest advantage, and that would seem to be Wiley Mills. I know Wiley. Her husband Michael referred Elise to me. She's a very responsible person, and it's probably no coincidence that Elise has not cut her off."

"Yes, but she has her own family and, as far as I know, a full-time medical practice. How much can I reasonably expect her to do?"

"We'll just have to see," said Dr. Massie. "Dr. Mills and I can talk if you'd like. I'd suggest ways in which she might regain Elise's trust to the point she can convince her to go back on her medications. This is paramount. As you say, Elise is driving this delusion about you and her building, and the drugs will go a long way to make this construct less appealing. And I can almost guarantee you that your aunt won't perpetuate the delusion on her own."

In Milos's view, this was the first useful thing Dr. Massie had said.

"The best treatment for her now, for both of them, would be in an inpatient setting," continued Dr. Massie, "but we have to assume for the present that's not going to happen."

"The best treatment for Elise, maybe, but not my aunt. Once I get her home—"

"You have to realize," Nan Massie interrupted, "that it took years for your aunt to reach this level of susceptibility to Elise and also that she has character traits that allowed it to happen. This is not a criticism—what happened took a preponderance of qualifying circumstances—but this situation, it's a folie à deux really, cannot be instantaneously resolved."

Folie à deux, Milos repeated to himself. He knew close to no French, but it sounded like "pas de deux." Last month he and Dawn had taken Kristy to a ballet for children. Afterward the director had explained that in a pas de deux, two dancers could achieve greater heights than one. Quite the opposite of what was happening between his cousin and his aunt.

"There's someone else in my family . . ."

"Yes?"

"Nothing. It's not important."

Dr. Massie waited—that shrink silence that said, "I know more about you than you know about yourself." Oh to hell with it, thought Milos, he would never see her again.

"My mother. Elise is related to me through both sides of my family, because my mother was also my father's cousin. My mother had . . . something wrong with her. That's why I went to live with my aunt and uncle. I'm only bringing this up because I . . ." Milos gave himself a moment. "I have three children."

Dr. Massie shook her head. "I've never met your mother so it wouldn't be appropriate for me to comment. There are genetic predispositions to some types of psychotic and mood disorders, but—"

Milos put up his hand to stop her. "It's all right," he said.

✦

During their phone conversation that evening, Wiley said that—just as they had both expected—Elise and Irena had refused to be admitted to Mt. Sinai Hospital. They had simply ignored Wiley's attempts to persuade them. In the end, Irena had retreated behind her screen, and Wiley had talked Elise into helping her clean the apartment.

In the background, Milos heard a little girl start to cry, and Wiley said she had to get off. First, though, she told Milos what she had found in Elise's kitchen. Balled up like wastepaper on the dish drainer was a summons from the New York County Supreme Court. Elise's mortgage company was starting eviction proceedings. When she'd shown Elise the summons, Elise had laughed. "You actually believe that?" she had accused.

"Oh, Christ," Milos had groaned. "What's the date on the summons?"

"May twenty-first. I have it here."

"I need to see it right away. I'm going to call you back with the hotel's fax number."

When he saw the eviction notice, Milos had to concede there was little he could do. Sitting up in bed and using the hotel's laminated checkout instructions for a writing surface, he composed a response to the clerk of the court, attempting to defer Elise's hearing. How could he represent her when she wouldn't get within fifty yards of him? And even if he could talk to her, he strongly doubted she had any evidence to support her case. To come up with a defense, Milos would have to resort to some improbable story. After all, there were only two tenants left in her building of ten units, the florist downstairs and someone on the second floor.

With the new baby, Milos didn't have the free cash to pay Elise's arrears. A postponement was the best he could do. He sealed the envelope and took it down to the lobby, where he arranged for a messenger to pick it up first thing in the morning. Back in his room, he didn't fall asleep until sometime after two A.M.

In his dream, Milos was with his mother on the shore of Lake Michigan. It was very hot, and they were in the water, although Milos didn't know how to swim. Farther out from where he dog-paddled in place, Milos spied Katrina's head disappearing under water, then emerging, each time closer. Finally she called him to come join her, but he could do no more than tread water, panicked by the effort it took to stay above the surface.

Milos had been having dreams about his mother ever since the Saturday morning five months ago when his uncle Stepan's cousin Pavel had called from Kutná Hora to tell Milos that Katrina was dead. She had died in the institution where she'd spent so much of her adult life. Pavel had pronounced Katrina's life a tragedy. To Milos, Katrina was little more than a stranger whose story he had followed. He found it sad that she hadn't stayed in the United States, where with modern care she might have had a better life. But he had been a young boy when she'd left, and later the Party would have made it impossible to bring her back to America. Milos didn't blame himself. After his father had been killed in 1968—on his way to buy a cigar—he had watched his mother immerse herself in a hidden place, a vaporous and scrambled inner existence that obliged her to look at him with glazed eyes, if at all. Then his grand-mother, a woman Milos had never met before, came to take his mother across the ocean.

Powerless as a boy to help his mother, and not entirely willing as an adult, Milos woke from this latest dream in a panic. He swore to himself that he would not run out on his aunt Irena, no matter how dependent she might now become.

Milos and Wiley were due to meet shortly after noon, but what was he supposed to do until then? Unable to go back to sleep, he dressed and went to walk about the neighborhood. The early-morning sunlight cast geometric shapes in subtle colors, pale yellow and ivory, onto the facades of warehouses and abandoned bars. It shone on a new glass-fronted office building. Walking along the all-but-empty streets, Milos understood how people might be seduced by this city—a place where long-standing and brand-new buildings managed to strike a surprising accord.

Just after seven, he began to walk uptown along Eighth Avenue. The city was waking to a clear day: a succession of store owners lifted security gates that squeaked and clattered; two supers chatted as they hosed the sidewalk in front of their buildings; a truck driver stacked crates of soda onto a handcart; joggers zigzagged around early-rising pedestrians.

By the time he reached the flower district and breathed in the scent of enriched greenhouse soil, Milos had regained a hopeful feeling. He pressed Elise's buzzer and waited. No one answered. Milos buzzed again, then went to the corner to call. Probably he should have tried this first. Right as he stepped into the phone booth, though, he spotted his aunt and Elise—still in her cast but now using only a cane—emerging from the Wendy's across the street. Good—they had gotten themselves out; this was an encouraging sign. He stepped up to the curb, smiled warmly, made sure to keep smiling, and waited for them to cross the street. When Elise caught sight of him, though, she grabbed Irena's arm and came to a halt in the middle of the crosswalk. She steadied herself by bearing down on the hood of a taxi. The driver tooted his horn. Elise jumped, then banged on the cab with her fist.

Even from across the street, Milos could see in his aunt's expression an odd clash of alarm and resignation.

"You slime-bucket!" yelled Elise. "You'll never get my building! Not a fucking chance in hell!"

Milos stepped forward, but stopped when the traffic light turned green. The taxi driver revved his engine. He blared his horn. Elise managed a 180-degree turn. Hobbling with Irena in tow, she disappeared back inside Wendy's.

Waiting at the curb for the WALK signal, Milos tried to gather himself. He could follow Elise into Wendy's, where there was no telling what kind of scene she would throw, or he could let her think she had won this skirmish. Taking this approach, he could bide his time until the right strategy occurred to him. He turned and left the block.

Now he had no destination. He continued to walk in the direction of the traffic, stopping a passerby to ask the direction of Central Park. The woman pointed uptown, where he was headed, and told him he had a full thirty blocks to go. He thanked her and kept walking. The sights and sounds of the city no longer absorbed him. Thoughts rushed forth ungoverned, overlapping. If there was a theme, it was how destructive he had managed to be since his arrival. He dreaded meeting Wiley later today; in one way or another she would have to pay for his attempt to see his aunt, to talk to his cousin.

Milos berated himself for failing to predict a realistic outcome for his mission. Yet who could predict anything in this situation? He saw now that Irena had become part of Elise—not the long-ago Elise of great promise but the volatile one, the Elise of embittered rages, of delusions and desperate lies—a woman who thought of herself as prey in a crowded jungle. She had turned Milos into the ultimate predator. Amazingly, his aunt had stood beside her as she did this.

Walking along, Milos reflected that he was up against a wayward gene so powerful it might surface in bodies generations away. He thought of each of his children in turn, particularly of Samantha, so restless she often seemed hunted. He picked up his pace, weaving around those who impeded his progress.

Stopping finally at the Central Park Zoo, he wandered among the exhibits of various animals. His aunt Irena's mind was sound, he reminded himself. She had raised two children, propped up a husband often lost to introspection, worked in the outside world. She had belonged to a book club, and as far as he knew was still in a political discussion group.

She had maintained loyal friends, Berta and Magda Kriz, two women who had done well since coming to America, two exemplary Czech-Americans.

Standing in front of a row of cages, looking on absently as a zebra emptied his bladder—a seemingly endless affair—Milos arrived at a strategy. Whatever its worth, it was his single plan; he had no backup.

Chapter Sixteen

June 9, 1990

Berta's butterflies started in the cab heading to Milos Blazek's hotel near Ninth Avenue. It was an apt idiom, a fluttering of diaphanous wings in one's stomach. Before this morning, she had used the term to describe *other* people's nervousness and fear—Irena's first granddaughter's fear of kindergarten, the jitters of Magda's young students before they performed a scene from Molière in front of an audience. She identified their butterflies to show them that a term existed for what they were feeling; they could console themselves that many others had felt the same way. Now Berta had to console herself for her own butterflies, and she was doing a poor job of it.

To distract herself while the cab waited its turn to enter the Midtown Tunnel, Berta reflected back to when she and Magda had first met Irena. It was the beginning of January, just after New Year's in 1959. She remembered this because one of Berta and Magda's New Year's resolutions had been that they would finally sew new curtains for all the rooms in their semidetached home. They had gone together to Kopecky's Fabric Shop in downtown Laflin to pick out material. After they had made their selections, they'd gotten into a conversation about three-player Mariáš with the clerk, a woman about their age. Both sets of their parents, it turned out, had played the card game back in Bohemia. The very next week Irena had invited Berta and Magda over to her house. After that, they'd had a standing Saturday game until Berta and Magda had each moved to Chicago.

Those were the days when Berta was not as conscious of her appearance; every week the three of them had indulged in homemade pastries. By the end of the sixties, they had switched to those awful boxed mixes. Berta recalled how impressed Irena had been that Elise's first roommate at Princeton was connected to the Pillsbury fortune. She had made a point of bringing up the girl—Debbie Curtis, was her name—every time she served something made from a Pillsbury mix. When they were alone, Berta and Magda used to make fun of the bragging that went on about that child, her 147 IQ as assessed by the Stanford-Binet test, her inquisitiveness, her ability to sustain concentration, her knack for foreign languages, on and on. As irritating as the sisters found this boastfulness, they would never dream of saying as much to Irena. They had nothing against Elise, and they well realized that without a challenging job and with a perennially distracted husband, Irena needed a consuming hope around which to fashion her existence. From time to time, especially in recent years, Berta had found herself feeling sorry for her friend, and that sorrow had in turn made her feel disloyal.

When the cab drew to a stop in front of the nondescript hotel where Milos was staying, Berta's butterflies quickened to the point of making her almost physically ill.

Once Berta had checked in and gone up to her room, she tried to gather herself together. Seated on the edge of the bed closest the bathroom, she looked around her. Too much mauve. The wallpaper had a clear vinyl finish. Who knew what the poor women in housekeeping had to wipe off its surface. There were few of the amenities Berta was used to when she traveled for the *Tribune*—no clothes iron, hair dryer, or coffee machine. Just twin beds, a dresser, a luggage stand, a closet with five hangers affixed to their pole, and a television set that had to be twenty years old. Berta supposed that Milos was in little mood to think about his surroundings. Abruptly, she slapped the dresser top, putting herself on notice. You're here for a reason, she thought, and quickly stood up.

Less than ten minutes later, Milos was at her door. Berta had not seen him since he'd moved to California. Now he had three little ones, and all traces of the exuberant boy had left his face. Young as he still was, his hair was beginning to recede from his temples. He tried to smile, but the effort only showed his tension. He stepped forward to give her an awkward kiss, then sat down on the bed opposite hers. "So," he said.

Berta looked at her watch. "Eleven fifteen already. Where are they now?"

"At the building, I'm sure. They go out as little as possible."

"And what about the old college friend?"

Even though Berta had just announced the time, Milos glanced at his own watch. "She's taken off several days from work for this. If she's not there already, she's probably on her way."

"Good."

"I haven't told you how grateful I am," Milos said.

"Please, I've known your aunt for over thirty years."

"Still, you couldn't have expected this. It's quite a situation."

Who could deny that? Berta nodded.

"Aunt Irena has always been close to you and Magda. If this doesn't work . . ."

"We have no reason to think it won't," Berta said, although she was overwhelmed with doubt. "What will you be doing while I'm over there?"

Milos's shoulders sagged; he caved in a bit at the stomach. "I'll have to stay here. Can we arrange a time for you to call?"

"Of course. Let's say three? But then still, it might not be possible. There are so many unknowns."

Milos seemed to consider this. "Yes, but I think that once my aunt sees you, you'll get a pretty quick idea of the direction it's headed in." He handed her the set of spare keys to Elise's building that he had gotten from Wiley. "Remember," he said, "try calling and then ringing the buzzer first."

Before Berta had left Chicago, Milos had told her that she might have to use these keys to get in. That was when the gravity of the situation had truly struck. When she had called Magda, laid up with the flu, the keys were the first thing she'd brought up. "I might have to actually break *in* on them," she had told her sister.

After a coughing spell, Magda had given Berta her advice. "Bring kolaces," she had said. "Stop on your way."

(*223*)

Berta knew that it was to avoid just this kind of earnest opacity that Milos had called Berta instead of Magda. Still, the bakery was on her way to the airport.

A half hour after seeing Milos, Berta found herself struggling to enclose her body, her purse, and the box from Zelenka's Bakery into a foul-smelling phone booth at the end of Elise's block. She dialed Elise's number and got her answering machine. The outgoing message might have been recorded by the world's most stable person. It was both direct and hearty. Berta's pulse raced as she came that much closer to having to use the key Milos had given her. Right as she was about to hang up, a woman's voice, clearly not Elise's, interrupted the message.

"You must be Wiley!" Berta exclaimed, relieved. "This is Berta Kriz."

"Where are you?"

Berta told her.

"I'll be right down," Wiley said and hung up.

Berta stepped out of the phone booth. Someone, poor soul, was waiting to use it. He would be irritated first by the smell, then by Berta loitering about, but it couldn't be helped.

In a couple of minutes, a blond woman wearing an oversized denim shirt approached her, peering closely. They shook hands, looked at each other solemnly, and—without either of them betraying the slightest change in mood—began to laugh. Not an ironic chuckle, but full-throated laughter. Berta was shocked at herself. Yet over what stranger circumstances could any two people meet? For Berta's part, the burden of her accountability was almost too much to bear. She wondered if Wiley felt the same.

"I told them I was running down to give something to my husband," said Wiley, the first to recover. "Are you ready? Did Milos tell you what to expect?"

"It sounds like I can expect precious little at this point."

"That pretty much says it. We're busy cleaning up the apartment. At least I've put them to work, even if Elise is doing it just to please me. We'll just have to see."

As a news and feature writer for the *Chicago Tribune,* Berta had been in more than her share of oddball situations. Just last year she had interviewed the son of a man whose two-room apartment was floor-to-ceiling newspapers through which he'd carved navigation tunnels. His building superintendent had discovered him dead in the tunnel leading to the bathroom. (After that story ran, everyone in the *Tribune*'s metro section had cleared their cubicles of excess paper.) But Berta was not on assignment for the *Tribune,* and despite the juvenile behavior that had just come over her and Wiley Mills, this was not a story she would ever make light of.

On her way up to Elise's apartment in the rickety old elevator, Berta felt her dread mounting. The most familiar of her friends, the little-changing Irena Blazek, had become someone else. Berta had no idea how to approach her.

Wiley pushed the door open before Berta could gather herself. There to the right of the elevator was Irena, sitting on a folding chair and rummaging through a box of pottery. Shawnee, Berta recognized, from the 1950s. An unwholesome-looking little dog came running up, barked twice, then sniffed at Berta's ankles before she was fully out of the elevator.

"Look, dear," Berta said to Irena, as if she had just seen her ten minutes before, "kolaces from Zelenka's." She extended the box for Irena to see. A tiny gust of wind escaped her throat, leaving a vacuum.

Irena looked up. She put a hand to her unwashed hair. A cream pitcher in the shape of a husky sailor slipped in her other hand, but she managed to save it from falling.

An accelerated pulse ticked in Berta's neck, mesmerizing her during the passing moments when no one knew what to do next. Finally Irena said, "My eyes are playing tricks."

"Where did *she* come from?" Elise demanded of Wiley. Berta heard only her voice; she didn't want to look around for her. "Who told her to come?"

"I did," Wiley lied.

Irena set down the pitcher and stood up. She looked down at what she was wearing, a stained cardigan and baggy jeans. Irena never wore jeans. Irena owned an indigo fox coat.

"Aren't you going to take it?" asked Berta, still holding out the box. "I had him put in a few apricots, but mostly they're poppy seed, your favorite."

Elise came forward to stand in the ray of sunlight at Berta's feet. "Get out," she commanded. "Get out of my building."

"Elise, it's me," said Berta. "I've known you since you were eight years old."

"We know who sent you. And how long you've known *him*."

"Elise, your mother needs something of her life back."

This came from Wiley. It startled Berta in its simplicity, yet she understood; sometimes the more layered a situation, the greater the need to reduce it to its starkest elements.

"This is *Elise's* building," Irena reminded Berta, rallying all fragments of an authority she never possessed.

"Of course it is," said Berta. "And it's an impressive accomplishment."

Irena blushed, powerless to suppress the expression of her pride.

"She's manipulating you," Elise warned. Then she turned to Wiley. "I told you—get her out of here."

Berta worked the string off the bakery box and put it in the pocket of her cotton blazer.

Elise lunged forward, whether for the box or for her, Berta couldn't tell, but Wiley came between them. "Stop it!" she commanded Elise.

"It's all right," said Berta. Then, to Elise, "I haven't come here to hurt you in any way, dear. I know you can't believe me, but I'm saying it anyway." She opened the box from Zelenka's. "Let's all have one."

"Zelenka's in East Chicago?" Irena asked.

"Of course." Berta attempted a smile. "There's another one?"

"Fuck your kolaces!" shouted Elise. "Get out of my building!" Dragging her cast, Elise made her way to the front door and a stainless-steel wall panel with many buttons. "See this one?" she asked, pointing to the largest button on the panel. "I press it once, and five cop cars pull up front."

"Come with me to Mt. Sinai," Wiley pleaded. "They'll calibrate your medication, and you'll be able to function again. The world will settle down for you. I'll visit you every day until they get it right. You've recovered before, Elise, and you can again."

"*You* get calibrated!"

Berta had never seen Elise like this. Years of Irena's evasiveness had shrouded the depth of her daughter's troubles. The Kriz sisters well knew that something was wrong; they even knew that from the Northwestern years on, Irena had from time to time lied about Elise's endeavors, but standing witness to the raw effects of her disease cast the misfortune into a fully dimensional tragedy—and into a netherworld that Berta had to restrain herself from fleeing.

"Why don't we all have one?" she repeated, never in her life less hungry. She opened the box and showed the kolaces to Irena.

Irena leaned forward to peer inside.

"They haven't changed their recipe in all these years," Berta said, "and they never will."

"But yours and Magda's . . . no one makes . . . I remember when I first tasted . . ." Irena glanced at Elise, standing behind Berta, then stopped speaking.

Berta closed her eyes to silently thank her sister for telling her to stop at Zelenka's. She needed to listen to Magda more often.

"Let them at least have a visit," implored Wiley of Elise. "You and I will continue working, and then she'll leave. All right, Berta?"

"Yes, of course. We'll have our kolaces, and then I'll leave."

"Let's go clean the windows in 2F," Wiley said to Elise.

Elise laughed. Berta had rarely heard such a derisive tone, nearly maniacal. "You think I'm dense? I'm not setting one foot out of here."

"Dense?" said Irena. "You're highly intelligent, Elise, you must never forget this. Your IQ is 147—that's in the genius range. You have accomplished many fine things."

Low genius, thought Berta, merely to give herself a moment's respite.

"We'll clean in here, then," said Wiley quickly. "There's still plenty to do. Let's keep going with putting the kitchen in order."

Berta turned to look. This was what passed for a kitchen in New York City, she reminded herself. "Are there any dessert plates?"

Wiley stepped forward and took two paper plates from a dusty cellophane pack in the cupboard. "I'm afraid these will have to do."

"I'm leaving the box here for when you two need a break," Berta said, as if everything about today's visit was ordinary. She put one poppy-seed kolace on a plate for Irena and took an apricot one for herself. Then, without waiting to be invited, she took the plates and walked to the screen behind which Milos said Irena had been living.

Sitting side-by-side on the unmade bed, Berta and Irena ate in silence, except for the appreciative, even greedy sounds Irena made. Irena had lost a good deal of weight; Berta was glad to see her eat.

"They got a new cat at Zelenka's," Berta remarked. "She seems young, they must have gotten her as a kitten. To replace Máslo, remember when she died last fall? You said it was from obesity."

"I know he sent you," Irena said. "Maybe it was not your fault. Maybe you didn't know what you were getting into. The horrible tangled nest of lies. You knew Miloslav as a boy. Could you tell he was going to grow up to be a con artist? I did my best, Berta. Don't you remember how I always did my best with him?"

Irena's hand fidgeted in her lap, and Berta covered it with her own. Irena looked down, puzzled, then slipped her hand out from under Berta's and reached over to her nightstand for her roll of Tums.

"He was here, you know," Irena continued. "That's how bold he's become. He came here to throw his cousin onto the street and me along with her. But he's gone now. Elise made it clear he should go."

Berta had resolved to steer as far from the delusion as she could. She had heard the point of view that you were supposed to play along with a delusion, but her time in New York was limited. "Was I right?" she asked. "Zelenka's kolaces never change. Death, taxes, and Zelenka's kolaces."

"It was his envy. The boy is supposed to have the superior intellect, isn't that right? But it didn't turn out that way."

"When was the last time you saw Kristy and Samantha?" asked Berta, trying to keep her tone conversational. "You must miss them. And you haven't seen the new baby yet, have you?"

"They're *his*," Irena answered.

"I remember Kristy at your sixtieth birthday party, with those pigs in sleeping bags of hers. Do you remember that?" Berta smiled.

There was a clatter from the front of the apartment, some words spoken in Russian, a bit of mirthless laughter, a curse word in English.

Finished with her kolace, Irena put the paper plate on the floor and nudged it with her heel, half concealing it under the cot, where Berta had spied other dirty plates. Best to ignore this, she thought, hoping her face didn't show her dismay. She had managed so far not to stare, to ignore the distracting rash on Irena's arms as well as her clothes—her mismatched socks, her stained and pilly cardigan that could have come from a Salvation Army bin. Likewise, she had registered without a sign

Irena's uncorseted breasts drooping unevenly in the cardigan, the gray skullcap of undyed hair, her cracked lips.

"She was a cute little girl," said Irena. Then she sighed. "But she's changed."

"They all change at a younger age these days. Already at the preteen years they're changing. Magda sees it all the time in her students. Insolent and indolent both, she likes to say."

"Who needs it?" asked Irena.

"But Kristy is your family, and at the core she's still a child," said Berta. "You have all sorts of contributions to make to your grandchildren's lives."

"Her father is trying to destroy us. You don't know the half of it. Not even the tip of the iceberg."

There was little choice, decided Berta, but to change the subject again, to say anything that shot through her thoughts; who knew what combination of images in Irena's mind might bring back a hint of longing for a well-reasoned existence? "Guess who's joining the Chicago Symphony?" she asked.

Irena peeled down the Tums wrapper and popped out a lozenge. She put it in her mouth and stared at the inside of the folding screen.

"Petr. They offered him a permanent post, and he's finally sick of traveling. Hallelujah. He'll be fifty-three next month."

"Everyone but my daughter has a stable life."

Berta repositioned herself on the cot, scooting backward so she could lean against the side wall. "He'll get comp tickets for every performance. You've always loved the symphony, Irena. Remember the Young People's Concerts you used to take Elise to at Orchestra Hall? Once or twice Magda and I went with you."

From her new position, Berta had a view of Irena's face in three-quarter profile. She saw her head drop and then the loose skin around her jaws quiver. She saw a high flush creep from Irena's neck to her hairline, and she sat by helplessly as Irena's upper body was seized by a silent rumble, and her face contorted from the effort of withholding the expression of her grief, perhaps the only show of extremity that was not permitted in this room. Berta leaned forward to touch her, then thought better of it. She wanted Irena to feel her rooted beside her, to feel the simple permission one body could grant another. After a while, Irena lifted her head. "My radiant little girl," she said.

"She has an illness," Berta said as quietly as she could. "She's done a remarkable job of fighting it. Soon she'll be able to continue fighting."

Irena sat there, not making a move. The two of them heard Elise's curses coming from the kitchen, along with Wiley's voice, alternately sharp and soothing. Irena slid back alongside Berta. Their feet were suspended in the air, like the feet of small children on big chairs. Irena turned to Berta. There was the slightest upturn at the corners of her mouth, a faint sense of bemusement that Berta just now appreciated as having always been part Irena's manner. "How's Magda?" she asked. "How's Frank?"

Chapter Seventeen

The jet turned to take its place in the runway lineup. Milos buckled himself into 14C. This afternoon, Berta and Irena—flying less than half as far—would also secure their seat belts, probably as soon as the aircraft began to back away from the gate.

Berta had told Milos she would not read the book she'd brought, that she would talk to Irena all the way back to Chicago. Don't mention my family, Milos had cautioned. No, no, she had said: just food, a little gossip, some Eastern European politics, whatever will distract her.

That's good, Milos had said. Still, all the way back to San Francisco he berated himself for never having devised a backup strategy for a plan that could just as easily have failed.

"Forget about it!" Dawn said when she picked him up at the airport six hours later. "It worked, didn't it?"

Chapter Eighteen

June 1995

The closest Irena had come to breaking her promise to herself
and to Dr. Lowry was on the afternoon of her seventieth birthday—her
last day in Plzen. It happened while she was sitting at an outdoor café
not far from the Church of St. Bartholomew, writing postcards home.
She had finished hers—to Miloslav, Dawn, and the children; to Reyna
Kopecky and two other friends—but Magda and Berta were still writing, their heads bowed at identical angles. Irena had one postcard left,
a photograph of the lagering cellar at Pilsner Urquell, where her father
had worked as a young man. It would have been nothing to write a few
words to send off to Elise. After all, she knew how to get in touch. Just
last month, Miloslav had surprised her by tossing off Elise's address. His
tone had been as offhand as the minute before, when he had mentioned
that Kristy was signed up for tennis camp and Stevie had started reading
one-syllable words.

Irena could scribble something about Plzen, her birthplace and the
city that she had talked about throughout Elise's childhood. The sun
was bright, tourists were smiling; why shouldn't she pick up the pen and
write a postcard to her daughter?

Irena and the Kriz sisters had been in Plzen for a week, and there
was much to describe. She could tell Elise how smart the city looked, all

decked out for its seven hundredth anniversary. She could write about her younger cousin Martin, with whom she was staying. Elise might be interested to know that he was no longer struggling to make ends meet, that he had started managing a team of laborers at Škoda Auto. She could write that Panasonic was set to build an assembly plant in the industrial zone of Borská pole next year—that there would be hundreds of new jobs. Maybe Irena would mention that she and Berta and Magda had visited the two-year-old University of West Bohemia, and it was full of students with smiling faces. She would tell Elise that this Plzen was not the grim and poor city in which she had grown up. And she would also mention Praha, where the three of them had been last week.

The only experience Irena would not relate to Elise or to anyone else was her visit to Karlstein Castle. She had gone there alone on their third day in Praha. Intending to spend the morning and most of the afternoon at the castle, she had taken an early train from Smíchov Station. It was a pleasant forty-five-minute ride along the Berounka River.

Irena had been unprepared for how she would feel when the hilltop Karlstein Castle came into view. From afar, she was able to identify the different parts—the Great Tower that Stepan had worked on the longest, the Chapel of the Holy Cross, the Well Tower he had loved. Details had crowded Irena's brain—she'd found herself recalling the number of panel paintings of saints inside the chapel and the dimensions, in meters, of the Great Tower. She could virtually hear Stepan's voice describing the banquet hall and royal bedroom. Then had come a jolt of grief so powerful that Irena had to look down at her lap to steady herself. As the train approached the town, she had sped through the spectrum of emotions she'd had on account of this castle throughout her married life: resentment and jealousy, boredom, occasional satisfaction, and finally pride that Stepan's years of work had yielded the tidy triumph she came to realize he was seeking.

From the Karlstein train station, Irena had walked behind a group of tourists to the village. The shops there offered Bohemia crystal, marionettes, T-shirts, and costume jewelry—the identical souvenirs sold in Praha. While the other tourists went on to take the twenty-minute walk up the hill to the castle, Irena had gone into one of the shops to pick out presents for the children: for Kristy a glass paperweight with a cardboard Karlstein Castle inside, for Sam a marionette of King Charles IV, for Stevie a coloring book of the castle rooms along with a big box of crayons. She had the shop send the presents directly to San Francisco. Imagining the children's pleasure as they opened packages that had come all the way from Europe had lifted her spirits for the first time that morning.

Then Irena had settled herself at a table on the sidewalk in front of a small restaurant. Seated next to her had been five robust, middle-aged Americans, four men and a woman, laughing and discussing their morning on the course at the Karlstein Golf Resort, which was right over the hill. Irena had heard about these golf tourists, the flocks of them who had been driving rented cars from Praha since the resort opened two years before. She had imagined Stepan there beside her, stock-still while he listened to these hale-and-hearty golfers going on about birdies and bogies. She'd known how disgusted he would be at the notion of wealthy Americans riding in mechanized carts toward the little balls they had scattered over the knolls, his beautiful knolls.

No, Irena would not write to Elise about her trip to Karlstein Village. She had been too heartsick to ride up the hill in a horse-drawn carriage as she had planned. Instead, she'd walked back to the station and had taken the next train bound for Praha. Writing her postcard, she would not mention Karlstein Castle at all; instead she would write about the new museums and galleries opening in Plzen, a topic Elise would enjoy. So easy. Pen to card. Stamps. Post office around the corner.

Of course Irena knew that Dr. Lowry thought she was not quite ready to get in touch with Elise. He had taught her about what he called "the negation of self" and the role it had played during those unearthly months in New York almost five years ago. If, when she got home, she told him that she had dropped Elise a line during her trip, he would give her a look that he'd imagine to be neutral but that would manage to communicate his disappointment. During their sessions over the last four years, almost five, he had cautioned Irena repeatedly that she must have no contact with Elise—should even try to avoid news of her. It would not be forever, he always added.

For the first couple of months following Irena's return to Laflin in 1990, Elise had called her every day, sometimes two or three times a day. From the very beginning of their sessions together, Dr. Lowry had planted in

Irena's mind the incredible idea that she simply not answer the phone and not respond to Elise's messages. After some convincing, Irena was able to admit that her daughter was in what Dr. Lowry called a "florid state," that her behavior was dictated by her delusions. But it was not Dr. *Lowry's* daughter who had no one in the world but him, nor was it Dr. Lowry's idle evenings that were being interrupted by pitiful appeals over the answering machine. Despite her better instincts, Irena had picked up the phone every time. How could she fail to do so when she knew that at the sound of her voice Elise would breathe a sigh of relief and settle right down?

After a while, though, she began calling at two, three, and four in the morning. When Irena picked up, Elise would start in on her new theory that the only reason her mother had given her the McDonald's money was so that in the end she could join up with Miloslav and Massie and the others to steal the building away. Propped up in bed, barely awake, Irena had endured her daughter's screaming at her. Once or twice she was able to make Elise see the irrationality of her theory, but then Elise would call the next night even more worked up and with precisely the same accusations. This went on for a month. Finally, Irena did what Dr. Lowry had wanted her to all along: she got an unlisted phone number. When letters began to arrive, she marked them with the rubber stamp she had ordered from Laflin Gifts & Stationery. There was not a soul to whom she could describe what it felt like to bear down upon this stamp and see the words RETURN TO SENDER next to her own daughter's name.

Many times during the following two years, the impulse to call Elise had been so strong that Irena had had to leave the house. Rather than stay at home where she could so easily pick up the phone and dial, she had more than once found herself roaming the aisles of the A & P she had left not two hours before, looking for items she might have forgotten.

All the previous times she had longed for contact with Elise, the impulse had arisen from the enormity of her despair, when she could not physically contain the reality of their estrangement, when she felt that the very essence of her daughter was seeping out of her, like magma splitting a rock. Several times, when it was too late to leave the house and she'd had nowhere to go, Irena had called Dr. Lowry. Weeping, she had told him she would go out of her mind if she could not find and contact

Elise that minute. Dr. Lowry had talked with her until she thought she might be able to hold on till their next appointment.

But then, so gradually that she could not at any point mark the difference, things began to change. She did a little dressmaking and started to enjoy her leisurely chats with her customers. To learn how to make her tiny savings go further, she had joined an investment club for widows. After the women had learned as much as they cared to, they had continued to meet, simply to be in one another's company. They rotated hosting their get-togethers, and they always served coffee and home-baked pastries, much as she and the Kriz sisters had years before. One of the group members, Dora Joysen, became a good friend, and she and Irena went into Chicago together to see plays at the Goodman Theatre. Irena never for a moment stopped missing Elise, especially her sweet smile, but that impossible longing, so physically painful, began at last to recede.

Now, light-headed from the beer and the sunshine, Irena picked up her pen. "Dear Zlatíčko," she began.

"All done!" announced Magda. "This one he'll get after we're in France."

So far, Magda had written to Frank every day of their trip.

Berta had finished her postcards, too. She gathered them into a neat stack. "How are you doing there?" she asked, looking over at Irena.

"Give me another minute," said Irena, taking a sip of beer. Ordinarily she wasn't much of a beer drinker, but Pilsner Urquell was the pride of her city. How could she, a native, turn up her nose at Plzen's major export?

Berta craned forward to look at the postcard Irena was writing. The sisters exchanged glances.

"Do you really want to do that?" Berta asked Irena. "Think about it."

A shot of adrenaline lurched through Irena. Instinctively, she covered the postcard with her hand. "What do you mean?" she asked.

"Remember what Dr. Lowry said. You have to tread very, very carefully."

"*Carefully?*" snapped Irena. "It's been almost five years, and I haven't tread at all." *Trod.* She remembered too late.

"We just don't want there to be any chance you'll spoil your birthday trip," Magda added, lowering her eyelids.

What did these childless women know, thought Irena, not for the first time.

"Read us what you wrote to Miloslav's children," continued Magda, clearly trying to distract Irena.

"You two need to have more faith in me," Irena insisted. If she knew the buses better, she would go back to her cousin Martin's house on the other side of the city. Instead, she took the postcard with the photograph of the lagering cellar in 1840 and tore it up, leaving Berta and Magda to watch the bits shower over their beer bottles. "There. Happy now?"

Irena's first day in Paris served only to bear out her suspicion from years earlier that if she ever visited Paris with the Kriz sisters, she would feel nothing so strongly as her own absence. Now she had acquired a term for that too-frequent sense that her identity was crumbling: Dr. Lowry's "negation of self." It was fine for Berta and Magda to want to show Irena the neighborhood around the Sorbonne where they had spent five of their growing-up years, but they also became loud and excitable and over-friendly, speaking too long in French to anyone who would listen. They showed Irena the building where their father had taught and the nearby high school they had attended. Berta took them to the corner where she had seen Samuel Beckett, and Magda pointed out the apartment building on Rue des Carmes where she'd lost her virginity. Irena was compelled to answer with a knowing smile, to disguise her surprise that Magda had not lost her virginity to Frank.

While she was wondering how many lovers Magda and Berta had had, the Kriz sisters insisted that Irena join them for coffee with a friend from their youth in Paris, now a retired linguistics professor named Christian Briard whom they had called from Praha. They met him at a brasserie on the Rue Bonaparte. He was a tall, solemn-faced man dressed in a tailored suit. After the Kriz sisters introduced Irena, the majority of the conversation was in French. The three of them appeared very comfortable with their reunion. Irena sat silently, looking at passersby on the street. It was not unpleasant, yet for all she was acknowledged, she could have been one of the dressmaker's dummies at Reyna Kopecky's old fabric shop.

The following morning, Berta called Irena's room in the small hotel where they were staying on the Rue du Bac. "Ready for *petit dejeuner*?" she trilled.

Irena lied that she had been up all night with a stomach bug and would need to sleep in.

A minute later Magda called, her voice as hearty as Berta's had been as she too trumpeted *petit dejeuner* and declared that once Irena had some tea she would be good as new. She reminded Irena they had only three more days in Paris. That's right, Irena agreed, and if she didn't take care of herself this morning, she wouldn't be good for any of them.

In the months after Berta had brought her back from New York that terrible June in 1990, Irena had begun to understand the intricacy of what Berta had done, the risk she had taken for their friendship. Yet she had been unable to bring herself to contact either sister.

Slowly, Dr. Lowry had helped her to see the connection between her despair over her future and her response to her daughter's escalating crisis. (To people on the outside, Irena came to realize, the association must have been obvious all along.) Throughout this period Dr. Lowry helped her understand that in the end she had opted for Elise's reality, chosen it of her own free will.

In all of Irena's working years—her long weeks in the bottling division of Ruff Brewery while Stepan was in trade school, the years spent raising her daughter and nephew, running her household, selling fabric at Reyna Kopecky's, and occasionally taking in outside sewing—in all those years, Irena had not worked so hard as she had with Dr. Mitchell Lowry in the two years after Berta brought her home from New York. During that time she had had no energy left for anything that did not help her to lay claim to her own private existence.

At home she read library books, novels the librarian at Laflin Public had pointed her to when Irena had asked for books by American writers from some earlier time, a time when writers didn't try to pass off their feelings as stories. She had ended up with works by Mark Twain and Theodore Dreiser, by Sherwood Anderson and Willa Cather. She had kept a notebook by her reading chair so she could copy down certain lines, lines that comforted her and ones that stimulated her to think: "I am a lover and have not found my thing to love," from Sherwood Anderson. From Willa Cather, "The dead might as well try to speak to the living as the old to the young." Sometimes Irena had brought the quotes in to discuss with Dr. Lowry. She'd had a hard time parting with the books. She would renew them for weeks after she had finished reading them; they were like the bulwark on Stepan's Karlstein Castle, a special wall to protect against invaders.

The Kriz sisters, even Berta, who had dropped everything to come to New York with her offering of kolaces, had no privileges during the nearly two years that were nothing but shame and hollowness, a few sustaining words from a group of long-dead authors, and a man to whom Miloslav sent monthly checks. The books were not enough to keep Irena from periods of great yearning. She had asked Dr. Lowry how people could ache for experiences they could not describe and had never had.

Not until she had resumed her dressmaking and had joined up with the other widows did Irena find the courage to call Miloslav. Despite her great resolve to preserve her dignity, she had broken down twice, confessing to him that no amount of apologizing could make up for what she had done to him, how unforgivable her betrayal had been. Miloslav had not uttered a word of reproach. He was the surprise of her late life. In the weeks that followed, Irena had talked to all of them: Dawn, Kristy, Samantha, even Stevie, whom she had never met. Each exchange had been brief and guarded, except for the one with Stevie, who told her he knew all the words to "Do Your Ears Hang Low?" and proved it by singing the song from beginning to end. That Christmas, Irena had flown to San Francisco bearing presents for all of them. Every Sunday now, she spoke to each member of the family who was at home. Six months ago, Samantha, already nine years old and a remarkably steady child considering the sort of toddler she'd been, had brought one of her little friends to spend a long weekend with her. On Friday evening, Irena and Dora Joysen had taken them to Chicago to see a revival of *The Wiz*, and Sam and her friend had burst into the song "Ease on Down the Road" for the rest of the weekend.

Shortly after making that first call to Miloslav, Irena had decided it was time to face Berta and Magda. She had missed them, and she missed the reassurance she got from their long-shared history. It was easier to first call Magda, who had not flown to New York to rescue her. Magda's response was as remarkable as Miloslav's had been—she had invited Irena to come with her and Berta to hear Petr play that same night.

Yet this morning in Paris these three years later, Irena had had enough of the Kriz sisters. It wasn't the first time on the trip she had felt this way, that she needed a break from them. Over time, she had learned that Berta and Magda were nothing like the vulnerable spinsters she was certain she'd met decades ago, when she had helped them pick out curtain fabric at Reyna Kopecky's. Married or unmarried, they approved of themselves and their place in the world; they had never required Irena's good graces to bolster them. Rather, Irena had required theirs. That was why this morning she could not suffer through *petit dejeuner* in the city they repeatedly called "our Paris."

After another hour's sleep, Irena put on the navy linen dress that flattered her bustline and the expensive shoes, the rubber and latex-soled Mephistos that Miloslav had sent for her seventieth birthday, along with a card that called them the Greek god of walking shoes. How French did she have to be to walk to the corner and have a little breakfast? She could say *petit dejeuner* as well as the next person. She could say *s'il vous plaît* and *merci*.

She went to the brasserie at the corner of Rue du Bac and Rue de Grenelle, walked in, and sat down at a table next to a window. Magda had told her that in these places you have to pay just for the privilege of sitting down, but she didn't care. It was the week of her seventieth birthday; if she didn't deserve a little indulgence on such an occasion, when did she? A waiter approached her table. It was just a touch thrilling that merely by sitting down Irena had commanded his attention. She ordered *petit dejeuner*. If the waiter thought her Czech accent with American overtones was ridiculous, he didn't show it. He offered what Irena made out to be a choice between coffee and tea. Despite being a tea drinker, she chose the coffee. She knew from Berta that French coffee was strong. Today she would need a push. Today she didn't need to be distracted by pain in her knees.

When everything came—the single croissant and miniature baguette, the butter and marmalade and café crème—Irena ate and drank slowly. She looked out at the boulevard but also in the opposite direction, at three men standing by the bar. One was having coffee; the other two were drinking some kind of liquor. It was barely ten A.M. In Chicago, Irena would never be in a place that served liquor at ten A.M. There the men drinking would be unshaven, their grammar terrible, their vocabulary mainly curse words. They would have scars that raised questions about their past. In such a place, Irena's pulse would accelerate, and she would long for the protection of her dead husband. But here on this corner in a good section of Paris, all seemed right with the world. The men spoke in quiet tones; one actually wore a beret, and Irena imagined they could drink all day without losing their sense of civility. The shortest of them caught Irena watching, and he nodded to her pleasantly. Not a smile, yet more acknowledgment than she had gotten from Professor Christian Briard.

Turning her attention back to the boulevard, she suddenly became conscious of what she might look like to others, an elderly woman having morning coffee. She thought about her parents, both of whom had died in their half of the two-family rental in Quincy, Illinois. Her father had been fifty-nine, her mother sixty-two. Now here she was, their seventy-year-old daughter, enjoying good health in the world's most beautiful city—a fact that felt to Irena like a small miracle.

Irena laid down a few francs as a tip. To her, the amount seemed insulting, but the guidebook had been clear: tips in France were optional, more of a gesture than anything else. Then she got up, walked to the corner, and approached a man wearing sneakers. In English, she asked the way to the Seine. The caffeine had left a buzzing in her temples, a bit of a racing heart, but enough excitement that she wondered why she had abstained from coffee all these years.

Following the Rue du Bac in the direction the man had said, Irena felt a stab of pleasure when she reached the Quai Voltaire. She had seen so many reproductions of the Seine and—at the Art Institute of Chicago—at least two Impressionist originals. Asking directions from another American tourist, she headed toward the Pont Neuf. It was all remarkably easy. In the Mephistos, her feet were not tired. Her knees did not ache.

Bookstalls lined the street that ran along the Seine, as Irena knew they had for two centuries. At one, she bought a print of an engraving of Notre Dame, forcing herself to go through with the purchase even though she could do no more than point and say *s'il vous plaît*.

Once she crossed the bridge to Île de la Cité, Sainte-Chapelle was right there. Reaching the upper chapel, she was able to discreetly join a group of British tourists whose guide was lecturing them in a French-accented English about the stained-glass panels. Irena enjoyed history; it was interesting to hear the stories from the lives of one or two saints and to learn how the panels were protected before the invasion of Germany during World War II, but she soon drifted from the group to sit on one of the wooden benches set along the wall. It was a day of clouds and sun, and she was mesmerized by how the intricate glass panels changed colors, fading to indistinct and somber tones when the sun retreated, then glowing with the rich hues of the original glass when it poured forth, shedding blue, yellow, and purplish red over the pattern of fleur-de-lis on the ancient floor. Tourists came and went as Irena lingered, making her private predictions about when the resplendent sunlight would next arrive. Every time it reentered through the arched windows, she willed the sunlight to fall directly upon her; she wanted to savor the last degree of warmth it had to offer.

"I slept practically the whole day," Irena told the Kriz sisters when they arrived back at the hotel. She hated telling a lie but had to follow up on her earlier one.

"You're better, though?" prompted Magda.

"Much." With some effort, she asked what they had done that day. She heard about buying chocolate truffles and gift bags of herbs at the Mouffetard Market. She heard about their outing with another old classmate, a man in the government who was divorced and who had flirted in French with Berta. She heard about the pictures they had seen at the Petit Palais.

"Are you all ready for tonight?" Berta asked.

Irena thought of claiming she was still woozy, but found herself wanting to rejoin the sisters. They had tickets to a concert at the Czech embassy, on Avenue Charles Floquet. Ever since she had reunited with Berta and Magda, she had been to the symphony many times and had learned a thing or two about music. These tickets were a gift from Petr. His friend Nicholas Someone, who had retired last year from the Chicago Symphony Orchestra, was in a trombone ensemble. No other horns, Berta had said. Irena couldn't imagine it. Trombones always made her think of

marching bands, the band from Gymnázium Ludka Pika, one trombon-
ist short after a Jewish boy had been taunted out of the brass section.

The three of them took the metro to the Seventh Arrondissement.
Even after her journey to Île de la Cité and back, the walk to the embassy
didn't bother Irena. Her arthritis had been undetectable all day. It was as
if on the occasion of her seventieth birthday, fate had restored the carti-
lage to her joints, the lightness to her step.

The recital was to be held in a large room with French windows overlooking a park, a lovely one whose name Magda said but Irena swiftly
forgot. When Irena and the sisters arrived, the trombonists were not at
their post at the front of the room, where four chairs and four music
stands had been set up. They were milling about in the small crowd of
their audience, waiting to be introduced.

The Kriz sisters approached their brother's friend, who looked
vaguely familiar to Irena. They each kissed him on both cheeks and
introduced him to Irena; his name was Nicholas Popova. During the
introduction he clasped her hand tightly between both of his. Irena
glanced down and was astonished to realize it had been years since a man
had held onto her hand like this.

As Irena looked up at him, her cheeks burning, it struck her how she
knew him. He was the musician who had explained the role of the brass
section at the Young People's Concerts in Orchestra Hall over thirty
years ago. Before the concert had begun, he had picked up each horn—
the trumpet, French horn, trombone, and tuba—and had played on it
the same few bars from "Twinkle, Twinkle, Little Star." He had asked the
children to compare the sound of the horns. If a boy or a girl looked at
him blankly, he played two of the instruments again and explained the
differences, using words like *high, low, mellow, buzz, color, brassy.*

Six-year-old Elise had not looked at Nicholas blankly. She had compared the sound of the tuba to an elephant walking and the French horn
to a lost person calling out in a cave. All these years later, Irena remembered how Nicholas's eyes had lit up when her daughter spoke. He had
laughed at her associations and had invited her onstage to try the tuba,
which he held up for her. She was frightened, clearly skeptical, but after some encouragement she put her lips to the mouthpiece and blew as
hard as she could. When the enormous sound emerged, she had jumped
away. Nicholas Popova had applauded heartily, and Elise was thrilled.

An embassy official went to stand up front. People took their seats. The man introduced the ensemble, the Four Temperaments, in both French and Czech. He gestured to them and backed away. All but Nicholas Popova assumed his place. Looking around at his audience, he gave a brief history of the ensemble, spoke about the different trombones onstage— tenor, bass, and alto—then announced they would start with Bach's "Fugue in D Minor," originally written for the organ. After Nicholas sat, the four men lifted their trombones. Irena felt an inward shudder; the sight of these instruments pointed like weapons toward the people in the front row did nothing to put her in the mood for Bach. And the first few notes intruding on the silence did seem like an assault. But as soon as she adjusted herself to the sound, tempered by the mutes all four trombonists used, the music grew as familiar and lulling to her ear as a tale she had heard many times before. There was a passage of three repeating staccato notes and another layer that answered those notes. The tones that came from Nicholas Popova's tenor trombone in particular seemed authoritative in their unexpected grace. The expression on his face as he played showed the passion of a much younger man. As she watched him, Irena found herself blushing that her one hand had been nestled for several moments within his two. She shifted her attention out the window, to the park shadowed in near dark and the buildings beyond, their interior lights twinkling. Recalling her afternoon in the upper chapel of Sainte-Chapelle, Irena was amazed that at her age a day could turn out to be so abundant.

Back at their hotel, Irena said good night to Berta and Magda in the tiny elevator and rode up to the next floor. Inside her room, the bedside lamp was turned on, as she had left it. On the desk were the postcards she still hadn't mailed, as well as the new one, the replacement she had bought for the card she'd torn up in Plzen.

> Dear Zlatíčko,
>   I want to tell you I'm in Paris with the Kriz sisters. Do you remember the man who let you come onstage to play the tuba at the Young People's Concert? He gave a recital here tonight, at the Czech embassy! Trombone. The picture on the front is the brewery in Plzen, where we were last week.

Irena tried to think what to say next. She let her pen hover above the postcard until her hand felt heavy, and she lost the keen attention that had made this a day she knew she would remember, even sometimes conjure before she fell asleep back in her house on Kozna Street.

Your Maminka, she signed.

Chapter Nineteen

On most mornings, the seagulls let Elise near them—came close enough to peck at the bread crumbs she emptied out of a bag from Krshinev Bookstore on Brighton Beach Avenue. It was her friends the babushkas who had introduced her to the seagulls, and now she was in love. She recognized them by the subtlest differences in their white-and-dove-gray markings, and she had names for them all. It was cold today—spring was yet weeks away—and she had an unobstructed view of the gulls hopping about. Come Memorial Day, that would change. In the meantime, though, Elise and the babushkas—Masha, Ester, Batsheva, and Leda—all fed the seagulls, but they did so separately, having chosen shifts without saying a word about it.

The seven A.M. shift was Elise's. Perfect. Every night when she went to bed, she looked forward to seeing her seagulls in the early morning, when no one else was around. The first time she had gone, she'd brought Brodyachaya Sobaka—a big mistake, the results of which any five-year-old could have predicted. Sometimes Elise simply didn't think. (No doubt it was the high doses of each of the three drugs she was now on—Topamax, Clozapine, and Depakote.) By the next day, though, the seagulls had forgiven her, had gathered around as they did this morning, eager to eat a breakfast for which they did not have to work. Their gratitude, Elise told herself, was implicit in their daily presence. And well they should be grateful. Who but Elise and the babushkas would spend time each day bundled up in long johns, thick sweaters, and decades-old furs so the seagulls' lives would be free of the least burden? Despite the gulls' sense of entitlement, Elise and the babushkas found them lovable. They were energetic, self-important creatures who returned the affection of their harem merely by not running away. Elise admired them. If she needed to be slobbered over, Brodyachaya Sobaka would accommodate her any moment of the day.

This morning, though, Elise's time with the seagulls needed to be cut short. Besides the new tapes she had to transcribe and lunch with Dimitri, Wiley was coming out after work, all the way from Mt. Sinai. They would have a drink at one of the places on the boardwalk. Wiley would have vodka, she *should* have vodka, and Elise, not drinking these days, would have cranberry kissel. Then they'd go back to the apartment, where Elise would serve borscht and smoked sturgeon.

Elise had been living in Brighton Beach—also called Little Odessa after so many Ukrainians, mostly Jews, had settled there in the late 1960s— for almost three years. As much as she and Wiley had talked about it, and as much as Elise had returned to Manhattan to see her, Wiley still hadn't made the trip. Although tonight's visit did not come under the best of circumstances, it was nevertheless an occasion. Elise knew Wiley would be tired from her day, from the long subway ride, but she hoped she would be open to all Elise planned to show her—starting with her two favorite nightclubs along Brighton Beach Avenue. She would take Wiley in before the action began, so that she could see the tables set out with their plates of pickled cabbage, chopped liver, and creamed her-ring with onions. She would see the garishly decorated stages where later there would be a floor show and performances from visiting Russian stars. Elise would introduce Wiley to the nightclubs' owners. No doubt Wiley would figure out that Elise had slept with Alex—although only twice, when his wife was back in Odessa for a visit almost three years ago. Now Elise just indulged Alex's flirtations and his vulgar remarks. It was the least she could do; his only son, Denis, had been killed in a gang fight.

Elise planned to take Wiley into the little groceries, where she also knew the owners. She would translate the Cyrillic labels on all the caviars, and maybe Wiley would select one. Then, after they'd had their drinks at whichever of the boardwalk restaurants Wiley chose, they would button up their coats and walk back to Elise's apartment by way of the beach. She would introduce Wiley to the seagulls; they'd feed them with bread from the restaurant.

Wiley deserved so much more than Elise could possibly give her on this or any other visit. Elise had her to thank for the apartment in Brighton Beach. When Elise had first heard the apartment was available through Sanctity Housing, a social service agency, she had refused to go to their offices in downtown Brooklyn for an interview. Wiley had virtually pushed her into a cab. She and the social worker at Mt. Sinai had worked hard to get Elise into the Sanctity Housing system. Independent living like this was a rarity, Wiley had said. Did she want to end up in a group home, for Christ's sake? They both knew she should not be in a group home. This was decent housing for people who had to be on SSI but could manage primarily on their own. It was scattered site housing; she would have her privacy. And this particular apartment would allow Brodyachaya Sobaka. If Elise didn't go for the interview, Wiley had warned, then that would be it—she'd done all she could for her.

Elise had held out from moving until the city marshal's office had put the final eviction notice on the door of her sixth-floor apartment. There had been a stay to the eviction, and then an appeal, which was lost. Someone had stepped in to conduct the appeal for her, someone from the New York office of a San Francisco–based firm. Wiley had tried to tell her it was Milos's law firm, but Elise had thought Wiley and Michael had hired the lawyer.

Once or twice in the last months it had struck Elise that Wiley was telling her the truth, that Milos *had* conducted the appeal for her. The thought released such a sweep of shame that she found herself running on the boardwalk all the way to Coney Island, trying to outrun its power. Milos was no longer merely her cousin; he had become something else, a subject as voluminous as any she'd tackled in her academic life, the first subject that utterly intimidated her, that froze her in her tracks at the same time it made her want to flee.

Before the Mt. Sinai clinic doctors had changed Elise's daily regimen of drugs, she had begun to cycle at eighty miles an hour: smelling scents that weren't in the air, hearing voices, thinking she was uptown when she was downtown, seeing auras, smashing objects she suddenly found offensive. She had felt racy and nauseated half the time, and it wasn't until this year, when Mount Sinai's outpatient doctors had replaced her Tegretol with Topamax, that Elise started to feel what she imagined was the approximation of a normal balance. In gratitude, she had sent the clinic flowers, an arrangement of mixed lilies that was striking but not so lavish as to make them think she was manic.

Since the Topamax, Elise had experienced eight months of freedom from any symptom at all. She did her best not to anticipate the other shoe dropping. Even from her new standpoint of feeling grounded, though, she couldn't summon the courage to remember the worst of her episodes. She knew only that they were like what Anna Akhmatova said about translating, the episodes of seizing gave her the sense of eating her own brain. The opposite poles of depression and mania had devoured her equally. There had been states in between these poles that Elise some-times wished for—days that granted a cascade of small epiphanies and a sense of her own delightfulness—but she could sacrifice such days for whole months in which the simple workings of common sense became a marvel to behold.

✦

Elise had spent the morning and half the afternoon preparing for Wiley's visit. She had cleaned her three rooms thoroughly. No one would ever guess the apartment was paid for by SSI. A few weeks after she had moved in, she'd rented a U-Haul and had driven up to some public building wreckage sales in Connecticut. She had gotten a stained-glass window she installed herself, once the landlord gave her permission. A gargoyle now hung on her kitchen wall, and a small glass chandelier was suspended from her bathroom ceiling. Best of all, she'd found half a dozen cherrywood bookshelves with beveled glass doors. She had spent hours arranging her books in alphabetical order by author. When she got to the Sanja Kenovic volume of poems that had won her the Kaminsky Translation Prize, she didn't linger over it but placed it quickly on the shelf, beside *Khrushchev Remembers*.

Before Wiley came, Elise dusted all these books and every one of the Shawnee pieces displayed on two long benches in the living room. They were what remained of the pottery Elise had shattered five years ago. Her favorites had somehow survived, among them the Puss 'n Boots planter, a sailor creamer, and a pink ashtray in the shape of a boomerang.

After dusting, Elise went into the kitchen to scrub the appliances and straighten the cards in the postcard display she had mounted next to the gargoyle. Many of the cards were from her former students, pictures of attractions in different Russian cities. The rest were from her mother, starting with the first Elise had received last year, the one showing the Pilsner Urquell Brewery in Plzen. The moment Elise had spotted her mother's handwriting on that card in her mailbox, she'd felt her pulse ticking in her neck—rapid and uncomfortable, like moth wings flickering under her skin. It had taken her nearly a month to answer. Yes, she was better, but that did not mean she should rush to call Irena the moment she heard from her. In the past she had contacted her shortly after emerging from a bad period and had ended up regretting it. Besides, what could she possibly say to her mother after all this time? I'm sorry for making you believe the unbelievable; I'm sorry for throwing away your life savings and then accusing you of plotting to take everything I had; I'm sorry that after you cast your every cell toward my boundlessly bright future, I'm now living off disability and feeding seagulls?

When she considered what she had put her mother through, Elise always experienced a blast of self-loathing that threatened to set off a new round of trouble. So far each bout of her illness had been worse than the one before. She had to try as hard as she could not to despise herself on account of her mother. She tried to think of Irena as if those months in New York had never occurred. Lately she had been remembering more about her earliest days with her mother, how Irena had taken her into Chicago to see and hear things that she herself had never seen or heard.

It had taken some time, but one day she'd answered Irena with a postcard of her own. She told her about this apartment a block from the ocean and about the new drug combination. Every couple of months since then they had exchanged cards.

✦

Shortly after midnight, Elise and Wiley were sprawled on the couch together, relaxing in a position reminiscent of their college days. The couch was from Goodwill, but it wasn't bad, a nice pale green that Elise had had steam-cleaned. She sat slouched on one end, and Wiley lay across it, her feet in Elise's lap. She had let Elise take her to the bookstore to say hello to Dimitri, whom she had met once in Manhattan, but that was all. At Elise's apartment, Wiley had had some borscht. She couldn't make herself eat the sturgeon. Maybe tomorrow they could do the other things Elise had planned, she said. For now she just wanted to lie here and do nothing. Her gaze fell lazily on the Shawnee collection. "If Brodyachaya Sobaka had any taste," she said, "he'd get rid of those with one swipe of his tail."

"He knows just how far he can go," answered Elise.

Hearing his name, Brodyachaya Sobaka came up to the couch to sniff Wiley's legs and wag his tail.

"He certainly doesn't look like his namesake," Wiley commented.

Elise beamed. Immediately following the initial success of her first combination of drugs, the one with Tegretol, Elise had attended to Brodyachaya Sobaka. She'd had him dewormed, gotten medicine for his ear infection, bought vitamins that were good for his coat, taken him to a groomer and, finally, to six sessions of dog training. The effect was as if *he* had been put on a winning drug combination. He looked healthy and handsome and had far fewer episodes of hysteria.

"Since he graduated, he's too polite to touch anything," Elise said. "He doesn't even touch the plants," she added, looking at the standing and hanging plants crowding the window facing her street that ended at the beach.

"It looks nice in here. You're doing so well," Wiley praised.

"For now," Elise reminded her. She took nothing for granted. The drugs had side effects that could catch up with her. Her blood cells, the weight of her bones, her sense of balance; everything could begin to rage at once. "But I have to—"

An unfamiliar sound—a brief gasp—erupted from Wiley. She was crying. In all these years, Elise had seen Wiley cry perhaps one or two times, and then briefly. She looked on, silent, until Wiley stopped.

"Maybe if I were younger," Wiley managed to get out, "but I'm forty-five already."

"We both are," added Elise.

Wiley gave her a look. Elise knew what it meant; this isn't about you for once.

"And the kids are both at hard ages. Travis is already a junior. How can I stop him from going out with his friends and doing who knows what? He answers me in the same simple sentences he used when he was four." Wiley wiped one eye with the heel of her hand. "Sabrina's thirteen, and you know what *that's* like. Neither one of them needs this."

Elise had always been amazed by what Wiley managed to cope with in a single day. She wanted to banish all of Wiley's responsibilities, to make her Queen for Eternity, to present her with a Maytag washer-dryer and the consecrated permission to rest on her laurels.

"He's not fit to eat Brodyachaya Sobaka's turds," said Elise.

Wiley laughed, a garbled sound, but laughter all the same. "And it's such a cliché, for Christ's sake—turning me in for a newer model! What am I supposed to tell people?"

Elise rubbed Wiley's feet. "Tell them he's a walking cliché," she said.

"And get this," said Wiley. "He wanted *me* to tell Travis and Sabrina."

"Men are not evolved creatures. When did you start thinking they were?"

"Well, maybe not evolved the way women can be, but I thought Michael was at least responsible. Imagine trying to get me to do his dirty work."

"Is he all moved out?" Elise asked.

"All except for what he's getting while I'm out here. I told him not to take the kids with him. Why should they watch him going through our closet?"

"You poor baby."

"No baby, not by a long shot."

"Poor savior of babies?"

Wiley snorted.

"Remember what your father said about women?" Elise asked.

"He said plenty of things."

"You know what I mean—about why he was so hot for you to go to Princeton. 'The female mind is as nimble as a gazelle.'"

Wiley smiled. "Oh, right, it became one of our riffs. You used to say, 'the hooves or the tail?'"

"Right. And you used to say, 'asleep or awake?'" Elise paused. "You'll get through this," she assured. "Your mind's as nimble as a gazelle."

"A lot of good that's done me."

In the morning, Wiley came with Elise to feed the seagulls. It was a clear day, windy, but the most temperate of the week. They brought bread for the gulls and Danishes for themselves. As they scattered crumbs, Elise narrated the unfolding scene, pointing out the most aggressive thief, the couple—Horace and Heloise—who did everything in tandem, the gull who had been injured in the last storm, and the albino one. Wiley tossed out her breadcrumbs, but her expression was dull and her responses flat.

"Let's go over there." Elise pointed to the cabana off the boardwalk.

Early as it was, two old men, one of them Ester's husband, Max, were in their parkas playing chess on the concrete table closest to the entrance. Elise waved hello and settled with Wiley at the other end, on the ocean side.

As soon as they sat down, Wiley said, "All the years you go through with someone you're certain has character, and then you turn out to be wrong."

Elise sat back. The word *character* was not in her lexicon. It was one of hundreds of words that belonged to the province of the mentally stable. Nonetheless, she nodded her head for Wiley to continue, nodded as a dozen shrinks had done for her.

"You hear stories from other marriages, and the whole time you're being sympathetic . . . you hope you don't look smug. I never even thought, 'There by the grace of God go I.' It wasn't by anyone's grace; I just thought I was immune. What an asshole I was."

"He's the asshole."

"And now I have to draw on my higher self, which is currently about half a centimeter, so that I don't bad-mouth him to Travis and Sabrina."

"Ugh. I couldn't do it."

"Yes, you could."

Elise wasn't sure what to say next. She took the Danishes out of the paper bag she'd been carrying. "These are good. Have one."

"I can't. Consider it a compliment I was able to eat your borscht last night."

"Do you still love him?" asked Elise.

"Elise. How can you expect me to answer that?"

Elise knew the question had perhaps been too direct, but she also knew Wiley forgave her. "Try, though."

It was far from the first time that, in a stable period, Elise had asked to be educated on the basics of romantic love, specifically on aspects of Wiley's relationship with Michael.

"I can't. I see red every time I think about the whole thing, which is all the time. Even the sickest preemies don't have my full attention. It's dangerous. I should ask for a leave."

"What do you think will happen?" Elise asked.

"He's going to marry her." This time Wiley's tears streamed down her face as she took a long, mute swallow of air, then paused before the sound of her sobs ricocheted in the cabana, overwhelming the ceaseless noise of waves slapping the shore. Max and his chess partner looked up, then quickly back down at the pieces on their table.

This was what she herself had sounded like, Elise realized, declaring her misery in a hundred public places. Yet the sound was coming from Wiley, her rock, and it scared her. She wanted to run back down to her seagulls. Wiley had been Wiley and Michael for almost twenty years; this would destroy Wiley, would make her question everything, would push her off a cliff.

Wiley snatched the napkin from underneath her Danish and turned toward the ocean to blow her nose. She grew quieter, but Elise saw her shoulders heave. No, Elise told herself, this will not ruin Wiley. It would ruin you, would push *you* over the edge. She reached for Wiley's arm, prodding her to turn around again. "What can I do for you?" she asked. "I would do anything."

In return, Wiley stroked Elise's hand. "I know you would," she said. "I think I need to skip today, if you don't mind. I'm sorry. I think I just need to go back to Manhattan and check on my preemies. Is that all right? Will you be all right?"

There came that seed of terror, that hard little kernel that settled in Elise's gut, warning her that without Wiley's calming presence she would experience nothing but panic, that she would have to exert untold effort to recoup some version of herself she could live with. They'd had plans. They had decided last night. Elise would show Wiley more of the neighborhood; she would introduce her to the babushkas; they'd take a lunch break with Dimitri. Suddenly she was on her own.

"Elise? Will you be okay?" Wiley repeated.

"Yes, I'll be fine. Go see your preemies. I'll call you tonight."

The day after Elise had moved into her apartment in March 1993, she had gone into the Krshinev Bookstore to find Dimitri Shiroff. She had approached a man about her age who was unpacking a box from East-view Publications. "Dimitri?"

He had thick gray hair that fell over his eyes. His eyeglasses reminded Elise of James Joyce's in the pictures she had seen of him; he had pushed them up his nose as he raised his head to answer her. "Yes?"

"I'm Elise Blazek." She had felt no need to elaborate, only to extend her hand, which he'd shaken heartily.

Ever since Dimitri had called one day during that hideous winter in 1990 to tell her that *Grey Is the Color of Hope* had come in, they had talked every month or so. Whenever Elise felt well enough to trust the words on a page, she had called Dimitri to order a new book of poetry or a memoir by a dissident poet. One day she had asked him how the bookstore was doing, and he told her he had gotten a bank loan and bought out the owner. Besides that, he'd said, he had gotten tougher on the new émigrés. If they spent too much time lingering in the store without buying anything, he reminded them there was a library nearby, that they could browse there for as long as they liked. Slowly, as the new émigrés found work, they began to buy books.

"So what brings you all the way out here?" Dimitri had asked. Elise told him she had just moved to Brighton Beach. She did not elaborate. He had looked surprised, but in a matter of weeks they began having lunch together several times a month.

Elise found out that Dimitri had come to New York in 1972. A young professor of Russian literature in Moscow, he had soon found out his Ph.D. and two years teaching at Moscow University was of no use to anyone but himself. While he was looking for a teaching job—first on the university level, then high school—he stayed with his parents in their three-room apartment on Brighton 6, one of the streets leading to the boardwalk. He and his father fought all the time. After a while, Dimitri stopped looking for a job. Most days he stayed in his room drinking beer in front of a black-and-white portable television set or playing cards with other unemployed émigrés. It was not until his parents told him that his uncle Sergi had been granted a visa and would be moving into Dimitri's room, not until they actually kicked him out, that he had found the job managing the bookstore he now owned. Since then his father had died of a stroke and his mother had moved to an efficiency in Brighton House, a residence for the elderly near the boardwalk.

For her part, Elise had told Dimitri everything, avoiding only the subject of her family. Hearing voices, shedding her identity, racking up debts, stealing into private buildings, sleeping with strangers, destructive rages, hospital stays—these she could relay with a curious dispassion, as if they were the broad strokes of someone else's life history. Her tiny family was another matter. They were breathing connections to her biography, to her childhood before she got sick. She had brushed off his questions about her family. During one lunch, when he seemed about to press her, she had changed the subject to a research project she was planning.

That was when Dimitri had told her about the mahjong club that met in his mother's efficiency. He had known that the mahjong club was the place for her to go, that there she would find what she was look-ing for—the piece of Soviet history the babushkas embodied. He had taken her to meet the club members that very day, and that night they'd become lovers.

Maybe her gratitude for the babushkas was why they had become lovers or whatever they were—a couple, an anti-couple, each insistent upon his or her own measure of distance, yet regular lunch companions and recurrent bed companions. Now Dimitri's blue terrycloth robe hung on a hook in Elise's bathroom. Sometimes she caught sight of it and was surprised by how much it reassured her. Other times she threw it on a pile of clothes on the closet floor and shut the door.

From the first day Dimitri had introduced her to them, the babushkas seemed to like Elise. Nevertheless, it took them months to agree to talk to her on the record. Each gave a different reason for refusing.

Dimitri's mother, Leda, had said that as far as she was concerned, the remainder of her days would be devoted to mahjong, her grandchildren, and her great-grandchildren. If she wanted to bring all that up again, why would she have tried for fourteen years to get out?

Ester had said it made Max nervous when people came over, and he didn't like it when she went out for hours, either.

Masha said she wouldn't do it unless the others did, and even then would only consent to be interviewed in Russian.

Batsheva had been the firmest. Why should she tell a perfect stranger her business, she asked. Elise, a U.S. citizen, had the luxury of researching the regimes that had destroyed the rest of them.

Over the months, various factors had gotten the babushkas to change their minds. Leda was the easiest; she'd changed her mind one Sunday when Elise and Dimitri came over, and Elise gave her two-year-old great-granddaughter a family of matreshkas—nesting dolls—a mother, father, and seven children.

For Masha, it was Sanja Kenovic. She had asked to borrow Elise's translation, surprising Elise with her love of poetry. When she had done well with the English, gotten through the whole book, Masha was suddenly Elise's friend.

Ester finally agreed for a reason that had nothing to do with Elise. Her grandchildren, she complained, couldn't care less about her stories. One of them had told her to stop talking about Russia; it was, Ester quoted her granddaughter, like totally depressing. "So if they won't listen now, maybe they'll listen after I'm gone," Ester had told Elise. "I'll tell Max to have his friend Leo come over and keep him company." Elise was grateful, but she could not drive out the memory of herself as a teenager—like Ester's granddaughter, groaning every time Irena had brought up the country of her youth.

It was Batsheva's sense of noblesse oblige that had gotten her to capitulate. One day at the grocers close to Brighton House, Batsheva had greeted Elise by grasping her shoulder from behind. Startled, Elise had dropped the wallet in her hand. Her Medicaid card fell to the floor. Batsheva knew what the card was for. Neither a shy nor a diplomatic woman, she had asked Elise why she was on Medicaid. Standing in front of the dairy case, Elise told her. When Batsheva narrowed her eyes, her tired expression became shrewd. She informed Elise that she had noticed a few things. For one thing, who wore shoes like that? Two days later she called to tell Elise she would participate in the project. Her tone had carried a certain rhythm Elise recognized from other times, the distinct cadence of Batsheva's condescension. Elise hadn't cared. The routes to her goals had always been many and varied.

The interviews had been going on for over a year. Mostly Elise interviewed the babushkas individually, but sometimes she asked them questions in a group. Perhaps those sessions were the most illuminating. Elise could observe the differences between the stories the babushkas told her alone, and those they told one another. Even here in the States, safe in their residence for the elderly and their sturdy brick apartment houses, they could not tell one another the truth. Under Stalinism, the way a person survived, particularly if he was Jewish, was merely the flip side of how his neighbor perished. Inform or be informed on. Everyone was an edge away from the opposite fate.

The doctors at Mt. Sinai, including Wiley, had advised Elise not to think about her project in large-scale terms. "Take it a day at a time," said one psychiatrist. "Let it find its own shape," Wiley had told her. "Don't put any pressure on yourself." Elise understood that the ambition of someone with her history was suspect, but did that disqualify her from accomplishing anything at all? The book she envisioned mined the experience of the refuseniks here, in Israel, and in Russia, where some remained. Many had surely told their stories before but not, Elise was convinced, the way she would tell their stories. There was more than one way to live on parallel planes, and Elise understood the mechanics of subterfuge in a way most American interviewers would not.

This afternoon's transcribing was going slowly. Wiley had left hours ago, and Elise was only a quarter of the way through Masha's last session. Masha's parts always took longer because Elise interviewed her in Russian, then translated the transcriptions. This time, Masha had surprised her by talking about poetry.

"All the best poets were censored at one time or another. But the Secretariat was so unpredictable, you didn't know when the poets would be on or off the list."

Some poets must have always been on the list. How did they reach an audience?

"They were out there, but no one talked about it. You know, I heard Anna Akhmatova once. It was 1949, only a month after her son was arrested. Everyone knew about that arrest. Akhmatova was so desperate she started to write poetry praising Stalinism. That just shows what a person can be driven to. She thought if she did that, they would release him. Lev, his name was."

She couldn't have really thought that.

"I'm not so sure. I've learned that desperation changes the way a mind works. It can make a brilliant mind stupid."

Where did you hear her?

"At a reading right outside of St. Petersburg. Underground—not safe, I'm sure. I can't imagine what I was thinking. But I was thirty-one and thought of myself as very bold."

What do you remember?

"I remember her hair was gray, and she no longer had the face from all the portraits. She was fifty-eight by then, but if you looked hard, you could still see her beauty. I remember being so lost in worshipping her that I didn't hear the first couple of poems. It was easy enough to make an idol of her. Half of the Soviet Union was in love with her. It wasn't like it is here; we were a country that very much needed our poetry. I was hypnotized. Did you ever hear her voice?"

Yes, I've heard the recordings.

"Then you know what I mean. It wasn't until the third poem that I really began to hear."

And what was that? Which poems did she read?

"I don't remember all of them. Except for 'Everything.' I do remember that one."

Elise's neck ached, and her legs were stiff. It was getting late. She thought she would walk to the beach, then return to Masha's interview when she came back.

"Out, Brody?" she asked.

Brodyachaya Sobaka immediately rose to shake off his nap and wag his tail.

Wrapped in her old raccoon coat, Elise let Brodyachaya Sobaka lead her to the boardwalk, then down the steps. Once on the sand, she took off his leash. It was nearly dark. She dug her bare hands deep into the pockets of her coat. The wind was sharp. Her eyes filled, and her nose stung. There wasn't a person around. It was closing time at the bookstore; she could turn around to get Dimitri, ask him to walk with her. He liked the cold, he would come. Fear shortened Elise's breath and made her feel the hollowness of her throat. Still after three years, the look and sound of the ocean at night, no sunlit objects or voices to distract her, was terrifying. Yet she continued to walk along the beach at night, as if her own fear was a dare she was obliged to accept.

Watching Brodyachaya Sobaka running ahead of her, she thought about the poem "Everything." She remembered it well, from as far back as her sophomore year. There were several English versions; she could no longer recall who had translated her favorite. She especially loved the final stanza. As much as the poem had to do with the totalitarianism Akhmatova lived under, it also described what Elise sensed right now, in this far more open society, alone with her dog at the ocean. "And something miraculous will come / close to the darkness and ruin / something no one, no one, has known / though we've longed for it since we were children."

Brodyachaya Sobaka ran up to Elise with something in his mouth. A bone of some kind, wrapped in seaweed. Elise made him drop it. They had walked for long enough. It was after six, and Elise remembered with some alarm that she was supposed to call Wiley. When in all these years had Wiley promised and failed to call *her*? She clipped Brodyachaya Sobaka's leash to his collar and quickened their pace to a run.

Inside her apartment, still wearing her coat, Elise headed for the phone. Between the tones the keys made when she pressed them, she thought she heard something, a hoarse voice gaining and fading. She stopped pressing the numbers and listened.

"Hello? Hello? Zlatíčko, is this you?"

Acknowledgments

I'm fortunate to have friends whose continuous support, love, humor, and intelligence have encouraged and cheered me throughout the writing of this novel. Some have read *Radiant Daughter* at various stages. Jean Casella is a superb editor, whose vision is sharp and perceptive at a bird's-eye view and meticulous when narrowed in on details. Yona Zeldis McDonough, Selma Rayfiel, and Marian Thurm each read with insight and care, and I profited from their suggestions.

Thank you to the staff members I worked with at Northwestern University Press; each offered valuable advice and all were responsive and lovely: Heather Antti, Henry Carrigan, Rudy Faust, and Jenny Gavacs. I'd also like to thank Barbora Dvorakova for her help with some Czech terms.

I have a dream agent. Judith Ehrlich works in a way too rarely seen, nurturing not only the project at hand but the writer over time. There have been moments, numerous ones, when her faith and persistence have made all the difference.

By being herself, Helene Kendler makes it possible for me to take my eye off the roiling, precarious world long enough to try to make a shred of sense of it on the page.

Patricia Grossman is the author of five previous novels.
Brian in Three Seasons (2005) won the 2006 Ferro-Grumley Award.
She lives in Brooklyn, New York.

green press
INITIATIVE